Nina Milne has always drea[m]
Mills & Boon—ever since sh[e]
with her mother's stacks of Mills & Boon
romances as a child. On her way to this dream
Nina acquired an English degree, a hero of her
own, three gorgeous children and—somehow!—
an accountancy qualification. She lives in
Brighton and has filled her house with books—
her very own *real* library.

Justine Lewis writes uplifting, heart-warming
contemporary romances. She lives in Australia
with her hero husband, two teenagers, and an
outgoing puppy. When she isn't writing she
loves to walk her dog in the bush near her house,
attempt to keep her garden alive, and search for
the perfect frock. She loves hearing from readers
and you can visit her at justinelewis.com.

HIS PRINCESS ON PAPER

NINA MILNE

BREAKING THE BEST FRIEND RULE

JUSTINE LEWIS

MILLS & BOON

First published in Great Britain 2024
by Mills & Boon, an imprint of HarperCollins*Publishers* Ltd,
1 London Bridge Street, London, SE1 9GF

www.harpercollins.co.uk

HarperCollins*Publishers*, Macken House, 39/40 Mayor Street Upper,
Dublin 1, D01 C9W8, Ireland

His Princess on Paper © 2024 Nina Milne

Breaking the Best Friend Rule © 2024 Justine Lewis

ISBN: 978-0-263-32127-2

03/24

HIS PRINCESS ON PAPER

NINA MILNE

MILLS & BOON

To my grandmother (Mamama) and my mum,
for both being such fun, good, loving grandmothers.

CHAPTER ONE

HIS ROYAL HIGHNESS PRINCE ROHAN, unwilling heir to the Kingdom of Sarala, glanced around the small cargo plane as it landed on the tiny, mostly disused airfield and then turned to smile at the pilot.

'Thank you, Amit, old friend. I appreciate the lift. And the privacy.'

'Any time, Ro. And good luck. If you need a quick escape, you know where to find me.'

The words, though said half in jest, had an uncomfortable element of truth—there was a chance, slim but there, that Rohan would need an escape route. Not just him, but the whole royal family of Sarala. If Sarala decided to copy the almost unprecedented step that its neighbouring island of Baluka had taken—and declare itself a republic, deposing the incumbent royal family.

As if sensing his friend's thoughts, Amit shook his head. 'It'll be all right, Ro. I've spoken to my family, to other people, and they don't want Sarala to become a republic. They're happy with the status quo, and with your parents. They are good, just rulers who look after the island and the people. Sarala is mostly prosperous and peaceful— why rock the boat?'

Rohan smiled at his childhood friend, son of the palace head gardener and one of the very few people on Sarala who treated him like a normal human being, not a prince. 'I don't think it's my parents who are the problem. I think it's the next generation.' He shook his head. 'No, that's not fair.' His older sister, Marisa, wasn't at fault, after all he was the heir. 'It's me.'

He closed his eyes for a moment, recalled exactly why the people saw him as a problem, remembered the glare of publicity, the relentless coverage of the breakdown of his disastrous marriage, the descriptions of him as 'cold', 'brutal', 'heartless'—a bridegroom wedded to duty, a frozen-hearted prince with no sympathy for his 'persecuted bride'. The photos of his then wife, Princess Caro, tears in her wide green eyes, anguish etched on every beautiful feature.

The memories streamed through his brain and triggered the searing sensation of remembered humiliation, the deep tearing wound of betrayal. But the humiliation, the pain, he had at least been able to keep private—not one person knew the truth of his marriage and none ever would.

He opened his eyes, saw his friend's expression of sympathy. Amit had no idea what had really happened but he would be able to guess how much Rohan had loathed the public analysis of his private life. The whispers and rumours, the swirling speculation, the hidden conversations and sideways looks.

Now he spoke. 'Maybe it's time to fix that, put the past behind you. Spend some more time on Sarala, show the people what you're really made of.'

Problem was, Rohan wasn't sure what he was made of, other than flesh, blood, bone and other wobbly bits, just like anyone else. And he couldn't see why that would impress the people, who had already judged him. That was why he had left Sarala; his parents had been adamant it was the only way to kill the scandal once the divorce was finalised and he'd been forced to agree, despite the uncomfortable sense that it looked as though he were fleeing.

So he had spent the last three years abroad as Sarala's ambassador, and whilst doing that he'd made a new life for himself, a life he loved—one that had now been upended by his recall to Sarala. An unwelcome recall, but he accepted the necessity. He closed his eyes, hoping against hope that this was a temporary necessity, suspected deep down that it wouldn't be.

'I'm not sure they'll like what they see,' he told Amit now.

'That depends what you decide to show them,' his friend said somewhat cryptically, but before Rohan could ask what he meant Amit glanced down at his phone. 'I've asked a friend of mine, Jamal, to pick you up and take you to the palace. Someone I trust,' Amit continued. 'He's there now.'

A few minutes later Rohan stepped onto the tarmac of the tiny airport, relieved to see that there was no waiting fanfare, no reporters here to record the returning son. Relieved that Amit's trust in his friend wasn't misplaced—there had been no tipoff to the press. He glanced around and headed towards the small, discreet dark car parked in the shadows and climbed into the passenger seat.

'Good evening, Your Highness.' The young man sounded nervous and Rohan smiled quickly, even as he wished his royalty didn't affect people.

'No need for formality. Please call me Rohan.'

The young man in the driving seat looked surprised but nodded, before executing a faultless turn and making his way to the main road, as Rohan assessed the mirrors, checking for signs of pursuit or interest.

'I don't think anyone can know that I am giving you a lift. I told no one.'

'I appreciate that.' He glanced at Jamal's serious expression. 'I don't want to cause any unrest or a stir until I have a chance to speak with my parents.' Speaking of whom, it was time to let them know what was going on, now it was too late for them to arrange a ceremonious welcome, if that was what they had planned. He messaged them.

Change of plan. My flight arrived this evening and I am headed to the palace now.

Jamal nodded. 'I understand.'

There was silence after that and Rohan looked out at the dusky night sky, the indigo darkness of a Saralan night, inhaled the familiar scent of lush sweet flowers that wafted in through the open windows. The smell of home, and for an instant he wished he could be here anonymously, could simply come and go unseen. Or at least only be seen when he chose to be seen.

Instead, he watched as the imposing gates, set in the vast stretch of whitewashed walls that surrounded the palace of Sarala, loomed ahead.

'I'll walk the last bit,' he told Jamal, not wanting to expose this young man to the security officers who would be patrolling. 'I'll get in via a side entrance. And thank you.'

'You're welcome. Amit speaks highly of you and I am glad to have met you.'

'You too.'

Ten minutes later, he approached the side entrance, where he was met by a stiff-faced guard. 'The King and Queen are expecting you in the Throne Room.'

Of course they were. The Throne Room, with its long mahogany table, its dazzling gilt-edged throne, the paintings on the wall of former rulers, the ancient tapestries woven from the silk for which Sarala was justly famed, the room where formal negotiations were carried out, visiting dignitaries met to display and be awed by the weight of royalty, the evidence of the dynasty of the Kamodian family.

So this was to be *that* sort of meeting—the return of Prince Rohan, Ambassador for Sarala, not a family welcome. Well, what had he expected?

Rohan loved his parents, he did, and they loved him. But he knew that for them the most important thing, the thing they loved the most, was Sarala, and this meeting would be about Sarala.

'I will call for someone to take you there.'

'There is no need. I know the way.' Yet his footsteps lagged as he scrunched across the gravel driveway, heard the rhythmic flow and fall of the water feature, and saw the dimly illuminated shapes of the hedges and bushes of the landscaped garden. For an absurd moment he looked up at the sky, in the foolish hope that Amit would swoop down in his plane and essay a rescue. But the dusky Saralan sky showed only the glitter of stars and the curve of the moon.

He entered via a side entrance and made his way down the long marble corridors of the palace to the throne room. Opened the door to see his parents at the table that stretched across the marble floor, and he looked from the two thrones on a dais across to the stained-glass windows that depicted kings of yesteryear.

King Hanuman and Queen Kaamini rose and stepped up onto the dais in front of the thrones and he joined them, knelt for the traditional blessing.

'Amma, Papa,' he murmured and then stood and waited as his parents returned to the table, sat and then motioned for him to follow suit.

His parents' eyes rested on him and he could see the

hint of approbation, the searching glances, the disapproval at his attire—jeans and a T-shirt.

His father's voice, though, was measured. 'It is good to see you, my son. But we would have preferred a more official arrival.'

'Your message said you wished for my urgent return. Given the situation with Baluka, I thought it made more sense to arrive unofficially.'

'Well, the important thing is that you are here. And here to stay. Your mother and I are recalling you to Sarala. Permanently. It is time for the heir to return home. Time to show the people that you are ready to settle down and learn to rule.'

The words sat like cold stones in his belly. Even though he'd known this would come—had known it all his life.

'You have done good work in the past few years and been an excellent ambassador for your country. Now it is time to show that you are capable of being a prince and a ruler. To do your duty.'

The weight of that duty, the mantle of royalty, seemed to descend on his shoulders. A duty he'd been born to and would carry out. Because he did love his country, this exotic, lush, beautiful island, producer of the finest silk in the world. And if he wished he'd been born a mere citizen rather than a prince it was a wish that was futile and pointless. And he understood that. If he wished the law could be changed to reflect modern times and allow Marisa, older than he by two years, to be heir, he knew better than to voice that wish.

But he could at least try to buy some time.

'I understand you wish me to be here more, but I would prefer not to leave my recent duties as ambassador incomplete.' Didn't want to leave the life he'd made—more importantly, the business he'd built. His business, one his parents were unaware of.

'There are more important duties now,' his mother said. 'It is time to provide Sarala with an heir. That is why you will marry.'

'No.' The denial came from deep within; he couldn't— wouldn't—make the same mistake twice.

Both parents raised their eyebrows in a synchronised movement that would have been comical at any other moment than this.

'I am not ready,' Rohan said. Not now, not ever.

'This is not about you. The kingdom needs an heir, needs continuity, needs certainty. A ruler who is here and present, taking no risks, and who has sons to follow him.' His father's voice was even and brooked no refusal.

The Queen continued. 'The monarchy on Baluka fell because there was no heir. Just a distant cousin many times removed who the people did not want. And so they stormed the palace and the King and Queen had to flee.' There was outrage in her voice, but also a thread of fear, one that touched Rohan with sympathy, even as a visceral, raw panic assailed him. A cold sense of inevitability. Yet he tried.

'I do understand, Amma, and in time…'

'There is no time. The preparations are already in hand,' his mother continued. 'Tomorrow you will meet your bride.'

Rohan stared at his parents, opened his mouth to protest.

'This is not about what you want; it is about what Sarala needs,' King Hanuman said, his voice deep with emotion and a certainty that his son would understand. 'This is about your duty.'

The following morning

Her Royal Highness Princess Elora of Caruli stared at her reflection, amazed that the years of training were still holding good, that somehow her countenance retained a serene expression, when inside, anxiety, nerves and panic fought for victory.

Somehow, she was even managing to focus on her mother's words, perhaps in the vain hope that Queen Joanna was going to tell her this whole thing was a joke. That she *wasn't* about to meet Prince Rohan, that there was no question of marriage.

Panic swirled and soared again. How could she marry Prince Rohan when the very idea filled her with cold dread?

Perhaps her mother sensed her turmoil. 'Elora. You understand the importance of this meeting. You must please Prince Rohan, show him you will be a worthy bride. This marriage is necessary and you will do your duty.' The words were a statement, not a question, uttered in the cold, distant tones she recognised so well, ever since the death of her twin brother. How she wished Sanjay was still here now, that he'd grown up alongside her. 'This is your chance to do something for your country.'

The word *finally*, though unsaid, seemed to hover in the air, flashing neon.

'I understand.' And she did; an alliance between Sarala and Caruli was vital for both islands now that Baluka had declared itself a republic. For centuries the three neighbouring islands had veered from friendship to enmity until in recent decades they had settled to a civilised alliance of sorts. Uneasy sometimes but an alliance.

But, of course, now everything would change and no

doubt Sarala was as shaken as Caruli by events. And so her parents and Rohan's parents had come up with this. A way of joining forces.

A marriage to tie the royal families of the two islands together. No matter the idea filled her with terror—marriage to Rohan, the prince who had already driven one wife away, resulting in a divorce that had fuelled public speculation for years.

'Elora.' Her mother's voice was tart. 'Are you listening?'

'Yes, Mama. And I do understand.'

'Then make sure you impress on Rohan that this marriage must take place. Soon.' The older woman's perfectly made-up face scrunched into a frown of disapproval. 'It is ridiculous that he has insisted on seeing you alone. Make sure you say nothing wrong, show him what a good future queen you will make. A future queen and mother to his heir. Because there has to be an heir, Elora. A son.'

Elora tried to keep her face serene, her body relaxed. Marriage did indeed involve more than a political alliance. As for getting an heir, her mother, of all people, knew that it wasn't that easy. Queen Joanna had tried for years, undergone secret fertility treatment until finally the miracle had happened and an heir had been born. Along with Elora—an unnecessary addition to the family but tolerated, loved even, until Sanjay's death.

What if pregnancy wasn't that easy for Elora either? There could be inherited problems; her mother knew that. Knew too that Elora's periods were irregular.

'I can't guarantee that. Perhaps it is better to tell the Saralan royal family now about...'

'No.' Her mother's voice was sharp and she glanced around as though the walls were sprouting proverbial ears.

'There is nothing to tell. Within a year you will have a son. I am sure of it. You will be like your sister.'

Elora held her tongue, didn't point out that Flavia was her half-sister. Flavia was the King's daughter from his first marriage to Queen Matilda, who he had divorced in order to marry Elora's mother, Queen Joanna.

Flavia had lived with her mother until Sanjay's tragic death had left Caruli without an heir. Once it had become clear that there would be no more children from Queen Joanna, Flavia had been recalled to the palace. Not because she could inherit, but because it had become imperative that she marry and produce an heir. Which she had duly and dutifully done, and now her son Viraj was five years old and heir to Caruli.

Now it was Elora's turn to duly, dutifully marry to produce an heir for Sarala. She understood that, but what if she was unable to carry out her duty in full?

'But perhaps we should at least have some tests done.' Her words were tentative; questioning her mother was not something to be undertaken lightly.

'No.' The reply was sharp, bringing back memories of other sharp words—words of censure, words that had caused pain, however much Elora knew she deserved them. 'There is no need and if anyone found out, rumours would fly. You are creating problems unnecessarily.' There was a slight pause and her mother gripped her arm. 'You have caused enough damage.' The words were said so softly it took Elora a second to absorb them, their meaning impacting with a dull, agonising thud even as the Queen continued. 'Do not do more. Then one day Flavia's son will rule Caruli and your son will rule Sarala.'

Now the Queen smiled, a frosty smile but a smile nonetheless, and it was a balm for Elora, and a promise that perhaps one day she would see the mother she remembered from when Sanjay was alive. A mother who had smiled often, and if that smile had mostly been for her brother there had still been leftover warmth and diluted love for Elora.

Perhaps she could win some of it back. By doing her duty. Perhaps she *was* worrying too much, making a problem where none existed.

'Enough talk,' her mother said now. 'I will take you to the meeting room. Remember, Elora, behave with decorum. Show him that you will be a good, dutiful wife.'

Good. Dutiful. Was that what his first wife had pledged to be? Princess Caroline—so vital, so beautiful, so talented and then so tragic.

Elora took one last look at her reflection. Long blonde hair, carefully clipped up into a tidy, sleek, glossy chignon. Dressed in a lehenga, the long, full silk skirt the teal blue of the Carulian flag, embossed with a pale pink diamond pattern and topped with a short, cropped blouse, lavishly embroidered, her bare midriff and arms artfully covered by a gauzy teal chiffon scarf. Her skin enhanced with the slightest tint of pink so that she didn't look deathly pale. She knew she burned too easily, her looks unusual for this island, courtesy of some European ancestor and her mother's English ancestry. Grey eyes a swirl of emotion, and she closed them in a rapid set of blinks to clear them, dug her nails into the palms of her hands to ground herself and keep the growing anxiety at bay.

'I'm ready,' she said.

CHAPTER TWO

ELORA FOCUSED ON taking one step at a time, heading for the Treasure Room, where she was to meet Rohan; her parents had chosen the venue, presumably to remind Prince Rohan that Caruli had just as much treasure as Sarala. With each step, her feet, clad in light embroidered slippers, felt as though they were encased in lead. But still she kept going, told herself that was the only way forward literally. And there was no other direction she could go. This meeting was inevitable, unavoidable. She was doing this for her country. One foot forward. Focus on getting the walk right, demonstrate the grace and poise expected of a Princess of Caruli.

If she kept that focus, she would be able to press down the anxiety that swirled inside her, the currents darker and stronger than the usual everyday nerves she'd learnt to live with. As always, she imagined the barrier holding it down, holding it at bay. An iron bar of control. Because if she allowed that barrier to yield she'd lose it, would show her weakness.

She could never let that happen again; it had been her weakness, her fears that had led to Sanjay's death—Elora could never forget that. Never forget and never forgive herself.

One more graceful step and they reached the Treasure

Room, where a staff member waited to push the heavy wooden door open.

Once inside, Queen Joanna looked around the room then turned to the staff member. 'The room has been checked?'

'Yes, Your Majesty. By three different people, including Mr Ashok.'

At the mention of the palace's security officer, Elora knew that her mother had been making sure there were no recording devices in the room, no possibility of a reporter having somehow infiltrated the palace.

The Queen nodded in dismissal. 'Please be sure to tell Prince Rohan this before you bring him here.'

Elora tried to calm her breathing, allowed herself one clench of her fists, dug her perfectly manicured nails into her palms. Nails painted a nice, neutral pale pearl colour that wouldn't call attention but would garner approval at their perfection.

She dug them in hard, needing the pain to distract her. Looked around the room as well, knowing she needed something to focus on, so if she felt the situation slip from her grasp she could find something to ground her. What better than the portrait of her brother Sanjay, aged eleven, painted just weeks before the fatal accident? After all, nothing could ground her more than the memory of her twin, the ache of missing him still so raw the pain seared her.

She saw that her mother too was looking at the portrait and a wave of sympathy engulfed Elora; her mother's pain at least equalled her own. The loss of her precious son, the heir she'd produced after so much grief and hope.

'Mama…' she began, but wished she hadn't as the Queen turned to her and Elora almost recoiled at the look in her mother's eyes, the flare of cold dislike.

'Do your duty, Elora, and do not make a mess of this. This marriage is necessary.'

And a redemption. Perhaps a way to alleviate her mother's deep, abiding disappointment that it was Sanjay who had died instead of Elora.

But now her heart started to beat faster as the heavy door swung open. To her surprise, it wasn't the equerry who entered, to precede and announce the arrival of the Prince.

Instead, a man she had no difficulty in recognising entered—a man she had briefly encountered years ago at official events, though mostly from a distance as political relations had been going through a strained period. A man she recognised more from the various articles and media posts she'd read.

But the pictures hadn't prepared her for the reality of him now in the flesh. Rohan was tall, his thick dark hair cut short but with a spiky uplift that suggested it was tamed from a tendency to wildness. His face was chiselled, the brown eyes, so dark as to be almost black, held an assurance and a coldness that made Elora shiver.

But it was a shiver caused by something else as well, something she was unable to define, causing her to grip the edge of the nearby chair, making her study him feature by feature. A face that looked etched in marble, all hard lines. The jaw was determined, the nose an aquiline jut—the only thing that looked out of control was the thick dark hair.

For an instant she was aware of his lightning scrutiny and something jolted in his eyes, the coldness charged with a flash of…heat, of surprise, arrest… Elora wasn't sure as it vanished as swiftly as it had arisen and he stepped forward towards her mother.

'Your Majesty.'

The Queen was frowning. 'I apologise for my equerry. He was instructed to bring you and announce you.'

'Please don't blame him. I prefer to announce myself; I made that clear to him. I would also like to thank you for agreeing that this meeting could be in private.'

Elora managed to restrain herself from an unladylike and audible gulp of shock. His words had been perfectly polite but insistent and the slightly dismissive tone had been unmistakable. If her mother had had any plans of remaining as chaperone they were being thwarted. But he'd had the grace at least to ensure there was no staff member present to witness any possible skirmish.

The Queen gave a regal inclination of her head. 'Your gratitude is noted. Please do not abuse the trust we have put in you. We will see you before you leave.'

'Of course.'

Elora watched as her mother left the room, glanced quickly at the picture of her brother, turned to face Rohan and waited in silence.

'I thought it would be better if our first meeting was in private.' His voice was deep, courteous but hard.

'As you wish,' she murmured. 'I am pleased to meet you again.'

'Are you?'

The question startled her and her eyes widened as she met his gaze, saw the sardonic rise of his eyebrow.

'You can be honest, Elora. That's why I wanted this meeting to be unchaperoned. Without convention and fanfare.' He glanced around. 'Shall we sit?' he suggested, his tone brusque, the words a statement rather than a question, and for a moment she was tempted to refuse, say she would prefer to conduct the conversation standing.

But that would be counter-productive, not what a dutiful wife would do. Plus she would rather be seated. So, without further comment, she headed to the two chairs arranged around an antique table placed in front of the ancient sword, its silver blade gleaming in the sunlight that streamed through the windows, causing the rubied hilt to gleam blood-red, displayed on a table draped with the Carulian flag.

Rohan eyed the sword before sitting. 'The sword that apparently slayed one of my ancestors,' he said.

'Centuries ago,' she replied. 'Isn't there a jewel-hilted dagger in the Throne Room of Sarala?'

'There is. I believe peace was eventually restored back then through marriage.'

'So, hundreds of years ago, a prince and princess sat together like this—maybe times haven't changed as much as all that.'

'All those years ago, that prince and princess had no choice; they were bringing years of bloodshed to an end. We do have a choice. You have a choice. That is what I am here to say. To ask. Are you being forced into this marriage?'

The direct question took her by surprise and she hoped she managed to conceal it as she tried to work out the best answer, found herself buying time with an apparent assumption of innocence. 'Is that a proposal?'

Elora took some satisfaction from seeing that the answer had wrongfooted him, and his lips relaxed into a near semblance of a smile. Suddenly she could almost see the prince who had graced the covers of various celeb publications in the past three years, recently with his arm around a beautiful woman.

Almost. Before his brown eyes hardened once more.

'No, it's not,' he said. 'It's a question. One I'd like a straight answer to.'

Elora paused, considered her options and saw the impatient movement of his fingers as they drummed the side of the chair.

'It's simple enough. Yes or no?'

'It's not that simple,' she snapped, then realised the tartness of her voice and drew a breath. But he wanted honesty, didn't he? 'If you want a single syllable answer, then no. I am not being forced.'

After all, her parents couldn't drag her kicking and screaming to the altar; there was no question of force. Unless the force of duty counted. Or the force of hope—the hope of redemption. The hope that if she did this, she could in some way make up for the death of her brother, for being the twin who had lived. If this marriage meant her parents could show her some forgiveness, some warmth, could be proud of her, then that hope would propel her to the altar.

He studied her expression for a moment then nodded and she took the opportunity to speak. 'Now can I ask you a question?'

'Of course.'

'Do you *want* to marry me?' He opened his mouth and she raised a hand. 'A straight answer, please. Of one syllable.'

That made him pause and now he did smile, a real smile that changed his whole expression and stance, warmed the brown eyes as he looked at her. Really looked at her, and there was that funny little shiver again.

'Touché,' he said.

'You mean it's not that simple?' she asked with exaggerated emphasis. 'You either do or you don't.'

'I don't want to marry anyone,' he stated.

'Then that includes me and the simple answer to the question is no.'

'Only you're right. It's not that simple,' he said.

'Isn't it?' she asked. 'If you don't want to marry me, why are you even here?'

Anxiety threatened and it was an effort to keep her voice steady. If Rohan decided not to go ahead with this marriage her parents would never believe it wasn't her fault. Maybe it would be. But…it would also free her from marriage to a man she didn't know and, from all she'd heard of him, didn't even want to know. A man whose visage was now grim, lips set in a firm line, brown eyes cold.

'Because, as I said, this isn't personal. I have no wish for marriage but I accept that it is a necessity. The dynasty must continue. As such, a marriage to a Princess of Caruli makes sense, given the political situation. As, most likely, our predecessors figured out.'

Sadness and a sense of bleakness touched her even as she appreciated the honest assessment of the situation.

'So perhaps I should change my answer to yes. I do want to marry you.'

The sadness intensified as she wondered what it would be like to be loved for oneself, wanted for herself, not because she was a Princess of Caruli.

'And you?' he asked. 'What of you? Do you want to marry me?'

The words seemed to rush through her head, so portentous she wasn't sure she could even breathe. Marry him. Marry a man who did not love her, did not even like her or know her. Marry a man whose first wife had run from him, and who had since been linked with at least two other women, both beautiful celebrities, as Princess Caro herself had been.

'Like you, I accept the necessity of a marriage.' The words sounded stilted and forced, even to her own ears. For a moment the future stretched before her, bleak and grey—life with a man who believed in duty, a cold man who was marrying her through necessity. As she was marrying him, she reminded herself.

She glanced at him now, realised her hands were clenched in her lap and quickly relaxed them. He was studying her and now he frowned, and she couldn't help it, a small shiver of apprehension ran through her at the cold darkness in his eyes, the formidable set to his lips.

'Or perhaps there is a better question. Do *you* want to marry anyone else? It seems clear from your reaction that you do not want to marry me.'

The question was so unexpected it jolted her out of fear and an image crossed her mind, the floating wisps of a dream.

'I...'

'Elora—' his voice harsh '—I need the truth. Is there someone else?'

She managed to shake her head, but the hardness remained in his eyes, his gaze unwavering, as though he wanted to probe her mind. But she could see shadows there too, shadows that spoke of suspicion and anger. She knew that she would have to explain something, however much she didn't want to.

'There isn't anyone else.'

After all, where would she have found the opportunity to meet someone, given her sheltered upbringing? The closest to romance she'd ever got was a few hasty kisses with a visiting minor royal, mostly motivated by an extra glass of wine and a burning desire to at least experience a kiss, to come a little closer to her imaginings. And the experience hadn't been unpleasant, but neither had it lived up to her hopes and dreams. Not that her hopes and dreams had any basis in reality, but they were precious to her, and now she knew she had no choice but to expose them.

She could see disbelief grow in his eyes. 'It is hard to believe that, given your expression.'

How could this have happened? What was it about this man that unsettled her so much that she had lost her ability to dissemble, to hide all feelings behind a cool mask?

'It is still the truth,' she said firmly. 'There is no one else. It is simply...with this marriage, I have to put aside any dream I had of some*thing* different, however much I knew the dream to be impossible.'

To her surprise, she saw understanding in his eyes as they softened slightly.

'What was the dream?' he asked.

'It doesn't really matter—it's foolish. Just an idea. About a life where I can be less of a princess, less of a public figure.' Allowed to slip into anonymity, where she could find a job that didn't require her to have any sort of public persona whatsoever.

'A life where you can marry someone else?'

His voice was way gentler now, but his eyes were still hooded, dark, calculating and Elora knew she had to dissemble, that this was rocky ground, an emotional minefield she didn't understand.

'That wasn't something I had considered—I'd got as far as imagining living in a small house or an apartment, not a palace, of popping to the grocery store, maybe growing my own vegetables in an allotment.' There was no need to tell this dark, brooding prince about the shadowy mythical figure on the periphery of her dream. A gentle man, someone average, who maybe wore glasses, had a slightly receding hairline, someone with a kind smile. Someone who didn't know Princess Elora, someone who knew just Elora.

'It was an alternate reality, not one that could ever come to fruition.'

'Unless, of course, Caruli became a republic.'

Elora shook her head. 'And that is not something I can ever wish for.' How could she betray her very heritage, voice any desire to remove the crown from her parents' heads, to deprive her nephew of his birthright? 'So truly I know that was nothing but a foolish dream.'

Yet she could still see some doubt in his eyes and, without even thinking, she leant forward, reached out and touched his hand. 'Truly,' she repeated, the word ending on a slight gasp.

What had just happened? The feel of his hand under her fingers, the firm strength of his flesh sparked something she didn't recognise, an unfamiliar wave of heat, a clench of her tummy muscles that caused her to snatch her hand back. She looked down at it, shock, surprise and that strange heat widening her eyes, then glanced up at him, saw something in his eyes, a flash of an unfamiliar response she couldn't identify. Though whatever it was sent a shiver rippling over her skin.

Using all her willpower, she pushed the feelings down. Just as she knew how to hold anxiety at bay, so she would this, whatever this was. She forced her expression to become neutral, to wear the cool, impassive princess mask.

'That's the truth,' she said. 'There is no one else I want to marry.' She held his gaze, kept her voice level.

'OK,' he said, and he too now had himself in hand, no scowl, no emotion, and then for a moment his face lost some of its hardness. Perhaps there was even a hint of compassion in his dark eyes. 'I'm sorry, Elora, sorry that the dream of normality isn't possible. Whether you marry me or not.'

Her eyes narrowed. She didn't want pity. This was her choice as much as his and his hardship as much as hers. This was her future and, dammit, she was going to at least try to make the best of it.

Somehow.

Bracing herself, she forced a smile to her lips, a smile that could pass muster as genuine, tried and practised for use at all social occasions.

'So I guess we are going to do this?' she said, keeping her voice light and steady.

'I guess we are.'

'Was *that* a proposal?' she asked.

There was a pause and then he smiled, a small smile admittedly, but at least his lips upturned. And there it was again—she found herself looking at his mouth, studying that upturn, and a funny, unfamiliar sensation twisted in her tummy.

'I suppose it was.' Then the smile vanished.

'I am sure you pictured something more romantic than this. But I can see no point in dishonesty or hypocrisy. So I will not be going down on one knee with violins in the background.'

Elora heard the bitterness in his voice, wondered if he had done that for his first wife. All she remembered was the announcement of the engagement—that had been done with plenty of pomp and ceremony.

But what she, and probably everyone, remembered most was not the beginning of the marriage but the end—the stories that had swirled and grown. Stories of a beautiful wife, a celebrated actress with an adoring fanbase, already a European cinema idol, driven desperate with misery at the reception she'd received from the royal family. A woman who'd wished to continue with her career, the idea apparently frowned upon. Stories of how she had thrown herself on her husband's mercy, begging for help and release from the marriage. Stories of an escape plan, of night-time car chases and private helicopters. Speculation had been rife and, through it all, Elora's sympathies had been with Princess Caro, and she had hoped once a divorce went through that the Princess would find peace. Had been pleased when, a year later, there was news that she had remarried.

But there would be no escape route for Elora. No romance and no escape. But no matter.

She inclined her head now. 'There is no need to apologise. There are more important things to think about here than romance.'

'Yes, there are. If you are sure you wish to go ahead with it, we need to discuss how this marriage will work.'

This marriage—he didn't even use the word 'our'—and that was...wrong.

He'd clocked her reaction. 'What's wrong?' Yet the words themselves were said neutrally, almost with a dash of impatience.

'Nothing is wrong. But this marriage...it's not an abstract. It's our marriage.'

He shook his head. 'It is, but it isn't personal.'

No way could she let that go. 'Actually, yes, it is. Personal.' She needed to say this, now. He'd said he wanted honesty. Well, that went two ways, and this might be her only chance to have a proper conversation with him before chaperones and occasions took over. 'We're people.'

'No, Elora. That's the point. You are a princess. I am a prince. We are marrying as representatives of our countries. Sarala is wedding Caruli.'

'Yes.' She took a deep breath. 'But it's still personal. Part of this marriage is about the need for an heir.' Gritting her teeth, she found courage from somewhere, knew her cheeks were tinged with pink even as she spoke the words. 'Or perhaps it's better to say Sarala needs an heir, which means Sarala is also bedding Caruli. And that is personal. Up close and personal.'

Especially given at some future point she was going to have to explain, or she supposed he would figure it out, that she had never been bedded before.

If her mother had heard these words she would be horrified; perhaps Rohan was. But he didn't seem horrified. Instead, he was looking at her...differently. There was no coldness in his eyes now; they held an intentness, a focus, as if he were seeing her properly for the first time. Considering 'up close and personal'. Seeing her as a person and, for some reason, instead of filling her with disquiet, it was sending a little ripple of sensation over her skin. She caught her breath on a sudden gasp, but met his gaze full-on, tried to read what she saw there.

Then it was gone and he raised his hands.

'You're right. I'm sorry. That is a fair point. I want you to know that we can take our time with that side of things. We won't do anything until you're ready. Until we're both ready.'

'OK. Thank you.' Only as she looked at him now she was aware of just the faintest shiver of...disappointment? Ridiculous—what did she want? Rohan to carry her over his shoulder caveman-style to the bedroom? The image threatened to take hold in her mind and she pushed it away. Dear Lord. What was wrong with her?

She focused on what he was saying next.

'So, on a practical note, we should announce the engagement as soon as possible. I have no doubt our parents have got it all planned out. A pageant, a show, the sooner the people know the better.'

Elora frowned. She opened her mouth to speak and then closed it again. After all, it sounded as though the decision had been made.

'Don't you agree?'

'I… I'm not sure…'

But, before she could continue, the door swung open and an equerry came in. 'Announcing Their Majesties King Gaurav and Queen Joanna.'

Her parents.

CHAPTER THREE

ROHAN ROSE TO his feet, but not before he'd seen the change in Elora. Her face just seconds before had shown animation, a desire to share an opinion despite her clear anxiety about doing so. Now it was as though it had closed down, her expression remote, distant, an ice princess.

Thus she had looked when he'd entered the room, until... Until their gazes had locked and then there had been a flash, something in her clear, cool grey eyes, light as a single raincloud on a summer day.

He gave his head a small shake; the imagery was ridiculously poetic.

But something was going on. Because the remote ice princess façade had changed in the past half an hour. Perhaps encouraged by the knowledge that this was her chance to be honest, she had been surprisingly direct. Which was useful, because at least he knew what he needed to know. No one was forcing this bride into marriage.

Not that his first wife had been forced. Though that was what Caro had claimed at the end, in desperate self-defence of her betrayal. She'd said that he had coerced her, bullied her. At first he'd been stunned that anyone would believe that to be possible; Caro had been a famous actress when he'd met her, a friend of his older sister, a woman with a string of celebrity relationships behind her. Yet she had played the role of persecuted heroine so well, the press, the public...everyone had believed her.

But Elora was doing her duty of her own free will. As was he. As had their ancestors all those generations ago. Though she, like him, had expressed the wish for a normal life. The knowledge that she felt as he did had forged a strange tenuous connection, even if it was one there would be no point in discussing.

He stepped forward to kneel before his prospective in-laws for the traditional blessing and then rose to his feet, shot one more look at Elora, saw her glance at a portrait on the far wall before turning to bow her head in respect towards her parents.

King Gaurav stepped towards Rohan without even a glance at his daughter. 'Rohan. We thought it was time to join the meeting. There are details to sort out that need our presence.' The King's voice was assured, a man in no doubt of his authority. Like Rohan's father, he carried an aura, a sense of power and a sense that that power was deserved. A blood right.

Rohan knew that he lacked that surety, could not put his hand on his heart and say he deserved the power that came to him simply because he had been born the son of a king. It was a different matter at the negotiation table or in a boardroom full of business people. A different matter when he was acting on behalf of his country to promote it. There, Rohan knew his worth. Knew he was good at his job.

But here, standing by the ancient sword, surrounded by reminders of rulers gone by, it was possible to feel awed by the majesty of royalty, sense the aura of this King of Caruli.

Queen Joanna stepped forward and Rohan studied her. Saw the resemblance to Elora—the blonde hair, though now courtesy of an expensive hairdresser and toned to an ash-blonde, the grey eyes the same colour, but Queen Joanna's held hardness and calculation. She was still a beautiful woman, but her lips held a line of ingrained disapproval as she regarded him.

She spoke now. 'We will announce the engagement tomorrow—I assume you have brought appropriate clothing and necessities to remain here a few days. If not, we will, of course, be happy to send for them.'

Rohan frowned; he'd expected haste but not to this extent, especially not on this island. After all, he knew that Elora's older sister had given birth to a son. Prince Viraj was five and Caruli had an heir, had its succession in place.

On the other hand, this was what his parents had advocated—for Sarala, speed was essential. After all, he was not exactly beloved of the people of Sarala; it was better now than in the aftermath of his divorce, but he still had much to prove.

In which case, perhaps there was little point in delay; hadn't he himself said that to Elora only minutes before? Baluka had declared its republic status—time for royalty to strike back.

He sensed the smallest of movements next to him and turned to look at Elora, but her expression remained calm, serene and accepting.

Yet, minutes before, Elora had also had something to say, an opinion she'd wanted to voice. Why had her parents made a point of cutting their tête-à-tête short? Why the insistence on an announcement tomorrow? Why was the King acting as though his daughter wasn't even present in the room, as if she had no say? Rohan believed Elora had told him the truth, that she wasn't being forced to the altar. But what if he was wrong?

There was no doubt that she was different in her parents' presence. In addition, there were further things he'd intended to discuss with his prospective bride, rules he'd wanted to set in place for the structure of their marriage. True, these things could be deferred until after the announcement but...

All his negotiating instincts were telling him he was being corralled. *They* were being corralled.

'Actually,' he said, and then stopped at the look of surprise on the King's face. 'Actually,' he repeated, 'I believe such an announcement is a little premature.' He raised a hand. 'Your daughter and I have agreed in principle to marriage. However, there is still much I would like to discuss with the Princess, prior to an official announcement. In fact, I was just about to ask her if she would do me the honour of having dinner with me tonight.'

There was silence, which Rohan made no move to break. He'd stated his position.

'Dinner.' The Queen uttered the word as though she'd never heard of the idea before. 'The two of you.'

'Yes. I would be delighted if the Princess came to Sarala and the palace there. Alternatively—' and now Rohan couldn't help himself '—if you give me access to the palace kitchens I would be happy to prepare a meal.' With luck, the suggestion would distract the Queen sufficiently from the idea of giving permission.

'Or perhaps, Mama—' Elora spoke for the first time since her parents' arrival '—I could cook for Rohan.'

'Then tomorrow, of course, we can meet to discuss the timing of an engagement. Like you, my parents are eager for an early announcement,' Rohan offered.

There was silence and now, finally, the King's gaze flickered to his daughter and then straight back to Rohan.

'Very well,' the King said. 'But tomorrow we need to finalise details. The people need to see this alliance.'

Elora bowed her head and the Queen stepped forward. 'Come, Elora.' She turned to Rohan. 'Dinner will be at seven-thirty. I will send a staff member to accompany you to the dining room. In the meantime, I hope you find the suite to your liking.'

A clear dismissal and equally clear injunction to remain in said suite until dinner, and Rohan accepted that. He had work to do after all. Work. Again, a bleakness settled over him. Would his work now have to come to an end? The business he had put so much into—would he have to sell up, liquidate? The thought filled him with a frustration that twisted his gut even as he knew he had to face the impending destiny he'd never wanted.

At precisely seven-thirty there was a knock on his door and Rohan went to open it, and smiled a welcome to the young man outside. He was slightly surprised when the palace staff member merely bowed the smallest of bows. 'Your Highness, I have been sent to escort you to dinner.' Somehow, the words managed to convey the utmost disapproval of both Rohan and the enterprise whilst still maintaining a rigid civility.

Perhaps, unlikely though it seemed, he was a budding republican. Whatever the reason, Pamir, who disclosed his name with palpable reluctance, maintained his distance for the whole journey down the magnificent staircase and along the palace corridors, past the imposing line of paintings and the gilded wooden panels.

He knocked at a door and this time Rohan decided to let him do his job and announce him, which he did with suitable words but a definite lack of fervour. Yet when he bowed to Elora his face creased into a genuine smile and Rohan blinked, waited until Pamir had left and turned to Elora. And blinked again, but for a different reason. Because there was no mistaking it this time—the gut punch of sudden, unexpected desire.

Dressed now in a more casual traditional *salwar kameez*, the calf-length, high-necked tunic a teal blue colour, with a floral pattern to reflect the teal, pink and white colours of the Carulian flag, over teal loose-fitting trousers, Elora looked beautiful, but it was more than that… Mere beauty wouldn't spark this sudden visceral reaction. Her glossy pure blonde hair was still pulled up but the style was slightly softer, allowing a few tendrils to escape, to frame the classic oval-shaped face. Her grey eyes seemed almost luminous and widened as she met his gaze. Now his eyes dropped to the curve of her lips, noted the generous shape, and the urge to step forward and pull her into his arms nigh on overwhelmed him.

Though of course he did nothing of the sort. Feet planted firmly on the ground, he tried to regroup, to find his usual poise, to regain control of this dinner and its agenda. This would be a marriage of convenience and he knew all too well from bitter experience how important it was to set rules in place before the event.

He nodded towards the door from which Pamir had departed. 'You have a definite fan there.'

'I have known Pamir all my life. The three of us played in…' She broke off and he knew she must be speaking of her brother, Prince Sanjay, whose life had tragically ended in an accident aged eleven.

'I'm sorry—' he began.

'Thank you.' Her voice was colourless but definite, the spark that had been there just seconds before extinguished.

'But there is no need to say any more.' She clearly had no intention of expanding on the subject and he didn't blame her. Yet he'd seen the flash of raw grief in her eyes, knew the memory had triggered a pain he couldn't fathom. Elora and Sanjay had been twins and he couldn't imagine what his loss must have meant to her. He wanted to offer comfort, but he sensed it wouldn't be welcomed. Especially not from him.

'Please be seated, Your Highness,' she continued, her voice both formal and aloof. 'The food is in chafing dishes to keep warm. I will serve you when you are ready.'

'No.' The refusal was instinctive. 'I am happy to serve myself.'

'As you wish.' She bowed her head and his eyes narrowed as he wondered if her parents had spent the day instructing her on how to behave at dinner. To present herself as a dutiful wife-to-be, allay any doubts that Rohan might have.

'That *is* what I wish. I also wish to apologise. When I asked you to dinner I didn't intend for you to have to cook it yourself.'

'It was no trouble.'

'Is that the truth?' He asked the question abruptly in the hope it might provoke an honest answer.

'Yes.' And this time her voice sounded more definite. 'I enjoy cooking.'

He studied her expression. 'For real? Or do you think that is the "right" answer? I would like us to continue to be honest with each other.'

He gestured with one hand as he spoke to emphasise his point, just as she did the same as she opened her mouth to speak, and, before he could pull back, their hands collided. It was the merest of accidental brushes and yet the effect caused him to hold his breath. It had sparked a current, a shimmer in the air that made them both look down at their hands as if in wonder.

She recovered herself first, fast enough that he wondered if he'd imagined the whole thing, though he knew he hadn't. On his part, anyhow.

But better to ignore it. Until he'd figured out what to do about it. On the one hand, of course it was positive if he and Elora were attracted to each other, but…he had no wish for an attraction that felt so…intense. An attraction that had the potential to distract him from what would be way more important in this marriage. Structure, rules, control.

'It is the truth.' Her voice was slightly breathless and this time she kept talking, he guessed as a distraction from whatever had just happened. 'Honestly, I've always liked to cook. When I was a child I spent as much time as I could in the palace kitchens and one of the sous chefs befriended me. Pamir's mother, in fact. She showed me how to bake and I loved it. Then…' she paused a fraction of a beat '…later, as I grew older, the kitchen became a place where I could be me. When I cook, I stop being a princess. If that makes sense.'

'It does,' he said. That was how he felt when he was involved in his business, where he was simply Rohan Carmody, a name he'd derived from his royal dynastic name, Kamodian.

'It's a chance to create something in different ways. You can follow a recipe or adapt it or have a go at making things up from scratch. Can suit your creation to your mood.' He knew that her love of cooking was genuine; there was real enthusiasm on her face and the animation gave her vitality and assurance. 'When I'm cooking I can kind of zone out from real life.' She stopped and bit her lip as if in annoyance at giving away too much. 'Anyway, as I said, it was no trouble to cook tonight.'

'Now I do believe you and I am looking forward to eating what you've cooked.' He hesitated. 'But is it OK if we talk first? So I'm not distracted by the food.' It was going to be hard enough not to be distracted by the tug of awareness that was refusing to disappear, even in the flow of conversation.

'Of course. Please go ahead.'

'Shall we sit?'

She nodded and they sat at the perfectly set dining table, a centrepiece of flowers exuding both colour and a light pleasant scent. Linen napkins and silver cutlery gleamed and there were candles in the elaborate silver candlesticks.

'So what room is this?' he asked.

'This is known as the meeting chamber. The history books say it is where important lords would be invited to private conversations—near the kitchen so that one trusted servant could bring food and drink easily and safely. It is used for similar purposes nowadays. I like it because I used to sit in here and read recipe books.'

For a moment he could picture a younger Elora sitting with legs curled under her, hiding from the realities of the palace and escaping into a world of ingredients.

'This feels like a good place then. I felt we were interrupted this morning before we'd had a chance to finish our discussion of what happens next. When I suggested we announce the engagement soon I got the feeling you disagreed. When your parents suggested it, though, you said nothing.'

'Nothing I say would change my parents' minds.' The words were a simple statement of fact, not bitter.

'OK. But *I* will listen. And if we are in agreement together, we will be able to change their minds. I will listen,' he repeated, sensing her reluctance and seeing the doubt in her eyes. But not just doubt, surprise as well at his words. Clearly, Elora wasn't used to being listened to. That or she hadn't thought he was the sort of man who paid attention. He waited, let the silence speak for itself, then risked a smile. 'But I need something to listen to.'

Then she gave a small smile of her own and he felt as though there had been some level of acceptance.

'Fair point,' she said. One more second to marshal her thoughts and then, 'I understand why this marriage is a good idea. For our countries.' If not for them. The words were unspoken but no less poignant for that. 'But the idea is to reassure the people that the monarchies of Caruli and Sarala are stable and present and will continue. That the rule of their kings will go on fairly and justly, so there is no need for a republic.'

'Agreed.'

'But I believe it is about more than that. Reassurance that something will continue is not enough to make people not want change.' She paused, seeming to replay the sentence in her head. 'Even people who support the monarchy may not want it to continue as it always has.'

Rohan stared at her, struck by the observation and its truth. He himself felt like that, so did Marisa, and there was every chance that Elora's older sister Flavia did too. So if they, as the younger generation of royals, felt like that, so too would the people.

'They want to see that we've moved with the times, that some things have changed since our ancestors' days.'

Elora nodded and for the first time that day she smiled a real smile that lit her grey eyes and revealed an unexpected dimple in her left cheek and a sudden breathless-ness threatened him.

'Exactly. And seeing us rush into marriage won't show that at all. Two people who don't know each other. Some people will decry it as a political move that insults their intelligence, others will dislike the idea that two young people are marrying simply for political reasons, others will feel that we are being forced into it and that that is wrong.' She hesitated. 'I know that is what Pamir feels; that is why he was so reticent with you. He is fond of me and he suspects what is going on and he believes it is wrong for me to be rushed into marriage, especially…'

She broke off abruptly and Rohan had little doubt about what words she'd cut off and a sudden surge of anger ran through him.

'You may as well say it, Elora. Finish the sentence. He doesn't want you to be rushed into marriage, especially with me, given my reputation as a terrible husband.' Terrible didn't really cover it, but he'd rather be thought of as a cruel, unfeeling bastard than for the truth to be known. And it seemed clear that Elora believed every one of those rumours and speculations, believed in the portrait the press had painted, and for an instant that fed the anger, turned it into an ice-cold hurt, even though he knew he could hardly blame her. 'I get it. The press may take this and come up with a sacrificial lamb story, which isn't what we want at all.'

'I don't think we can ignore that the people, especially those on Caruli, may feel that. I am their princess.'

And much as he loathed having to ask the next ques-tion, he knew he must. 'What about how you feel? Do you see yourself as a sacrificial lamb?'

'No.' But the denial held a thread of doubt and now the

anger and hurt morphed into sudden compassion. How was Elora supposed to know the truth? If she believed even one half of the speculation she was probably terrified of him.

'Elora, look at me. Please.' She raised her head and did so. 'I don't want to discuss my previous marriage—it is water under the bridge and in the past.' A past he would not revisit. 'But I promise I will do my best to be a good husband. You have no need to be afraid of me.' He could only hope the words rang true, even as he knew they were words he would say even if they weren't truth.

Her grey eyes looked into his, unreadable pools of shimmering silver, and she gave a small tentative nod. An acknowledgement, he hoped, that she had at least registered the words, so perhaps something had been achieved, a small measure of trust, however fragile.

'So now I'd like to hear how you think we should present this marriage to the people.'

'As a positive thing, so we need a positive spin.'

'What sort of spin?' He knew he wasn't going to like this.

'A romance.'

Rohan stared at her, every instinct crying out against something so patently ridiculous. 'You want us to spin a romance, pretend we're in love, act all lovey-dovey.' He couldn't help the horror in his voice. 'It won't work. No one would believe it.'

'Why not?'

'Because I am not a romantic type of guy.'

'I get that.' Her voice was cool, nonjudgmental, and against his will he felt sympathy for her. He wondered if she had ever dreamt of romance, but reminded himself that she must have known a political marriage was most likely for her. 'You don't have to *be* romantic, you just have to pretend. This would be the story. Now Baluka has become a republic, it is natural for you to be recalled. It is also natural for our families to confer, to work together and to want to show the people that we are good rulers with a plan. Agreed?'

'So far,' Rohan said cautiously.

'So, as Sarala's ambassador, you have come to Caruli today to meet my parents and discuss ways for Sarala and Caruli to work together. Whilst you're here you also meet me and we...' Now she blushed. 'We like each other and you ask me to dinner.'

As he looked at her, somehow, that whole fiction didn't seem so impossible. Because, dammit, something was going on here. If he'd met Elora back in London, if she hadn't been a princess, and there'd been this zing of desire, maybe he would have asked her to dinner. Or maybe he wouldn't, because he wouldn't have trusted the intensity of the desire. He knew desire didn't last, still recalled the wild, heady days of his marriage to his first wife. After Caro, he'd taken a different approach to relationships—attraction, sure, but nothing that wasn't under control. Nothing that made him care.

Undaunted by his silence, she continued, though her voice faltered slightly. 'Then we go from there. We plan various dates; we can use them to get out and about. I can show you Caruli, you can show me Sarala. It will be great publicity, and give us a chance to give our views, travel around, and show the people who we are, who the next generation is.'

Rohan studied her, saw the intensity in her grey eyes. Her arguments were lucid and made sense and he was struck anew by the difference in her here and now, compared to the princess he'd met earlier in the day. Was aware again of that simmer of desire, knew too that desire was only an added complication. Right now, this marriage had to be all about measured decisions, about avoiding another disaster like his previous marriage.

'Those are all valid arguments,' he acknowledged. He knew too what she wasn't saying, that her way would show the world that this would be a different marriage to the one that went before, that she was no sacrificial lamb, that she was going into this marriage of her own free will. Proof would be in the spinning of a romance.

'So do you want to go ahead?'

Did he?

Aware of her steady gaze, he considered the strategy.

CHAPTER FOUR

THERE WAS A long silence and although Rohan's expression was impassive Elora sensed he was considering the idea, assessing the pros and cons and its viability. A look of weariness crossed his face, weariness mixed with distaste, and she felt a pang of hurt—a hurt that years of practice enabled her to instantly mask. A quick glance down at her folded hands was enough to allow her to put the expression of serene acceptance back onto her face. At least he had considered the idea, not dismissed it out of hand.

Yet when she looked back up she saw that his dark eyes were watching her.

'It is a good idea...'

'But?' she asked. 'But it is too much effort and will be too difficult for you to pretend to be attracted to me. I understand.'

Elora was sure she had kept any note of bitterness from her voice—after all, she did understand. But what she hadn't expected was the crack of laughter that greeted her words and she couldn't keep the surprise from her face.

'What's so funny?'

Rohan shook his head. 'That's not what I was thinking. At all. I mean you're right—it will be an effort, but not because I can't pretend to be attracted to you. That won't be a problem.'

Elora bit her lip, held back the urge to ask what he meant. Did he mean he was attracted to her? The idea sent an unfamiliar shiver down her spine, clenched her tummy muscles, caused her eyes to linger suddenly on his lips, his hands, the sheer strength he exuded.

Get a grip. He'd said it would be easy to pretend—all that meant was that he knew how to act, play to the camera. But... The way he was looking at her, right here and now... There was heat in his dark eyes. She was sure of it. Nearly sure.

Though how was she to tell, to know? She had no idea how to play this game, no inkling of the rules. All she did know was that she had no intention of making a fool of herself.

Keeping her voice cool, she said, 'I'm glad to hear you are confident in your acting skills. You'll have to give me some tips. If we go ahead with this. So what were you going to say?'

She kept her gaze neutral, her chin at a slightly defiant tilt, and waited.

'I was going to say that I am not sure you are truly aware of what you are taking on. Not just with me but with the press. Your idea means we will be on show, playing the part of two people falling in love, and we'll need to be convincing because, trust me, the press will want its pound of flesh and they'll be scrutinising every move, every word, every look, and it won't always be under our control. They will rake things up and speculate, and that can be difficult. I can't let you go into this without really considering what you will be putting yourself through. And the consequences if we can't pull it off.'

She saw the shadows cloud his eyes and knew he spoke from bitter experience, remembered exactly how the press had torn into him, their persistence, the stories and opinions and... For a second, sympathy threatened. Until she recalled the facts—or at least what had surely been the facts. Princess Caro had accused her husband of cold-hearted cruelty. And Rohan had never once, personally or through a spokesman, so much as issued a denial, had made no comment whatsoever, made no attempt to put his side of the story, never refuted a single one of the claims.

Never given his side, presumably because there was no side to give.

But now, as she looked at him, Elora was aware of a sliver of doubt as to his guilt. Cold maybe, but cruel? He'd shown no sign of cruelty, but then again, he'd said himself he was a good actor—maybe all of this, the dinner, the meeting was an act. Judging by the grim set of his mouth now, she had little doubt that he could be ruthless

'I understand that the press will be intrusive and ever-present, but there is not a lot they can do to hurt me. My past is an open book.' She took a deep breath. 'But I understand this will be difficult for you, so really it is your call. If the inevitable coverage of your first marriage will be too...' What word to use? Her brain spun as she saw the set of his lips, the darkness in his eyes '...painful I understand that.'

The wrong adjective, though she suspected any word she'd picked would have been wrong as the grim expression hardened.

She hurried on. 'But maybe you could come up with a way you want us to combat it.'

'We will not speak about my first marriage. Not to the press, not to anyone.'

Elora bowed her head, pushed down the sudden surge of anxiety that threatened. Because when Rohan looked like that, so formidable, so withdrawn, the doubts could only multiply. What was she getting herself into?

'Understood,' she said. 'The decision is yours. I would like to try the fake romance angle, but again it is up to you.'

There was a second of hesitation and then he nodded, held out a hand. 'Then we have a deal.'

Elora hesitated. Doubt shot into her head—what if her mother was wrong and Elora did have fertility issues? No. She would not think that, would not let an anxiety, a weakness affect this decision, use it as an excuse to allow her not to marry this man, do her duty. Earn redemption. Her mother was right; she had done enough damage already. The memory of her words jolted pain through her and also a dose of determination. She would do this for Caruli, and maybe her mother would show her some respect, some semblance of affection. Perhaps her father would feel something positive about her.

Abruptly, she put her hand out, watched as if in slow motion he took it in his, and then she wasn't sure what happened. It felt as though a current shot up her arm at his touch, as if she could see sparks fly, and her reaction was so extreme, so out of her comfort zone she couldn't cover it. She dropped his hand and stared at him, wide-eyed.

'I... Food...' she gabbled. 'Now we've made that decision, let's have food.' The idea calmed her as she thought about the meal she'd prepared, ran through the components, the menu, and she managed to rise with her usual poise at least mostly intact.

Rohan nodded, though she was sure he rose with unseemly haste, after a quick glance down at his own hand. But by the time they returned to their seats with their loaded plates he seemed unflustered, sat down and waited for her before tasting his own food. She saw the surprise in his eyes as he chewed and swallowed and then looked up at her.

'This is amazing.'

Now she smiled, a real smile, because she knew he wasn't faking this. 'Thank you. I'm glad you like it. It is a Carulian speciality with a royal history, so it seemed appropriate.'

'Tell me.'

'So, years ago, Carulian kings were avid hunters—as you know, Caruli is known for its wild horses and royalty liked nothing better than to go out hunting. But they also liked to eat the meat as fresh as possible, so they would take their royal chefs with them on the hunt. Royalty also wanted their meat to be properly cooked and to smell good. Not always easy for a chef presented with a freshly killed boar or deer. So this dish was born—basically, those chefs figured out they needed to carry a whole host of ingredients with them and as time went on they perfected the recipe. Apparently, King Aadarsh about a hundred years ago chased the royal chef around the eating area because the dish was too bland.'

'Well, I promise I won't be chasing you round the table because of that.'

There was a momentary silence and Elora bit back a mad urge to ask if there were any other reasons why he would chase her round the table, and pushed away the idea that she probably wouldn't run very fast.

'You wouldn't need to,' she said without thinking, re-played the words in her head and hurried on. 'I mean, one of the ingredients in this is hot chilli peppers, along with cumin, coriander, melon seeds, peppercorns, ginger. Oh, and it isn't made with wild boar any more either—I've used chicken, and I've added my own twist. Lime and a bit of paprika.'

'Well, the whole thing is incredible.'

'And these look good too.' He pointed as he spoke.

'I cooked the bread in the tandoor oven, the rice is just plain but I've made it as fluffy as possible and there is a simple *raita* to go with it. I thought that would cool it down. I don't know how hot or spicy you like things.' She looked at him. 'Your food, I mean. Obviously.' *For heaven's sake.*

For a moment she thought she saw a gleam of amusement in his eyes.

'So, do you cook a lot? For family?'

Elora shook her head. 'My parents don't really understand or approve of my cooking. They believe there are more important things to do.'

'Do you agree?'

'Of course. I understand that part of being a princess is a lifestyle that involves having a palace chef and kitchen staff. But I do love cooking and it can be a useful skill. That's why I decided to…' Elora broke off, aware that she was so unused to anyone showing an interest in her that she'd nearly said something she had no intention of sharing.

'Why you decided to do what?'

'Nothing. It doesn't matter.'

'Then why can't you tell me?' The question was eminently reasonable.

'Because it's not something I've told anyone, so I'd rather keep it to myself.'

'OK, but, for the record, you can trust me. We've just made a deal to fake a relationship, to get married.'

'As a deal,' Elora said softly. 'We still don't really know each other. Trust has to be earned.' And she didn't know if she could ever trust a man who'd treated his ex-wife as he apparently had. A man who had made it clear that marriage was off-limits as a topic to his soon-to-be second wife. 'Would you tell me something, share a secret with me?'

'It would depend on the secret.'

'There you are. This is a secret I propose to keep.'

'Fair enough, and I agree that trust has to be earned.

But there are some things that we will have to trust each other on going forward.'

'Such as?' She heard a heaviness in his voice, and suddenly the enormity of what they were planning struck her anew. She took another forkful of food and focused on identifying the flavours. The slight bitterness of the cumin, the tart lime, the sweetness of the smoked paprika and the bite of chilli all grounded her.

'I need to trust that you will behave appropriately; you cannot cause any scandal. Your reputation must be spotless. Not only now but throughout our married life. No scandal, no negative publicity. And that means fidelity. If you have any doubts about that, then this will not work. The press will sniff out any indiscretion and I will not tolerate seeing my wife splashed across the papers with another man.'

A sudden anger lacerated her at his tone and at his words and Elora narrowed her eyes. 'I understand you don't know me, Rohan, but I wouldn't do that to you or anyone. There will be no indiscretions. And,' she couldn't help adding, 'I am not the one with the track record of being splashed across the papers with a partner. So can I check where you stand on the fidelity front? One rule for you, one for me?'

After all, she knew that was the way of the world. Her sister's husband had been rumoured to have had an affair, but the expectation had been that Flavia would forgive and forget. She had a suspicion that her own father had strayed even as her mother had turned a blind eye, too worried that her husband would divorce her for failing to produce another heir.

Anger flared in his eyes for a moment, but no way would she back down.

Then, unexpectedly, Rohan's expression relaxed, his lips even turned up in the smallest of smiles. 'Fair point and fair question. In answer, I play fair. I will not expose my wife to the humiliation of seeing me splashed across the papers with another woman. You can trust me on that. Can I trust you?'

'Yes.'

But as they looked at each other she knew that, once again, these were only words. Trust did have to be earned over time. But maybe for now they needed to believe that it was a possibility. But how to make that start? She had to try.

Perhaps he felt the same, as he leaned over and gently covered her hand with his own. 'Then that's a good start.'

The words accentuated the sense of warmth, of promise that his touch was generating, causing a swirl of conflicting feelings. A heat, a desire that caused her to tentatively reach out and cover his hand in hers in acknowledgement.

She heard his own swiftly concealed intake of breath, which he tried to mask by clearing his throat, and her whole being was focused on their still clasped hands, dwelt on the sensation of his skin beneath hers.

'A good start,' she managed, and now she wasn't even sure what they were talking about any more. Her lips had parted and his dark gaze focused on her mouth and she was leaning forward, and so was he and she knew she needed to break the spell. She pulled her hands back and for a second she froze, their gazes enmeshed, and then she scrambled ungracefully to her feet.

'I... How about dessert?' She gave what she recognised herself as a slightly breathless laugh. 'Luckily, it's ice cream.' *Really*, Elora... Perhaps she should suggest they bathe in it? 'Well, not ice cream, more of a *kulfi*. But I even got cones.'

'Then I have an idea.' She wasn't sure if she was imagining it, but his voice held something, something that surely couldn't be shock. 'Why don't we go for a moonlit stroll?

You can show me the palace gardens.' His voice gained assurance. 'It could be a part of our story. We have an evening stroll and eat ice cream.'

'Good idea.'

'And we could talk as well.'

'About what?'

'About next steps, a more detailed plan, and exactly what we need to do to pull this off.'

It was a good point. If they were going to pull this off in the face of intense press scrutiny, they would need to be convincing. Would have to act as though they liked each other—would have to act as though they were attracted to each other.

That could be crucial, the make-or-break pivot.

Problem was, right now, Elora didn't understand what was going on, had a horrible suspicion that she was actually really attracted to Rohan. It was an unforeseen development and she had no idea what to do about it. In which case, she would have to pretend to be pretending about an attraction she had no desire to feel.

And then her gaze lingered on his lips, fell to his hands, imagined them around her waist, tugging her body against his, pictured her lips parting, her own hands in his thick, dark hair, pulling him closer... Elora gulped, felt heat rush to her face and over her body. The flush of awareness signalled a sense of panic, and from somewhere she pulled a final vestige of poise and could only hope that Rohan hadn't clocked any of her ridiculously out of control reactions.

'Sure. Good plan,' was the best she could come up with as she forced herself to walk from the room with all the grace and poise she had spent so many years cultivating, and which this man was threatening to dismantle in mere hours.

CHAPTER FIVE

ROHAN TOOK A deep breath as he watched Elora leave the room and head for the kitchen, aware of the need to pull his thoughts together, pull *himself* together and stop being so poleaxed by a brush of their hands, so distracted by her lips.

Because they had to figure out how to make this fake romance plan work, however much the word *romance* set his teeth on edge. He recalled the futile, gauche, unwanted romantic gestures he'd made in an attempt to fathom his first marriage and he could almost taste the bitter after-taste of humiliation. He'd been a fool, a credulous fool, and he'd paid the price.

But this was different; this was a planned romance.

An illusion.

One that made political sense.

He looked up as Elora returned, carefully holding two cones, each topped with a light green scoop. He rose and headed towards her, and there it was again, a hum, a zing, a visceral reaction triggered by…by Elora. He wasn't sure if it was the gloss of her hair, the grey of her eyes, the tilt of her chin or the tantalising scent of rose petals. What-ever it was, it kept catching him unawares, shocking him with its volatility.

He took his proffered cone, noted how careful they both were to avoid even an accidental touch.

'Thank you.'

'You're welcome. Follow me. I agree we should see the palace gardens. They are illuminated and a truly beautiful place to walk. I've grown up with them and they still fill me with awe. If we need to, it will be easy to describe a romantic stroll there.'

'Sounds ideal.' He tasted the *kulfi* and turned to her, genuinely distracted from his thoughts. 'This is also amazing.'

For a fleeting second she smiled, and then her eyes narrowed slightly. 'You don't have to say that.'

'I know that and I wouldn't lie. We're trying to build trust, remember? This is truly delicious. Another Elora twist?'

'Yup. I put pistachios and almonds in it, and a little bit of cocoa powder.'

'I'd forgotten how much I like *kulfi*. The past few years I've not had it so I've settled for ice cream, but this…' He looked down at the light green concoction and could see the flecks of nuts in it. 'I should probably know this, but what's the actual difference?'

'*Kulfi* doesn't include eggs and uses full fat milk so it's creamier. It's also denser because it's simmered overnight and it isn't whipped. It apparently originated in the sixteenth century. They used to mix the ingredients, put it into pots and bury them so they'd get cold.' She gave a sudden smile. 'Sorry, I like knowing the origins of food—it's just so incredible to think that people all those centuries ago ate a version of what we are eating right now.'

He walked along the trellised pathway, under the arches, lush with deep green foliage, inhaled the heady scent of the flowers and saw the riotous, gorgeous mix of colours that seemed to glow iridescent in the moonlight.

'Perhaps a prince and princess centuries ago walked along this path eating that version,' he said.

'That's a nicer image of the past than blood and gore and daggers and swords,' she said. 'These gardens were built by one of my ancestors, King Eshanth, for his wife, who was apparently one of the most beautiful women on the island. They married for love and these gardens were an ongoing work of art. They built three terraces and planted an amazing number of trees and a mix of flowers. And this.'

She came to a halt and so did he, stunned by the magical backdrop ahead of him. A waterfall cascaded over a stone parapet, the water a melodious gush, an illuminated flow that twinkled and glittered, lit by strategically placed lights in the niches behind it.

'It's magical,' he said.

'Straight out of a fairy tale,' she replied as she finished her last bit of *kulfi*. 'So we have a perfect setting for romance, but how are we going to make everyone believe the romance itself is real?'

They headed to a bench set close enough to the waterfall to be bewitched by its beauty and for the noise to be an accompaniment rather than an impediment to conversation. The bench itself nestled on a patio area vibrant with shrubs and bushes. And suddenly as he turned to her all he could think was that the setting, beautiful though it was, served only as a backdrop for her beauty. The moonlight glinted off her silvery blonde hair and highlighted the delicate strength of her features—the wide brow, her luminous grey eyes and lips that seemed to beg to be kissed.

He had to focus, had to keep talking…

'Well, a key point will be to convince them that we are attracted to each other.' He sounded like a pompous professor but that was better than succumbing to the urge to kiss her.

'How?' The question was blunt. 'You said earlier you weren't worried about pretending to be attracted to me. You've clearly already figured it out. So tell me.'

'Well, actually...' Rohan paused, suddenly wishing he still had the *kulfi*, something to distract him. All his aplomb had disappeared and although the evening had a pleasant breeze he felt perspiration threaten, his collar seeming to tighten around his neck as she looked at him expectantly. 'That's not exactly what I meant.'

Her grey eyes were wide and, dammit, he couldn't tell what she was thinking.

'So what did you mean?' There was the slightest frown on her forehead, her lips upturned in what could be an encouraging smile. And now he seemed incapable of tearing his gaze from her mouth. Forcing himself to look away, to focus on the rush and cascade of the waterfall, he tried to decide what to do. He'd been planning on telling her the truth, admitting the damned attraction, but standing here, looking at her wide-eyed innocence, he knew he couldn't. Or wouldn't.

Thoughts ran through his head at lightning speed. Unless the attraction was mutual, and he was by no means sure it was, the knowledge could spook her, couldn't help but make her feel awkward. Better if she believed for now that the attraction was as fake as the romance. Something to be worked on.

But it was more than that, he acknowledged to himself deep down. To tell Elora of this attraction would be to give her power over him. Even more so if it were onesided. He'd believed Caro had been attracted to him, had

thought his own feelings had been reciprocated, and he'd
been made a fool of. Because he'd ceded control.

He wouldn't take that risk again. He didn't understand
his awareness of Elora, the visceral tug of desire that he
couldn't seem to control. Well, he would learn to control
it, tame the volatility. Would also try to figure out how
Elora felt about him. And then would be the time for complete transparency.

Right now, the most important thing was to convince
the world that their relationship was a real one, and that
meant keeping things under control. So he needed to think
fast, because Elora was still looking at him expectantly.

'I meant that we are both used to being on public display and as such we are used to projecting feelings that
aren't real, or hiding feelings that are. So, between us, we
should be able to figure out how to make the press believe
this is real.'

Elora's gaze was steady but he'd swear something
flashed across her eyes. Hurt? Disappointment? Or perhaps it was simple relief.

'You're right in that I know how to project certain feelings, but faking attraction is new to me.'

'Me too, so I guess we'll need to practice.'

Even as he said the words, he realised how foolhardy
they were.

'Practice how?' There was a definite hint of panic in
her voice. 'Practice what? I mean, it's not as though I'm
going to be plastering myself all over you on a first date.'
There was silence and now she'd said the words the image
filled his mind, of her doing exactly that, her body against
his, her hair tickling his nose, the delicate tilt of her head
as she looked up at him, lips parted.

Hell. Rohan focused on staying stock-still, and realised

that he wasn't the only one with a dreamy look on their face. Elora was staring at him, her grey eyes wide and slightly out of focus, as if her mind might be headed down the same path as his.

Rohan gritted his teeth. All he wanted to do was lean forward and kiss her but…he wouldn't. Dammit, he would show himself that he could control this, because he would not let this marriage be governed by desire in any way at all, wouldn't let attraction make him lose sight of anything, let it con him into believing he cared or, worse, that he was cared for. This marriage was going to be played by the rulebook and he had every intention of making the rules.

Digging deep, Rohan found the prince capable of banter and charm, of lightness and flirtation. 'So, on which date do you think plastering is acceptable?' he asked, careful to inject a light tone to his voice, hopeful that this would deflate the sudden tension in the air, relieved when she tilted her chin and met his gaze full-on.

'There will be no plastering,' she said. 'That isn't how a Carulian princess would behave in public, however modern she is.'

'And in private?' The words fell from his lips without thought and her face became tinged with pink.

But she didn't miss a beat. 'Right now, this princess is only concerned with her public image. And,' she continued, and now her voice was matter-of-fact, in control, 'I don't think we need to worry too much—we won't be expected to do any lovey-dovey stuff on a first date after all.'

'No, but we need to at least look comfortable.'

She raised her eyebrows. 'Comfortable? That sounds like a pair of cosy old slippers. We're meant to be giving people something to be excited about.'

'I get that, but nervous isn't a good look either.'

'I am not nervous.'

In lieu of a reply, he stretched out a hand and she shifted backwards, nearly lost her balance, grabbed the table edge to steady herself and glared at him.

'You caught me by surprise.'

'Doesn't matter. We could get caught on camera in an unguarded moment. And there needs to be a spark.'

She looked at him, jutted her chin out. 'There will be. I've got this. I just need a little bit of time. To adapt. You were right, I do know how to project an image. By tomorrow there will be sparks galore. But first we need to run this past our parents.'

He thought for a minute. 'Let's get your parents on board first. Sarala needs this marriage slightly more than Caruli does. So if your parents agree, my parents should follow. Would you prefer to talk to them on your own?'

Elora looked at him as though he were mad. 'I don't think that's the way to go,' she said.

'Why not?'

'It doesn't matter. It would just be best if you present the idea. That's all.'

'I need more than that. If you want me to negotiate to convince them, I have to understand more about the dynamics. If there's anything I should or shouldn't say or do, I need to know now.'

He sensed her reluctance, but then she nodded understanding.

'Basically, it will be best if you do all the talking. Say it is your idea, your plan—if they believe that, they are more likely to go along with it. More likely to see the positives. Leave me out of it as much as you can. Play the overbearing prince card.' As she rose he'd swear he heard her mutter, 'Well, that should come easy.'

* * *

Elora felt her heart thud against her ribcage as they entered the Treasure Room. She glanced sideways at Rohan, aware of an illogical urge to take his hand. To offer comfort or give it? Neither made sense. Rohan looked completely confident, no sign of nerves, apart from perhaps a slight tautening of his jawline. As for comfort—why would she expect to get that from Rohan's touch? Or maybe she just craved that touch, which was mortifying, seeing as he had made it plain that any attraction would have to be faked. In any case, she had no intention of reaching out; to do so would do nothing but court her parents' disapproval. They would see that as unnecessary, an unbecoming display of emotion.

Enough. She stepped forward and bowed her head in greeting to her parents, but not before she caught the sharp glance her mother levelled at her. Her father, as always, ignored her, kept his gaze averted, focused on Rohan.

'Thank you for seeing us so late,' Rohan said. 'We thought it would be courteous and useful to tell you what we have decided.'

King Gaurav's eyebrows went up. 'I would be interested in hearing what you *discussed*.'

Rohan's smile was still assured. 'Of course we value Your Majesties' opinions,' he said smoothly.

'So tell us your thoughts,' the Queen said.

'I believe that the people would not welcome a rushed marriage, would not wish to see their Princess pushed into a political marriage with a man with a reputation like mine. I think it would therefore serve the purpose of both Sarala and Caruli if we offer them a romance. A fairy tale—this would give both the Princess and myself an opportunity to make a number of public appearances in a positive light and then announce our engagement when, hopefully, it can be welcomed by the people as a real alliance.'

The Queen's face darkened and Elora felt a sense of dread, though a quick glance at her father's face showed her that he was considering the facts. She knew that in public the Queen would never question the word of the King. Even in private she had become less assured since Sanjay's death, had lived in fear that the King would divorce her and remarry for an heir. Perhaps he would have if Flavia hadn't had a son, if there wasn't now an heir. But there was and her mother had regained some of her lost authority and influence. But not all.

The King nodded. 'Your words do make some level of sense. I have heard from my own sources and there is much in what you say—there is a feeling that we royals must modernise.' He sighed. 'I am now too old a dog to change, but your generation and the next perhaps should make a start.' For a fleeting instant his gaze rested on Elora and, as always, skittered away again. Grief tugged at her heart. Sanjay had been her father's pride and joy, the beacon for the future. Her mother resented her, but her father... Elora believed he simply wished her away, could not bear the sight of his daughter and the memories she evoked of all he'd lost.

'So you agree to the plan?' Rohan asked.

'I agree to the commencement of the plan, but we will need to monitor the results. If adverse publicity is generated or anything looks to be going wrong then the engagement will be announced immediately.'

Rohan nodded. 'I agree that we should evaluate how the idea is going in two weeks and discuss the best way forward from there.'

Elora held her breath, as aware as everyone else in the

room that her father was used to being agreed with one hundred per cent without caveats, but the King gave the smallest of smiles.

'Very well, young man. Have it your way. For now. Provided, of course, your parents agree.'

'That shouldn't be an issue. So we can start tomorrow.' Rohan turned to Elora but before he could speak the Queen interceded.

'Elora looks tired and I would like the chance of a mother-daughter chat before we sleep. I am sure you wish to apprise your parents of events. I will finalise plans for tomorrow and you will be contacted as to arrangements.'

Elora focused on keeping her expression neutral even as she felt anxiety surge. Mother-daughter moments were rare but only happened when Elora had displeased her parents by more than the fact she simply existed. But she would weather the scolding, the lecture, the hectoring and if she could she would do as her mother wished. At least, whatever happened, her father had consented to the plan.

Next to her, she sensed Rohan's glance and looked up at him, aware of her mother's gaze.

'I will see you tomorrow, Your Highness,' she said.

'Until then,' he said. 'And thank you for today.' And he smiled at her, a real smile that held warmth and…a sense of promise… It was a smile that tingled her toes and surprised her.

Elora smiled back, watched as he left the room, aware of a sudden desire to run after him, and perhaps he sensed that because at the door he stopped and turned. But the Queen rose and headed to Elora, her lips thinned, her grey eyes cold and hard.

'Come,' she said and, reaching out, she turned her daughter away from the door as she raised a hand in dismissal.

Elora turned her head and she too raised a hand, knew it would be better to simply get the mother-daughter moment over with.

She followed her mother through the second door and up the spiral staircase to the room the Queen used for private meetings, turned to her mother and braced herself as she registered the anger on Queen Joanna's classically beautiful features.

'Fool,' her mother spat, stepping forward. 'Have you let that Prince's handsome face turn your head and shed what few wits you ever had? Don't you see what he is doing with this "modern" plan of his?'

'Actually, it wasn't his plan. It was my idea.' Elora had no idea why she'd even revealed that. Usually, it was best to just listen to what her mother had to say, but the words had stung.

'I don't believe that for a minute, but if it is true then you are an even bigger fool than I thought you were. You have played straight into his hands. Do you really believe he will marry you now?'

Elora stared at her mother. 'I don't understand.'

'Then let me explain.'

CHAPTER SIX

THE FOLLOWING DAY, Rohan looked at the text he'd received three hours after leaving Elora the previous evening, not from Elora herself but from a 'royal events coordinator', asking him to meet the royal family for a 'meet and greet', followed by official photographs, prior to leaving with Elora for a visit to a mango farm. After a tour there, Elora would return to the palace and then he would take her for dinner.

At least he'd insisted on arranging the dinner himself and he'd spent the morning doing exactly that.

He checked his phone again, aware of a wish that it had been Elora who had messaged him. He'd had a feeling the previous night that he shouldn't leave her, but what could he have done—whisked her away from her parents? On what grounds? The meeting had gone well and it was fair enough that the Queen had wanted to spend time with her daughter.

Yet unease lingered, however irrational, and remained with him as the official car drove up to the steps of a side entrance to the palace, leading to a pillared patio area where the royal family awaited him.

Official photographers were already in place, his arrival recorded with all due pomp and ceremony, and he forced himself to smile as he climbed out of the official car. He made his way up the sweeping stone steps and looked up to meet Elora's eyes and now his smile turned genuine, but even as his gaze rested on her he was aware of something…wrong.

Though he couldn't place it. She looked beautiful, her salwar kameez today a teal tunic patterned with the national bird of Caruli, a golden myna, over dark flared trousers. Her lips upturned in just the right way, the smile held the exact right mix of pleasure at seeing him, tempered by a hint of shyness. Just as a princess should look at someone who she might, just might, be attracted to, and who might, just might, be attracted back.

The illusion was perfect but it was wrong, however right it looked. Or he was completely overreacting and overthinking—that was also a possibility, but his instincts, honed by years of ambassadorial and diplomatic duties, were usually pretty spot-on. But the important thing was it looked right and he wouldn't be the one to mess it up.

He smiled again and turned to the Queen, who touched her hand to his shoulder in the traditional greeting that granted a level of familiarity. The cameras clicked one last time before staff members ushered the press away to give the family some privacy. Queen Joanna waited, then gestured to a young woman standing next to her.

'This is Her Royal Highness Princess Flavia, mother to Prince Viraj.'

Rohan studied Elora's sister, or half-sister to be precise, and could see a superficial resemblance, though the two women were completely different. Flavia's glossy black hair was pulled back in a bun, her eyes dark brown, though she shared her sister's long dark lashes. Like Elora, her expression was regal and remote but her eyes held a tinge of bitterness he recognised all too well. He'd seen the same expression in the mirror during his marriage breakup. Rumours had circulated about the state of the royal Carulian marriage, but the speculation had died or been killed off and on the surface all was well between the couple—he hoped that was the truth. He smiled now, greeted Flavia and then turned to the dark-haired boy next to her, solemn-faced and upright despite being only five years old.

Rohan grinned at him, recalled being five, being the heir and being on show. 'I am very pleased to meet you. Are you coming with us today? I bet you'd love to climb a mango tree and pick some mangoes.'

The little boy's face lit up, just as Rohan realised that was the wrong thing to say—he could sense the disapproval radiating like a laser from the Queen. And so could Viraj, as after one swift look at his grandmother he shook his head.

'I am sorry, I cannot. I have lessons this afternoon.'

'Plus climbing trees is not what princes do,' the Queen said.

Rohan thought that Flavia was going to say something, saw Elora step closer to her half-sister, and instead Flavia pressed her lips together and put a gentle hand on her son's head.

'Perhaps another day we can do something different,' he suggested. 'Something we can all agree on.'

'I would like that,' the little boy said, but Rohan sensed from his tone he had no expectation of it actually happening.

'So would I,' he said firmly. 'Let's shake on it.'

Viraj smiled and stuck his hand out to shake Rohan's, before stepping back to stand by his mother. Rohan caught Elora's eye and she smiled at him.

A real smile this time and it caught him unawares, froze him to the spot.

'The carriage is here.' The Queen's words broke the

spell and he turned automatically, aware that the photographers would be back and taking pictures in earnest. In that second, before the photographers approached, he saw the Queen take Elora's wrist in a quick grasp, lean forward and whisper something, her expression retaining a smiling serenity.

But, whatever she said, it caused Elora distress, the look of resignation, sadness and weary acceptance fleeting but definite, and then it was gone as she stepped forward towards him, towards the waiting phalanx of photographers. There she was next to him, and awareness of her proximity tightened his gut. He glanced at her once, saw that she looked relaxed as she faced the cameras, yet he sensed a tension in her body as she waved and smiled.

The tinkling of bells indicated the arrival of the horse and carriage and within seconds a lavishly ornate carriage appeared, the body black and gilded with gold leaf, the massive wheels also lined with gold, the two horses a glossy ebony black, their manes plaited, their bridles glinting gold in the sunshine. The turbaned driver was perched high at the front.

As he pulled the horses to a smooth stop in front of them, Elora stiffened, her whole body taut, but she continued forward and Rohan was sure no one else would have seen her very slight hesitation. But something was going on, he just didn't know what. Wasn't sure if it was her mother's words, the sheer symbolic enormity of taking the first step of their fake story, the first step towards a marriage of duty, or the mass of photographers.

As they approached the carriage he nodded the staff member away and held out his hand for Elora so he could help her in, saw surprise flash in her eyes, followed by a gleam of appreciation as the cameras clicked around them.

And yet he hadn't done it for the cameras but because he'd sensed that she was troubled. Once seated, she smiled a lovely smile at the driver.

'Hello, Jaswant. Thank you so much for being here.'

'You're welcome, Your Highness. The journey should be about twenty minutes.'

Twenty minutes spent looking out at the lined streets, smiling, waving… The whole thing, as always, made Rohan feel slightly ridiculous. Though he made sure to keep a lookout to assess the level of support, and noted a few in the crowd holding anti-monarchy placards.

In the promised twenty minutes they arrived at their destination and Elora turned to him.

'Ready?' he asked.

'Ready.'

This time he waited as someone came to the door to let Elora out, watched as she descended gracefully with a friendly smile, and then his door was open and he stepped down, braced himself for more photographs, tried to offer a smile that held enough charm to bely his reputation of being cold and unfeeling without looking as if he was trying too hard.

Before he could figure out if he had it right or not, Elora had made her way to his side and, in an easy gesture that looked completely natural, she took his arm and gave him the smallest of pinches. Hell, it took him by surprise but it worked, focused him, as she smiled and beckoned the press forward.

'Hey guys, just to let you know I'll be showing Prince Rohan around Caruli over the next few days and he'll be returning the favour in Sarala. I'll make sure you're kept informed of our official itinerary. So we're going in here for a private tour for a couple of hours then back to the palace.

Whilst I have you all here, can I also say how glad I am to be showing the Prince one of our best, high-quality exports. When we leave here, I know Pria and Kamal, owners of this lush farm, will have made sure Prince Rohan is an expert on organic mango farming and a definite fan of their mangoes in particular.'

'I'm looking forward to it,' Rohan said. 'And also looking forward to showing Princess Elora Sarala.'

With that, they made their way towards the farm entrance and, once inside, Elora led the way to an open paved courtyard enclosed by a low roofed farmhouse, the brick walls topped with terracotta roof tiles.

'This looks almost Mediterranean,' he said.

'It's all eco-friendly,' Elora replied. 'The bricks are actually made from local soil, and Kamal got the tiles secondhand from a local builder when someone was replacing their Mediterranean roof. There's no cement so that water drainage can be maximised—Kamal and Pria have done loads of courses in how to run a farm on ecological principles, so they are experts on utilising rain harvesting strategies. All the spaces in the paving have been carefully thought out.'

'That's impressive,' Rohan said, looking around with interest.

A woman who Rohan estimated to be in her fifties emerged from the front door and headed towards Elora, a beaming smile of welcome on her face as she embraced her in a massive hug, one Elora returned with fervour, before turning to Rohan.

'This is Pria, my old nurse.'

'Less of the old, missy.' The woman turned to Rohan and gave him a long appraising look before turning back to Elora, her expression neutral and, not for the first time, he wished that people wouldn't judge him by his reputation. 'I spoke to your mother,' she said. 'The Queen instructed me that you should take Rohan round the farm on your own.' Pria hesitated, glanced at Elora's set expression and back to Rohan. 'But if you'd rather have some company then I am happy to come along.'

Elora smiled but shook her head. 'It's fine. I don't know anywhere near as much as you, but I can give Rohan some information.'

'Then you head straight back. The whole family want to see you and I'll have freshly made mango smoothie all ready.'

'That sounds amazing,' Rohan said. 'I'd love to hear more about the way you run the farm.'

Pria eyed him with evident scepticism in her brown eyes and Rohan nodded firmly, wanting to show this woman, whom he instinctively liked, that he wasn't the monster she believed him to be.

'Really.' Rohan glanced around. 'I am genuinely interested. I was wondering if you'd ever thought about inviting guests, paying guests, to see what you do. You've got the space to build accommodation and I think people would be genuinely interested. Just like I am,' he added for good measure.

That got the very smallest of smiles. 'I think that's a good idea; I just haven't managed to persuade my husband. Yet. I'd be happy for you to say your bit.' She turned back to Elora. 'You sure you don't want me to come?'

'I'm sure. I'll be fine.'

She'd be fine, fine, fine. Elora didn't feel fine. She was dreading this conversation—a conversation her mother had instructed her must happen, the order given. Last night, she had been convinced that her mother was right, that Elora had been a fool, a dupe, a pawn...but now, in Rohan's presence, it didn't seem as clear-cut. Which was ridiculous and proved her mother's point—maybe he was messing with her head.

For a while they walked in silence, a silence she appreciated as she let the familiar scents and sights soothe her mind, bring her a semblance at least of calm. The walk past the long earthy enclosure where Pria kept her hens and roosters, the brightly coloured birds each with their own individuality clawing the ground as they strutted about, clucking at intervals. Then past the cattle and alongside the small lake, a habitat for wild birds that skimmed the silver-blue water, under the overarching branches of the massive banyan tree.

Then they entered the lush beauty of the mango orchard and Elora inhaled the sweet scent of the nearly ripe fruit, interlaced with the turpentine nuance of the dark green leaves. Looked up at the spread of the trees dotted with the pink and yellow of the mangos. Rohan too gazed and she sensed his interest as well as his appreciation of the sight and smells.

'They should be harvesting,' she said. 'But they gave the pickers a few hours off to ensure our privacy.' She gestured upwards. 'They use the leaves as well—though I am not completely sure about the details of how they are picked. They have been used for medicinal reasons for centuries—apparently, if you burn them, the smoke gets rid of hiccups and is good for sore throats. And they are a source of Vitamin C, and they are great for cooking. Pria makes a wonderful chutney.'

She paused to take a breath. She knew she was rambling because she was nervous, and dreading the prospect of the conversation ahead. She wanted to talk about the beauty of their surroundings, to forget the doubts and bitterness of her conversation with her mother.

'Pria uses the mature leaves to make a *torana*, or gateway, at the entrance to the farmhouse. They are supposed to bring good fortune because of their cleansing energy.'

'You're close to Pria, aren't you?' Rohan asked.

'Yes, I am. Pria has been...good to me.' She had been the only one who hadn't changed towards Elora after Sanjay's death, the only one who'd still loved and cared for her and tried to understand Elora's searing loss and grief. But not even Pria knew the full truth about that day—if she did, perhaps she would not have been so sympathetic. 'She liked you,' she added.

'Really?' Scepticism came across loud and clear.

'Really. She wouldn't have let us do this unchaperoned otherwise.'

'Despite what your mother ordered?'

'Despite that,' Elora said. 'Pria is one of the few people who doesn't always listen to my mother. Unlike me and Flavia.' She turned to him. 'You were very good with Viraj. He liked you too.'

'I liked him. What do you think he'd like to do with us?'

Surprise warmed her and then the penny dropped.

'I guess whatever you think would be a good publicity stunt.'

Now he stopped and there was anger in his dark eyes. 'Excuse me?'

'Isn't that why you suggested it? Why you were nice to him?' Doubt assailed her at her easy assumption as his frown intensified into a full-blown scowl.

'I wouldn't do that. Wouldn't use a five-year-old child who is already overexposed to the public by sheer dint of his birth. I meant that as a genuine offer—if Viraj wanted to spend some time kicking a football around or climbing a tree or any other "normal" five-year-old thing. That was it and I would strongly veto any publicity around the whole thing.'

There was absolutely no doubting the sincerity of his words and now she reached out and laid a hand on his arm. 'I'm sorry. I jumped to an obviously wrong conclusion.'

'Why?'

Because that was what her mother had told her, had grabbed her wrist and told her not to be fooled by a man proven to be a cold, ruthless monster.

But how to say that? So, instead, 'Because everything we do, every smile, every word is an illusion. That's why I spent two hours last night researching the best way to flirt and use body language that implies attraction.'

'I appreciate that, and I agree that everything *we* do in public is an illusion, but not the words I say to a five-year-old child. And not the words we speak to each other in private. Everything I have said to you in private has been honest.'

But how could she believe that when her mother's words were still ringing in her ears?

'Yesterday I thought we'd at least taken the first steps towards trust. So what has happened since then? Did your mother say something in your mother-daughter chat?'

Elora could see no real point in prevarication, knew this conversation had to happen.

'Yes.'

'What did she say?'

Now she came to a halt, stood under a branch weighted with the round, luscious fruits.

'She wants me to tell you we need to announce the engagement now.'

She expected him to ask her why, what her mother's reasons were. Instead, he reached out and gently tipped her chin up so their gazes met, the touch fleeting and gentle and sending her spinning.

'What do *you* want?' he asked.

Elora's eyes widened in shock. No one ever asked her what she wanted. 'I don't know. I don't know what to think.'

'OK. How about we try to figure it out?'

She nodded, felt a sense of shyness. 'There's a place we can sit. It's where the pickers stop for a rest.' Minutes later, they were seated on a bench that surrounded one of the circular wooden tables, placed in a clearing at the edge of the orchard.

Rohan turned to face her. 'So what's going on?'

'My mother thinks you're playing me.' A memory of Queen Joanna's contemptuous expression loomed.

He thought for a moment and then shook his head. 'I may be being obtuse, but I don't get it.'

Neither had she at first. 'She thinks you aren't announcing the engagement because you're hedging your bets. That there's a high risk you'll string me along then back out, leaving me looking a fool.'

'But why would I do that?'

What to say to that?

Her mother's voice was in her ear.

'Get real, Elora. The more he gets to know you, the less likely he is to marry you. He's used to women of a different ilk. What if his last girlfriend turns up? Marrying a non-royal is suitably modern, isn't it?'

The words had been venomous.

'The thing Sarala needs most is an heir. Rohan may well decide he's better off with a beautiful Hollywood ce-

lebrity. Like his first wife, like his girlfriends. Women you can't hope to live up to.'

Elora couldn't, wouldn't, repeat those words verbatim.

'Because you may get a better offer,' she said. 'Or find someone better suited to being Queen. Or your parents may find you a better option.'

'That won't happen. I spoke with my parents last night—they very much want this marriage and they completely bought into the "romance" idea. Not just my parents but my sister too. Marisa loved the modernisation idea, and using our romance to get out and about. So I'm sure she'll have some "date" ideas for us.'

Elora blinked, tried and failed to imagine the Carulian royal family having the type of conversation Rohan was describing.

'OK. I accept your family are on board right now. But things change.' She looked towards the tree opposite them, the tree she and Sanjay had used to climb. 'Or...you may decide not to get married. You don't want to get married—you told me that yourself. If things look like they are sta-bilising on Sarala if the backlash isn't as we feared, then you might decide you can afford to wait for a while.'

She looked at him now, braced for...she wasn't sure what. Anger? Agreement? But all she saw was a serious look of intent.

'Do you really think I would do that to you?'

She met his gaze full-on. 'You are the one that said it isn't personal. So would Sarala do that to Caruli?'

To her surprise, he gave a sudden smile. 'Touché. But, as far as I'm concerned, I have made a commitment to you. *And* Sarala has made a commitment to Caruli. I won't walk away from that. I won't break my word.'

'Even if a better bride comes along?'

'Even then. Once a deal is made, it is made... I would like to think my word means something.'

But did it? That was the question. There was the Queen's voice again.

'He has shown the worth of his word with his first marriage. He is not a man to be trusted; I am sure Princess Caro would vouch for that. You need to secure him fast.'

As if reading the doubt on her face, he shrugged. 'Clearly, it doesn't.' The words were said lightly but she sensed that the idea hurt. He thought for a moment, his expression unreadable. 'How about I share a secret? Not anything soul-baring, but something important. A good-will gesture.'

Elora looked at him; she knew what her mother would say—that it was a meaningless gesture. But she didn't believe that—could sense that sharing a confidence on any level wouldn't come easy to him. But they had to start somewhere and he was willing to make that start. That had to mean something.

She nodded. 'OK. Tell me a secret.'

Rohan leant forward slightly, rested his forearms on the table, and she was suddenly oh, so aware of him, the bulk of his body that exuded strength, the sheer clean, muscular lines of him, the swell of sculpted biceps under his shirt, the solid shape of his thighs next to hers. The canopy of the trees, the smell of the mangoes and the warm heat of the Carulian sun.

'So...' he said, and stopped. 'Very few people know this.'

'For what it's worth, you have my word that whatever you are going to tell me I will keep confidential. Completely.'

'Yesterday you told me a bit about your dream—about

what you'd do if you weren't a princess, your alternative life. Well, this is about mine.' Now her attention was completely caught and she looked at him, willed him to keep talking. He inhaled deeply and then, 'I've set up my own business,' he said and she could hear pride in his voice even as he gave a small self-deprecating laugh. 'It's not a global multi-million venture or anything, though I wish I could make it into one, but it's a solid, profitable enterprise.'

'Tell me.'

'I haven't done it as a prince, I've done it as Rohan Carmody and so far, through various legal loopholes and thanks to a couple of trustworthy business partners, I've hidden my name and identity as much as it is possible to do. I know I can't keep it secret for ever, but it was important to me to see if I could do it, and I knew my parents wouldn't approve. Wouldn't believe that a prince could also be a businessman. Wouldn't see the point in starting a venture I won't be able to continue, a venture that has nothing to do with Sarala.' There was resignation in his voice and she felt a pang of sympathy, understood all too well. 'So, there you are. That's my secret.'

'You can't leave it there. Tell me more. What sort of business is it? What are your plans for it? How did you start it?'

'You really want to know?'

'Of course I do. I am full of admiration.' The idea that Rohan wanted something more than the role allotted to him by fate, had actually got it together to do something about it was admirable. More than that, it was relatable, made her feel closer to him. The real him.

'It's a tourism business. When I was sent abroad as an ambassador it was to promote Saralan produce, improve our trade links, win more lucrative export deals for our silks. Make our small island more global, more well known. I enjoyed it, enjoyed the negotiations, and doing something for Sarala that I'm actually good at.'

Elora couldn't help but wonder if that had been a reference to his disastrous marriage and the negative publicity or something deeper.

'But I also realised I loved the travelling aspect of the job, I loved exploring different places and cultures and I was lucky, I got to do it as a prince and experience the most fabulous resorts and hotels on offer. But because I'm not that well known I could also sometimes be an ordinary person, a tourist who mingled with everyone else.'

'So you became interested in tourism?'

'Yes. It all started because I got to thinking how much more Sarala has to offer. And I wondered why we don't offer more tourism opportunities, given how much money it can generate for the economy. It all got me thinking, but then I realised I didn't really know anything about the tourism industry at all. So I figured I needed to find out more.

'I did a lot of research and I went and spoke to people who know what they are talking about. That is a perk of being a prince—it opens doors. I spoke to hotel magnates and government ministers and I got more and more interested in the idea.

'And then I was travelling somewhere and we passed an old rundown hotel and there was something about it—it looked like an opportunity to put some of the things I'd learnt to the test. Could I create a place where people would want to stay?'

'And did you?'

'Yes. And I loved every minute of it. It was an old rundown building but it had such amazing potential and it was…exhilarating. Costing it, getting the necessary finance, planning, designing…and I got involved in the actual building work. Knocking walls down, gutting rooms.'

As he spoke, Elora could picture it, imagine him, dark hair dust-covered and tousled, hammering, pounding, getting his hands dirty in a way princes were never supposed to. And watching him relive the experience sent a funny little buzz through her, seeing his face relaxed, his deep voice full of enthusiasm and pride.

'Then there was the marketing, the planning—I loved watching the hotel transform and take off.'

'Can I see it? Do you have pictures? A website?'

'Sure.' They shifted closer as he pulled out his phone. 'So this is what it looked like before.' And as he scrolled through the pictures, talked her through the transformation, she sensed his utter dedication to the project, to the business.

'I love it. Each room is so unique and yet they are all equally beautiful and they all have a little twist. The chandeliers in room seven are breathtaking and I love the rooftop room, with a porthole to the stars.' She reached out to enlarge the picture and her fingers brushed his and she couldn't withhold the small gasp, triggered by the sudden rush through her body. Now she realised how close they had somehow got, so that all it would take was an infinitesimal shift to be pressed right up against him.

She should move away, but she didn't want to, his tantalising nearness too tempting, so instead she cleared her throat and managed to ask the next question. 'What about food? Can I see the menu? When I have time, I try to cook food from abroad but I never know if I manage to make it authentic and of course I end up adapting the recipes to use more local ingredients.' She was rambling but she couldn't help it, could sense the tension in his body too, saw the care he used as he pressed the requisite buttons on his screen, angled the phone so she could see it.

'We do theme weekends,' he said. 'Not every weekend, but say for Halloween or Christmas or Independence Day…'

She read the menu out loud. 'The Valentine's menu features aphrodisiac ingredients, beautifully prepared with sizzle and spice and includes oyster risotto, chilli foie gras and a decadent dessert to share, complete with dark chocolate, passion fruit and a hint of ginger to hot things up.' There was a silence and then, she couldn't help it, she started to laugh and, seconds later, he followed suit.

'What were the chances of me randomly selecting that menu?' he asked, shaking his head. 'I'm sorry.'

'Don't be. I can't remember the last time I laughed like that.'

'Me neither.'

And there it was again. As their gazes met she was oh, so aware of him, his closeness, the planes of his face, the dark intensity of his eyes, which were fixed on her now, scrutinising her with such intent she gave a small shiver and somehow, with a sense of utter inevitability, they both moved at the same time.

Then, before she could even think about what she was doing, their lips met and for a glorious moment she was lost in a tumult of unfamiliar, unexpected pleasure. Dizzying sensations flooded her as her lips parted and he deepened the kiss, evoking a yearning need she'd never felt before.

That realisation trickled through the vortex of feelings, enough to trigger an escalation of panic. What was she doing? She had no idea. Couldn't fathom the depth of these exquisite needs that twisted her stomach, made her want to throw caution to the wind. *Oh, God.* Had she made a com-

plete fool of herself? Rohan was an experienced man—
for him, a kiss would mean nothing, was simply a way of
passing the time. Now, he would know for sure what he
could only have suspected—the extent of her inexperi-
ence—and mortification burned.

From somewhere there also burned a determination to
ensure damage limitation, to somehow keep the tattered
remains of her dignity. Finding her inner strength, she
pushed down the surge of desire with relentless force, focused on the tree she and Sanjay had once climbed, on the
vista that reminded her of childhood lost, and she found if
not true calm, then the ability to project it.

She shook her head. 'Turns out you don't need to actually taste the Valentine's menu to break the rules. I did
promise not to plaster myself all over you on the first
date—looks like we didn't make it that far. But probably
best if we don't do that again when so little has been decided.'

What would her mother say? She could hear the light
contemptuous laugh in her head, the sarcastic applause.

*He played that well, distracted you with a tiny bit of
charm and you're putty in his hands. For God's sake don't
let the man seduce you before he dumps you.*

She rose to her feet. 'Thank you for trusting me, your
secret is safe with me, and now we'd better get back to
Pria. The mango smoothies will be ready.' She managed
what she hoped was a light laugh. 'And on the way back
I'd better tell you something about mango farming.'

CHAPTER SEVEN

ROHAN KNEW HE should say something, do something, but as he rose to his feet all ability to speak seemed to have deserted him as he tried to figure out what the hell had just happened. He hadn't planned to kiss Elora; it had been the very last intention on his mind. The whole idea had been not to spook her by seeing if their attraction was real.

Well…that was out of the window, but it wasn't Elora who was acting spooked. It was him, because the un-planned kiss had blown his mind and his senses out of the water. And now…now he wasn't sure what was going on. One minute he'd been gloriously kissing her, the next she'd withdrawn and had swept the entire kiss under the proverbial carpet. Was hotfooting it back through the trees at a rate of knots, talking about mango farming as if she were a bona fide tour guide.

'Elora. Stop.'

She broke off.

'I am genuinely interested in this, but…'

'There are no buts. We are about to spend time with Pria and her husband and they will expect me to have told you something about the farm they are so justly proud of.'

'I get that and I've done the research. I spent a couple of hours last night getting some facts. So I can tell you that the farm aims to be self-sufficient as well as produce tonnes of produce per year for sale. They also produce bananas, lychees and many other fruits, they grow vegetables and spices and are renowned for their organic and eco methods. I want to discuss all this with Pria and I would really like to talk to them about how they could expand, have paying guests who learn from them and have an amazing experience. But, right now, that isn't what I want to talk about.'

'That's why we're here,' she said flatly.

'Perhaps we should have thought of that ten minutes ago. When we definitely were not talking about mangoes or anything else. I think we should talk about the kiss.'

For a surreal moment he thought she would ask, *What kiss?* Then, instead, 'I don't think it is worth discussing.'

'Because it was so displeasing to you?' he asked, stung.

'Because it shouldn't have happened. For all I know, you kissed me to mess with my head, distract me, confuse me...' She broke off.

Anger flashed through him that she could believe that, after what they'd shared, after the laughter, after he'd told her about his business, and then the anger morphed into a pang of hurt and an alarm bell rang at the back of his head. What was going on here? Anger, hurt, laughter... kisses. This was spiralling into emotions he had no wish to feel. This marriage was not supposed to be emotional— he would not step onto that rollercoaster again. But neither would he let this go. He could see the confusion, the wariness in her grey eyes. And he understood—her mother had planted seeds of doubt in her mind and he couldn't blame Elora for believing them. He knew his reputation was hardly stellar.

'That kiss was unplanned. I shared a confidence with you in good faith in the hope it would demonstrate that I am on the level. I have no wish to mess with either of our heads. All I want is to get on with this charade and complete our deal for the sake of our countries. You can choose to believe that or not. I truly hope you do, but I do understand that you may have reservations. It's your call.'

Elora closed her eyes and took a deep breath. 'I'm sorry,' she said simply. 'You did trust me and I truly appreciate that and what you told me. As for the kiss, it's unfair of me to dump all the blame on you… I was there too. And you're right. I need to decide—so I say let's stick to the plan. I don't think announcing the engagement now is the right idea. But perhaps as well as evaluating in two weeks time we can tell my parents we plan to announce the engagement in a month.' She gave a small smile, but he sensed it was a genuine attempt to call a truce. 'Does that sound fair?'

A temporary trust earned and a compromise that would hopefully satisfy her mother. That made sense.

'Agreed. And Elora?'

'Yes?'

'I promise that kiss was not planned. I didn't mean to mess with your head or make things more complicated. I'm sorry.' For a moment he relived that kiss, the sheer unbridled, glorious joy of it, 'But it is hard to regret something so…enjoyable.' The word didn't do it justice, but somehow he needed to keep it in perspective. It was a kiss.

She bit her lip, looked down and then back up again, slowly unclenched her hands and nodded. 'Then I guess the best thing we can do is put it behind us.'

'That sounds like an idea.' Though he wasn't sure how easy that was going to be. It felt to him as though Pandora's box had been opened, and once open it couldn't be closed again. There was no way he was forgetting that kiss in a hurry.

'Now we really had better go,' Elora said. 'Pria's mango

smoothies are worth hurrying for. She puts a secret ingredient in that she won't tell me and...' She gave a sudden smile. 'If you can convince Kamal that paying guests are a good idea Pria will love you for ever. Then after that we need to prepare for our dinner date. Where are we going?'

He smiled at her,, suddenly aware of a sense of anticipation, one he tried to damp down. It was just dinner. Just like the kiss had been just a kiss. In which case, why was his body still taut, his gut still clenched with desire, his mind still blown? 'It's a surprise,' he said.

Elora was none the wiser a few hours later, as she surveyed her wardrobe and tried to figure out what on earth a sheltered princess should wear on a surprise first date.

She closed her eyes and tried to pretend this was real—that Rohan had asked her on a genuine date. If the illusion was real. If that kiss had been to him what it had been to her. To Rohan, it had meant nothing apart from an unplanned 'enjoyable' moment. He'd been unaffected, able to impress Pria and Kamal, and discuss the prospect of expanding the farm's business with an enthusiasm she now understood. Tourism was something that Rohan genuinely felt a passion for.

Whereas the kiss had meant nothing—to him, such kisses were commonplace. After all, he would have experienced hundreds, if not thousands, of kisses that had been way more 'enjoyable' with women he'd *wanted* to be with, not a woman he was stuck with through duty.

But to Elora the kiss had been...magical, a few minutes of sheer new sensations that had unlocked a part of her she'd never known existed. Which was mortifying. In the extreme. And yet here she was thinking about it again and now a sudden sense of defiance touched her.

It was true that she'd never be a woman he'd choose to marry, but dammit, she could maybe at least make him believe kissing her would be better than 'enjoyable'. She closed her wardrobe door with a decisive thud and frowned, thought for a moment and then pulled her phone from her pocket and texted a message. A few minutes later she was heading along the corridor towards the three-bedroom annexe where Flavia resided.

She wondered, hoped, she'd made the right decision. She and Flavia weren't close, but they had never really had the chance. Flavia had lived with her mother after the King had divorced his first wife, and Elora had seen her older half-sister only rarely. Then Flavia had been recalled to the palace when Elora was seventeen and soon after that she had been married, and a year after that Viraj was born.

In that time Elora had wanted to get to know Flavia better, but somehow nothing had ever come of it. Her mother had told Elora that Flavia blamed Queen Joanna for the divorce and that resentment extended to Elora.

But instinct told Elora her mother was wrong, and now she was putting that to the test, asking her sister for help. As she approached her sister's quarters, Flavia pulled the door open.

'Hi.'

'Hi.'

They both spoke together and Elora gave a slightly nervous laugh in the ensuing silence as each studied the other.

'I'm glad you messaged,' Flavia said.

'Really?'

'Really. Tell me what you need.'

'I need an outfit that will make me look as though I have dressed up for a date.'

'And you don't have anything like that?'

'No.'

'Because the Queen doesn't think you need it and the outfit you have in mind isn't one she would approve of?'

'Exactly. I want to look…attractive.'

'For Rohan?' There was no judgement in her sister's voice.

'I want him to notice me. Properly. Is that silly?'

'No, it isn't.' Flavia reached out, laid a hand on Elora's arm. 'I'm not sure what is going on between you and Rohan, but it seemed to me earlier that you have already got his attention.'

Elora sighed. 'Not really. He accepts he has to marry me and I think he is making the best of it, but just once I'd like him to see me as a person, not a Princess of Caruli.'

'I get that,' Flavia said, and there was both understanding and sadness in her voice, and for a moment Elora wondered if she was thinking about her own marriage. But, before she could ask, Flavia gave her head a small shake and then she smiled. 'I completely get it and I have just the right outfit in mind.'

Rohan was ushered into the Treasure Room and announced with due pomp and ceremony. He waited for the equerry to leave and stepped forward to greet Queen Joanna and Flavia.

'I am sure Elora will be here soon,' Flavia said in a soothing tone, and Rohan could swear she gave him the smallest of secret smiles as she scrutinised him.

'I expect my daughter to show punctuality,' the Queen said.

'Perhaps I am a little early,' Rohan replied, just as the door pushed open and he saw Pamir in the doorway, an especially wooden expression on his face.

'Her Royal Highness the Princess Elora,' he said and stood to one side.

Rohan heard a sudden almost choking sound and realised it came from his throat. Dressed in a shimmering golden lehenga set, with a long swirling skirt and a cropped blouse that left her midriff bare, she looked... Elora looked... He couldn't come up with any adjectives, any words at all. For the first time he understood the cartoon characters whose eyes popped out on springs.

He continued to stare, saw her loose hair cascading in waves to touch her bare shoulders, bangles encircling her slim arms and a gauzy dupatta scarf complementing the whole, along with strappy jewelled sandals.

He blinked as Flavia cleared her throat meaningfully and he looked away and saw Queen Joanna's face. Well, Elora had surprised him, but, unfortunately, she had clearly also surprised her mother, whose face had screwed up into a look of utter displeasure. But, before she could speak, Flavia broke into speech.

'Elora, we were just wondering where you were. I think Rohan is worried you'll be late. He has a reservation, but he won't tell us where.'

She moved towards Rohan as she spoke and gave him a small unseen nudge.

Somehow gathering himself, he nodded. 'Flavia is right. We'd better get moving. The car is waiting outside. The driver is my own personal security officer so Elora is in safe hands.' He spoke evenly but made sure there were no pauses as he ushered her towards the door. Elora swivelled and as he looked back he saw Flavia give them both the thumbs-up sign and then a shooing motion.

'I suggest we walk fast,' he said sotto voce and they half walked, half ran down the marble corridor, through the door and towards the waiting car. It was only once they were inside that she turned to look at him and he couldn't help it, he began to laugh and soon she joined in.

'I didn't think we'd make it out of there,' he said. 'So what's going on? I thought your mother was going to throw me out and forbid the date.'

'I borrowed the clothes from Flavia. My mother expected me to wear one of my more "usual" outfits. Not this.'

There was a silence and Rohan said softly, 'I like this.'

Suddenly, just like that, the car seemed to shrink, the air seemed to thicken and his heart started to beat faster.

'Good. I thought it was more appropriate for the vibe we are trying to project,' she said hurriedly as if she too felt the tension in the car rise and simmer and she continued, her voice slightly breathless, 'I thought about it and if we want the press to take an interest and pick up the romance idea there is no point in me dressing the same way I always do. We want to demonstrate that we are no longer doing this for diplomatic reasons. This is a date, not a business dinner. It's personal. Dressing like this seems to mark a clear line between what I wore to the mango farm.'

'Well, whatever your reasons, you look stunning,' he said as the car glided to a stop. He pushed the intercom button. 'Thank you, Danzi. Fabulous driving, as always. I'll message you when we're ready to be picked up. If there are any press, we're going with option U.'

'What's option U?' Elora asked.

He answered in a murmur, after he'd walked round to open her door for her. 'The one where we are unusually polite. The alternative is option ST. Screw them.'

Elora smiled up at him just as the cameras flashed as she climbed out of the car.

But though he'd meant the words to hold humour, as he saw the press surge in, memories of past encounters threatened and, as if she sensed it, she kept her hand on his arm as they turned to the cameras and the bombardment of questions.

'So what's happening? Is this a business dinner? Or a date?'

'No comment,' Rohan said, and she gently pressed down on his forearm, forced him to stop as she spoke to the journalists.

'Ask us tomorrow. We may have figured it out by then,' she said lightly, and smiled at the reporter. 'And watch this space,' she added as she pressed his arm again and they started to move towards the restaurant door.

CHAPTER EIGHT

ROHAN INHALED DEEPLY. 'You handled that well.'

'Not really. The press have always been kind to me, so it wasn't hard.'

She glanced towards the hustle and bustle of the busy restaurant, where heads were already turning. 'This bit will be more difficult for me,' she added, 'Whereas you are most used to it. Being the centre of attention with a date, in a multi star restaurant.'

'Actually,' he said, 'I have it planned a little differently.'

Elora was right. Back in New York or London, or wherever he'd been staying, he had got used to wining and dining women in a public setting, had been adept at using that publicity to promote Sarala as best he could. But here, today, he had no wish to be on show.

He turned to smile at the proprietor, a man in his thirties, with trademark slicked back dark hair and a beaming smile. 'Rohan.'

'Michel.' Not that he had originally been called that, but it was the name the public knew him by and, whilst he wasn't a global name, he was definitely famed throughout this part of Asia.

'Everything is ready for you and the Princess.'

Elora beamed. 'I can't believe I'm meeting you. I am star-struck—I have always wanted to come here and I loved your latest book. Your take on a chicken *cafreal* was absolutely incredible.'

Michel beamed. 'I am overseeing your food myself,' he said. 'But now follow me.'

He led them away from the dining room and Elora turned an enquiring glance to Rohan, who smiled what he hoped was an enigmatic smile. To his own surprise, anticipation swelled inside him as they climbed the spiral staircase and he realised he was looking forward to seeing Elora's reaction. He tried to tell himself this was all an illusion, but knew he wanted, hoped, to bring a real smile to her face, the one that sparked her eyes and also narrowed them ever so slightly, wanted her to see that he too had put some thought into their date this evening.

Once again, a warning bell clanged in the back of his head, but this time he shut it down. There was nothing wrong with wanting to be nice.

They reached the top of the stairs and stepped out onto the terrace, bathed in the golden rays of the evening sun. Leading to their table, by the side of the surrounding stone wall, there was an arched trellis, woven with a selection of foliage and bright flowers he'd chosen from the local flower market. Teals and pinks mixed against dark green to show the colours of the Carulian flag, alongside whites and reds to represent the colours of Sarala. The table itself was placed to optimise the view of the waterfront, the dark blue of the sea glinting with silver against the deep golden yellow of the sand. It was simply but beautifully set, the glass top strewn with flower petals.

Elora looked around, wide-eyed, and then gave a small gasp. 'It's beautiful.'

'I can't take credit for this,' Michel said with a note of regret. 'This was all Rohan. I told him I would offer him a job.'

'It's magical,' she said. And the smile she turned to him was all Rohan could have hoped for.

'There is a cocktail all ready for you with some snacks. The first course will arrive shortly.'

With that, Michel left and they walked over to the table.

'Mango margarita,' Rohan said as he handed her a glass. 'Made with a mango given to me by Pria.'

'Really?'

'Really. I told you, I am a man of my word.'

'That makes this extra special.' She sipped the drink and gave an appreciative sigh. 'Perfect.' She gestured around. 'All of this is perfect.' She reached for her phone. 'It will look amazing on social media, a perfect setting for the charade.'

'Wait.' He reached out to move her hand out of the way and they both stopped at the touch, looked at each other across the small circular table, tension shimmering in the warm evening breeze as the sun began its descent, casting a deep glow across the sky.

Now he couldn't help but remember their kiss. How could he not, when she was so close, when he could smell her perfume, when he could see the satin sheen of her bare shoulders, the delicate planes and shadows of her collarbone, and his fingers tingled with a desire to run over the delicate contour, to drop kisses on the bare skin to provoke again that wonderful, glorious, joyous response?

He forced himself to stay still, not to spook her, but there was an answering flare in her grey eyes and a slight quiver in her body as she too fought to remain still.

'Yes?' she said, her voice a little breathless.

He held her gaze, held the moment. 'You're right, this will look good on social media, but I didn't just do it for that. I did it for you. I picked the flowers in the market with you in mind.' Had even tried to match the scents to the elusive, tantalising perfume she wore. 'That's the truth as well.'

'Then thank you. You got it dead right. It's all I could have wanted from a first date.' She gave a small laugh. 'Even a pretend one.'

Before he could reply, he saw the door to the terrace swing open and a waiter appeared, balancing a tray.

Rohan welcomed the interruption, not sure what he would have said next, because right now this didn't feel fake. He wasn't sure how it felt.

Elora smiled up at the waiter, clearly also relieved by the distraction, the chance to change the mood, and soon she was engrossed in a discussion on the starters, a selection of snacks chosen to go with the cocktail.

The waiter left with a promise to return with the main course and the 'perfect wine' to go with it.

'These look perfect,' Elora said.

So do you. He bit back the words, aware of how cheesy they would sound.

'Tell me about them.'

'Weren't you listening?'

'No,' he admitted. He'd been too busy watching her, seeing the expressions flitting across her face, the focus as she'd discussed ingredients and textures.

She gave him a slightly puzzled look and then pointed at the plate. 'So we have kachori puff pastry filled with a spiced onion filling and then fried. The main spices are the fennel seeds and the nigella seeds, so they will have a slightly bitter flavour offset by some chilli powder and then the sweet chilli chutneys to dip them in. We also have long green chilli peppers stuffed with potato and deep fried. And finally, another deep-fried offering, lentil vadas, with spinach, chillies and ginger.' And now Elora did reach for her phone. 'But before we start we need a picture with the cocktails and the remains of the sunset. Then we *need* to eat. I can't believe you managed to get a table here.'

'I didn't. I was a bit flummoxed until Michel mentioned they are thinking about renovating the terrace so they can expand. I asked to see it and came up with the idea.'

Elora picked up a stuffed chilli and took a bite. 'Well, when you taste this you'll be glad you did!'

He realised he was already glad, perhaps too glad. But he couldn't help but enjoy her appreciation of the food, the venue and the occasion. Watching her sample each savoury snack, he savoured her enjoyment more than the actual food itself. He had to get a grip; it was time to get this dinner at least a little on track.

'I thought we could use this opportunity to discuss the future,' he said. In part to reassure Elora that he was serious about their marriage, despite her mother's concerns. 'Use the time to look forward, make plans, set rules.'

'Rules?' Now the smile dropped from her face, her expression wary, and for a moment he regretted his words, steeled himself to continue.

'Yes.'

'I wasn't aware a marriage had rules as such. We've already agreed there will be no scandals or indiscretions, that we will be faithful. What other rules could there be?'

'Perhaps "rules" is the wrong word. Expectations would be better.' He would not make the same mistakes twice. With Caro, he'd made so many incorrect assumptions and she'd accused him of smothering her, crowding her, not giving her space. He'd got so much wrong; he wouldn't again.

'Our marriage is an agreement, a contract, and I want us to figure out the terms, what we both want from it, apart from a means to bring our countries together, apart from an heir.'

There was the slightest of pauses as she looked down to her empty plate, took the last sip of her cocktail.

'OK. That makes sense.' She looked up. 'I'll pop to the bathroom and I'll have a think whilst the main course arrives.'

Elora looked at her reflection in the small private bathroom Michel had put aside for her use. Saw the sparkle in her eyes, looked down at what she was wearing, and knew she was in danger of letting an illusion mess with her head. For a while there, as they had sipped cocktails in the rays of the setting sun, it had felt all too real.

But it wasn't. This wasn't a romance. It was an arrangement and she knew she should be grateful that Rohan wanted to set some rules—rules he was consulting her on. It made sense. With rules in place, their marriage had a chance of being way more successful than so many marriages based on love. Expectations could be managed—she closed her eyes—or could they? Rohan was expecting an heir—what if that was an expectation she could not fulfil? She couldn't afford to think like that. Her worries were just that—worries, that might prove to be utterly unfounded. She couldn't jeopardise this agreement, which was so important for her country, because of a worry.

So now she would pull herself together. Go and set some rules.

By the time she returned to the table the main course was already in place.

Rohan smiled. 'The waiter said to tell you that Michel would be happy to discuss ingredients and methods with you later, and he is even willing to give you his personal email and number.'

'He may live to regret that.' Her smile was friendly but cooler than before; she knew she had herself in hand now. 'So—the rulebook,' she said. 'Where do you want to start?'

'How about you tell me how you see your life once we are married?'

The question made reality loom;in a few months she would be married to the man opposite her, would have vowed to spend the rest of her life with him. She closed her eyes briefly and focused on this moment, concentrated on the taste of the food, the texture of the *appam*, the pancake served with the vegetable *ishtu*. She ran through the ingredients. Rice flour for the *appam*, coconut milk used in both *appam* and *ishtu*, the sauce spiced with cloves, cinnamon, coriander. The crunch of the cauliflower, cut into perfect bite-sized chunks, the potato, soft but not too soft.

Enough, Elora. Answer the question.

'I assume we will live on Sarala.'

He nodded. 'Yes. Though I am hoping to continue some of my ambassadorial duties, as well as keep an eye on my hotel. So I may spend some of my time abroad.' She waited, aware of a hope that he would suggest she travel with him. Instead, 'So you needn't be worried that you won't have your own space. You will. There are a number of royal residences we can live in—the one I have in mind has plenty of space so we can have separate quarters.'

Elora didn't understand why his words weren't making her happier. When the plan for this marriage had first been mooted she'd have been filled with relief at the idea of keeping everything as separate as possible.

She gave her head a small shake and looked up at him. 'That sounds ideal,' she said firmly. Rohan was giving her a chance to live her own life, something she had always wanted to do, and she would take the opportunity with both hands instead of letting a sunset mess with her head. 'I would also like some autonomy in other areas, though I will, of course, carry out all my royal duties. Do you have any idea what they will entail?'

'Similar, I imagine, to what your mother and sister carry out on Caruli. There will be royal visits, events, you will be on the board of various charities and take on other duties as they arise.'

Such as being a parent—mother to the heir of Sarala. The idea was not one she wanted to contemplate, and the guilty knowledge that it might not be that easy sent a burgeoning anxiety straight through her.

'That all sounds as I expected, but I would like to do more than that.'

'In what way? Do you want to get a job, pursue a career?'

'Not as such. I don't feel working for a salary when the royal family already holds so much wealth is necessarily fair, given I do not already have a career of my own. I meant I would like a more hands-on role than my mother has. Rather than being on the board of a charity I'd like to play a more active part.'

'I have the feeling you have something in mind.'

Elora hesitated. 'Yes, I do.' He said nothing, simply held her gaze, and she knew the choice now was hers. To trust him or not. He could do no more to advocate that trust than he had already done. She closed her eyes, put her mother's voice out of her mind and made that choice. This man was offering her a fair shot at a partnership. This was not, could never be, the marriage of fairy tales, but it could perhaps still be a happy union. 'But I'll need to explain, and to do that I will need to share a secret with you.'

'For what it's worth, you have my word that whatever you are going to tell me I will keep confidential. Completely.'

He'd echoed her own words of earlier back to her and she got the message. He'd trusted her, she needed to return the favour. And she would. 'Thank you. Because it's not just about me.' If he did betray her, she wasn't the only one who would be in trouble.

'Right, here goes.' She pushed her empty plate to one side, took a sip of wine and started.

'A few months ago, I was at an official function, a fashion show featuring a designer from Caruli, a protégé of my mother. During the show there was a protest; a woman ran into the event, brandishing a placard. The message was simple—she was saying that the cost of a single outfit would feed her family for a month.

'She was hustled out but…it made me think. My mother told me that it was sheer nonsense, that families like that needed to learn to budget better, manage better, and that Caruli is one of the most prosperous islands in the region. I knew that the latter fact was true, but that's all very well for the eighty-five percent of the population who are OK— what about the rest? I was also ashamed to realise I don't really know how much it costs to feed a family.'

'It's not your fault. How could you or I know? We aren't taught things like that.'

'Then we need to find out for ourselves. How can a royal family rule if they don't understand how real life works for most people?' She paused, suddenly aware of how passionate she sounded, knew that her parents would have deemed this conversation unseemly and closed it down, taken her words as an insult, an unacceptable criticism.

'You're right.' She looked at him almost suspiciously,

the words so unfamiliar she thought there must be an edge to them. But he continued, leaning forward, and she could see real interest, that he was listening. 'So I take it you did some research.'

'Yes, I did. And that protester was right—her maths made sense. But I also learnt more about the fifteen per-cent of people who don't have enough money. I learnt about food banks and the struggle to get help and I have tried, really tried, to get to grips with it. Though I know how daft that sounds, sitting here at one of Caruli's best res-taurant's sipping cocktails.'

'It doesn't sound daft. But I hope you don't feel guilty about it—you were born royal—that wasn't your choice and the lifestyle we have comes with the territory.'

'But it doesn't, or it shouldn't, come with the territory to ignore those who are struggling. So I decided I wanted to do something. However small.'

'What did you do?'

'I tried to think of something I could do in my capac-ity as princess, but my mother vetoed any involvement at all. She said I mustn't do anything political, especially when there was already unrest on Baluka. Mustn't "rouse the rabble".' Elora had disagreed so profoundly with her mother's words that for once she had nearly argued back, nearly shown some moral backbone. But in the end she'd simply bowed her head, whilst resolving to find a way. 'So I found a soup kitchen and I volunteered there as a private citizen called Preeti Bannerjee. They have no idea who I really am.'

Rohan stared at her. 'But how on earth have you pulled that off?'

'I have help from a member of staff who is also a friend.' She knew he would guess it was Pamir but she didn't name him. 'His wife lends me her clothes. We are a similar build. I even have a wig, a very realistic one, I may add. So I am a brunette rather than a blonde, I dress in jeans and a top, an outfit Princess Elora would never be seen in, and it works. Pamir covers for me and so far, it has worked. I help out, I cook—sometimes when I can I take the left-overs from the kitchens. I give as much of my money as I can without arousing suspicion and I love it.'

'Good for you. You are doing a good thing.' He leant back and lifted his glass. 'To Preeti Bannerjee. I hope to meet her one day.'

'It doesn't feel like I'm doing enough, though. I want to do more—and there is so much to do. So I was thinking, hoping, that if…when we get married I could be more in-volved. Not as Preeti Bannerjee but as myself. Perhaps ar-range charity fundraisers, try to raise awareness, if I can't continue with the more hands-on work. Unless, of course, your parents veto it.'

'They won't,' Rohan said. 'My sister Marisa has always been a champion of the less well-off inhabitants of Sarala.' He paused. 'Though with Marisa it's hard to tell if it's be-cause she cares about their plight or she thinks the poor are more likely to be anti-royalty. Sarala is less prosper-ous than Caruli—Marisa has been telling my parents for a while that they need to think about the percentage of peo-ple who may feel they would be better off in a republic.'

Elora's attention was caught. 'So your parents listen to you and Marisa?'

'They probably listen to Marisa more than me, but yes, they listen. They don't always agree, but they will let us have our say.'

Elora tried to imagine that—parents who at least listened, paid attention, believed you had something to contribute.

'In this case,' Rohan said, 'I think they would welcome your involvement. You can discuss it with them over the next few days.'

'Yes.' Though in truth she couldn't imagine doing anything of the sort. She was nervous enough at the prospect of leaving for Sarala the next day, staying with King Hanuman and Queen Kaamini.

Rohan looked at her. 'Don't worry. My parents will welcome you. They are pleased the marriage is going ahead.'

Pleased that their son who had no wish to marry was willing to do his duty. Duty—that was all this was about. This charade. The reminder was perhaps opportune as the waiter brought out the dessert, a beautiful concoction of ice cream topped with strawberry meringues and tiny dark chocolate truffles, presented in a rose gold bowl for sharing, complete with two heart-shaped dessert spoons.

It was nothing but a prop, to sustain an illusion that masked a political necessity. And she mustn't forget that. Elora reached for her phone again, kept her voice cool and businesslike.

'So the plan is to leave for Sarala tomorrow afternoon, after we have a "romantic" picnic breakfast, and then spend some time with Viraj as planned. I thought we could do some baking; I think he'd like that. Also, that way, we're in the palace kitchens and no one can change it into a publicity stunt. That's the agenda.'

An agenda, the perfect word for a planned romance, an illusion that would melt away once the marriage was sealed. Melt away like the ice cream in front of them, and the glint from the heart-shaped spoons seemed to mock her as she took the picture.

CHAPTER NINE

ROHAN WOKE UP, stared up at the ceiling and realised he was smiling, realised too that he was looking forward to seeing Elora. With a frown, he swung his legs out of bed and headed to the bathroom. Yes, dinner had been enjoyable, but this was ridiculous. All of this was part of a plan, an agenda.

Half an hour later, he walked down the majestic treelined avenue, the chinar trees covered in a dense foliage of verdant green, followed Elora's instructions and soon saw her kneeling under one of the trees, spreading a blanket on the ground. A picnic spot, chosen in the hope that one or more of the gardening staff would spot them and release a picture to social media.

As she saw him approach, she opened the wicker basket next to her, pulled out a container and opened it.

'That smells incredible,' he said.

'I've made *dosas* with a potato filling and to follow I've made a fruit salad. Hopefully, the kitchen staff will also have taken note and plenty of speculation will be swirling.'

'Good. I think so far, so good?'

'I hope so,' she said as she handed him a cup of coffee. 'But perhaps we should do a social media check.'

He nodded, pulled his phone out and started to scroll as he bit into the *dosa*. 'This is delicious.'

When she didn't respond, he turned and saw that she was intent on reading something.

'Elora?'

The sharpness of his tone penetrated her concentration. 'There's an article on Celebchat.' A massively popular site that covered hot celebrity gossip.

Quickly, he found it and started to read.

How does Princess Elora measure up? Let's check the Dateometer!

Rohan scanned the article under the headline, wondering how the reporter had unearthed the series of photographs, all of him on a series of first dates. A grainy old photo of him aged eighteen with a girl he barely even remembered, and then his first date with Caro. His twenty-three-year-old self was staring across a table, a ridiculous look on his face of adoration, obsession, utter absorption, and he flinched as he looked at it.

Caro had been two years older than him in age, and at least five years older in experience, already a well-known actress, a near household name, a friend of his sister. Marisa had asked Caro to 'look after him' and so she'd contacted him, then asked him out for dinner, and then everything had spiralled. She'd reeled him in, revelled in her all too easy conquest of him, used her undeniable ability to entice and promise and pull back and it had left him a quivering mess ruled by his hormones.

He pulled himself back from this trip down memory lane and turned his attention to the next photos. There he was, opposite a woman he'd dated for about six months, just after the divorce, a Hollywood actress. The next photo

showed his most recent relationship, a model he'd gone out
with for three months.

His expression in those photos was clearly posed for
effect, his smile assured and charming, and his dates had
been equally playing to the camera.

And then there were two photos with Elora, clicked as
they were entering the restaurant and again when they
came out. They were both smiling, and he tipped his head
to study the images more clearly.

'I think we did OK,' he said. 'We're smiling, we look
as though we like each other and...' He broke off, clocked
how still she was before she turned to look at him.

'The photos are fine.'

Her voice was tight and he saw she was still staring at
the screen and he followed suit, readi the article below. A
quick précis on who each woman was, and then the conclusion.

> *There are no photos of our Princess on previous*
> *dates—this is her first foray into the world of dating.*
> *How will she fare?*
>
> *Our gallant Princess can hold out some hope that*
> *she measures up not too badly in the looks depart-*
> *ment...but does she have what it takes to hold Ro-*
> *han's eye now she's caught it?*
>
> *What does this sheltered, inexperienced princess*
> *have that Princess Caro didn't?*
>
> *Can she compare to Hollywood royalty or the*
> *Queen of the catwalk?*
>
> *Only time will tell, but let us know what you think.*
>
> *Answer the poll: Does Princess Elora have what*
> *it takes?*

Rohan looked up, saw the set expression on Elora's face and thought carefully about his next words.

'I think we could have come off worse than this and in fact I am sure that we will as this "romance" progresses.' He was counting his lucky stars they hadn't delved into his previous marriage in any detail, hadn't regurgitated all the old stories and scandals.

'I know it could have been worse.' But her voice was colourless. 'Plus it is irrelevant. We will marry whatever the poll says.'

'A poll that will be carried out by people who know none of the "contestants",' he pointed out. 'Plus the very fact the poll exists proves that people already believe in our romance. That's a good thing, right?'

'Yes,' she agreed. 'So far, so good. So let's get on with our day. Would you like some fruit salad?'

'Sure.'

But as they ate, despite the fact that Elora maintained a spate of light social conversation, Rohan couldn't shake the idea that something was wrong, that the article had upset her way more than she was letting on. He just didn't get why.

'Are you OK?' he asked eventually as they packed up the remains of breakfast.

Her eyes widened, her smile the perfect pitch of bewilderment, her eyebrow slightly raised. 'Of course. Why wouldn't I be?'

He could let it go—should let it go. If the comments had upset Elora there was nothing he could do. He'd warned her the press would be intrusive before they had embarked on this venture. Plus he was probably imagining this. There wasn't anything in the article to upset her. She couldn't be jealous because she didn't care about him—this was a fake relationship.

And yet… 'I don't know,' he replied. 'But I know something has upset you.'

'How can you know that?'

It was a good question.

'Because you look…too calm, too unruffled. It's your frozen face. Your Ice Princess face.'

'I am a princess.'

He ignored the intervention, 'And when you read the article I saw you clench your hands. You do that when you're upset, then you pretend to be busy with something whilst you retreat behind your princess mask.'

She'd recovered herself now, the grey eyes cool and guarded.

'Of course it upset me for a moment. I'm not used to being discussed in such a way. But then I got over it. You did warn me what I was letting myself in for. I'll just need to have a thicker skin and not let it affect me.'

All very sensible words, but…

'It's not that easy,' he said. 'I know how sometimes things the press say hit a nerve and if you let those words fester they end up sticking with you, in your head. So how about you tell me what upset you and we can make sure it's in perspective?'

'Did you ever talk to anyone about the press stories about you?'

This was approaching ground he didn't want to traverse but it was a fair question.

'No, I didn't. Because I didn't have anyone I could talk to. You do. You have me. Or if you don't want to talk to me, talk to Flavia or whoever. Because if you don't you will end up brooding on it. And the next article will be worse and so on. And it will end up affecting us and…'

She raised a hand. 'OK, OK, I get it. But it's not that easy. It's awkward.'

He rose to his feet. 'I've got an idea. Maybe it will be easier to talk somewhere else. Not here, surrounded by reminders of royalty. Let's go for a walk. To the local spice market. As two normal people. Put on your Preeti Bannerjee clothes and I'll go incognito as well. Everyone will think we're still on the grounds—we'll be back in a couple of hours. I'll meet you by the North Door in twenty minutes.'

Twenty minutes later, they were walking along the dusty road away from the palace and Elora felt a weight lift from her, felt free in a way she only could when she shed her princess persona. Right now, no one was giving them a second glance—they were just a couple like any other amongst the busy bustle and throng of people.

Street vendors shouted their wares from the small stalls that lined the dusty road, voices were raised in the everyday barter and haggling over goods, cups of masala chai tea, potato pakoras, books, comics, a hodge-podge of offerings laid out for all to see. A few lone cattle roamed, seemingly unsupervised, people walked balancing goods upon their heads, mums holding babies cocooned to their bodies, dressed in bright saris that splashed the landscape with colour. Tourists and locals dressed in more Western clothing, young girls chattering as they walked to school.

And next to her was Rohan, dressed in casual jeans and a T-shirt, a baseball cap on his head, and a wish caught at her that they were actually a normal couple, that this wasn't yet another facet of the illusion they were conjuring.

But it was. She was a princess, an 'inexperienced, sheltered' one, a gauche woman who he was with because he had to be, and a million miles from the other women in his life. The type of women he'd chosen, and therefore she could never measure up to them.

The phrases from the article, the photos of those other women streamed through her brain and darkened the sense of lightness and in that moment she knew he was right. If she didn't talk to him about this it would affect their relationship. No, not a relationship—their agreement.

She looked up at him. 'OK, you're right. I think we should talk about the article. I'm just not sure how to start.'

'Would a cup of tea help?'

'Yes.' It would give her something to do, distract her if it got too embarrassing. 'Please.'

A few minutes later, cup of chai in hand, she tried to gather her thoughts.

'I know it was written as a frothy, gossipy article, to draw in readers, to get likes, et cetera, et cetera, but the writer had a point. I *am* an inexperienced, sheltered princess. The other women in your life weren't.' And that made her feel inadequate, small, as if she could never measure up. The way he'd looked at Caro had twisted her up inside, had made her face the fact that he had loved his first wife, whatever had happened later. And the other two women— he'd looked happy and relaxed with them, he'd chosen to be with them. Beautiful women of the world, all three of them talented celebrities in their own right. 'So how am I going to hold your attention? You chose all those other women.' She asked the question as impassively as possible, as though she were trying to pose a logical question. She wouldn't admit inadequacy to a man who clearly didn't know the meaning of the word.

'And we have chosen each other.' He looked down at her and she realised they'd slowed their steps, were attracting a few glances, and as he realised too he gestured towards the shade of a large amaltas tree, glorious with golden flowers, and a place where they could stand unnoticed. 'This isn't about "holding attention" or comparing you to other women. We have agreed to get married, to forge a marriage that is based on respect and liking and the rules and expectations we have set out. This is about you and me.'

'But we have chosen each other because of our positions. You said it yourself. Sarala is wedding Caruli. The other women in the article—you chose them because you wanted them, because you were attracted to them. Because of who they were as people. So how will we make it work long-term? How can you be faithful to someone you are marrying out of duty? How can I hold you? I'm nothing like any of those women.'

'I don't want you to be like any of them. This isn't about comparisons.' He reached out and took her empty cup from her, placed it on the ground and took her hands in his. 'Our marriage will be about you and me. I won't be comparing you to other women in my life. They are in the past. You are my future.'

'For better or worse.' She gave a laugh she recognised as brittle. 'Even that feels like a comparison.' She shook her head. 'How can I not compare myself to them? The article was right—they were all stunning, accomplished women. Experienced women. I had to watch videos on how to flirt and body language, just to prep for our date. We are faking attraction—you were really attracted to those women. We have kissed once and it was "enjoyable" and that was probably due to the novelty factor.'

She paused for breath and he jumped in.

'There's something *I* need to say.' He hesitated. 'And it's awkward for me.'

She looked up at him in patent disbelief, but saw that he meant it, there was discomfort in his expression and colour touched and heightened the planes of his cheekbones.

'Go ahead.'

'I'm not faking the attraction.' He blurted the words out. 'And that kiss. It went way beyond enjoyable. It knocked my socks off.'

He must think she was daft.

'Yet *you* described it as enjoyable,' she pointed out. 'You don't need to be kind, Rohan. I wasn't fishing for compliments.' Now her mortification was complete and she tugged her hands away.

'I am not being kind.' He dragged a hand over his face. 'I didn't say anything before because the level of attraction took me by surprise, and I don't like surprises,' he said. 'That's the honest-to-God truth. Kissing you blew me away with its intensity. The volatility made everything feel unpredictable and right now I figured we don't need that.'

Could she believe him?

'I also wasn't sure how you felt about the kiss. If you'd hated it and I'd told you the truth it would have made you uncomfortable, and that would make everything complicated.'

It made sense and she sensed that it wasn't a lie, but that didn't mean he wouldn't exaggerate to make her feel better. Yet she also heard uncertainty in his voice, as though he really didn't know how she felt about the kiss.

'I didn't hate it,' she said softly.

'And the attraction?' he asked. 'Does it exist for you or is it all faked, learnt from videos, acted for the cameras?'

She owed him truth. 'It isn't fake, but I don't understand it. As an innocent, sheltered princess, my experience of attraction is limited.' She jutted her chin out, hated the admission she was about to make. 'I've only ever kissed one other person. Once. I don't know what's normal. Plus I don't really know you. It doesn't make sense to me that I should be attracted to a man I don't know at all. And I'm not sure I like that. That kiss…it spun my head and I'm not sure I like that either.'

That kiss… The memory swirled around them now, catching her in an intoxicating net of remembered desire. She looked at him, standing there, his dark hair dappled with glints of sunshine, so vital and alive under the trailing branches, and somehow everything faded into the background—the noise, the bustle, the heat and warmth of the early morning sun washing over her, the scents and sounds of the nearby market. The heat of chillis burnished in the sun, the sweet scent of mangoes, the call of the vendors— all combining in this moment.

Sensations roiled and churned inside her, along with so many questions. How could any kiss be as magical as she remembered it? Especially with a man she hardly knew, a man so far from her dream man. Was Rohan lying to her, trying to make her feel better? How could kissing her, with her paucity of experience, possibly blow his mind, this man who had kissed Hollywood royalty, the queen of the catwalk and Princess Caro, a woman he'd loved?

And so… The words came, a command more than anything else.

'Kiss me again,' she said, seeing surprise touch his eyes and his expression and then understanding. 'A planned kiss.' A kiss to test her memory and his word. 'Not for the cameras, not as part of a charade. A kiss between us. As people. A kiss we choose.'

'You sure?'

Of course she wasn't sure, but she was damned if she'd back down. 'I'm sure.'

He smiled at her now, a toe-curling smile that somehow also held warmth, reassurance and a promise that caught her breath.

'Don't look so worried.' The smile was in his voice too as he reached out and smoothed away the frown she hadn't even realised was there. The touch sent a shiver through her and then, oh, so gently, he ran a thumb over her lips, his skin a little hard, a little calloused, and she knew why, from the manual labour he'd put in.

The feel was exquisite and now her eyes widened as she saw his brown eyes darken and burn with desire, a desire that was for her, his gaze so intent, as though all he could see was her, truly her. Everything faded so that it was just them, nothing else mattered but this moment, and she stepped forward into his arms, looked up at him in wonder. Then he was kissing her and she was kissing him and all thoughts stopped, her whole being subsumed by the sensations that engulfed her as his lips met hers, gentle at first, teasing, tantalising, and then she was pressed against the hard length of him and he deepened the kiss in answer to her demand and she was lost.

Until finally the beep of a horn, the whiz of a bicycle going too close to them, the caw of a bird—she wasn't sure what it was, but it pulled her back to reality and she stepped back on wobbly legs, reached out to place a hand on his arm, not wanting to lose the connection, looked at him as she tried to calm her ragged breathing. He looked as shellshocked as her, desire still burned in his eyes and his breathing was as uneven as her own.

He gave a shaky laugh. 'Now do you believe me? The attraction exists.'

Her own laugh matched his. 'I think the attraction has a life of its own.'

As her heart rate slowly came down she was aware that her whole body was conflicted, a part of her glorying in the aftermath of sensation, but another part of her aware that she wanted more—more kisses, more pleasure...just more. The feelings were jagged and demanding and for once she was finding them hard to control, the iron control failing. Which was causing a sense of panic. Her ability to tame her anxieties, her fears, her emotions was part of who she was. Her hands clenched and she saw his gaze flicker to the movement and the panic increased. This man not only had caused this but he was also able to read her. In a few scant days he had upended strategies that had taken years to hone and she felt exposed, vulnerable.

'I think you were right. This is too volatile, too unpredictable, and I'm not sure either of us is comfortable with it.' The idea triggered a sense of sadness—wouldn't it be wonderful to have had this reaction to a man who wanted it, welcomed it, wanted to be with her and vice versa. A man who she could walk off with hand in hand, run to the nearest hotel and take this further, secure in love and trust.

Well, that wasn't happening and it never would. Their marriage would be an agreement, a contract where they managed expectations, but she had no idea how to manage this attraction. Her only comfort was that neither did he.

'Then let's try to keep it under wraps,' he said. 'For now. Until we get to know each other better.'

'That works.'

'But...' he gave her a smile now '...attraction is a good thing. It will be a good part of our marriage. A very good part.'

His voice sizzled with promise and it occurred to Elora that keeping attraction under wraps might not be as easy as all that. All she could think to say was, 'Let's go round the spice market.' Maybe the smells, the colours, the familiarity of the ingredients would distract her, somehow ground her.

CHAPTER TEN

ROHAN TRIED TO focus on the market—the smells, the hustle and bustle, the raucous cries of the competing sellers hawking their wares, the brightly coloured mounds of turmeric, cumin and chilli powder vibrant in their contrasting hues. But to little avail. His whole mind was filled with Elora, the simmering awareness of the woman walking next to him, an urge to throw caution to the wind, take her by the hand and book them into the nearest hotel.

Insanity.

Surely he had learnt from the mistakes of his youth, where he'd been blinded by desire for Caro, dazzled by a lust he'd never experienced before, a hostage to his hormones and libido. And all along he'd been played by Caro, a woman with way more experience, and she'd enjoyed his devotion, enjoyed making him play to her tune.

He shook his head. Elora was not like Caro—nothing like her. She wasn't deliberately manipulating him; she was just as confused as he was. And, more to the point, he wasn't Caro—he would not rush Elora or use this attraction to influence her in any way. And he would not let either of them make the mistake of mistaking lust for love. No one was getting hurt in this marriage. Attraction would be sidelined until they had everything else in place. Because he could sense how troubled she was, knew that he was the cause of that trouble. That something that should be good and positive was becoming complicated.

'Elora?'

'Yes.'

'Are you feeling any better about the article?'

'I'm not sure,' she admitted. 'I'm glad that the attraction exists and is mutual but…it also seems to have complicated things. And it still doesn't really solve the problem. We haven't chosen each other. How can you help but compare me to them?'

'I won't. I don't want to, any more than you can compare these vegetables.' He gestured towards the wicker baskets heaped with firm red tomatoes, bunches of long, thin green chillis, dark green okra and the bitter gourd. 'This one is bitter, this one is hot, this one is long, another is short.'

'I don't think your analogy holds. People don't only eat one vegetable—they enjoy a variety. Because one day you may want bitter, another sweet.'

'And you can get that from one particular vegetable,' he said. 'You can use chillies to make something hot and spicy that blows your mind, another day you could deseed it and have something gentler, another day you could make a sweet chilli sauce or… And you can be faithful to one seller of all vegetables.'

Now she stared at him and he shook his head. 'OK. You're right—this is a terrible analogy. What else can I do to try and help, apart from promise you I would never compare you to anyone else, because you are unique? You are you.'

But he could see his words still weren't helping.

'I'm not sure. I think…part of the problem is that I have no knowledge of relationships; I've never had one. So, even if I want to, I have nothing to compare you to, so I don't know if I can believe you.'

The words were simple and yet they hit him like a sucker punch on the back of his previous thoughts. When he'd met Caro he'd never had a relationship, had mistaken lust for love. He'd got married expecting the whole happy ever, hadn't had a clue how to manage his feelings or accept he'd got it wrong. Had tormented himself with jealousy over her previous relationships, had been a mess.

'Can you tell me something about yours—not your marriage, I understand that's off-limits—but perhaps the two other women in the article? I'm trying to figure out how we can work when I'm so different to the type of women you choose to be with.'

'What do you want to know?'

She shrugged. 'I'm not sure. How did you meet? What went wrong?'

'I met them both at parties. I met Charlotte at a premiere of one of her films. She approached me, we got talking and ended up having dinner the next day. It was a very straightforward relationship. She had never dated a prince, she said it was on her to-do list. We got on, we liked each other, both of us knew it wasn't serious. We went out for a bit, did a few interviews where I promoted Sarala and she promoted her film. Then, when she landed her next starring role, we decided it was time to go our separate ways. Completely amicably, no drama, no fuss.

'It was much the same with Marianne—we met at a party, got on, decided to have some fun. She decided to end it a few months ago, when the unrest first broke out on Baluka—we had a conversation about possible outcomes. She decided it was best to call it a day. I think she had hopes of becoming a princess, but once she realised that could lead to becoming a deposed princess she bailed.'

'Did you mind?'

'Not in the slightest,' he said truthfully. 'I'd always been clear that marriage wasn't on the cards. I did choose to be with them, Elora, but I never saw them in my long-term future. They were casual relationships.'

She nodded, a small frown on her forehead. 'Did you ever love them?'

'No. I liked them. I enjoyed their company and I don't regret my time with them, but love was never in the mix.'

'So it was like a temporary contract. A different agreement to ours, with a different rulebook. But essentially the same idea.'

'Perhaps. But the idea behind our marriage is permanence.'

'So the poll is flawed. I will hold you because I am the Princess of Caruli.'

'I can't change the fact that we are marrying for political reasons, but I can say that I truly believe that what we are creating now will give us a bedrock, the foundation to a successful marriage.'

'But you didn't manage that with Caro.'

'No, I didn't. But you aren't Caro and I have learnt from my mistakes.' He pressed his lips together, grateful that Elora didn't push it, even more grateful and a little bit surprised when a minute later he felt her hand slip into his as they continued to walk round the market.

'I'd like to buy some things to give to your parents,' she said. 'Just everyday things from the market, or maybe I could buy some ingredients and cook something for them?'

Without even meaning to, he squeezed her hand, grateful for the change of topic. It was as though she not only respected but understood that he didn't want to relive the bad memories.

'That's a good idea,' he said.

And as they walked and looked at the stalls and discussed what she could make, as they walked back to the palace holding a bag of food, he wished that they really could be Preeti Bannerjee and Rohan Carmody. But they weren't and later today he would return to Sarala, to the island he was destined to rule, however little he wished for that destiny.

Once back at the palace they slipped inside and Elora glanced at her watch. 'We're late. We'd better hurry. My mother disapproves of unpunctuality.'

Rohan nodded and within ten minutes they were both back downstairs and at the door of the reception room. No wonder no one recognised Preeti and Elora as being one and the same. Elora looked a million miles from the woman he'd walked hand in hand with, and yet when she'd met his gaze he'd seen a glimmer of his Elora.

Whoa. His? Stop right there.

Elora wasn't his.

'We'd better go in,' she said, and there was a hint of trepidation in her voice.

They entered, to be met by a disapproving look, aimed at Elora. 'You're late.'

'I apologise, Mama. I was preparing for the journey to Sarala.'

'That is no excuse. A princess shows respect through punctuality. I expect you to remember that.'

'Yes, Mama.'

Rohan opened his mouth to at least take some of the blame, but, before he could, Elora gave her head the smallest shake and he knew it was a signal to let it be.

The door opened and the equerry announced Flavia and Viraj, who, Rohan noted, were not reprimanded for their lateness.

'Hello, Viraj. I've been looking forward to seeing you,' Rohan said and the little boy beamed, just as the Queen spoke.

'There has been a slight change of plan. Viraj, you will understand. I have agreed to a meeting with a local pro-royalist group; it is a good publicity opportunity and a chance to remind the people there is continuity.'

Rohan glanced at the little boy, saw the beam fade to disappointment and then resignation, saw Elora look at her sister, then her mother, and open her mouth as if to protest, saw the look the Queen gave her, so cold that Rohan instinctively stepped forward.

'Actually,' he said, 'I don't think that will work.'

The Queen's grey eyes glittered, but courtesy dictated a civil answer. 'Viraj understands that duty comes before pleasure—there will be other times...'

'Not like today,' Rohan said firmly. 'I know and I appreciate your daughters' and your grandson's desire to do their duty, but I also believe that sometimes, where possible, it is acceptable to make sure pleasure is part of life and that makes the duty more pleasurable. I made a promise to Viraj and a prince always keeps his promises. Or at least this one does.'

Flavia stepped forward. 'Perhaps Viraj could spend some time with Rohan and Elora, so the Prince can keep his promise, and I will speak with the delegation, and then we could carry out a photo opportunity.'

'That way, pleasure and duty are covered.'

Viraj entered the fray. 'Please. I promise I will do everything right for the photos and I will do extra studies as well.'

Rohan said nothing else, but he admired Viraj's intervention, giving the Queen a reason to relent under the guise of being a doting grandmother, without losing face.

'Very well.' The words were snapped but they were an acquiescence. 'Elora, make sure you take good care of Viraj.'

'Of course, Mama.' Elora's voice was even but he could sense the tension, saw her put a hand behind her back, knew she was clenching it. Though by the time they left the room she was smiling down at Viraj. 'Ready to make cake?'

'Yes, please.'

'You can be chief chef,' Rohan offered.

'Yes, Your Highness.'

'You can call me Rohan.'

'Are you sure? Grandmama says…'

'Well, Grandmama isn't here. And I am giving you permission to call me Rohan.'

The little boy nodded. 'My tutor says I must make a good impression,' he explained. 'Because one day you will rule Sarala and I will rule Caruli. So it is important you see that I am strong and sensible.'

'Perhaps it is more important to make sure that we are friends,' he suggested, wishing with all his heart that this little boy could be just that—a little boy. 'And to have fun.'

Viraj looked unconvinced. 'But if I have fun, how will you take me seriously?'

'I promise I will take you seriously, but we can have fun as well. All of us together.'

They had reached the kitchens now. 'OK,' Elora said. 'Aprons on and let's get started.'

Rohan watched how carefully Elora listened to Viraj's questions. Instead of telling him what to do, she helped him read the recipe, figure it out and let him do everything, his tongue poking out in concentration as he measured the flour.

'I got it wrong.'

'Hey. That's OK.'

'But it's not. Princes can't get things wrong.'

'Yes, they can,' Rohan said. 'Because sometimes that's how they learn. If you don't get things wrong, how will you ever learn to get them right? The important thing is to learn from your mistakes and not beat yourself up about them.'

'Is that what you do?'

'It's what I try to do. So just have another go at the measuring and this time I'm sure you'll get it right. But if you don't you can have another go.'

Half an hour later, the cake was in the oven.

'Now for the best bit,' Rohan said. 'We scrape the bowl and eat the cake mix.'

He waited for Viraj to swoop on the bowl. Instead, the little boy turned a worried face to him. 'I think it would make me ill. That's what Grandmama says. She told Mummy off when I ate some raw cookie dough and...'

'Then maybe it's best if we don't,' Elora said quickly. 'We can eat the cake instead when it's ready.'

Rohan glanced at Elora and saw that her expression mirrored Viraj's, a mask of worry.

'OK. New plan for the cake mix.' He was making this up as he went along now. 'We'll use it to make a diplomatic pact of friendship. Everyone grab a spoon.' Dammit, he was going to make Viraj and Elora have at least a little bit of fun. He handed out the spoons. 'Hold your spoon up and repeat after me. We vow to be friends.'

Elora gave a sudden smile and nodded at Viraj, who held his spoon up and repeated the words.

'And now,' Rohan said, 'to seal the pact.' And, quick as

a flash, he'd scooped up a bit of cake mix and dabbed it on Elora's nose and then on Viraj's. 'Now, you do the same.'

And suddenly Viraj was giggling as he dabbed the blobs of cake mix and Elora's low chuckle joined in. Then somehow Rohan dipped his fingers in the flour and swiped at Elora's cheek and everyone was laughing as Elora chased Viraj across the kitchen, and they were so immersed they didn't notice the door swing open until a voice rang out, 'Announcing Her Majesty Queen Joanna.'

Rohan saw Elora freeze for an instant before swiftly stepping in front of Viraj, who instantly raised a hand to his face to wipe away the evidence.

'What is going on here?'

'Nothing, Mama. We have made the cake.'

'And now you are running around like fools,' the Queen said. 'On a slippery floor, where Viraj could slip, fall, get injured. Is this how you take care of the heir to Caruli? Is this what you teach him? To make mess, be disorderly?'

'Grandmama, it is not Elora's fault.' Viraj stepped out from behind Elora.

'Yes, Viraj, it is. I foolishly entrusted you to her. Now go—you need to prepare.'

'But...'

'It's OK, Viraj. Go,' Elora said. 'I will see you later.'

The Queen waited until Viraj left and turned back to Elora. 'I am disappointed, Elora.'

'I am sorry, Mama.'

Rohan knew he needed to say something. He had been so taken aback by the Queen's overreaction that he'd stayed silent.

'Actually,' he began, 'this isn't all down to Elora and Viraj was just having a bit of fun.'

The Queen turned to Rohan and managed a wintry

smile. 'I appreciate your intervention, Rohan, and I will take your words on board. However, we do things differently here on Caruli and it is important that everyone understands how Viraj is to be treated. Elora does know. I will speak with her on your return from Sarala.'

Rohan opened his mouth and then saw that Elora had turned her gaze on him, a plea in her grey eyes, and he knew she wanted him to say no more, even if it were in her defence.

'Yes, Mama,' she said.

'Now, please go to the stables and prepare.'

'The stables?'

'Yes. You are all going to ride in procession to the ferry. The people always love a horseback procession. Please don't be late.'

'Um…perhaps I should stay here, clear up the kitchen and I could…'

The Queen's expression of exasperation caused Elora to break off.

'I have told you what needs to be done. Do it. The cake is not important. Switch the oven off and I will ask someone to come and sort out the mess in here.'

Rohan clenched his teeth together, wanted to throw all traditional respect for his elders out of the window seeing the pallor of Elora's face.

He waited until the Queen swept out and turned to Elora, who raised a hand. 'It's OK, Rohan. Please leave it. I need to go and get ready. I'll meet you at the stables.'

Without another look at him, she left the room.

Elora studied her face in the mirror, made sure every trace of flour had gone, that the mask of make-up she'd applied hid her pallor. At least now her hands were no longer shaking, at least she'd made it out of the kitchen and to her room before the panic had hit, before the onset of the shallow breathing, the pounding of her heart, the beat and throb of fear in her chest and at her temples.

It had been the shock of it. Usually, she had warning of when she would be in the proximity of a horse, advance notice that she would be required to ride. But today it had been sprung on her, with no chance to do her usual preparations. But she'd have to manage, could only imagine her mother's wrath if Elora collapsed in an undignified heap. And Rohan—she didn't want Rohan to know about this, didn't even want to acknowledge it herself. For a moment the image of Sanjay on that last day threatened and she pushed it down—couldn't afford to let that memory in now or she wouldn't be able to enter the stables, let alone ride.

One more swig of her herbal remedy against panic, two more minutes of deep breathing and then she touched the talisman she carried everywhere with her. Sanjay's ring— a beaded ring they'd made together as children.

Now she was ready. As she headed down to the stables she was entirely focused on her breathing, on projecting an aura of calm, knowing the horses would sense even the slightest hint of nerves. But she managed a smile for Viraj, safely ensconced on a horse with a groom behind him, ensuring his safety.

Rohan stepped towards her and she saw the questions in his dark eyes, relieved that at least he would ascribe any tension to the encounter with her mother. 'You OK?' he asked, and the warmth in his voice warmed her.

'I'm good,' she said as a groom brought her horse towards her, and she saw with relief that it was Jaswant, the one person who knew the depths of her fear of horses, the one person who had shown her sympathy, helped her to manage over the years. Without him, she had no idea how she would or could have coped.

He helped her onto the horse, kept a soothing hand on the thoroughbred until the last moment. 'He'll be good,' he said briefly, the words he used every time, words that held a promise that Elora believed.

She waited as three members of the pro-royalist group were also helped onto horses from the stables, saw their excited faces, as photos were taken, managed to play her part and smile, grateful that Jaswant was still standing nearby.

And then they were off and all she focused on was getting through the ordeal. She told herself the journey was at least short, and a glance at Rohan showed her that he rode with an assurance and confidence that meant he should be safe. Viraj too would be OK, held firmly in place by one of the palace's most experienced grooms. And she was flanked by them, so the crowds weren't focused on her.

But, in some ways, perhaps that made it worse because now, as she saw the crowds cheer Viraj, captivated by his youth and the knowledge that they beheld their future ruler, knowing she wasn't being watched made it harder for Elora to keep her smile in place.

Now, all she was aware of was the immensity of the horse beneath her, the power of the creature's muscles, the height from the ground and the horrible knowledge of how easily everything could go wrong in a heartbeat. And with that treacherous thought came a sudden flashback to that awful day…the smell of the horses, her own terror, the realisation that she was going to fail, that she would not be able to keep her fear of horses in check. And then Sanjay, wanting to help her…and in the process, in a scant few minutes, tragedy had struck.

Oh, God. She felt herself sway in the saddle, was suddenly aware of an outstretched hand—Rohan's. Strong, safe, secure, and it galvanised her. This time she would not cause further tragedy. Straightening, she put her smile back in place and somehow made it through the rest of the journey to the ferry port.

And only now did she really think about her destination, recall that now she and Rohan were taking their charade, their illusion, to Sarala, an island where there was more unrest, an island where Prince Rohan was regarded with suspicion, and new anxiety rippled through her.

CHAPTER ELEVEN

As THE FERRY approached Sarala, Rohan stood next to Elora and regarded the looming coastline, the familiar curve of sandy beach, the angles of the tree-lined hills.

He loved his country and yet, the nearer they came, he felt a heaviness in his chest, a heaviness caused by the sure knowledge that he didn't want or deserve the destiny his birth had conferred on him, that he was not cut out to rule this land, though he would do his very best. He'd always known it, but he'd accepted his fate as inescapable. That acceptance was harder now that he'd found something he did want to do. But there was no hope of that; this he knew deep down, though he would try his best to persuade his parents that he could take on a dual role—run his business and fulfil his duties as heir.

He looked down at Elora, standing next to him, tendrils of blonde hair rippling in the sea breeze. There had been no opportunity to speak on the journey, the hour taken up in the charade, speaking to fellow passengers, posing for photographs, all of which Elora had done with grace and poise and friendliness. Despite the fact he knew she'd withdrawn, and how could he blame her after that scene in the kitchen? He wanted to speak to her about it, but he was waiting for a chance to get her in private.

But first there would be the arrival party, the greetings

with his family and then... 'Later today,' he said, 'I plan on visiting a temple—an old temple on Sarala, a place I always go to when I get home. Would you like to come? It isn't part of the publicity—no press, no photos.'

'Yes, I would. As long as I won't be intruding.'

'You won't. I'd like to show it to you.'

The words were nothing more than the truth; it was a place where he found peace and perhaps Elora would too.

'But first we need to get through the fanfare of our arrival.'

And it was indeed a fanfare, as they left the ferry with a smile and a wave to the people waiting, walked towards the car that would take them to the palace.

The press was out in force and one of the reporters threw a question. 'Princess Elora, how was your first date? And Prince Rohan, how does Elora measure up?'

He tensed and next to him he felt Elora's nails pinch his arm in warning, as she stopped and turned.

'It is very early days and right now our priority is to show each other our islands. We will be doing a number of state events together, because we are hoping to show our people that we are here and hoping they will put their faith in us as the future. And we are here to listen. And...' she raised a hand '... I know that didn't answer your question. As first dates go, it was...pretty good and you'll be glad to know that His Highness measured up to *my* expectations. Other than that, a princess doesn't kiss and tell.'

Rohan knew it was time to say his piece. 'All I can say is that if the Princess agrees, I am hoping whilst she is here to take her on date number two and three and four. As for measuring up, Elora is in a field of her own and I would never presume to compare her to anyone, and I'd appreciate it if none of you did either.'

It was the best that he could do and even that wasn't easy, given what he wanted to do was take the reporter and kick him into the sea. But, instead, they continued their walk to the waiting car and then smiled and waved their way to the palace.

There on the steps were his parents and Marisa, waiting to greet them. Marisa stepped forward.

'Welcome, little bro and Elora, it's lovely to see you again.'

'Indeed.' Queen Kaamini stepped forward and took Elora's hands in hers. 'Welcome, Elora. The King and I look forward to getting to know you better over the next days. We also have a number of events planned.'

'Amma! Give Elora a chance to get her bearings,' Rohan said.

'No, Rohan. It's fine. I like to have as much preparation time as possible. I would be happy to discuss the agenda for my visit.'

'But first I will show Elora to her room. I have put you next door to me. I hope that is all right.'

'That sounds wonderful.'

'It does,' Rohan said. 'Now, though, I am taking Elora to the temple.'

His sister's gaze flicked to him and he saw the hint of surprise that he was taking Elora to a place that usually only he and she now visited. He had never even taken Caro there. But he knew if they didn't go now, they would get swallowed up in royal duties and he would never have the chance to find out what was going on.

'We will be back in a couple of hours and then we are all yours,' he said.

'I will hold you to that,' the King said. 'There are matters to discuss.'

Rohan bowed his head, then gestured to Elora.

'Where is the temple?' she asked as they left the palace and headed towards the car port that housed the royal fleet of cars.

'Not far. It is on the palace grounds, but if we are to be back in time it will be better to drive.'

After ten minutes he parked by the side of the road near some woodlands. 'We can walk from here.'

As they headed through the woods the air was scented with the evergreen smell of the trees that provided a welcome shade from the heat of the sun. They walked in a silence broken only by the sound of birds, the metallic note of the coppersmith, the tap of a woodpecker and the chatter of the parakeets.

She looked at him. 'Your family were so welcoming. I appreciate that.'

'They are relieved that our marriage is going ahead, relieved that we are here. As long as Sarala is served, my parents will always be gracious.' He replayed the words and then shook his head. 'That was discourteous of me. My parents are good, kind people who I love and who love me. But what you do need to understand about them, now you are being welcomed into the family, is that however much they love me, however much they love Marisa, they love Sarala more. And they would admit that freely—they see no wrong in it.'

'But at least they show grace and love,' Elora said.

They reached the temple now and she slowed. 'Oh, I didn't realise it would be so...old. It feels awe-inspiring, like stepping back in history.'

'It was built back in the tenth century. At some point a ruler let it fall into disrepair, perhaps when war and fighting meant there was no money, and in recent times it has been difficult to justify spending money on a temple that is on private palace grounds.'

'Yet it still holds such beauty,' she said softly as they both looked at the remains of what once must have been a vast edifice. But Elora was right—what was left was still a thing of beauty. Stone steps led up to a rectangular base, with beautifully carved stone pillars that rose majestically to support a now moss-laden domed roof.

'I come here to think. It's a place my grandfather used to bring me to. He didn't have a lot of free time, but when he did he'd come here with me. I think its age puts things into perspective, makes me feel part of a whole pattern, part of Sarala and all its traditions and the history it is steeped in.'

'History both good and bad,' she said. 'History that is in the making right now, and not only for us, for royalty, but for every single inhabitant on this island. Centuries ago, we fought and battled for our independence from each other, to prevent our ancestors from taking our lands and seas. Now, Baluka has battled for its republic, for democracy. And people died, not soldiers on the battlefield, but people caught up in history, people in the wrong place at the wrong time—one person got caught in a wave of protests and was trampled underfoot.' Her voice broke. 'When I think about that, that person and their family, it all seems so unfair. Yet some would say there is always a price to pay. For freedom.'

'Or to keep power,' he said.

'But that's not what it's about, is it?' she asked. 'I don't think our parents want power. I know I don't. I think they just believe in their divine right to rule and they believe they are blessed to be given it.'

'And in return they give their all to ruling, do their best

to be just and bring good to the people and the land. And they would sacrifice anything to do that,' Rohan said.

'And I suppose that's why your parents love you but love Sarala more.'

'And why your parents guard Viraj so carefully.' He hesitated. 'I want to apologise for earlier. When I suggested he had fun, encouraged the food fight, I didn't mean to bring down your mother's anger on your head.'

'It's OK.'

'But I wish you had let me explain—and, more than that, to perhaps make your mother see that what we did wasn't wrong. That poor child was only having a little bit of fun. My parents let me have some fun. If I had said something...'

'It would have made no difference,' Elora said with a weariness in her voice that touched his heart. 'Could even have made things worse. If you had defended me, my mother would be more likely to veto any further suggestions we spend time with him. Viraj would suffer.'

'So in future I have to stand back and allow your mother to say whatever she likes to you? I'm not sure I can do that.' He hesitated. 'I don't know Queen Joanna or the ins and outs of your relationship, but sometimes when people are naturally autocratic it is better to stand up to them, rather than just accept it. I know that is difficult in our culture, where respect for our elders is so important, but perhaps your mother isn't even aware of what she is doing. Next time, maybe it will *help* if I speak to her...'

'No!' Now Elora's voice was sharp and, realising it, she lifted a hand. 'I know you want to help, but truly it will be better to leave it. Anyway, hopefully, after our marriage my mother will change, but if she doesn't it's OK. I don't mind.'

He looked at her, wondered how she could not mind. 'I may need more than that. I am not sure I will always be able to hold my tongue. You will be my wife—how can I stand by and not defend you?'

The question appeared to catch her by surprise. 'We can make it part of our agreement,' she said steadily. 'That you are allowed to stand by, that that is my expectation of you.'

'Then you will need to explain. I cannot agree to a term I disagree with and don't understand.'

She sighed now. 'My mother has never got over Sanjay's death. I'm not sure that she ever will—either of my parents. Sanjay was their...hope for the future, their pride, their joy. Their world, I suppose you could say.'

'And he was your brother, your twin. I cannot imagine the pain of your loss.'

'No,' she said simply. 'I don't think anyone can unless they have experienced it. But for my parents it wasn't only the loss of a child. It was the loss of the heir. Made worse by the fact my mother didn't fall pregnant again. She was forty when Sanjay died and she still hoped for years that it would happen, but it didn't, and because of that she slowly became more and more bitter and despairing. And afraid.'

'Afraid of what?' The penny dropped before she had answered. 'She was scared your father would divorce her and remarry.'

'Yes. After all, he'd already done it once. He divorced Flavia's mother because after Flavia she had a number of miscarriages. He met my mother whilst he was abroad and what started as an affair became serious and he decided to marry her. Decided that it was worth the risk of a public backlash, gambled that the people would forgive him once an heir was born.'

'That must have affected Flavia very much.'

'It must have, but she has never spoken to me about it. She went abroad to live with her mother. She only came back when Sanjay died. Because that was her duty.'

'To return and marry and produce an heir,' Rohan said.

'Like you. And once she had Viraj my mother's position was more assured. But I don't believe either of my parents, especially my mother, will ever get over Sanjay's death. And I'm his twin, the one who is still here, I am a constant reminder to them of that loss. They lost him and they were left with me, and they wouldn't have been human if they hadn't wished it had been me who died. My father can hardly bear to look at me—when he does, it is with such sadness, such weariness I could weep. My mother shows her feelings through anger because every time she sees me it causes her pain and grief.'

His heart tore at her words—words he wanted to refute and deny but he knew he couldn't. He'd seen how her parents were around her, couldn't even put his hand on his heart and say that his parents wouldn't be a little the same. But he knew too that, however much they grieved, they would never treat their remaining daughter with cruelty, would never stop loving her.

'They are wrong,' he said flatly. 'To grieve the loss of a son, the loss of an heir, is understandable, and I feel for them, but to treat you badly...that is wrong. This is all wrong.'

'Perhaps, but it is as it is. That too is part of our tradition. I am sure in centuries past so many kings and queens cursed and rued the day a daughter was born instead of a longed-for son.' She shook her head. 'I don't want sympathy. I am just trying to explain why I don't wish you to challenge my mother or stand up for me. Nothing can change how she feels about me, but if telling me what to do, belittling me, gives her any comfort then let her have it.'

He frowned, and wondered why she was so accepting of her mother's attitude. It was almost as though she felt she deserved it, and yet that made no sense.

'It still is wrong. If we have daughters, I swear to you, here in this holy place, that I will love them. I will love them for being the individual human beings they are, I will love them because they are my child, part of me, and I will never curse, regret or rue that they are a girl. I need you to believe this. To trust me on this if you can't trust me on anything else.'

He saw confusion in her eyes and then the sparkle of tears as her lips parted.

'I...' Then she looked away for a moment and back at him. 'I do believe you.'

He frowned, sure that she'd meant to say something else, and then she rose to her feet and repeated the words. 'I do believe you. Thank you. And I will do everything to make this marriage work.' And, reaching up, she kissed his cheek, the touch so gentle, so sweet, he thought he felt his heart ache.

They stood hand in hand for a long moment and then, as if to break the spell, she stepped back and glanced at her watch.

'We'd better get back.'

He nodded agreement and with one last backward glance they headed to the car.

CHAPTER TWELVE

ONCE BACK AT the palace they were pulled into an instant whirlwind of activity. First, they had a meeting with both King and Queen to outline the events planned for the next days, complete with allocated time slots left for 'romance'.

'We thought we'd leave that bit to you,' the Queen explained, 'but if you need any props or organisational help let us know.'

'I think we'll manage,' Rohan said quickly, and Elora smiled, taking it all in. His family were so different from her own, their conversations easy and courteous, with a teasing tone that would be unimaginable in her own home.

Then, once the meeting was done, Marisa entered the room. 'I'll take you to your room,' she said.

Elora followed Marisa through a palace that was in many ways like her own home in Caruli, marble-floored, portraits on the wall and a massive oak staircase sweeping to the second floor.

'Here you are.' Marisa pushed the door open to a spacious suite of rooms, her suitcase already placed on the king-sized bed.

'Thank you.'

'It is we who should be thanking you. Not every princess would agree to take on my brother. I understand it's a tall order, and I assure you Rohan is a good man. But we are grateful—Sarala needs this marriage and a marriage that strengthens an alliance with a neighbour in these times is welcome. Now all we need is an heir.'

The words sent that familiar shiver of anxiety through her, an anxiety already triggered by the conversation with Rohan by the temple. Because that had shown more than a desire for an heir—there had spoken a man who wanted a family, be they sons or daughters. And she'd been so close to sharing her fears with him, telling him the truth about the possibility of fertility issues, but in the end she couldn't take that risk.

'I understand,' Elora said. 'I understand too that it is important to make the people believe that Rohan is a good man. With the times as unstable as they are, they need an heir they trust to rule well.'

'Yes.' For the first time in the conversation Marisa glanced away, her gaze fixed on the window, looking out towards the capital city. Elora wondered for a moment how Marisa felt about the law that meant she could not rule simply because she was a female, despite the fact she was the elder. 'We are hoping that this romance idea will help with that, show him in a softer light. But I should warn you that it will not be easy. Here on Sarala, there are more republican sympathisers—there is more poverty here— but also there is animosity towards Rohan, an animosity my brother has done little to allay.'

Because he was guilty? The idea that she had been so sure of just days ago no longer seemed so easy to believe. How could the man who had kissed her, held her, and promised to love daughters as much as sons, be the ruthless prince portrayed by the press? The husband who had terrorised his wife into flight.

Yet it had happened—the foiled escape, the divorce—

and never once had Rohan given his side of the story. Did Marisa know the truth? It was a question Elora wouldn't ask. If Rohan did not wish to share the facts with her then she would not go behind his back to discover them. Nor would she ask Marisa to betray her brother's confidence, even assuming he had confided in her. Probably not, given Caro had once been, maybe still even was, a friend of Marisa.

'If the animosity is deep-seated it will be difficult to shift.'

'Yes, but at least my parents are well liked. I doubt the people would move against them, but it is the future we must protect. Caro was a popular princess, which means you will have to work extra hard to win their liking. The best way to do this is to have an heir.'

That word again, and she had to deflect the subject.

'That takes time. In the short-term, what would you advise?'

'Be as natural as possible. If you believe in Rohan, people will see that and they will take that seriously. Play the romance card, but don't overdo it. Make it all as believable as you can. As you know, Caro was my friend, but that doesn't blind me to her faults. She and Rohan were always ill-suited. Caro likes drama and she likes being at the centre of it and, as a born actress, she is an expert at creating drama and illusions. I suggest you skip the drama and create better illusions. And get Rohan on board. He can't stand the press; you'll need to keep him on track. I'll help as much as I can.' Marisa smiled. 'But now I'll leave you, give you a bit of a chance to process things before dinner. And good luck.'

Elora had the feeling she'd need it.

But over the next days her luck held. She and Rohan attended the events organised by his parents, charity galas and walkabouts, visits to factories, and in between they fitted in a couple of 'dates', a dinner at a small local restaurant and a trip to a theatre to watch a performance by a local playwright. Both venues had been suggested by Marisa and both felt very public—Elora and Rohan on show as they chatted to fellow diners and theatregoers. Press coverage was neither enthusiastic nor vitriolic; Elora had a sense of suspended judgement.

On the fourth morning of her visit she entered the breakfast room, once again enjoying the fact that here on Sarala there was less pomp and ceremony, no need to be announced. But she sensed a very different atmosphere to what she was used to here, the tension evident—Rohan's expression stiff and grim, his parents' resolute. The Queen dabbed at her mouth with a napkin.

'So what are the plans for today?' Elora asked, needing to say something. 'I see we have romance slotted in.'

'*I've* planned a picnic,' Rohan said, managing a smile. 'I thought we were due a date where we aren't on show.'

'However, I have arranged for a horse and carriage to take you to your destination,' the King said. 'With Carulian horses, descendants of a gift from your grandfather to my father.'

It took all her years of training, all her experience of controlling anxiety to allow her to smile. 'Thank you. It will feel like another sign of the alliance between our countries.'

'You'll also be able to assess how many protesters line the streets and how many supporters,' Marisa said. 'Far easier in a carriage than a car.'

'There will also be plenty of security present.'

'Undercover, presumably?' Marisa said and the King nodded.

'A judicious mix. Enough that people are aware of them but not so many that it causes undue comment.'

'Where are we going?' Elora tried to sound casual, wanting to assess the length of the journey, and told herself it would be fine even without the familiar turbaned figure of Jaswant behind the horses. She would be in a carriage; it wasn't as though she had to ride a horse.

She saw Rohan's dark eyes rest on her thoughtfully, and then he answered. 'We're going to a royal nature park. Private land. And beautiful. About half an hour away.'

The words were said in his usual deep rumble, but she could still sense the tension in the room. Knew something had been said before her arrival at the breakfast table. She ate deliberately slowly, waited until the King, Queen and Marisa had exited the room and then turned to Rohan.

'What happened?'

At first, she thought he wouldn't answer. Then he shrugged. 'I told my parents about my business and, in brief, they have instructed me to close it down or hand it over to someone else.' His voice was matter-of-fact, but she knew how much it would hurt, recalled the enthusiasm, the vitality he'd shown when he told her about the hotel. Knew how much of himself he'd invested in the business.

'What if you moved it to Sarala?' she asked. 'What if you built up tourism, resorts on Sarala?'

'I suggested that and Marisa backed that as a positive idea. That was when they said I should hand the business over to someone who "will have the time and energy to invest in it to maximise the benefit to Sarala" and that person cannot be me as I will need to put my all into preparing to rule and then actually ruling Sarala. That I must do my duty.' He cradled his coffee cup. 'Duty comes first.'

The unfairness of it all tore at her. Rohan was willing to

do his duty, to rule, to give up so much. To marry a woman he didn't want to marry, to move back here.

'Are you sure they won't change their minds?'

'I'm sure. They believe I need to focus exclusively on Sarala.'

'But your business was for Sarala.' She frowned. 'What if you start the business up now, whilst you are the heir? What if I offer to help? I can learn—if there are two of us, then...'

He looked at her and now his smile was genuine, warmed his dark eyes. 'Would you do that? For me? That isn't in our agreement.'

'No, it isn't. But yes, I would do that, because I know how much your dream means to you and I would like you to be able to fulfil at least a part of that dream.'

'It's a kind thought, but I know my parents. They will not change their minds and I will not complain. Now, we had better make ready for the procession. The picnic at the end will be worth it.'

The finality in his tone indicated that the subject was closed and now...now she needed to prepare. Make sure she did her duty and didn't make a fool of herself.

Rohan helped Elora up into the carriage, aware that she seemed a little more tense than she had been on previous public outings on Sarala. Perhaps it was simply the whole waving and smiling gig. He'd been touched at her reaction earlier; it had felt good to know she truly got what it meant to him, but also understood that he had no choice. His destiny was unavoidable. As now was hers. His to rule, hers to marry him and carry an heir.

Once seated, he saw her flick a quick glance forward and he introduced her to the carriage driver. 'This is

Deepak; he has been working in the stables for ten years and he loves these horses.'

Then he concentrated on the crowds that lined the streets, observed the number of pro-republican placards amongst those who had simply come to watch their progress. But the protestors were peaceful enough, and Rohan was waving on automatic, his brain still conjuring ways to try to change his parents' minds, even though he knew it was a futile endeavour.

They were about halfway on their journey when he became aware that a group of protesters had started a chant and then everything happened all at once. A shout, the whinny of a horse as it startled, the whirr of an object lobbed from the crowd…a scream from Elora

Without thought, he had an arm around her and pulled her down. She must have been hit—the cry had been so full of fear. What the hell had been thrown? White-hot anger and panic converged inside him.

'Where are you hurt?'

The groom had the horses under control now, but the crowds were jostling with noise and exclamation and security was about to surround them.

She sat up, pushed his hand away. 'I'm fine.' She twisted in her seat. 'We have to go back.'

'Go back. Why?'

'Please…' Her voice broke. 'Please trust me. We have to go back.'

A moment's thought and then, 'Turn round,' he ordered.

'But Your Highness…'

'You heard me.'

'But…' Now it was the security officer. 'I am sorry, Your Highness, but…'

'Rohan—' Elora's voice was urgent '—please.'

'I said turn around. This is my call, my responsibility and, believe me, I will be listened to. Do it now.'

Security pulled away as the groom turned the carriage.

'Where do you want to go?'

'Back to where it happened. We have to stop Security from getting involved. I am not hurt. Nothing happened. This is my fault.'

In minutes they were back and instantly she scrambled down. He jumped down after her, beckoned to Security, who helped push through until they found the protesters circled by a ring of security officers.

'Please stand down.' Elora's voice was clear and incisive. 'I'm not hurt and I'm not pressing any charges. You can leave. I wish to speak to these people.' Elora was every inch a princess now, but she wasn't in her own country and Rohan stepped up next to her.

'Listen to the Princess. But stay within calling distance. And keep everyone else away.'

Once they had backed off, he turned back to Elora. 'Now what?'

'Now we talk to them,' she said. She was calmer now as she looked at the group of four, aged between eighteen and twenty-three at a guess, two boys, two girls.

'Are any of you hurt?'

'No. Why? Did you expect your security to hurt us?'

'No,' Elora said. 'But I understand how sometimes people can get carried away. If Security believed I had been hurt then it is possible they could have been overzealous. I just wanted to be sure.'

'Given you threw something at the Princess and could have injured her or caused an accident, I am not sure you should be so belligerent,' Rohan said. 'If my groom had lost control of the carriage there could have been a lot worse damage.'

'What did you throw?' Elora asked.

'A tomato,' one of the girls admitted. 'It wasn't planned. It was part of my lunch. It was in my hand and I heard the chanting and I saw the placards and I thought that I needed to do something and then, almost before I knew it, I'd thrown it.'

'A tomato is hardly a deadly weapon,' one of the boys said.

'My security forces weren't to know that,' Rohan pointed out. 'I wasn't to know that. The people here weren't to know that.'

'Also, it was a terrible throw,' another protester said. 'I didn't think it could possibly have hit you.'

'It didn't.'

Rohan glanced at her; he'd been sure she'd been hurt, but events had all happened so fast.

'But that wouldn't have mattered,' Elora said softly. 'Just by throwing that tomato, you could have caused a real accident. Security were surrounding you—it could have triggered further protest, violent protest, people could have got hurt, killed even. And I don't think you want any of that to happen, not from one impulsive gesture that had no real malicious intent, apart from to make me look silly. But sometimes our actions have unforeseen consequences. Anyway, I have an b idea.'

The protestors looked at her questioningly.

'I know there is more to this—if you are here protesting, some of you may be doing it on principle because you want the right to vote for your rulers, have a democracy. Others of you will have other reasons.' She looked at the girl who had thrown the tomato.

'My brother is ill—he has been waiting for a hospital appointment for nine months and he is getting worse. We don't have the money to go private. We have no insurance.'

'And these are all things that should be heard.' Rohan stepped forward now. 'My sister believes that we should hold meetings where people can come to us and tell us of cases like his, matters that need our attention. I will do what I can to make this happen.'

Elora nodded. 'In the meantime, you all have every right to make a peaceful protest.' She turned to Rohan. 'Thank you for listening, thank you for turning round and for asking Security to let us talk.'

Rohan could only admire the way she had somehow contrived to give him credit in public for something she had instigated. But he saw how she stumbled slightly as she turned to walk back to the carriage and knew on some visceral level that she was holding herself together by a thread. He wrapped an arm around her waist, knowing she wouldn't want anyone to suspect that she was struggling. Perhaps it was delayed reaction, though right now he was unsure what, exactly, had caused it.

'That was a good call,' he said, his voice deep and reassuring as they headed to the waiting carriage and horses, and now he could feel her tension, sense the clench of her muscles, hear the quickening of her breath. 'It's fine,' he murmured. 'We've got this.' He helped her into the carriage and his admiration soared again as he saw her pull herself together, sit straight and tall, a smile on her face as she looked around, but close up he could see her pallor and he knew what to do—the only thing he could think of to do.

He turned to face her. 'Look at me,' he said softly, and she did. 'Trust me?' he asked, and she gave a small nod.

And oh, so gently, he cupped her face in his hands and

almost before she realised what he was doing he leaned forward and kissed her, poured his admiration and warmth and reassurance into the kiss. And after a surprised second she responded, the kiss different from their others, though no less passionate. This one held sweetness and a low simmer of heat, building in a gentle crescendo of passion.

Eventually the cheers of the crowd penetrated the fog of desire and in joint consensus they pulled apart and, as they did, he said so only she could hear, 'That was for you, not for the cameras.'

'I know, but we may as well reap the benefits.' She sat back and he could see that the tension was gone, though he reached out and took her hand in his and held it firmly until they arrived at their destination.

CHAPTER THIRTEEN

ELORA LOOKED DOWN at the hand that clasped hers as the carriage drew to a blessed stop. Registered that his touch had calmed the turmoil inside her, knew that without that kiss she would most likely have baulked at remaining in the carriage, would have shown her anxieties and fears in public. And, worse, to do so would have escalated the situation, brought further attention to an incident that, in truth, was little more than trivial, though the underlying cause for protest was anything but.

'We're here,' Rohan said, and she looked around to see a wrought iron gate set in a stone wall. Peering through, she saw a beautiful lush garden dotted with flowering bushes, exuberant bursts of reds and oranges amongst tall exotic shrubs and trees, verdant with differing hues of green, the spectrum veering from lime to a deep, deep green.

'It's beautiful,' she said as she alighted from the carriage with a sensation of relief and they entered the peaceful, warm atmosphere of the gardens.

'And private. It will be a good place to talk.'

Elora glanced at him. 'Talk?'

'Yes. About what happened back there. I did as you asked without question, I trusted you, and now you need to trust me.'

He made it sound so easy, but trusting him meant shar-

ing things she had never shared before. Yet she did owe
him that. He had listened to her, had trusted her in a way
no one had ever done before, or at least not since Sanjay.
Her brother had trusted her implicitly, as she had trusted
him. But Rohan had helped her, allowed her to defuse a
situation, possibly avert tragedy, and so, 'You're right. I
do owe you an explanation.'

'No, I don't mean that. I want you to trust me, not because you owe me but because you can. I want to help. I
want to know.'

She nodded.

'Come, let's walk. There is a pagoda by a lake where
we can eat. And talk.'

As they walked she absorbed the sunshine and the
scents from the flowers, looked around and saw just how
much thought and care must have gone into these grounds.

'So does this belong to the royal family?'

Rohan nodded. 'Yes. We open it to the public regularly
throughout the year, but otherwise it is for royal use.'

She was grateful for the small talk and the companion-
able silence until they reached their destination, a picturesque blue lake, dotted with wild birds who skimmed the
water with movement and colour. Nearby was the promised
pagoda, a pretty circular roofed structure which contained
a small table and chairs, where they were soon seated.

'You were amazing back there,' Rohan said. 'You de-
fused a situation that could have turned ugly.'

She gave a small hard laugh. 'No. What I did back there
was defuse a situation I had created.'

'I don't understand.' Rohan poured a glass of the spar-
kling mango juice he'd brought and handed it to her and
she accepted it gratefully, let the cool, sweet liquid run
down her throat as the events of the past hour ran through

her head. Anxiety threatened again and she let the warm rays of the sun wash over her, but most of all knew she was taking comfort from Rohan's presence.

She tried to work out the best way to explain and, in the end, settled for the one fact that had impacted her life so much and for so long—the fact that had precipitated tragedy and loss.

'I'm scared of horses,' she said. 'Terrified is a better word.' And she could hear her voice crack with regret and guilt, the thread of sadness and resignation, and Rohan took her hand in his, said nothing, asked no questions, let her take her time.

'I always have been, though I don't know why. On Caruli, horses are an integral part of our culture and tradition. History speaks of kings and princes riding bareback across the island, of brave cavalries that fought battles, of loyal stallions. The royal stable has thoroughbreds with family dynasties of their own, going back hundreds of years. Carulian royalty love horses—it's a given, an important tradition, tied up with so much of our culture. Horses have always been seen as noble creatures. But somehow, from the moment I was taken to the stables, all I felt was terror. Which horrified my parents. Basically, I was told to get over it, that this was not allowed. Once they forced me to stay in a stable with one of the thoroughbreds. There was a groom in there with me and I am sure it was one of the gentler horses, but to me it was like being locked in with a monster.'

She saw anger cross Rohan's face and squeezed his hand. 'I know it sounds cruel and I would never do that to anyone. But to my parents my fear was inexplicable, a flaw in my make-up; they genuinely believed confronting it would cure it and, to a degree, it did. I was so scared they would shut me in again that I managed to learn to control the fear a little bit. I also gained a friend in the groom; he helped allay my fears in there.'

'But you are still terrified inside.'

'Yes, I am. But it was Sanjay who helped back then. He knew of my fear and he helped protect me from it. When he was there I felt safer and because he loved horses, had no fear of them, that helped me.

'But then…' She pulled her hand from his, clenched her hands into the grass, looked away from him, not sure if she could relive the memories, the searing pain and guilt.

'Elora, it's OK. I'm here. You don't have to carry this alone.'

But she did. This was her burden to bear and here and now she needed to face it, acknowledge it, and so she began to speak.

'Sanjay and I were eleven, which is the time for a coming-of-age ritual on Caruli. A time when we were to be given our own horses, entrusted to look after them, as they would look after us. Sanjay was so excited; he already loved the horse that had been chosen for him. He kept telling me it would all be OK, that I just had to get through the ritual, that he would be there. "All" I had to do was mount the horse and ride it through the palace grounds and then through a few of the streets so the public could see.'

'I imagine to the child you were then, that must have filled you with overwhelming fear. To get on the horse and then ride it alone. In public.' There was no judgement, just understanding, and when he looked at her she felt as though somehow he was reliving the experience with her, could see her as she'd been then, a small, scrawny, terrified little girl with two long blonde plaits, eyes screwed up, wishing, praying, that something—anything would happen to mean she didn't have to go through with it. Well, something had.

'We were in the stable area—Sanjay and me and Jaswant; he was an undergroom back then. Sanjay was on his horse and he was so confident so happy and I was so scared. And I was so full of shame as well, that I was such a coward. I knew I couldn't do it.'

She could recall the fear, the scent of her own sweat, wanting to laugh hysterically because she'd been told that princesses didn't sweat, they perspired. Could feel the scratch of her clothes and see the shining flanks of the horses, sleek and so powerful, so much stronger than her.

'Jaswant had managed to help me onto the horse, but then the horse reared slightly, could sense my fear, and I screamed. Sanjay saw and he wanted to help me.'

She could hear it now, his voice. *'It's OK, Elli, I'm coming.'*

'But for some reason he decided to try and dismount, probably thought bringing his horse over to me would spook me more. His foot somehow got caught in the stirrup and then he got tangled up, lost his balance and slipped, which made the horse bolt and Sanjay fell and hit his head.'

She could still hear the sickening thud.

'It all happened so fast and I was crying and Jaswant somehow kept his head enough to get me off the horse and catch the horses so no one got trampled...and I ran to Sanjay and I didn't know what to do—just prayed and prayed he'd be OK. But he wasn't—he didn't recover and he died two days later.'

She turned now, didn't want to see what would be in Rohan's eyes, but knew she had to.

'It was my fault.'

'No.' His voice was fierce, jagged, and she knew he

felt her pain. 'It wasn't. It was a tragic accident, a series of events that culminated in heartbreak. But it was not your fault.'

'If I hadn't screamed, if I had controlled my fear better, or maybe if I'd had the courage to refuse to get onto that horse in the first place, then Sanjay would be alive.'

'You don't know that.' Now he had his arm around her, holding her clasped to his side, and the sheer warmth and strength of his body gave her comfort. 'There are some people who believe the day of your death is set in the stars from the day you are born. It is possible that Sanjay's horse would have bolted regardless, perhaps during the procession. But, regardless of whether you believe that or not, it was a tragic accident and it was not your fault. Though I understand why you must think again and again about the what-ifs and wish you could change what happened.'

She nodded. 'For years I relived it every day. Jaswant never told anyone what had happened, never mentioned that I'd screamed or why Sanjay was trying to dismount. He has never even spoken of it to me. My mother believes it was somehow my fault but she doesn't know the facts.'

'So all these years you've carried this secret, this knowledge. I am so sorry, Elora, so very sorry.'

And now he shifted and he held her, her face against the solid strength of his chest, and for the first time in years she cried, wept and wept until she didn't have any tears left, and only then did he release her.

'So that's what happened today,' she said. 'It was nothing to do with the tomato. Something spooked the horse and it reared. That's why I screamed. It all happened at once. If I hadn't screamed, I doubt we would even have noticed the tomato, but then I was terrified that history would be repeated. That my fear would trigger a chain of events that would end in tragedy. Again.' She managed a smile. 'So thank you for helping me, for trusting me, so that didn't happen.'

'Oh, sweetheart, you don't need to thank me. What you have been through, what you went through today, and yet you acted with courage and good sense and such poise. You are a true princess, Elora.'

'Thank you.' She turned to look up at him and what she saw in his eyes made her gasp, a warmth that touched her to the core, and then, as their gazes meshed, something happened, the warmth changed nuance and sparked into desire, and now…now she was aware of his closeness, his proximity, his strength in a completely different way and awareness began to grow. She felt the rock-hard muscles of his chest and if she shifted that hand the accelerated beat of his heart.

She saw the glint of the sun on the deep black of his hair, the set of his jaw and the firm line of his mouth and now she knew with a glorious sense of inevitability what would happen next and she wanted it, needed it, desired it with every fibre of her.

Then they were kissing and this kiss was different, here, in this place of unspoiled nature, where they were all alone—a place where she'd shared something profound—and all that gave this desire, a depth, a sweetness and a heat and a sharpness that was impossible to resist or even want to resist.

Now their bodies were pressed together and her hands were fumbling, trying to get his T-shirt over his head, whilst not wanting to break the kiss, break the connection, and then it was done and her fingers were trailing over his bare skin, greedy and wondrous at the feel of his response as he pulled her closer, and then she was on top of him and all she knew was that she wanted more.

The ring of his phone pealed through the air and with an impatient noise he tugged it from his pocket and threw it to the ground. Must have pressed a button in so doing as it clicked to voicemail and there was Marisa's voice. 'Sorry to call, little bro, but I thought you needed to know. Caro called me—she's on her way to Sarala. I'm not sure why, but I couldn't dissuade her...'

The words were more than enough to break the connection that had seemed so all-consuming. Reality seeped in, cold and absolute, and she moved off him, rose to her feet and closed her eyes, rubbed a hand over her face, over her lips, then to her hair in a desperate attempt to undo the past minutes.

Caro.

The name was a reminder that, whilst she had bared her soul, she still knew nothing about Rohan's first marriage, he still had given her no refutation of the events outlined in the press, outlined by Caro—his first wife, the woman he'd once looked at with adoration.

'You'd better call Marisa.' Her voice sounded drained even to her own ears and he shook his head, rose to his feet and moved towards her.

'I will, but not yet. Not until I know you are OK.' He took a deep breath and then another. 'Perhaps it is a good thing we were interrupted. Before we got too carried away. Thank you for your trust in me today; truly, I value it.' Now he stepped forward and kissed her gently, a brief brush over her lips, and then he picked up his discarded phone and moved away from her.

Elora ran a hand over her lips and tried to think, knew she was too tired to do so clearly but questions pinged around her brain. Why was Caro coming back? How did Rohan feel about that? Did she want him back? Foolish thought—this was the woman who had fled from him, denounced him as a cruel husband. Caro. The woman he'd loved. Or so she believed. The woman he wouldn't speak about.

Rohan walked back to her and now his face was grim, reminiscent of the man she'd first met in the Treasure Room only a week before.

'We'd better get back to the palace. I've asked for a car to come and get us.'

'Thank you.' That was kind of him. 'But we should make sure it is an open-topped one. We should let the people see us—see that Caro's return has not affected us, you and me. Let the people see we stand together.'

He nodded. 'You're right.'

But she could see the wariness in his dark eyes, and perhaps it mirrored her own. Did they stand together? Could they when Caro was here to wreak who knew what damage?

CHAPTER FOURTEEN

ELORA OPENED HER eyes the following morning and felt a sense of foreboding. Since their return to the palace the previous day there had been an unease, a tension, a sense of waiting.

Because that was what they were doing—waiting to see what Caro would do. As the Queen had said, 'There is nothing to do but respond when we see what she does.'

The King had simply said, 'She is old news. She can stir up old news. There is nothing else she can do.'

Marisa had looked at Rohan and said simply, 'It's in your hands, Rohan. My advice is to stand your ground. Caro will be enjoying the idea she's got you on tenter-hooks.'

And Rohan... He had said nothing. Elora had no idea what he was thinking and she had decided not to ask, but hurt burned inside her. After what she had shared, after the previous day, she'd believed... Believed what, exactly? That something had changed? That there was a connection beyond the physical?

There wasn't. Or if there was it meant nothing. It was part of an agreement, a contractual marriage of convenience made for political gain. The romance was a charade, and now the test would be whether their woven illusion was strong enough to withstand the advent of Caro.

How was Rohan feeling? Was he looking forward to seeing his first wife again? Did he still love her?

The thought was enough to force her out of bed, though she decided to skip the family breakfast. She would text Marisa to let her know. The thought of sitting in silence, or sitting next to a man who was presumably brooding on another woman, was not conducive to appetite.

Instead, she went down to the palace kitchens, where she'd already befriended the staff, and requested a few pieces of freshly baked bread and a chunk of cheese. Then she set out into the palace gardens, wandered around, before settling on a small wooden bench next to a bush that blazed with bright red blooms.

'Psst! Elora!'

Elora turned her head and frowned, sure she didn't recognise the voice. Unless it was a staff member or Marisa disguising her voice. Hard to imagine Marisa doing that.

She stood up and looked towards where the voice came from, as a woman stepped out from behind the bush.

Elora blinked, wondering if she'd actually hallucinated her into being, but knew she hadn't. The beautiful woman with auburn hair cut into a sleek bob was undoubtedly Caro. The woman who she'd seen so many times on the big screen, admired as an actor for her ability to make every part she played so real, for bringing both beauty and talent to her work. But a woman she'd also seen on the pages of so many magazines, denouncing Rohan.

Caro put a finger to her lips. 'Don't call Security. I persuaded someone to let me in. His teenage son is a fan of mine so I signed an autograph and promised to send him a signed photo as well. Look, I really don't want anyone to get into trouble, and I'm not here to make a scene or cause trouble. I just want ten minutes of your time, that's all.'

Elora weighed up her options. Calling Security seemed pointless and surely would only generate potential negative publicity. Plus she was curious, wanted to know what Caro had to say.

'OK. Ten minutes.'

'Are you escaping the family breakfast? I'm sorry my arrival on Sarala has caused a problem.'

'You must have known it would.'

Caro shrugged elegant shoulders. 'Yes, but I wanted to talk to you.'

'You could have called, could have set up a video conference.'

Caro waved a dismissive hand. 'That isn't the same. I wanted to see you properly, and anyway you can hang up on a call or leave a meeting.'

'Fair enough. So what do you have to say?'

'Don't do it.' Now Caro's voice was low, urgent. 'I married Rohan because I thought he was something he wasn't. I was taken in by his looks and he made me feel as though I was the world to him, but then, once we were married, everything changed. I knew I'd made a massive mistake and I don't want to see you or anyone else do the same. I'm sure you think it will all be OK, that he will be a good husband, but he won't be. He made my life a misery, became a monster, and all I wanted to do was escape. I felt trapped, suffocated—don't make the same mistake I did.'

Her voice cracked, her beautiful face etched with remembered pain. 'Look at me now. I got away and now I'm happy, married to a man I love. Don't give up your chance for that, because *you'll* never be able to leave, he won't let you.' Caro laid a hand on Elora's arm. 'I know the King and Queen... With the situation on Baluka, I know how desperately they will now want Rohan to marry and produce an heir. I know as well how important that will be to him. To do his duty, do the right thing. But you don't need to be taken in, you don't need to sacrifice yourself. You deserve what I have now.'

Elora tried to think, tried to work out what was going on. Caro sounded utterly sincere. Elora would swear that she was telling the truth, or at least the truth as she saw it. What had Marisa said? That Caro created drama and illusions. Perhaps the reason she was such a good actor was her ability to truly believe whatever drama she decided to play out.

But what was she really saying? That *she* had felt trapped, that *she* had made a mistake, that *she* had believed she meant the world to Rohan. That she was happy now in a marriage based on love. But Elora still didn't know Rohan's side and it occurred to her now that no one did. Because he wouldn't tell it. So all Elora could do was work on what she knew of Rohan.

A man who had shown her nothing but honesty and truth even in the illusion they were weaving.

'Caro, thank you for coming here, for telling me all this. But the Rohan I know is different from the Rohan you describe. I trust in him. I cannot believe he will turn into a monster, trap me or suffocate me.'

'But that is what I thought, what I believed.'

'But Elora isn't you.' There was a rustle of leaves as Rohan stepped into view, his face unreadable. 'I apologise. I came to look for Elora. I didn't expect to find you here, Caro.'

'I came to speak to Elora. If you wish to call Security…'

'I don't. If you wish to come into the palace, you and Elora can continue your conversation there or here, or you can come and see my parents and sister. Or anyone else within the palace. You are welcome.' His voice was even.

'Welcome?' Caro's voice held an almost outraged surprise, as if Rohan wasn't playing his ascribed role.

'Yes, you are welcome. Welcome to say what you have come to say, tell the story as you see it.'

Caro hesitated and then shrugged. 'I will go.' She turned back to Elora, her green eyes wide and imploring. 'Please think about what I have said.'

'I will.'

With that, Caro slipped away.

'I will just make sure she really does leave.'

A few minutes later, Rohan returned.

'How long were you listening?' Elora asked.

'Just at the end. I really did come to find you, to see why you skipped out on breakfast. Did you mean what you said to her?'

'Yes.' Every word felt weighted right now, but Elora wanted to speak the truth. 'I wish you would tell your side, but if you won't then all I can do is make a judgement based on my knowledge of you. The person you are now.'

'I will tell my side.'

Elora looked at him warily, relieved when a small smile tipped his lips.

'Don't look so surprised. You showed a trust in me that I am not sure I deserve, but it seems fair to let you be the judge. You've heard some of Caro's side, now I will tell you mine.' He looked around. 'But not here. We are too likely to get interrupted.' He thought for a moment. 'There is an old disused barn out by the orchards. I used to hide out there as a kid. We can go there.'

Half an hour later he'd driven them through the palace grounds and parked outside the barn, led the way in. Let down the ladder leading to the hayloft and gestured to Elora to climb up.

'I can see why this was a good hideout,' she said as she looked around. 'The hay makes it cosy and warm and being up here is really private.'

He nodded. 'It seems like a good place to tell this story.'

They settled by the window, overlooking the orchards, with the palace looming in the distance. She studied his expression, saw no hesitation or regret that he had decided to tell her the truth about his marriage. There was a small frown on his face and she sensed he was marshalling his thoughts.

And then he began. 'When I met Caro I was twenty-three, *I* was the inexperienced, gauche Prince. I'd been out on a few dates, but never a serious relationship, or anywhere near. I'd gone abroad to Europe, my first time away from Sarala on my own, and that's where I met Caro. An actress, a serious actress at that, she'd been acting since she was talent-spotted as a teenager and she'd just had rave reviews for a film. She was only two years older than me in terms of age but about ten years older in experience. She'd left her family home at fifteen to be a model and she'd had a succession of high-profile relationships. Hollywood actors, a French politician, a Formula One driver. And for some reason her attention lit on me. I don't know why. Maybe she wanted to add a prince to her list. But soon we were dating. And I was bedazzled.'

'Of course you were. How could you not be?'

'I didn't know whether I was coming or going and I think that amused her, or perhaps it gave her balm. She'd come out of a messy breakup and there I was, willing to worship and adore her. And soon I asked her to marry me, because back then I thought that was the right, romantic thing to do. I wouldn't have dreamt of sleeping with her first. I wanted to show her I was different. That I had honour.' She could hear the self-mocking tone in his voice, and she could picture him as he had been then, in the throes of first love.

'At first she refused, but then she changed her mind. I don't know why—perhaps it was because she believed that being worshipped, me thinking the world of her, would be enough. Perhaps she wanted the glamour of being a princess, perhaps she thought it would help her career. She said it would be a fresh start, that she would be a princess who the people adored. But I thought she loved me. I was sure I loved her.'

Without thinking, she placed a hand gently over his and, oddly, it felt as though she were walking back through the past with him, that they were watching his younger self trying to navigate the emotional minefields of his first marriage.

'At first everything was blissful. I was completely in her thrall and Caro liked that. And it wasn't just me. She had—has—the ability to charm people, to make people believe they are wonderful. But…it's not real. I'm not sure when I realised it. Perhaps the day she stopped to help up a child, a staff member's daughter who had fallen over. She was loveliness itself. But two days later, when the little girl came to give her flowers, she couldn't really recall who she was, was a bit dismissive, and I saw how hurt the girl was. It wasn't a big thing, but to me it was the start. And soon after that I began to annoy her, and I understand why. I wanted to be with her all the time, wanted to read her poetry, wanted to do things together. And she started wanting her own space, her own time. Which was fair enough, but I didn't understand, took it as rejection. And I noticed her flirting with other men. She'd tell me I was being silly,

jealous, but then Marisa noticed it too. And other people—
I could see the funny looks, the hidden smiles.'

Elora could only imagine what that would have done to
Rohan, how hurt his pride must have been, how confused
and miserable and small it would have made him feel. His
wife showing favour to other men, people smirking, his
own love being repudiated, his romantic gestures met with
indifference, labelled annoying.

'So, yes, there were arguments. I ordered, begged,
pleaded with her, but she got more and more angry and in
the end she went home, back to Europe for a "break". Said
perhaps she would see if there were any acting opportunities. And when she came back she was different. I didn't
understand it. At first I was pleased because she stopped
flirting with other men, but she also stopped wanting to
be with me. Started sleeping in a separate room, said she
needed some time. I didn't understand, or maybe I didn't
want to understand, but things became harder. I could
see she didn't want to be with me, but then, suddenly she
changed again.'

His face was tired now, weary, the lips set in a grim
line, and Elora felt for him, knew these were dark memories that haunted him, understood all too well how that felt.

'Suddenly she was loving again. She asked me out for
dinner, took me to a place we'd gone to in the early days,
and I was so happy. And then, over dinner, she told me why
she'd been strange, explained her behaviour. She told me
she was pregnant, that it must have played havoc with her
hormones. I was so ecstatic I was going to be a father, we
were going to have a baby, and I wanted to shout it from
the rooftops, but Caro wouldn't let me. Said she wanted to
wait until she was absolutely sure she was safe, but she'd
wanted me to know. So of course I agreed not to tell any-

one, but then she refused to see a doctor, said there was no need, not yet. Told me not to worry, to be happy. We were having a baby and I was happy, but something still felt off. She still wanted separate bedrooms, didn't even want a hug, but I put it all down to hormones, focused on looking forward to being a dad. And I swear to you, Elora, I didn't care, girl or boy, I was just happy.' He shook his head.

'Anyway, then everything blew up. Caro said she wanted to go back to Europe. I asked if it was safe to fly and she lost the plot, said I was trying to imprison her, and it was soon after that that she tried to flee by night. Even though I had never said she couldn't go. And in the end I found out the truth—the baby wasn't mine.'

'Oh.' Elora stared at him, tried to imagine how that would have felt—the grief of believing you were going to be a father and then finding out you weren't. The searing pain of betrayal, the anger, the sadness, the whole gamut of emotions.

'She'd met someone when she was back in Europe, a director, but then he had rejected her so she decided to try to make me believe the baby was mine. That's why she didn't want to go to the doctor—in case it was obvious that she was less pregnant than she had claimed, but as time went on she believed she could wing it. Fudge the issue. But now the man had changed his mind, wanted her back. So I said she could go as long as she told no one about the man or the baby. I couldn't bear the humiliation or all the rumours, the DNA testing. So we divorced.'

'And you let the press rip into you, paint you as a monster. Why?'

'Because that was preferable to the truth. And it was better for the baby. Caro left and soon after she announced her new romance. They went travelling, she said she wanted to be left alone and then she had her baby, a home birth, and no one ever thought to question the timing because by then she and her husband were married and she was busy spinning other stories. Now they have another child and they are a happy family. Caro is acting again and she has it all.' He shrugged his shoulders. 'So there you have it.'

Now, finally, she felt she could speak. 'I'm sorry…so, so sorry. To believe you were going to be a father and then to find out you weren't. To have been betrayed on that deep a level—that goes beyond unfaithfulness. I know you don't want to speak of it but I'm still sorry you had to go through it.'

'That was hardest of all. Caro being unfaithful—yes, that hurt, but it hurt my pride. By then, I think I knew she'd never loved me. I don't think I ever loved her, not really. I loved the idea of loving her but, when it came to it, we never really knew each other. But when I thought I was going to have a baby, that was love…'

'And when that was taken from you, you were angry, but mostly you were grieving.'

'Yes. But now, telling you this, sharing it, you trusting me, me trusting you, I feel lighter. As though this is the foundation for our future, we will have a marriage based on trust and soon, hopefully very soon, we will be married and…' He grinned at her, and suddenly he looked lighter, younger. 'Hopefully, soon we will have a baby, a family.'

The words hit Elora like a punch in the gut. Rohan was talking about trust—mutual trust being the bedrock, the foundation of their union. And now she knew something she hadn't known before—that Rohan had already once been cheated of a baby, a family. Knew that this man wanted children, didn't care if they were sons or daughters. His words at the temple, sworn in a sacred place, had shown her that.

She was a fraud, and how could she let this man enter another union based on a lie, believing it was based on trust? For a long moment she looked at him, took in his masculine beauty, relived the feel of his lips against hers, their bodies pressed against each other, the glorious feel of his naked chest under her fingers, the sheer level of want and need and desire between them. Remembered too the way he'd held her as she'd cried, how he'd listened, how he'd engaged with her idea. Remembered the walk through the spice market, sitting by the temple, and she knew she was processing and storing those memories before she did what she had to do.

Knew too, with a sudden blinding clarity, that she loved him, loved the prince who had somehow, somewhere captured her heart. A heart that she could feel cracking inside her even as her brain made one last-ditch attempt to consider the arguments her mother had deployed, that she herself had deployed over the past days to justify a decision she'd known all along to be wrong. Thought now too of what her mother would say to her, the venomous hiss of vitriol and bitter displeasure, her father's weary resignation, another notch of disappointment on the list.

But it didn't change anything.

'We need to talk,' she said slowly.

CHAPTER FIFTEEN

THERE WAS A moment of silence as Rohan studied Elora's face. Perhaps she should look incongruous here amongst the hay bales, but she didn't. She just looked beautiful. And sad. And determined. And he had a sudden feeling of foreboding.

'I thought we were talking.'

'We are, and what you have shared with me… I appreciate more than I can tell you. I understand how hard it is to trust.'

Of course she did. She had spent the past decade and more keeping the circumstances of her brother's death a secret, unable to trust her parents or the people who should have been there for her.

'And that's why I can't go ahead with this marriage—our marriage.'

The words were so unexpected he simply froze and then in a delayed reaction they hit him, a missile he hadn't seen coming.

'Why? Is it something Caro said?'

She shook her head. 'It's what I haven't said.' She clenched her nails into her hands and then faced him, her grey eyes unwavering. 'There is a chance, a good chance, that I may have fertility problems. That there won't be a baby.'

'I… I don't understand.'

'My mother struggled to have a baby. In the end she had IVF treatment. No one knew—she went abroad to receive it. That resulted in Sanjay and me. It is possible that I have inherited her issues, though there is a lot that isn't known about inherited fertility problems. But it's more than that. My periods are irregular, patchy, and always have been. That makes it harder to conceive.'

She delivered each fact straight, no quaver in her voice, and as the import of her words hit him he could feel anger surge in his gut, cold and bleak, as he realised how close he'd come to being taken for a ride, conned again.

'Why are you only mentioning this now?' He could hear the ice in his voice as he moved away from her.

'Because when I wanted to at first my mother told me not to.' She raised a hand. 'I know that sounds ridiculous but…'

But he understood the influence, the power, Queen Joanna wielded.

'And I believed her reasons, thought they had validity. She told me not to create problems where they don't exist, that my periods are down to my foolish anxieties that can and will be overcome, that this marriage was vital for Caruli and that was what mattered. And so I put my doubts aside, told myself she was right.'

Rohan tried to think, but right now all he could see was the fact that Elora had not told him the full truth.

'And this week, when we discussed having children, when it must have become increasingly clear to you that Sarala needs an heir, that this is the duty I have chosen to embrace…' However heavy it was, however much he didn't want it, but the saving grace was having a child, a family. 'What was your plan if a child didn't come?'

'I had no plan,' she said. 'I just had hope.' Now she showed a flash of spirit. 'After all, do you know that you can have children?'

'No. But I have no reason to believe that I can't.'

'Touché. I deserved that. But when we first met I didn't know you. I didn't want to marry you, but I knew I had to. I thought that perhaps I was making excuses, looking for a reason to not do it. And then, each day that passed...' for the first time she paused, stared at him with eyes wide '...it became harder to tell you, so I buried my head in the sand. I was wrong and that's why I am releasing you from our agreement.'

'It's not that easy.' And it wasn't. 'We've spent a week spinning a mythical romance. How are we supposed to end it? We kissed in public, we've been on dates, we've made it clear we are an item. If we end it now, it will look as though either we have been playing them all along or that Caro has influenced your decision.' The anger was heightening now, but he recognised it was two-pronged— he was angry because he didn't want to end the agreement, felt doubly cheated because the idea of no marriage when he'd found the perfect partner, the person he wanted to marry, a woman he... He slammed the thought to a halt. A woman he had been dealing with in good faith, a woman who hadn't dealt fairly with him, and yet...as he looked at Elora, he knew he didn't want this to end.

'I know. But I will take the blame.'

'No.' Now his voice was cold. 'We cannot end the charade as yet. We will have to continue the pretence, the illusion, until a better time.'

'I... I don't know if I can do that.'

'There is no choice. It will give us time to work out a

strategy, a way to tell our parents. Your mother…' Whatever fault lay with Elora, she didn't deserve the backlash.

Elora shook her head. 'It doesn't matter. What I did was wrong, Rohan. I didn't do what I knew was right because I thought you wouldn't go ahead with the marriage. I know how ugly that sounds. But I wanted to show my parents that I could do something for Caruli, could earn some redemption.'

And, just like that, his anger dissipated. He understood why she had done what she had and he stepped forward, but stopped when she shook her head.

'Don't.' She managed a smile. 'I'll just cry. Because somehow, over these past days, I did believe we had a chance.'

'Maybe we still do. Maybe we should go ahead, marry anyway. Take the risk.'

'We can't.' Her voice was rock steady now. 'I've seen what it's like, what the desperation to have an heir can do. It would tear us apart and it's not fair on you. You are already sacrificing your dream, your company, what you want to do with your life, to do your duty. I can't make it harder for you, can't take that risk. You can't. Tell me the truth, Rohan. If I had told you from the start, wouldn't you have thought the risk too high? Wouldn't your parents and Marisa agree? Your sister would tell you that you have to do what is best for Sarala, and that isn't me. I'm potentially damaged goods.'

He broke off, closed his eyes, tried to think straight. What did he want? The answer was instant and true. He wanted Elora.

But Elora was right. Sarala needed an heir. Elora might not be able to provide one.

Or she might.

But the risk was too great.

And this wasn't all about him. What about Elora? What did she want? For her. Not for Caruli, not for her parents, not for a mother who didn't deserve a daughter like Elora, or a father for whom the need for an heir had overridden all else. She wanted a normal life, so perhaps, unbelievably, Caro had been right. Elora deserved what Caro had, a man to love her for herself, who could give her that normal life she craved. Relative anonymity where she could perhaps be more like Preeti Bannerjee than Princess Elora.

And that meant he needed to do the right thing.

He wouldn't condemn Elora to a life of being watched, the pressure of becoming pregnant, that monthly question with the eyes of the world upon them. Wouldn't subject her to blame if there was no child—or a daughter.

The Prince of Sarala would do the right thing for Sarala and for Elora.

'You're right. Our marriage is not possible, but we *will* need to continue the charade a little longer. But for now we will come up with a reason for you to return to Caruli. Perhaps we can say, or imply that I don't wish you to be subjected to Caro, or hurt in any way. So I will take you back and then return to Sarala alone. We will then let our romance "fizzle out".'

He could hear the coldness in his voice but he knew that was the only way he could do this, the only way he could go through with it. When every particle of his being wanted to tell her that it didn't matter, they'd take the risk.

Elora nodded. 'I...hope that things work out. I hope that somehow, some way, you can keep your company, at least partially realise your dreams. And when you do marry, I promise I wish you all the best and I hope with all my heart that you get the family you want and Sarala needs. I know you will be a good ruler and a wonderful dad. Thank you for the past week. I mean that. And Rohan, I'm sorry. I truly am.'

Five days later

Rohan sat outside the temple, tried to think about his grandfather, grey-haired and still upright even in his eighties. Remembered the last time the old man had brought him here.

'I have lived a long time, Rohan, and yet my whole life has been dedicated to Sarala, as yours will be too.'

A pause, and then, as if there was no connection…

'Marisa is a clever girl; she too loves her country. As my sisters did.'

His grandfather had been the fourth child and first and only son of his parents and, sitting here now, Rohan wondered what the old King had been thinking back then. Whether he had ever entertained the enormity of thought that was in Rohan's mind now.

Wondered too what Elora would think.

Elora… He could picture her so clearly, as if she were branded on his brain, just as he was beginning to believe she was branded on his very heart and soul. Because, however hard he tried to not think about her, she was always there. Waking and sleeping, she haunted his dreams and, wherever he was, the scent of jasmine, the taste of cumin, the glimpse of a woman dressed in teal…any little thing brought back a memory.

He'd like to have spoken with her about his decision but he knew in the end this decision was his and his alone. Enough pressure had been put on Elora to make decisions based on duty and sacrifice. He wouldn't speak with her until the dice were rolled and the game played out.

He turned as he heard the familiar footsteps of his sister.

'Hey, little bro, here I am, as requested.' Her voice was gentler than usual as she sat down next to him and he studied her face, almost as if he were seeing his sister for the first time.

'Hey. Thanks for coming.'

'No problem.' She eyed him for a moment. 'Is this about Elora?' She didn't even wait for an answer. 'Because if it's not, it should be. I don't know what you've done but, whatever it is, go fix it.'

'Excuse me.'

'For years I've felt bad. I knew Caro—I asked her to keep an eye on my little brother for me when he went to Europe for the first time. Look what happened.'

'You tried to stop me from marrying her,' Rohan pointed out.

'You didn't listen to me then. I'm hoping you'll listen to me now. I have never seen you as miserable as you have been these past days, not even during the divorce. I think whatever happened with Caro hurt your pride. I think Elora has broken your heart. You have moped about, barely exchanging a civil word with anyone, but your eyes, Rohan. They are racked with sadness and pain. So my advice is to do something about it. If you've been a fool, go and grovel and hope she'll take you back.'

Rohan stared at his sister and gave a rueful smile. 'I thought I was hiding my feelings.'

'You weren't.'

'So your advice. Is that personal advice or political advice? Do you think I should go and get Elora back for Sarala's sake?'

Now it was Marisa's smile that was rueful. 'It is a bonus that it will help Sarala,' she said.

Rohan inhaled deeply. 'Well, I have an idea that I think will really help Sarala,' he said.

One week later

Elora stared at her reflection, tried to somehow put some sort of smile on her face, a sparkle in her eyes, but for the first time that she could remember she couldn't. Missing Rohan was like a physical ache, one that no ability to act could help. But somehow, from somewhere, she had to find the Princess Elora façade to hide behind. Didn't want anyone to guess the truth—that she had somehow fallen for a man who didn't love her back, had succumbed to a love that could go nowhere, had no hope.

So somehow she had to find some inner strength, a way to face the world, when the news broke that the romance was over. She couldn't continue to hide in her room for ever, though that was exactly what she had been doing the past twelve days. Acting on Rohan's suggestion that they buy some time whilst Caro was in Sarala, whilst they worked out how to announce the breakup, saying she had come down with a bad case of flu, she had returned to Caruli. In the meantime, large bouquets of flowers, bunches of Saralan grapes and two beautiful silk scarves had arrived as gifts with all appropriate fanfare.

The press was, thankfully, distracted by Caro, covering a story of her dining with the Saralan republic party leader, but there were also pictures of a lunch with Marisa. There was speculation that Elora's 'illness' was to avoid confrontation, but the stories were on the whole sympathetic to all parties. And Elora had stayed in her room, tried hard to be strong, do all the right things, whilst inside she was sure she could feel her heart breaking.

And soon they would have to tell the world what she had already told her parents—that it was over.

There was a knock at the door and she looked up. 'Come in.'

The door opened to show Flavia, holding a box. 'Hey.'

'Hey.'

Flavia had been incredible over the past days—had asked no questions, had just been there. They had talked about the past, about Viraj, about Caruli, but Flavia hadn't spoken of her marriage and Elora hadn't spoken of Rohan.

Flavia handed the box over. 'Viraj and I made chocolate chip cookies. And, just so you know, I let him eat the cookie dough.'

'Good.' Elora managed a semblance of her real smile at the thought of her nephew, even as it reminded her of Rohan, the way he'd brought fun into his life. Another reminder of why he deserved the chance to have a family of his own.

And she couldn't help it, an image of Rohan holding a baby, looking down on the infant with pride and joy, filled her mind and then, to her own horror, tears began to spill from her eyes.

'Elora…' In an instant her older sister was by her side, holding her close. 'It's OK.' Her voice was soothing, almost as if Elora were Viraj, and after a few moments Elora gulped to a stop and moved gently away. 'I'm sorry, Flav…'

'Don't be sorry. It's good to let it all out. Is it Rohan?'

As she spoke, she handed Elora a tissue and Elora wiped her eyes and sighed. 'Yes,' she admitted.

'What happened? I know you said it was a mutual decision not to marry. But I thought maybe it was something to do with Caro.'

Elora shook her head. 'Caro tried to warn me off but I told her I trusted Rohan. But then…now… I love him, Flavia, and I've messed it all up and he'll never love me and he's going to marry someone else and… I am so miserable.'

'Whoa. Hold on, Elora. Does he know you love him?'

'No! And there is no way I am telling him.'

'Why not?'

The simple question floored her as she opened her mouth to answer but found no words would come.

Eventually, she said, 'Because there is no point. It's not his fault. He never offered me love or the prospect of it. Just a dutiful marriage. And now that wouldn't be fair to him.'

Flavia thought for a moment. 'Rohan is a good man, I think. I saw how he looked at you. I saw how protective he was of you when your mother treated you badly. Also, I saw him with Viraj—and that spoke volumes for his character. I think a man like Rohan maybe deserves to know that he is loved.'

Before Elora could answer, her phone pinged.

'It's from Rohan.' She scanned the message.

Elora, I need to speak with you. If you agree, I will send a friend of mine to collect you from the airfield tomorrow morning at about eleven o'clock. No need for secrecy, but preferably no fanfare or undue publicity.

'He wants to see me.' She looked at her sister. 'Presumably, he wants to discuss the best way of ending the relationship. Presumably also without fanfare and undue publicity.' The thought filled her with a bleakness that she knew was etched on her face.

'Will you go?'

'Yes.' She knew she couldn't pass up the chance to see him one more time, however much it hurt. 'I want to make sure this time there is no adverse publicity for him.'

'Think about what I said.' Flavia's brown eyes looked suddenly filled with sadness. 'Love is a precious thing.' She moved forward and gave Elora a hug. 'Whatever you decide, good luck.'

Rohan glanced at his watch for what felt like the millionth time in the past five minutes, and wondered how time could crawl so slowly. But she would be here any minute now, any second now, and there went his phone.

Amit, telling him that they had landed.

'She's amazing, Ro. I'm not sure what's going on, but don't let this one go.'

'Thank you, and your advice is duly noted.' Problem one: he didn't think 'this one' would want to stay. He headed towards the plane, aware that his heart was alternating between skipping and pounding; his pulse rate must be irregular enough to cause a doctor concern.

Then he saw her walking down the steps towards him, the elegance, the grace and the wariness all so familiar. His chest ached with the sheer happiness of seeing her again, even if he knew this might be the start of their final time together. He set his jaw. Not if he had anything to do with it.

'Elora, thank you for coming.'

'It seemed necessary and Amit was a charming companion. I was glad to meet him.' And for a second her smile, her true smile, dimpled. 'He told me about the time you and he did a midnight kitchen raid and mistook the flour for the sugar.'

'It made for an interesting cup of coffee,' Rohan conceded, knowing that Amit must have really liked Elora.

As if recalling why she was here, or at least why she thought she was here, Elora's smile disappeared and she looked around.

'So where shall we go to talk?'

'Just over here. But before we do, I want to give you something.'

CHAPTER SIXTEEN

'GIVE ME WHAT?'

'Come this way.' He led the way over to a small paddock and made a gesture. 'If I've got this wrong then please just tell me and there will be no offence taken.'

She stared into the field for a moment, tried to compute what her eyes were seeing. In the corner, contentedly munching at some grass, there was a pony—a sturdy, medium-sized, compact pony.

'This is Elsie,' he said. Now he sounded hesitant. 'She's eight years old and she needs a new home. I know she is a horse but, by definition, she is a small horse and in temperament she is nothing like Carulian horses. I thought she may help—that perhaps getting used to a small, placid horse would be helpful. I spoke with a few therapists and they said usually they would take it a little slower, start with pictures of horses, but seeing as you are already managing to ride horses and be around them, despite your fears, they thought this may be a good idea, as long as you take it slow.' His voice trailed off. 'But if you are looking at Elsie and thinking you want to run a mile, then we'll jettison the idea.'

Elora stared at the pony then looked up at Rohan and she couldn't help it, couldn't hold it back, felt a tear rest on her eyelash, before it dropped to fall down her cheek.

'Hey, I didn't mean to make you cry.'

'I'm not.' She blinked fiercely. 'It's just such a lovely thought.' The first time anyone had tried something positive to help her. 'Can I meet her? I mean, maybe not actually go into the field with her, but if you could get her to come to the gate, and I stand back, then I think I'd be OK.'

Rohan instantly pushed the gate open and she couldn't help it, her gaze caught and lingered on the muscled swell of his arm under the white T-shirt he wore, swept down the lean sinew of his forearm, and now desire entered the mix, simmered in her gut, somehow warmed by what he'd done.

Minutes later, he was leading Elsie over, nice and slow, and he stopped a little way away. 'Well?'

'So far, so good,' she said and she meant it. Somehow, seeing Rohan standing beside the pony helped; she could see the differences between Elsie and the royal horses but she could also see the similarities. The pony was still strong, still had large teeth—was still a horse. But when Elsie shook her head and then looked straight at Elora her brown eyes seemed friendly and she knew with every fibre of her being that if Rohan was gifting her Elsie then Elsie was safe.

And that gave her the courage to step closer. She was rewarded by a small whinny and she smiled, a real genuine smile, because this felt like a significant step.

'Thank you. Truly. This feels...like it may really help. A step in the right direction.' Almost as if he had somehow read her mind. It was one of the things she had determined in the past two weeks. 'Because I want to try to manage this anxiety better, not hide it and hope for the best, not simply get through each time I have to ride. I want to see if I can get to a point where I am no longer afraid. Or at least less afraid. So thank you. And I am sure Jaswant will help me with the pony.'

'He will. I took the liberty of speaking with him about housing Elsie in the Carulian stables and whether that would be possible. He said yes.'

'Thank you.' And she meant it, though there was a tiny bit of her—OK, a large part of her—that wished, some-how, she and Rohan could have Elsie, that he could be the person to help her, that they were in this together. Because somehow, imperceptibly, right now, that was how it felt. But that wasn't how it was and it was time to find out why she was really here. 'Truly. To do this for me is so incred-ibly thoughtful and that's one of the reasons I…'

She broke off, horrified by what she'd been about to say.

Next to her, Rohan stilled, looked down at her, and there was something in his dark brown eyes, something she couldn't read, couldn't identify.

'You what?' he asked. 'That is one of the reasons you…?'

Flavia's words came to her and suddenly the decision was easy.

'I love you,' she said simply. 'I didn't mean to tell you and I didn't mean for it to happen, but I love you. I love you because you are a good man, a kind, strong man who deserves to be loved. I know you don't love me, know you never promised me love, and I know it doesn't change any-thing. But there it is.'

'You love me?' he asked.

She stepped closer, reached up to touch his cheek. 'Please don't feel bad; I don't. I wouldn't change the past weeks. They've changed me and made me a better person.'

Now a smile lit up his face and as she made to move back he took her hands in his.

'Feel bad? I don't feel bad. I feel…ecstatic. Because *I*

love *you*.' He raised a hand and his smile grew, his eyes alight with a sincerity she couldn't question. 'And no, I am not just saying it. That was one of the things I wanted to tell you. Today. That I love you. I promise you, Elora. I love you with all my heart. And I'm a man of my word, remember?'

He was, and she knew he was speaking the truth, knew he wouldn't lie. That wasn't Rohan's way.

'After our conversation, after your return to Caruli, I missed you so much it hurt,' he said. 'And I knew then that I loved you. That I didn't care about the fertility risk, or whether we have boys or girls or any children at all. I just want you. Just you. Elora. Not the Princess of Caruli. You. It's entirely personal, nothing to do with your island or mine.'

'Why didn't you tell me?' she asked, and now reality began to seep in. Was he about to tell her that love was irrelevant, that it didn't change their duty? 'You said you had something else to tell me,' she remembered.

He nodded, kept her hand securely in his. 'Yes.' He took a deep breath. 'Is it OK if we walk and talk? I'd like for you to see this bit of land.'

She looked around, wondered why he'd chosen it. It was a large expanse of rough land, overgrown with grass and wild flowers and the occasional bush.

'Of course.'

'Right. Well, I did a lot more thinking and… I have stood down as heir to Sarala.'

'What?' Elora tried to absorb the enormity of his words—understand and take on board the fact that Rohan had decided to turn destiny on its head. 'But then who will become heir?'

'Marisa.' He said it simply. 'She is more than able to

take on the role and by rights it should be hers. She is the elder. And that is right.'

'But whose idea was it?' She turned wide eyes to him. 'You didn't do it for me, did you? Give up your birthright?'

'No, I didn't do it for you. I love you and I would have asked you to marry me and rule by my side regardless and I believe we would have made it work because of the strength of our love.'

'Then why?'

'I stepped down because I truly believe it is the right thing to do. It wasn't an easy decision to make.' His voice was deep, serious.

'I wish I'd been here. I wish you'd told me.'

He shook his head. 'This had to be my decision and mine alone. I couldn't put the burden on anyone else. But Elora, you were in my thoughts—you are the one who helped show me my way, my path.'

'How?'

'We decided that we couldn't risk getting married in case you couldn't have children, even though we didn't know for sure, one way or another. Because I need a male heir. That is wrong. We had other conversations about having daughters. About your father divorcing his wife to get a male heir when he had a daughter. That is wrong. Your mother wishing it had been you instead of Sanjay who died because he was the male heir. That is wrong. Flavia, unable to rule, only worthy to produce a male heir. My sister, older than me but not able to be heir because of her sex. Wrong again. The bottom line is Marisa would make a better ruler than me and she is older, and yet here we were, bound by tradition and history when we were supposed to be modernising the royal family. What was modern about any of what I have described?'

'Not a lot,' Elora said.

'It suddenly seemed crystal-clear what needed to be done. So I did it. Of course, if Marisa had said she didn't want to rule, well, then there'd have been a different problem, but she didn't.'

'But your parents—what did they say?'

Elora was so caught up in the story she only now realised that, somehow, they had come to a halt and were sitting, backs against a tree, right next to each other, reminiscent of their conversation under the mango tree weeks before.

'They didn't want to listen at first, but when they saw I was adamant, when I pointed out the number of times they took Marisa's advice, and when they knew I was standing down no matter what—they came on board. The past week has been about looking at the legal side, making it all watertight and working out how to make the announcement in the next few weeks. Marisa has gone away for a bit, to be out of the limelight until it is all sorted. And to have some time to herself before her life changes.'

'So now all I have to offer you is me. Not a kingdom to rule, not the chance to be the mother of a ruler. Just me. Rohan.' He shifted away from her. 'If that changes anything I understand. I know our marriage for you was a way to earn your parents' love and redemption. I can't offer you that any more. There is no reason I can give you to be with me now. Except love.'

'And that is the most precious thing you can offer me,' she said softly, her heart bursting with joy, with the knowledge that Rohan loved her, this prince of men, this man who could turn her insides to mush, this man who amidst the turmoil of renouncing a kingdom had found time to get a pony for her—a man who had changed her for ever.

He loved her. 'And that is what I offer you back. I love you, Rohan. I fell in love with you, not your title. I fell in love with the man who has been honest with me, a man who trusted me and made me trust him, a fearless man who wanted to stand up for me but also encouraged me to stand up for myself. A man who has bought me a pony to help me fight my fears. You haven't just listened; you've done something about it. You made me feel as though I am worth something.'

With that, he rose and pulled her to her feet and into the biggest possible hug. 'Elora you are worth so much, you are so brave and strong. You've lived your life with a near intolerable burden of guilt and with parents who do not deserve you and you have come out of it without bitterness, able to smile and care, truly care about people. To have the courage to stand up for your convictions and look to help people who need it. You've helped me more than I can ever say, allowed me to trust, to love, to be brave enough to do what is right, and brave enough to want to live my dream. With you.'

He smiled at her, a smile so carefree and light and happy, and she knew it matched the one on her face.

'I have spoken to Marisa and I thought I could run my company, but for the good of Sarala. This land we are on now, my company is going to develop into a resort; it will bring jobs to Sarala, and I will be involved in the designing, building...everything as well as promoting Sarala. And I want the profits to be ploughed back into the country, to help alleviate poverty, improve medical facilities. And if you want to be involved you can, but I respect that your dream is different, to have an allotment, and that is fine with me.'

Elora laughed and he looked at her with a question in his eyes.

'That dream—it's not valid any more. You've changed that dream. You see, now I believe I can make a difference, that I can be a princess and I can make my dream bigger. I don't have to be Preeti Bannerjee. I can be Princess Elora and I want to be part of your dream and I want you to be part of mine. I want to help, I want to make sure all those profits go to the right causes. Perhaps we can build a new facility. I have also contacted Michel, the chef, and we are in discussion about writing a cookbook together, and again the profits will go to good causes. And in this marriage of ours we will always share our dreams. And one of my dreams is to have a family, but now...'

'Now there is no pressure. We can take our time. We can adopt. We will have a family, Elora, and I know how happy we will be. We are going to have the romance of a lifetime. And every single bit of it will be true.'

She smiled at him. 'All we will have to do is be ourselves.'

And she knew that they would be the happiest people in the world. Elora and Rohan. As themselves. No illusion, no charade, just the reality of a love that would fill her heart for ever.

* * * * *

BREAKING THE BEST FRIEND RULE

JUSTINE LEWIS

MILLS & BOON

For my amazing daughter, Emily,
who brings me joy every day.

CHAPTER ONE

THE RAIN ALWAYS made Charlotte nervous. Today's torrential downpour, with water coming down in sheets and overflowing gutters, positively made her heart race. It was good weather for ducks. For the garden. And getting into fatal accidents.

She was safe in her gallery, she told herself. *Her* gallery. An old but light-filled space on a quiet Soho side street. She would have preferred a more prominent position to attract passers-by but could barely afford the rent on this space as it was. Though three years after opening she was still solvent, which was more than many commercial art galleries could say.

Customers didn't tend to wander past without purpose on days like this, so the afternoon was dragging. At times she fancied the clock was standing still. She tried to keep herself busy by digging around on the Internet for up-and-coming artists. The principle of her gallery was to find yet-to-be-discovered artists and help them on the journey to grow their careers, rather than chasing after already established names. It was a model that had proven to be successful and canny investors sought out her gallery and her advice. The bigger galleries watched her carefully.

A crack of thunder made her jump. She tried to take her mind off it by sending some emails, but her heart rate remained high.

The old wooden-framed glass door rattled open and her best friend, Ben Watson, appeared, soaking wet but carrying two coffees from the cafe across the street.

'Sorry,' he muttered as he shook his long, wet brown hair from his eyes, leaving a Ben-sized puddle on the floor.

Charlotte raced to the back office, retrieved a towel she kept on hand and passed it to him. He wiped his face, beard and hair and then hung his wet coat on the rack.

'Why are you out in this weather? By choice?'

Ben's apartment and studio were in Camden. He might still be in it, safe and warm. Working on his latest piece. Something was up.

'I came to bring you coffee,' he replied, passing her one of the cups.

'I'm grateful. But really?' Other people didn't hate the rain as much as Charlotte, but most didn't wander around in it without a good reason.

'No, I do have an ulterior motive. Something's um…happened.'

Ben's usually happy face looked tight. Concerned. The last time she'd seen him like this was just before he returned to Australia to see his father, who had suffered a massive and unexpected stroke. His father had passed away before Ben's plane landed back in Adelaide.

'Oh, no. What's going on?'

He sipped his coffee. His blue eyes were cast downwards, and his wet hair now slicked back off his forehead, which was furrowed. 'If you get an invitation to your mother's wedding less than two weeks before the event, are you even really invited?' he asked.

'Your mother's getting married? I didn't even know she was dating anyone.'

'Nor did I,' he said darkly.

Charlotte did a quick calculation. It had been just over a

year since Ben's father, David, had passed away, the September before last.

Ben's parents had been married for the best part of forty years. Charlotte hadn't met either of them. Ben rarely returned to his native Australia since leaving it at the age of twenty-one to pursue his artistic ambitions overseas and his parents had never visited him here, in London. Ben adored his mother, but his relationship with his business-focused father had always been tense. As had his relationship with his older brother, Will. Will had gone into the family business and neither Will nor his father had supported Ben's dreams of being an artist.

Charlotte suspected that most days Ben didn't give either his father or brother a second thought, but the old wounds were never far beneath the surface, especially when something like this happened.

Charlotte motioned to a seat and Ben sat down beside Charlotte's desk.

'Who's she marrying?' she asked.

Ben took out his phone, brought up a photo, and passed it to Charlotte. It was a photo of a happy couple standing near the ocean, the man's arm wrapped around the woman's shoulders, both beaming at one another, oblivious to the person taking the photo. Charlotte recognised the smiling woman as Ben's mother, Diane. The man was at least a foot taller than her and very handsome, but she didn't say that to Ben.

Instead she tried to find the right word. 'He looks…'

'Young?' Ben said.

'I was going to say hot.'

Ben glared at her.

'Sorry, but he is. Young and hot.'

'It's hard to tell from the photograph alone. I've looked him up. He's forty-seven. Fourteen years younger than Mum.'

Go Diane, Charlotte thought, but kept the opinion to herself.

'Half the age of the oldest person, plus seven. Isn't that the rule? So they're well within that.'

Over the four years they had known one another, Ben and Charlotte had discussed all of life's important questions, including who made the best coffee—Australians—the best way to end a relationship—quickly, clearly and politely— and what amounted to an inappropriate age gap in a couple.

Ben frowned. 'I'm not sure that rule applies to one's mother.'

'But forty-seven isn't that young. At least he's older than you.'

Ben dragged his hand through his still wet hair, slicking it back even further. He looked like a drowned dog, and sad eyes completed the picture. But no wonder, his mother remarrying so soon after his father's death and giving Ben practically no notice of the nuptials. Her chest ached for him.

'I'm not worried about his age,' Ben said.

'His hotness?'

Ben grimaced.

Perhaps this wasn't the right moment to tease him.

'It's not his age that's worrying me. Or even his...' Ben waved his hand over his phone. 'Or even his attractiveness. It just seems so quick.'

Charlotte agreed. A year did seem a little fast to be finding a new husband after the death of your husband of forty-odd years.

Charlotte's first and last serious boyfriend, Tim, had passed away seven years ago and she was yet to meet a man she could contemplate staying with for more than a few weeks, let alone marrying. People told her that she had mourned long enough, and her reply was always that people mourn at different rates. It seemed like an apt reply now, for the opposite reason.

'Did you even know she was seeing him?' she asked.

'I had no idea, but then I haven't been back to Adelaide since the funeral.'

'So the first you're hearing about her relationship with this man is the wedding invitation? Gosh.'

Charlotte had thought that Ben's difficulties had just been between his father and his brother, Will. She'd always believed Ben was on good terms with his mother. This news must be making him wonder about all sorts of things.

'It's my fault. I guess I wasn't around after Dad passed. I haven't been there for her, like I should've been.'

'Maybe not, but you came back to London with her blessing. You talk regularly, don't you?'

Ben nodded.

Younger man, older, richer but emotionally vulnerable woman. There was another theory they should canvas.

'Are you worried that maybe he's using her? That he's after her money?'

'Even if I was, it would hardly be my business to say. My father made it very clear I gave up any rights to the family business when I moved away. Besides, Dad was so tight about his money and Will's just the same. So much of it is tied up in trusts and other arrangements.'

'But she's still wealthy, isn't she?'

'Yes, but I don't even have to ask to know that Will must have insisted on an airtight prenup.'

'But it's not his money, surely? She must have her own money that your dad left her. Will can't be controlling her fortune.'

'I wouldn't put it past him.'

Charlotte bit her tongue. She'd never met Will, Ben's older and—according to Ben—super-uptight brother. When Ben declared his wish to go to art school, instead of work in the family company, his brother and father ended all financial support for him. However, being forced to work his way through life and support himself had made Ben focused and single-minded. He was now a highly successful painter, whose work was shown in galleries all over the world. Ben had found financial security and success his own way and Charlotte knew he was immensely proud that he'd done it on his own terms.

'Then what is it? What's really worrying you?'

The two old friends could speak honestly and openly with one another. He was more straightforward than any of her girlfriends, but no less close to her. She valued his advice and counsel and knew he did the same of her. Thankfully, she wasn't attracted to Ben nor he to her and their friendship was stronger and more solid because of it. Friendships she'd had with other men had been ruined in the past when either she or he had become attracted to the other. Charlotte was glad that neither she nor Ben had ever developed complicated feelings towards the other.

'I thought they loved one another,' Ben said, sagging. 'I mean, I know Dad was difficult, of course he was, but I thought Mum loved him. But what if she didn't? I mean, what if all this time she was actually desperately unhappy? Like I said, he wasn't an easy man to love.'

'Ahh. Right.'

Even though Charlotte had struggled after losing Tim, she did know that people dealt with grief differently.

'It is so soon,' Ben said.

'This doesn't mean she didn't love your father. Or that she was unhappy. Forty years is a long time to be married to someone. Just because she's found new happiness it doesn't mean what she had was any less special.'

Charlotte grasped the pendant around her neck and turned it between her fingers. The feel of the smooth, shiny silver between her fingertips always reminded her of Tim and centred her when she was uneasy.

'You can find new love without dishonouring the old.' Charlotte said the words, almost a repetition of what her mother kept saying to her, but her heart wasn't in it.

Ben raised a suspicious eyebrow, as though he didn't believe she was committed to the sentiment either.

'Why don't you just wait and talk to her? Reserve judgement before you meet him.'

'The wedding's in ten days! How much time will I actually get to know him? That's if I even go. This invitation? Is it a real invitation? Is she expecting me to come halfway around the world with so little notice? What's all that about?'

'Maybe...' Charlotte was lost for words. Ten days did seem unnecessarily hasty.

'See, you can't think of a good reason either,' Ben replied.

Maybe she couldn't at this moment, but she didn't want to discount the possibility that Diane might have a good reason for getting married so quickly. Even if she didn't, this wedding was an important life event and if Ben didn't go because of old wounds, or confusion or hurt or whatever reason, he'd regret it.

'She's your mother. You will go, won't you?'

Ben sighed. 'I don't know.'

'When were the invitations sent?'

'This morning. By email. Also, it's in Bali.'

'Bali? The island?'

He nodded. 'Bali, the island. In Indonesia. On the other side of the world.'

Charlotte had never been to Bali. It sounded warm, relaxing. She imagined friendly people, vibrant jungle and crystal-clear water. It probably had great food too, tasty spices and fragrant herbs. She began to salivate.

'Well, I think you should go. Even if she isn't expecting you to come, I think you should.' Charlotte looked out of the window at the grey London afternoon. 'Apart from anything it's a holiday. It'll be warm!' She'd do anything for a chance to escape the wet London autumn. Even go to an excruciatingly awkward family wedding. To feel sand between her toes. 'And I'll come with you.'

The words were out of her mouth before she'd thought twice. But she didn't regret them for a second.

Ben's eyes widened.

'You will? You don't have to.'

Her offer had been quick, but she was sure. Ben was her best friend and had been so supportive and helpful to her over the past few years: with advice on her gallery, cooking her warm meals, not to mention being a non-judgemental listener when she had to tell someone about her latest dating misstep.

'No, I really want to go. I want to be there for you.'

She couldn't read the look on Ben's face and tell if he was relieved at her offer or pained by it.

'And come on, Bali! A break in the sun! Won't that be great, with or without a wedding?'

He frowned. 'They're getting there in three days' time. Three days! That's no notice at all. It takes nearly a day to fly there.'

'So, we leave in two days.'

'Don't you want to go to the exhibition at the Royal College?'

She did, especially as it would be full of work by recent graduates and an opportunity to spot new talent before anyone else did.

'So we leave the day after that.'

'And the gallery?' Ben looked around. 'Who'll look after it?'

'Marcia can manage it for a week. Besides, this is an opportunity to travel, maybe find some new artists too. Ben, it's so perfect. We have to go.'

'Okay, but let me book.' He crossed his arms. She wanted

to giggle. He was trying to look firm, but he was still soaked and looked as if he'd been dragged out of a pond.

'Fine, but I'll pay you back.' She crossed her arms back and stood with her legs apart to let him know she was serious too.

Ben shook his head, but she didn't know if the shake meant, 'Of course you will pay me back' or 'I will definitely shout you'.

She'd argue about it later. Right now he was upset and stressed.

With his hair slicked back, she could see more of Ben's face than usual. He hid behind a brown beard, which in Charlotte's opinion was way too long, and wavy brown hair that was always in need of a cut. He had a distracted artist thing going on, with loose, fraying sweaters, dirty boots and hands that were perpetually splattered with paint. His dishevelled appearance didn't hurt his reputation, only seemed to enhance it. Ben was one of the most sought-after artists in London at the moment. Charlotte mused: talented men could get away with ignoring their appearance in a way that women couldn't. But under his apparently chaotic appearance, Ben was her rock. Solid, unflappable. The only time she'd seen him shaken was when his father had died.

And now.

The rain had eased by the time Ben left, as had her mood. She was going to Bali! Getting away from London at the time of the anniversary was a truly excellent idea. Escaping the wet cold British autumn for the sunny skies and warmth of a tropical island was such an obvious solution to her October funk she should have thought of it years ago. A few customers started wandering in and by the time she was closing up that evening the skies had cleared.

Warm, tropical. That was all she knew about Bali, but that was enough.

October was always hard in London. The change of season. The rain.

It had been a soaking October day when Tim had had his accident, sliding off his motorbike under a poorly timed lorry.

The accident had been quick, but the end hadn't been. He'd had several major surgeries, been in so much pain for weeks, before his body decided it had really had too much.

They had both been twenty-three.

She'd moved on slowly. In his last days, when it had looked as if his body was just not going to be strong enough to fight off the injuries and subsequent infections, he'd made her promise she'd find love again. But a second love had been elusive for Charlotte.

No one was quite like her Tim.

She tried though; if there was a man she could love as much as Tim, she was going to find him. She dated many men. So many her girlfriends rolled their eyes and her mother shook her head.

Only Ben didn't judge, and he understood why she always seemed to end things after a few dates. Ben had watched over her for the past four years, like a big brother. Not the superprotective older brother though, but a cool, watch-from-a-non-embarrassing-distance type of brother. Close enough to be there at short notice if things got uncomfortable. And always there to listen to her talk about any fallout afterwards. A perpetual singleton like herself, Ben understood the risks of committing too quickly to anything and why she was so cautious.

Yes, she had to go to Bali for Ben. He had always been there for her.

Her flat was only a few Tube stops away and she wanted to get home and start googling swimsuits. She had tentative plans to have a drink with a guy she'd met at a party a week ago—Dale? Dan? No, Don. The fact that she couldn't even remember his name was an obvious clue that it wasn't likely to be a date that would change her life. She sent him a message to cancel.

Hi Don. I'm so sorry, but something has come up and I have to go abroad for a bit. It's probably best that we don't start something I can't finish. C xx

Her usual sign-off. Her friends told her that she should just make it a signature block on her messages: Sorry, but I don't think we should start something we can't finish.

She meant it to be kind, to let the poor fella down easily. Let him know that she didn't want anything serious. She was under no obligation to commence a relationship with anyone.

Don replied right away.

Safe travels. Let me know if you want to catch up when you're back.

She sighed. Don was probably one of the nice ones. Just not the right nice one for her.

At home, she took off her high-heeled boots, skirt and bra, changed into sweats and made herself comfortable on the couch with her laptop.

She'd opened a browser and typed in 'tropical getaway swimsuits' when her phone pinged with a message from Ben. It was a link to a plane ticket from Heathrow to Denpasar, leaving in three days' time. She messaged him right back.

Business class! Ben!

It's a twenty-hour trip. Trust me, we'll need it. And I AM PAYING.

Are you sure? I didn't expect you to buy business class seats!

Do you want me to leave you in cattle class while I sip champers in business?

Charlotte was comfortable, but not so comfortable she could drop thousands of dollars on last-minute business class seats to Bali. It was so generous of Ben she hardly knew what to say so she simply typed XXX and clutched her phone to her chest.

Seconds later he messaged back.

You're doing me a favour. I'm really glad you're coming with me.

The exhibition was in a gallery in East London, featuring work of current and former students. Like all such exhibitions, the works were of wildly differing styles and quality. Ben's eyes were drawn to Charlotte right away. She was wearing a long, bright green jacket, a fitted black jumpsuit and bright red heels. She looked stunning, as usual.

She was studying a canvas that filled half a wall. He grabbed two glasses of champagne from a nearby waiter and walked over to her.

Charlotte was just the type of woman Ben could have fallen for, if he hadn't stopped himself, just in time. Because what business would someone as wonderful as Charlotte have falling in love with him?

Minutes into their first meeting he'd found himself drawn to her. They had met at a mutual friend's party, and she had stood next to him in a corner of a cramped terrace, where, for some reason he couldn't remember, she'd told him exactly what she thought about Picasso and his treatment of women, waving her hands around and nearly splashing her drink over him. Her beauty was obvious: long straight dark hair flowed down her back, colour high in her cheeks, naturally defining them. She stood straight and confidently.

Her intelligence was almost as quickly apparent as her beauty. Her dark blue eyes flashed with insight and thoughts about the world. Her passion for art came across next, which would have endeared her to Ben in any event. But it was their shared gently cynical sense of humour and appreciation of the ridiculous that he really adored.

Now, four years later and on the other side of London, he stood with Charlotte looking at a work by an artist he'd never seen before. The work was competent, but uninspired. He handed her one of the glasses.

'Are you all set for tomorrow?' he asked, knowing full well that she wouldn't be packed and that her flat would look as though it had been ransacked by a burglar.

Outwardly, Charlotte looked sleek and well put together. It was a mystery to him how such a well-presented creature managed to emerge from her messy flat each day. But that was Charlotte.

He was the opposite; he liked the spaces around him to be tidy and ordered but outwardly he was, as Charlotte called him, a bit of a scruff. He rubbed his beard. He couldn't even remember the last time he'd had a haircut.

Together, they would have made one put-together person.

She narrowed her eyes at him. 'I'll be ready. Besides, it won't take me long. We're going to Bali. A couple of bikinis and a dress for the wedding and I'll be set.'

Ben imagined Charlotte in a bikini and swallowed hard, quickly shaking the image away. He didn't think about Charlotte like that. He had built a wall around those thoughts. It was high and he didn't look over it. Let alone try to scale it.

The night they'd first met he'd been working up the courage to subtly ask if she was single, when another man had joined their conversation and completely monopolised Charlotte, charming her with stories about a recent trip he'd taken to Florence.

They had wandered away together and Ben had taken himself home, miffed.

Hadn't they got along well? There had been a spark, at least on his side. But no, she'd wandered away with some Lothario, old enough to be her father, and left Ben feeling confused and empty.

He'd run into Charlotte at an exhibition a week later; the art scene in London was big, but still small enough that you did come across the same faces. This time she'd approached him. She'd confessed she was scouting him out to see if he wanted to exhibit in her new space and they'd gone for coffee. They'd talked for hours, but this time, as prospective business associates, he'd been careful to stay professional. He wasn't going to play runner-up to the charmer she'd left with the other night. Or to any of the steady stream of men Charlotte seemed to date.

And then there was the night she'd told him all about Tim. A few months into their acquaintanceship he'd found her, after leaving a function, standing in a doorway, not moving. It had been raining heavily and he'd offered her use of his umbrella, but she'd refused. She'd grabbed his arm and held him back and they'd waited under the awning together until the rain had passed. It had been then that she'd told him all about Tim and the accident. From that point on Ben had realised Charlotte's heart was not free and his own heart would be safest locked away.

Because, despite what Charlotte might claim until she was out of breath, she wasn't ready for another relationship. The pattern quickly became apparent to Ben: Charlotte would meet a man—sometimes on an app, sometimes at a party, sometimes through work—and they would hit it off. Charlotte was beautiful, charming and great company. Men were attracted to her like bees to pollen. They would have a few dates—three was usually the limit but once or twice some poor fella had made it to four—and then Charlotte would pull back. Either because she could tell the man was not for her, or, sometimes, because she thought he might be. The thought of falling in love scared Charlotte so much that she had occasionally ended new relationships when she'd felt herself feeling more about the man. Charlotte didn't have any intention—consciously or otherwise—of falling in love with any of them.

And she told Ben about every single one of them. Where they went, what had been said, what she didn't like about the guy. If he *had* fallen for Charlotte, the last few years of his life would have been an utter misery. He knew that by keeping their relationship platonic he'd ensured that she would never push him away. By staying her friend, he would always have Charlotte in his life. And that felt like a win.

'What do you think?' Ben nodded to the painting they were standing in front of.

'Competent, but he's not telling me anything I don't already know.'

Ben smiled to himself. They almost always agreed on art. It was an unusually slick exhibition for recent students. The champagne was above par and there was a string quartet as well.

'I love strings,' Ben confessed.

'Really? I never knew that.' Charlotte tilted her head and studied him closely for a second. He felt his cheeks warm; that would be the champagne kicking in.

'There are lots of things you don't know about me.' He said it in a way that was half teasing, half trying to be enigmatic.

'Nonsense. I know you,' she said.

She did.

And she didn't. She knew more about him than anyone else on earth. But there was still a part of him that was locked behind a high brick wall that was impossible for even her to scale.

'Have you spoken to your mother?' she asked.

'Briefly. She's thrilled you're coming too.' Diane had gently prodded him for details about his relationship with Charlotte over the years, questions that Ben had simply rebuffed. But this time the questioning had been pointed.

'I've arranged you a one-bedroom villa. Will that be fine?' she'd asked.

'We'll each need a bedroom, Mum. I'll call them.'

'No, no, I'll take care of it,' she'd said, and he hoped that she had. Charlotte would not thank him if they arrived to find one bed waiting for them. If that was the case, he'd be on the floor.

'I hope I'm not intruding on a family occasion,' she said.

'Not at all. Besides, by the sounds of things there will be quite a few people there. I assumed it was some sort of elopement, but Gus's family and friends will be there as well.'

Given it was going to be quite a big affair, Ben still wondered what the rush was, but that was something he'd have to ask his mother face to face. Maybe it was Gus's idea, get everything tied up before Diane had second thoughts. Before Will could get the seal on the prenup. He knew he could call his brother and ask what was going on, but the thought of picking up the phone and dialling his brother's number made his mouth dry.

Maybe they love one another?

Ben felt like scoffing. Love? Did love really make you crazy or did people simply use it as an excuse for bad decisions? Ben had never met a feeling he couldn't analyse, unpack and use for his art. He'd never let his feelings for someone lead him to do anything reckless.

He supposed that was one thing he had in common with his brother.

As though she could see straight into his skull, Charlotte said, 'I'm looking forward to meeting Will.'

Ben's spine straightened at the mention of his brother's name. And the fact that he had piqued Charlotte's interest.

'What's the matter? He's your brother. I'm curious.'

'Nothing's the matter. But we're not at all alike.'

'Sure, sure, but you're brothers, close in age. Same parents. How different can you be?'

'Very.'

Eighteen months could make a lot of difference. Will was the golden boy. His father's favourite. Ben was an afterthought. A disappointment. He lacked his father's aptitude for numbers and his love of large ones, particularly those numbers with a dollar sign in front of them, whereas Will shared his father's passion for money and accumulating it.

Ben didn't understand their obsession and was called ungrateful and spoilt because of it. His father had never understood that Ben was never ungrateful, he would just rather be thinking about the way the world worked and studying how things looked and why. And most of all he loved creating and shaping things with his hands. Rather than keeping track of how much money he'd made.

Ben was well aware he'd benefited from his family's fortune: it had paid for his private school education. But his father had paid for Will's university tuition and refused point-blank to pay for Ben to attend art school. When Will had graduated, not only were his fees paid, but his father had bought Will a new car and an apartment of his own. He told Ben that Will deserved all those things because Will was working for him, but Ben always knew it was an excuse.

Ben had enjoyed a very privileged upbringing and lived at home while he studied. He'd never gone hungry, but it still smarted. Not the lack of money, but the love and respect the money represented.

Ben had worked through university, bartending, teaching high-school students and occasionally receiving secret handouts from his mother. Finally, at twenty-one, he'd completed his degree, with first class honours and the year prize.

His father had come, grimacing, to the graduation exhibition, literally dragged along by the hand by Diane.

'What a waste of time and money,' his father had said when he'd walked through the exhibition.

But someone didn't think Ben's art was a waste of money. *Someone* had paid the ludicrously high price Ben had placed on his prize-winning painting of his favourite beach. The painting had been commended for its unusual use of perspective and he'd been personally proud of the way he'd used the colour to evoke the mood. He loved that painting and had set the price at an exorbitant amount of ten thousand dollars, expecting no one to pay it and for him to be able to keep it.

To his amazement, a red sticker had been placed on the work early in the evening. The next day Ben had bought a plane ticket with the money he'd made selling that painting, flown to Los Angeles and never looked back. Since that day he had supported himself entirely, without a further cent from his family.

He was sometimes sad that he'd sold that painting to an anonymous investor, he'd loved it so much, but the fact that someone had been willing to pay him ten thousand dollars for something he'd painted had given him the courage to launch himself into the world. It made him proud to know that somewhere out there that painting was making someone happy. Ben had his whole career to thank them for, really.

Particularly his life in London, which he loved.

Los Angeles had been busy and vibrant. Then he'd moved on to New York, which had been exciting, but exhausting. In London he'd found a happy medium. Busy, crowded, the meeting place of the world. A magnet for all cultures.

London was confident, with statesman-like vistas, and history that caught in your throat. It wasn't as overtly beautiful as Paris or Venice, but it still had buildings that could take your breath away, laneways that would make you swoon and streets you wanted to dance along.

And above all, London had Charlotte.

At some point in his reverie she'd wandered off to look at another painting and had begun chatting to another man.

He watched from a distance, curious about what would transpire, but confident in the knowledge that tomorrow she would be getting on a plane with him.

CHAPTER TWO

WHEN THE CAR pulled up at the kerb Charlotte wheeled her suitcase towards it. Ben jumped out to help her with her bag and she did a double take.

What on earth?

Ben looked down and rubbed his bare chin subconsciously. 'Yeah, I know. I just got it done this morning. Is it awful?'

She looked at her best friend as if seeing him for the first time. She was so accustomed to seeing the bottom half of his face covered with a thick clump of soft brown hair it took her a moment to unscramble the new image before her.

'It's awful, isn't it? You hate it,' he said, groaning.

'No, not at all,' she said quickly. 'It's just different. Give me a moment to catch up.'

He lifted her case into the boot and closed it. They both slid into the back seat of the car and the driver pulled from the kerb.

She stole sideways glances at him. 'Why?' she asked.

'The heat.'

'Really? How hot will it be?'

'Hot.'

Without whiskers obscuring it, she could see his Adam's apple rise and fall as he swallowed, probably pushing down his anxiety about seeing his mother again.

It was the first time Ben would see his family since returning briefly for his father's funeral a year ago. Charlotte hadn't gone with him on that trip, but he'd been different since his return. Not a big change, only something that she, as his closest friend, had noticed. A sadness, partly, but also a deeper maturity. Charlotte had never lost a parent so she could only imagine that was what it was. She also knew that Ben's feelings towards his family were complicated—part anger, part guilt. They had never understood his passion—or rather his *need*—to paint. Those who were not artists often didn't, but surely a parent only wanted their children to be happy and fulfilled? Apparently, Ben's father had not, and Ben hadn't had the opportunity to make his peace with his father before his death.

She knew Ben didn't regret moving away though, breaking free from the Watson empire. He had been born an artist and so he'd had to leave in order to pursue his goals. It had taken a lot of courage to break free from his family's expectations, but that didn't mean he didn't feel some guilt about not being around to help with the family business, be a part of it.

Charlotte was immensely grateful for her own parents, who had encouraged to her to follow her passion and to study fine arts and art history. They were proud of her, and they also adored Ben.

'What did Don say when you told him you were going away for a week?' Ben asked. 'Or didn't you tell him?'

'Of course I told him, I sent him a message. And I told him it probably wouldn't work out with us.'

Ben nodded.

'Don't say it,' she said.

'I wasn't going to say anything.'

'But you're thinking, *She's dumped another guy.*'

'That's not at all what I was thinking.'

'What were you thinking?'

'I was thinking that at least you let the poor guy know. At least you didn't ghost him.'

'I always let them know,' she said. That was a half-truth. Sometimes she didn't call or message back. Particularly if the guy in question had been rude.

Ben smirked.

'There's nothing wrong with not messaging back. I'm only doing what millions of guys have done over the years.'

'And it wasn't nice when they did it either.'

London zipped by outside the window, the houses becoming smaller and sparser as they headed west to Heathrow.

'It wasn't like we had a relationship. I mean, we kissed a bit, but we didn't sleep together.'

Ben coughed.

'What was that about? You're one to talk. When was the last time you went on a third date? Or even a second?'

It did surprise her that Ben was still single. He was successful, fun and smart. Not to mention kind. He was one of her favourite people in the whole world and she knew his single status was not due to a lack of interest or trying by the women of London. Ben was as allergic to long-term relationships as she was, yet no one ever seemed to pressure him to couple up. No one, but no one, ever seemed to worry that, at thirty, Ben was single. When he failed to commit, people said that was just what men did, whereas when Charlotte declined a long-term relationship, people wanted to know what was wrong. Ben was single, but everyone said he just hadn't found the right woman. Charlotte was single but it was because of a character flaw. Or worse, the tragic dark cloud of Tim's death.

The double standard was unfair.

He met lots of fabulous women. Her friends, for starters. She'd introduced him to a few in the hope they would hit it off, but nothing had ever stuck. The lack of suitable women wasn't the problem—London was awash with amazing single women who were successful, bright, and beautiful—and no one thought Ben's reluctance to buy someone a diamond ring and a house in a good school district was a problem to be fixed.

Further, Ben didn't have a reason to avoid commitment—something in his past that had scarred him for life. No. He was just a man and society did not put the same pressure on men to couple up.

Maybe his reluctance was due to his family. He was cagey about them and visibly tensed each time she brought them up. Now she'd finally have a chance to meet them and find out if they were the ogres that Ben believed them to be.

Charlotte contemplated this as the car weaved along the motorway.

She was quiet as they enjoyed their champagne in the lounge and as they boarded and settled into their seats.

'When did you last go on a date?' she finally asked.

'Why?'

'Just wondering.'

'Oh, I don't know. A few weeks ago.'

'Who with?'

'Julie.'

'Julie, the vet from Croydon?'

He nodded. She thought that had been months ago.

She studied Ben. Despite knowing him so well, she still often got the feeling that he was holding something back.

Like his face, for starters. Ben had a jawline and it was sharp and strong.

And hot.

She fanned herself with her boarding pass as if she were some corseted lady who had never felt attracted to a handsome man before.

Which was ridiculous, because he was still Ben. The same Ben she'd seen yesterday at the exhibition. Drinking champagne with him at the East End gallery she'd felt nothing but a gentle buzz from the bubbles. But now, on the plane, her face felt warm, her heart rate elevated. And her stomach jumpy.

You're about to fly to Bali...no wonder you're a little on edge.

'Did she break your heart?' she finally asked.

'Who?'

'Julie!'

Ben groaned. 'No, she didn't.'

'Then why won't you talk about it?'

'Because she wasn't that important.'

It suddenly bothered her in a way that it never had before. Why was Ben single?

He was certainly good-looking. His eyes were blue and quick. And when he really studied something, they were deep and soulful. His hair was wavy and a lighter shade of brown, his figure solid but still lean. She'd never liked his overly thick beard much, but it was her own preference, and it didn't seem to bother other women. Charlotte often noticed women walk past them and give Ben a second look. The women would also often give Charlotte a quick appraisal, followed by a fleeting glance of disappointment.

Without the beard and with a more flattering haircut, he was...handsome. He had been hiding something under his too-bushy beard after all—impressive bone structure and full lips.

So why was he single? It was one thing for her to be. Committing to someone was difficult after losing her childhood sweetheart and the love of her life. But Ben had no reason not to be settling down with any of the lovely women Charlotte introduced him to.

Was he a bad lover? Was that it? Was he a horrible boyfriend? Unlikely. He was a good friend and, besides, as far as she could tell he was usually the one who was reluctant to take things forward.

The last time she'd set him up had been with her friend Kitty. They'd gone out twice, so twice his usual amount. But when a third date had failed to eventuate, she'd questioned them both.

Kitty had said Ben's heart was not for the winning, which was strange because Ben wasn't in love with anyone.

Ben had just told her that it wouldn't have worked.

But why?

What was Ben's problem?

She'd liked him the first moment they'd met. Not only was he easy to talk to, but they had lots to talk about. She had fallen into a relaxed and comfortable conversation with him. In the beginning she'd thought of him as a prospective client and then, for once in her life, she had a man who was a friend, who wasn't interested in anything more than that. And she adored him for it.

Charlotte studied him over the rim of her champagne flute. Ben was looking out of the window at the runway and sketching something in the notebook that was never far from him. It was his way of thinking, working and relaxing all at once.

'You know my friend Kitty?'

He hummed agreement.

'She's getting married.'

'Oh,' he said, but didn't look up from his sketch.

'Why didn't it work out with you two?'

Ben looked at her and pulled a face. 'What?'

'You went out a few times.'

'Yeah, but—'

The pilot came on the speaker to announce their departure just then, and Ben used the opportunity to avoid explaining.

Charlotte lay next to him in the flat bed on the long leg from London to Singapore, an eye mask covering her eyes, her dark hair half across her face, her chest gently rising and falling. They'd enjoyed a few more glasses of wine and dinner before Charlotte had done the sensible thing and changed into her pyjamas for sleep. She'd fallen asleep with ease, but now he nursed a Scotch and watched her.

He should get some sleep to minimise the inevitable jet lag on arrival, but his mind whirled.

He'd tried to make things work with Kitty; she was lovely, attractive, clever. But when he'd suggested they go back to his apartment for a coffee Kitty had crossed her arms and asked him what exactly he was playing at. Confused, he'd told her upfront that coffee really meant more wine, some kissing and perhaps something else. Kitty had told him outright that there was no point them dating when he was so clearly in love with Charlotte. He'd told her in no uncertain terms that he was definitely not in love with Charlotte. In fact, he'd spent ten minutes telling her all the reasons he was utterly, comprehensibly, and completely not in love with Charlotte, at which point Kitty had laughed, picked up her bag and strolled out of the restaurant.

But that had been three years ago, and he hadn't thought about it for two years and fifty-one weeks. He was glad Kitty was getting married, but didn't know why Charlotte was in such a snip about it all of a sudden.

She was plotting something. It was the uncharacteristic silences and the unusual looks she was giving him.

He hoped it wasn't a mistake bringing her to Bali. He'd wanted her to be close, but he also didn't need further complications this week. And Charlotte, somehow, brought complications with her.

Watching his mother marry someone else, having to deal with Will, that was enough for one person in one week. Would Charlotte make it easier to get through it all, or would her presence make it harder?

The flight attendant came past with cold bottled water and chocolate bars. He offered some to Ben, who shook his head.

'And would your wife like some for when she wakes?'

Ben opened his mouth to contradict the man, but then thought, *He doesn't care. The status of our relationship is not remotely relevant to whether Charlotte wants chocolate.* Ben just smiled, nodded and took the offered treats.

It felt nice.

Charlotte had thought Ben was exaggerating about the heat in Bali; she'd been to Spain and she knew what hot weather was, or at least she'd thought she did. The heat in Indonesia was intense, and the air was almost solid with humidity, weighing down on her like a thick blanket. By the time the car came to pick them up, she was already drenched with moisture.

The car took them from the airport, across the marina and down to their ferry. Ben had his face turned to the window and was letting the air rush over him. He'd left his baggy sweater behind and was now wearing a simple white T-shirt. His decision to shed his hair and beard before arriving at the equator now seemed genius. She twisted her long hair back but lacked a band to tie it off her neck completely. She har-rumphed.

She kept looking back to beardless Ben. It was still Ben, but also not, at the same time. For the first time ever she believed that Clark Kent could go unrecognised as Superman with his glasses disguise. How had she missed noticing this Ben? The thin white T-shirt he was wearing left her glimpses of his well-defined biceps and the soft brown hair covering his strong forearms, not to mention the dip at his throat, which displayed a hint of the top of his chest. Charlotte let out another harrumph and tried to blow air up her face to cool herself down. It had precisely no effect.

'Why did you grow the beard in the first place?' she asked.

He shrugged. 'Laziness?'

Ben wasn't lazy, though, he was driven and hard-working. He painted every day. If he couldn't paint, he sketched. And he sketched constantly, filling at least one sketchbook a week with drawing and thoughts. The man rarely stopped moving.

'I don't believe that,' she said and he laughed.

Even his laugh was different without the beard. She could see his smile properly, the lines around his lips. The dimple.

Ben had a dimple, she saw now. Just one, a gorgeous little dent to the right of his lips. She wanted to reach over and press a fingertip to it, but stopped herself just in time.

'Was it to hide your dimple?'

He looked horrified. 'My what?'

'Dimple. Just there.' She pointed to it. Her finger stopped just millimetres from his skin, but he flinched and she snatched her hand away.

It wasn't just the dimple she wanted to feel, it was his bare cheek. She wanted to run a finger down it, see if it felt as smooth as it looked. She also wanted, she realised with a further blush, to touch the ends of his unruly curls that bounced in a way his longer hair never had.

Oh, the heat was more discombobulating than she'd expected.

'When I first moved from Adelaide, it was easier. Cheaper. I wasn't flush with funds and I spent what little money I did have on paint and instant noodles. Not razors. And then I found I liked it. I looked older. People treated me more seriously. Investors expect artists to be bohemian. Not conservative.'

The look he was wearing now was hardly conservative. Sure, it wasn't the full beard and long locks he'd had two days ago, but it wasn't a short back and sides either. His thick brown curls went in all directions from the crown of his head, messy and untamed and licked at the nape of his neck. He still looked slightly unkempt. Ruffled. As though he'd just climbed out of bed.

And it suited him.

Charlotte's mouth felt parched at the thought. She searched her bag for a water bottle to sip. Couldn't find one.

'But you stuck with the beard, even when you could afford a razor?'

'Would you like to shave your face every day?'

She shook her head.

'It's freaking you out a bit, isn't it?' He held her gaze and her stomach did a strange floppy thing it never usually did when Ben looked at her. She looked away.

'No! Okay, I'm surprised, but it's not freaking me out, I just need time to get used to it.'

'You hate it, don't you?' he asked again.

She considered her answer. She didn't hate it, it really suited him. But he didn't look like the Ben she knew.

Which was ridiculous, because she did know him. Very well. She'd spent hours and hours in his company, talking, laughing.

Now, he looked like someone she'd swipe right for.

She would have to get past these strange new feelings because he was her best friend. After her parents, he was probably the most important person in the world to her and she wasn't about to ruin that with a silly crush.

She sought his eyes out. They, at least, were familiar, unchanged by his trip to the barber. She looked deep into them, blue and bright. Only now she saw that they were the same brilliant blue as the water the ferry was cutting across. With flecks of emerald the same colour as the lush greenery that seemed to cling to every spare surface on the island.

Locking gazes with hers, his irises suddenly opened with a flash, wide and seemingly large enough to look into her soul and read her mind.

Ben's eyes are gorgeous.

Oh, no.

That was not a thought she wanted him to read.

She looked down. Had his eyes always looked like this or had the Bali sun transformed them, brightening the blues and bringing out the occasional shards of tropical green?

What was going on with her?

'You do hate it. It's okay, you can say.'

'No, I don't hate it at all,' she said honestly. If it hadn't already been so hot, her face would have felt warm. 'I'm just getting used to it.'

That was all. By tomorrow, he'd be just Ben again. And her stomach would have stopped being so damned flippy. Her body temperature would be back under control.

It was a half-hour ferry ride over to the island they were staying on, Nusa Lembongan, just off the coast of Bali. They were greeted by a man in a small truck, who took their bags. He pointed to the bench seat and motioned for them to climb in.

Charlotte eyed the truck and Ben explained, 'There are no cars on the island, just some of these small trucks for transporting goods or tourists to their hotels.'

'If there are no cars, how will we get around?'

'Walk. Motorbike. Cycle.'

Charlotte flinched. She didn't cycle. She certainly didn't motorcycle. Not since Tim's accident.

'It's okay,' Ben said, sensing her fears. 'The villa is close to restaurants and cafes and everything else we need is certainly within walking distance.'

Ben was right, the truck only drove them a short distance from the ferry dock, up a low hill to their accommodation. They passed through a village, which was filled with numerous cafes and food stalls, and her worries about having to cycle her way around the island abated.

They were dropped off at a group of villas that Ben's mother had booked for the wedding guests. Walking into their villa was like stepping into a celebrity's Instagram feed.

Her room had a high wooden ceiling, like a tropical hut. The walls were made of glass and slid open to give the effect of the entire room being open to the ocean, which glistened vivid aqua blue below.

Just like Ben's eyes.

She closed her eyes and shook the thought away. She just needed a proper night's sleep. Once she had adjusted to the time zone...

Charlotte pushed open another door and found herself standing next to an infinity pool and across the pool Ben stood in his room, also staring, slack jawed, at the view.

'Oh, wow...' She exhaled.

Purple flowers climbed up the walls, a small table was laid out with a water jug, dripping with condensation, and next to it was a bowl of tropical fruit. For eating or decoration, Charlotte wasn't sure.

She stepped out of her room and onto the deck that adjoined both their rooms. 'This is amazing. Can we move here?'

'Sure.'

'You're joking, but I'm not,' she replied. 'I think you're going to have to pick me up and carry me home. I don't ever want to leave this place.'

'You might change your mind when you meet my family.' His jaw tightened and she could almost hear the sound of his teeth clenching, enamel on enamel.

It was strange, being able to see the muscles in Ben's face and neck react in a way she hadn't before. What else had she missed about him? What else had she failed to see in the man who was supposed to be her closest friend?

She shook her head. 'Unless they're serial killers, this place is still worth it.'

There was a knock at the door.

'Speaking of which.'

'Who is it?'

'I'm guessing it's the family.'

Ben drew a resigned breath and she wanted to reach over and squeeze his arm, but he turned and moved towards the door before she could.

Charlotte heard a middle-aged Australian woman cry, 'Benji, sweetheart, I'm so glad you're here.'

Benji. She smirked. She was never going to let him forget that. She took a big breath and pressed her hand against her stomach, which was suddenly jumping with nerves, though she wasn't sure why. She wasn't worried, she was just curious to finally meet Ben's mother.

Charlotte moved to the living room of the villa. Ben's mother held him in a tight hug, then pulled back so she could look at him properly.

'Oh, thank goodness you've shaved off that awful beard,' she said, and patted his face.

Charlotte stood by, shifting from foot to foot, feeling like an intruder watching the family reunion.

Diane clearly adored her son.

Ben turned and, spotting Charlotte, said, 'Mum, this is my friend Charlotte.'

Was it her imagination or did he stress the word 'friend'? As if there was no way she could ever be his *girl*friend.

Girlfriend.

The nerve-endings in her belly did another dance. This time a vigorous Charleston.

Before she could step forward, Diane let go of Ben and moved over to her.

'At last! The lovely Charlotte!' Diane held her hand out, and Charlotte lifted hers, expecting a shake, but Diane pulled her into a hug that smelled of Chanel N°5.

'I'm so glad to finally meet you.'

'Me too,' Charlotte replied into Diane's hair.

Diane was beautiful. It shouldn't have been a surprise—after all, Ben was not unattractive, especially since he'd lost his scraggly beard and cut his hair.

'Thank you so much for inviting me. And for this.' Charlotte spread her hands around.

'No, thank you. Thank you for coming and for bringing my prodigal son.'

Charlotte looked at the floor. Diane's comment was sincere; it was clear she knew Ben had taken some convincing to come.

'It's so beautiful.'

'Isn't it? I'm so happy here. Get changed and unpacked, then come and meet Gus. Will and Summer don't get here until tomorrow, so tonight it's just us.'

'Summer?' Ben asked.

'Yes, Will's girlfriend.'

'Will has a girlfriend? Will Watson?'

His mother swatted the air. 'Oh, don't be ridiculous. You know Summer, they've been together for years.'

Charlotte got the impression that Ben most definitely did not know Summer. The two brothers were more estranged than she had realised.

CHAPTER THREE

CHARLOTTE WAS RELIEVED to take off her London clothes and have a refreshing shower following the flight. She chose a light white cotton dress for dinner, and, once dressed, studied herself in the mirror. Her hair had doubled in size in the humidity, and she was unaccustomed to the volume. She tied it into a loose braid to keep it off her face and slipped on a pair of sandals.

She walked to the living area and found Ben waiting. He'd showered and changed as well, into blue shorts and a loose white shirt.

Ben in shorts.

His legs were more tanned than a Londoner's had a right to be in October, as if he couldn't quite shake his Australianness, even after all those years. The top few buttons of his shirt were also undone, giving her a view of much more of Ben's skin than she was accustomed to.

Not that it mattered. It was no big deal at all.

He must have read her thoughts because he rubbed his chin. 'I know, I know. I'll grow it back after the wedding.'

She stepped up to him and said, 'No.' Then, without thinking to stop and wonder if her gesture would be inappropriate, she did what she'd wanted to do since he'd first picked her up all those hours ago outside her flat. She lifted her index finger and touched his cheek. It was no longer freshly shaven, and with a smattering of stubble it felt like a fine sandpaper—rough, but far from unpleasant. She dragged her fingertip across it to get the full effect.

'No,' she repeated. 'Don't.'

For the second time in as many hours they locked eyes. The crease between his eyes deepened and he narrowed his gaze with a wordless question.

He exhaled, but neither of them moved. Instead, they simply stood at the door, with her finger resting against his chin, for a moment too long.

Finally, Ben turned his head away. 'We'll be late,' he said, his voice ragged.

He coughed and they left.

The restaurant was a ten-minute walk away and it was invigorating to be out and about, seeing this beautiful but unfamiliar place. Over the water, back towards Bali, the sun was setting into one of the most magnificent sunsets she'd seen in her life. The entire sky was lit up in pinks, oranges, purples. Not for the first time since their arrival they both stopped, awestruck by the view in front of them.

'I thought I knew what a sunset was. I was wrong. Have you seen a sunset like this?'

'Never. I want to paint it.'

She smiled. That was so Ben.

His work was his life. That was probably why he didn't want to date poor Julie. Or Kitty. Or any of Charlotte's friends. He was just too focused on his career. The answer to the question she'd been asking herself since London was as simple as that.

As well as the lack of facial hair, there was something else different about Ben tonight. And it wasn't as pleasant.

He was anxious. Stretched tighter than a new canvas, ready to tear.

For once, she had the strange sensation of feeling as if he

was relying on her to be the strong one, rather than the other way around. She needed to be calm for him.

In London he was a self-contained unit. Strong, always emotionally stable. Here she saw a quality in him she hadn't noticed before. Hesitation. Uncertainty.

Vulnerability.

When they reached the door to the restaurant, he stopped.

Ben was about to meet his new stepfather. The man that would marry his mother in less than a week. It was enough to make anyone pause.

She took his hand and squeezed it. It wasn't a gesture she made often but tonight demanded it. She wanted him to know she was there for him, as he'd always been there for her.

'We can turn around and go back, if you like?' She knew he wouldn't agree, but she wanted him to know it was an option.

'She's marrying this guy. What if he's awful?'

'Why would you think that?'

Ben didn't answer.

Because his father had been. Because his father had been difficult and overbearing and what if Diane had chosen another man just like him?

'If he's awful, we'll leave.'

'We can't do that.'

'No, you're right. But if he's really awful we'll just drink more. And we'll have more to talk about later.'

A smile crept over his lips.

'If he's nice, we'll have nothing to make fun of.'

He squeezed her hand but didn't let it go. She squeezed back and they entered.

Charlotte was more curious to meet Gus than she wanted to admit. Ben was nervous, but that didn't mean that she had to be. She was an objective bystander. Besides, she intended to get to the bottom of the surprising relationship between Gus and Diane. She was less intrigued by the age gap and more about why Diane had decided to remarry so soon after the death of her husband. Would Gus be a sleaze preying on a vulnerable woman? Or a gold-digger?

They were both about to find out.

Diane and her partner were standing by the bamboo bar when Charlotte and Ben entered, but they noticed them straight away.

Gus was good-looking and appeared more mature than his forty-seven years, with salt-and-pepper hair and a healthy tan.

He smiled broadly and confidently when he saw them enter. He used both of his hands to shake Ben's and kissed Charlotte on both cheeks.

Their table was on the deck, overlooking the water, and the brilliant sunset provided the backdrop.

'Gus knows this place well. Are you happy for him to order for us?' Diane asked.

'Do you like your food spicy?' Gus asked them both.

They nodded, but with trepidation. Everyone's definition of spicy differed. Gus ordered, speaking Indonesian.

'Most locals speak Balinese,' Diane whispered, 'but many speak Bahasa Indonesian and English too. Gus just spoke Bahasa.' There was a hint of pride in her voice.

Gus and the waiter shared a joke that no one else understood. He seemed to be on good terms with the staff.

The food was delicious and thankfully the waiters kept bringing cold beers. Charlotte preferred wine but Gus assured her that with spicy food beer was the best option. He wasn't wrong.

Plates of satay and rice weighed down the table and her mouth watered. The food was delicious and Gus was proving to be a good host. A positive tick in Charlotte's list.

With Ben clearly finding the situation strange, Charlotte

felt overly obliged to help carry the conversation. It was one of the reasons she'd come, after all, to be the lubricant and peacemaker in these awkward meetings.

But making conversation with Diane and Gus wasn't an effort at all.

Gus was ready to talk and, as part of her mission to subtly find out whether he was good enough for Diane, she quizzed him. He had lived an interesting life: he'd made a small fortune by the time he was thirty developing several computer programs in the tech boom at the turn of the millennium, but had then moved on to mentoring young entrepreneurs and had established a series of annual symposiums on all sorts of emerging technologies and ideas.

Gus was impressive, charming, and Charlotte could see why Diane had fallen for him. He was also mature and intelligent, and Charlotte could see why he'd be drawn to an older, but no less impressive woman, like Diane.

Gus was also making an extra effort to talk to Ben.

'I love your work, Ben.'

Charlotte felt Ben stiffen next to her.

'You do? Where have you seen it?'

'Will has one of your pieces in his office.'

'I don't think so,' Ben said.

'I'm sure of it. It's the ocean and a beach in the distance. From the point of view of a swimmer. It's so big.' Gus stretched out his hands.

Ben looked to Diane for confirmation, but she was suddenly busy beckoning the waiter. Charlotte didn't recall a painting of Ben's that would fit that description, but maybe it was one of his earlier works.

'Why choose Bali for the wedding?' Charlotte asked, changing the subject as it was obviously making Ben uncomfortable.

'We met here.'

Diane picked up Gus's hand. 'A year ago. At one of Gus's symposiums. I wanted to learn more about ocean waste management for our company, and Gus had organised a series of lectures on ocean conservation.'

Ocean waste management?

If you could be attracted to someone talking about that, it must be love, Charlotte thought.

'And it's one of the most beautiful places in the world, don't you think?' Gus asked Charlotte but he was looking at Diane.

'He does a lot of work for an NGO here. He won't tell you that, because he's too modest, but I'm allowed to,' Diane said.

Diane looked radiant. Her shiny grey hair was cut into a stylish bob and her skin was soft and fresh. The couple only had eyes for one another.

Watching them together over dinner, Charlotte had no doubts that Diane's feelings for Gus were real. And Gus clearly adored Diane and was not in need of her fortune.

Watching the pair of them made Charlotte believe that there was such a thing as soul mates. Two people so perfectly matched, two halves of the same soul.

She missed having that connection with someone, longed for it in her chest.

It was a concept she hadn't allowed herself to think about for years. Because if there was only one soul mate for everyone then hers had gone. Would it ever be possible to find someone else? Even if it was, did she want that?

She couldn't let herself get as close to someone as she'd been to Tim.

If she'd lost one soul mate, there was every chance she could lose another.

Charlotte was quiet as they walked back to their villa.

Or maybe she wasn't speaking because she knew he couldn't. The trip, the dinner, the whole day had left him tired in his bones. And then, to top it all off, there was that strange moment with Charlotte before dinner when she had stroked his face.

She'd slid her finger from his cheekbone to his chin and he'd felt every single one of the grooves in her fingerprint. Two hours and several beers later, he could still feel her touch like a burn.

He could tell his new look was throwing her; she looked at him as if he were a stranger. It hadn't been his intention to unsettle anyone. He had simply decided it was time for a change, something that would be more comfortable in the heat. There was something new in her eyes though. An intensity he'd never seen before.

Was it desire?

No. That couldn't be it. Charlotte was most definitely not attracted to him, and the absence of a beard wasn't going to change that.

Charlotte was not remotely superficial—just one look at the eccentric line-up of men she'd dated in the past few years proved that. The barrier between her and a committed relationship was much greater than just some facial hair. It was a dead boyfriend she wasn't over and an unshakable fear of falling for anyone else.

They walked the path through the lush undergrowth back to their villa. It rustled with unseen nocturnal animals.

'Are there snakes here?' she asked.

'Um… I'm not sure.'

She moved closer to him, and their shoulders bumped and for a moment her bare forearm brushed against his. At least in London when that happened one of them was likely to be wearing sleeves. Now her skin collided with his, soft and silky, strangely intimate.

He laughed to hide the fact that he'd really rather enjoyed the brief skin-to-skin contact. 'So it's okay for the python to attack me?'

'You're bigger. It'll take longer to wrap itself around you.'

As they reached the villa she said, 'So, we're safely out of earshot now. Tell me, what did you think of him?'

Ah, Gus. He'd managed to avoid that conversation for ten whole minutes. Ben's thoughts and feelings were colliding; he wasn't sure exactly what he thought. Even less about what he felt.

'He seems fine.'

'Fine. What a great review.'

'I just met him. That's all I've got. I'm happy for them, really.'

Gus did seem like a good guy, and Ben hadn't spotted any red flags—and he was certainly looking for them. Gus had only taken his eyes off Diane to respond to Charlotte's intense questioning. What did he do? Where did he grow up? What did he study? What were his hobbies? Favourite foods? Charlotte could have made Gus her mastermind topic after the evening was out, but Ben was grateful to her for handling the cross-examination because Ben couldn't ask those questions of Gus without appearing to be mistrustful or disapproving. Coming from Charlotte the questions seemed like nothing more than natural curiosity.

Ben was no longer ambivalent about Charlotte's presence, he was downright grateful. She'd been the one to nudge him through the doorway of the restaurant and having her beside him all evening had made him feel calm and centred. She had talked about herself too, and her gallery. The conversation had flowed smoothly and naturally.

Meeting your mother's new fiancé wasn't necessarily one of the most stressful situations in a person's life—Ben had certainly been through worse—but it was still unsettling and he was grateful Charlotte had been there to hold his hand.

Quite literally.

Ben flexed his fingers now.

Holding hands at that moment had felt so natural he only now reflected on the fact that it wasn't something they usually did.

It had felt nice. He rubbed his hands together, shaking off the sensation. Holding hands wasn't something friends did. Even good friends as they were.

'Ben, really. It's okay, we can talk about it.'

Ben sighed. 'I don't have a problem with the marriage.'

'I know.'

Ben slipped the key card out of his pocket and unlocked the door to their villa. They stepped inside.

'I don't care that he's younger.'

'Good.'

'I don't care that he's good-looking.' He put the key card down on the table with a little too much force.

She laughed. 'Ben, it's okay.'

Charlotte reached over and wrapped her hand around his forearm. His skin prickled. He wanted her to rub his arm. He longed to feel the friction between their skin.

'It's okay to find this situation weird. It wouldn't matter who she was marrying, it's the fact it's happening so soon after your father's passing. You're allowed to be sad about your father. You're allowed to have mixed emotions.'

He looked down at her hand, warm against his forearm. She rubbed her thumb against the soft skin under his arm, probably just to reassure him, but sparks shot through him. It was an effort to focus on the conversation. What was going on between them? Bali was having a strange effect on them both.

With effort he brought his thoughts back to the conversation and away from wondering what it would feel like if he too lifted his hand and stroked her arm...

'I don't want her to think I'm not supportive.'

'She doesn't think that. She's just glad you're here. That you've come. I don't think she wants to upset you either.'

'Dad was difficult; he caused lots of tension in my life and I never truly felt that he loved me. So I am glad she's found someone.'

Charlotte nodded.

'And he seems like a good guy. But that's all I've got.'

It was the truth. Jet lag, dinner and the beers were all catching up with him. There was an uneasiness inside him he couldn't place, but he knew it likely had to do with the woman in front of him. Stroking his arm with her soft thumb.

But now was not the time to try and analyse it.

Charlotte let go of his arm but leaned in and wrapped him into a hug. He leaned into it. He could ponder later on what was going on in Charlotte's mind. Right now, he was grateful for the touch, the support. Her warmth.

'Thank you for being here,' he said into her hair. She still smelt of London, of her shampoo. Of roses.

'I wouldn't have missed it.'

When they pulled apart, she stood on her toes and lifted her face to his.

'Goodnight,' she said, and kissed him. It was meant to be on the cheek, he was sure, but the kiss landed half on his cheek and partly on his mouth. An accidental brush was all it was, but he had tasted her lips. The last of her lip gloss, the beer she'd had with dinner, the salt from the light sweat that skimmed her skin. He brushed his tongue over his bottom lip, tasting her again. She turned and walked to her room, leaving him standing there, watching her go, wondering for the umpteenth time that night: what was going on with Charlotte?

Charlotte woke some hours later, drenched with sweat and wide awake even though it was still dark outside. The last thing she remembered from the day before was accidentally almost kissing Ben on the lips before stumbling to her room and falling into bed.

Accidentally, almost.

The edge of her mouth had touched the edge of his, enough that the sensitive nerve endings on her lips had felt the softness of his. The memory made her lips tingle and she touched them with her fingertip.

The same fingertip that had also stroked Ben's smooth cheek the day before as well. It was just a beard! Why was its absence making such a difference in the way she looked at Ben?

Steamy Bali was doing strange things to her brain. She and Ben were not casual kissing or hugging friends. On regular days, if he dropped into the gallery or if she popped over to his place for a meal, they'd greet one another with a wave. Ben wasn't overly demonstrative, and she understood that; he was Australian, she was British, neither nationality known for unrestrained shows of emotion.

On the few occasions they had kissed casually on cheeks— birthdays, celebrations and the like—it had been quick and his prickly beard had always been in the way.

This time was different. For starters, his prickly beard was gone, leaving only smooth, bare skin and exposed soft lips.

It had clearly been a mistake, a misjudged movement, a kiss on the cheek that had missed. These things happened. They didn't mean anything. She knew, beyond doubt, that Ben had not tried to kiss her.

Charlotte ran her tongue over her lips.

But what would it be like to kiss him properly? Not accidentally.

She shook the thought away as soon as it came to her.

Not Ben. She couldn't kiss *Ben*.

Ben was her friend, her rock. Her confidant. The person who cooked her dinner when she couldn't be bothered. The person who she could call, day and night, in any emergency. The person she could speak to about almost anything. Who would cheer her up when things inevitably turned sour with Ben, if not Ben?

Her parents and girlfriends had long since stopped being useful counsellors in relation to relationships. They couldn't understand why she just couldn't settle down with someone already.

It's been seven years, they would say. *Surely you're over Tim by now.*

The last part was implied, rather than spoken aloud, but it always hung in the air any time she'd mention that a date hadn't gone well or that she'd ended a nascent relationship.

Ben didn't judge her for all the false starts. Never implied Charlotte's standards were too high, as everyone else had.

'I think they have a club,' Kitty had joked once. 'The three dates with Charlotte Reid club. They'd like to say it's exclusive, but it's not.' Her friends had fallen over themselves with laughter in the wine bar at that one. From then on Charlotte had reserved discussion about her dates for Ben only.

Ben understood: he knew she just hadn't found the right person.

Sometimes she felt that she was getting there. She'd meet a man and he'd seem lovely and kind and then she'd imagine what their future might look like and that was usually the point at which things would start to unravel. Occasionally she might wonder if he could be the type of man she'd like to see more of, and this was harder, as when she imagined herself falling for him she'd be gripped with a type of fear and Tim would intrude into her thoughts more than ever. Tim when they first met, but also Tim in the hospital. Because was this new man worth the heartache? Would he be worth the pain? Or the worry? Maybe it was just better to end things and move on instead. Easier. Simpler.

Charlotte threw off the single sheet that had covered her

in the warm night and walked over to the window. The sky was still resolutely dark.

But it wasn't rainy, like London. Today would be a clear, bright day.

Unlike that day, a decade ago.

The details had taken for ever to emerge. First the phone call saying Tim had been in an accident, but not to worry. Then at the hospital, where the nurses had met her with solemn faces. Then finally, tense discussions with the doctors and Tim's parents.

Multiple fractures, internal bleeding. Long surgeries and ICU stays. Their initial fears gradually gave way to optimism, but then a roller coaster of emotions tossed her around physically and mentally. One day they might be planning rehabilitation, the next they were discussing nursing homes. Some days he was conscious and lucid, other days the pain was so much they kept him sedated.

Days turned to weeks and one day she was surprised to come out of the hospital and find that it was spring. And then he was gone. She still marvelled that even after all those months it was a shock when he passed. Marvelled at the fact that one moment he could be there, everyone discussing the next round of treatment and rehabilitation, and the next he was gone.

Charlotte dropped out of her teaching course, realising that, without Tim, she didn't want to lead the life that they had planned. And she looked back to her first love: art.

Life was too short to make conservative choices. Her dream job—the one she'd never believed she could do—was as a curator. Now, feeling strangely free and unburned by planning for a shared future with Tim, she dreamed even bigger—owning her own gallery.

She studied and she worked and she didn't stop to rest, living her life enough for two people.

With that thought, Charlotte decided to start her day. The clock on her phone showed five a.m. but her body clock was on a totally different time zone. And she was warm already. She decided to go for a swim.

Charlotte floated on her back, holding herself up with long lazy strokes and looking up at the sky, still dark blue but getting lighter. The strange, unfamiliar constellations were fading. This place was magical. Relaxing, sublime. Otherworldly. Something caught her eye, and she flipped upright. Ben stood on the patio rubbing his eyes.

'Sorry, I didn't mean to interrupt,' he said.

'You're not interrupting anything. I'm just cooling down. I'm sorry if I woke you.'

Ben was wearing boxers and a black T-shirt. His pyjamas. She'd never seen him in his pyjamas.

He's never seen you in a bikini.

Ben shifted from foot to foot and looked as if he was about to leave. This was silly. They'd be sharing a villa for a week; they'd have to get used to seeing one another with fewer clothes on. She swam over to the edge of the pool and lifted herself out. She turned her body and sat on the edge, dangling her legs in the water. She patted the space next to her. He looked around, but then joined her by the pool.

She looked down at her bikini-clad body. Was that why he couldn't meet her eyes? He was always a gentleman, she reminded herself, but they were on the equator and the temperature hadn't dropped below twenty-five degrees since they'd arrived.

'I take it you didn't sleep well,' he said.

'I did at first, but once I woke, I couldn't get back to sleep. You?'

'Same. We should probably try and get out in the sun today, get our body clocks to adjust.'

'Sure, what's on the agenda?'

'We're meant to have dinner with my family this evening, but nothing before that. We could go to Ubud, check out the crafts.'

Ubud was a town in the hills on the main island of Bali, known for its art scene. She wanted to go, but, after travelling around the world yesterday, she also longed to get her bearings just where they were.

'I'm happy to stay on the island and just explore here,' she said.

'Let's do that. I'm still adjusting to the time zone and, honestly, this place is just beautiful.'

Their feet dangled in the water and the last of the moonlight danced over the surface of the pool. She kicked gently back and forth and watched the ripples on the surface.

Her gaze slid over to his legs, bare and also gently kicking the water.

Her eyes travelled up from his big feet to his knees, which were covered in a light smattering of hair and a few drops of water. Without her realising what she was doing, her gaze travelled higher, to his shorts. His hands covered his groin. It was a strange posture to adopt; her hands were planted on the tiles behind her, which was much more comfortable than the pose Ben was in.

Why would he...? Unless?

No. Ben didn't think of her like that. They'd spent thousands of hours together over the years and he'd never reacted to her like *that* before.

But you've never been sitting next to him dripping wet in a bikini before.

Since that awkward and accidental kiss goodnight she'd been hyper-aware of her lips. Even now. She pressed them together.

The look he gave her asked, *What's the matter?*

And she couldn't answer him. She couldn't lie and tell him that nothing was the matter, because there was no denying something wasn't right. But she didn't have the first idea how to put it into words.

Ben was sitting there with his hands protectively over his crotch and she was wondering what it would be like to kiss him. That was what was going on.

But why? Were they different in Bali? Ben was sexy in Bali. There, she'd acknowledged it. Beardless Ben was sexy as hell.

She hadn't changed though. She hadn't shaved off a beard or transformed her appearance in any way, so why was he suddenly attracted to her?

It was the southern hemisphere and more than one thing was upside down.

'I think they'll deliver us breakfast soon,' he said.

'Yes, that's what they said.'

This conversation couldn't get any more prosaic.

'It looks like the weather will be nice today,' he said.

Wait, no, it could.

She turned to him, drew a deep breath and was about to say, 'What's going on?' when their gazes locked. She stared into the deep blue depths of his eyes, noticed the dark flecks that lay deep within. The sparks that danced across the surface.

She should look away; she didn't. Instead, her gaze dropped slightly lower, to his lips. Dusty pink, full. Her own tingled again.

He pressed his lips together, oh, so gently. Wetting them.

Before she realised what she was doing, she mirrored the gesture.

Oh.

Bali Ben was different. Bali Charlotte was too.

Slowly, as though testing the temperature of the water, she

lifted her hand to his face. Instead of simply feeling the new smoothness of his skin, she placed her whole palm against his cheek. He didn't move. Didn't flinch, just kept his eyes on hers, let her lead the way. She splayed her fingers, discovered how his cheek felt against her palm. His eyes didn't waver, though his lids became heavier. She slid her fingers across his temple and into his now short hair. It was soft, smooth, just like his cheek.

It was ridiculous, touching him like this, and for a moment she wondered if in her jet-lagged state she was actually still asleep. The sky was now a lighter blue. The colour of Ben's eyes.

If you'd asked her a week ago what colour Ben's eyes were, she would have said blue-grey. Now they were the colour of a tropical lagoon. The Northern Lights. A magnificent opal.

This was madness.

She took her hand from his face but in a flash his hand rose and held hers in place.

Don't stop, said the eyes that were the colour of a Bali sky at sunrise.

He was still, almost as though he weren't breathing, and reflexively she held her breath too.

She was looking so closely into his eyes she felt she might fall into them, their mouths close enough for her to see each crease in his pink lips, each pore in his skin. His newly bare, smooth skin.

She dragged her hand down to his chin, tilted it slightly and leaned in. She closed her eyes but their mouths still found their way to one another's. Her lips pressed lightly on his, but neither of them moved further, each waiting a moment to see what the other would do. She parted her lips ever so slightly, enough to excite a spark of friction between them, setting off nerve cells through her body. Finally, his mouth opened and his tongue slid gently across hers. His kiss was slow and measured, yet still had the effect of igniting sparks through her body. He tasted faintly of mint, but otherwise the taste was new, unexpected. He tasted of Ben and she liked it. Needing more, she opened her mouth and fell completely, wholly, irretrievably into the kiss.

Ben collapsed into the kiss. It was everything. Like a guilty dream but so much more because this wasn't happening during an early morning REM cycle, he was fairly sure this was happening in real life. Charlotte was kissing him.

Out of nowhere.

Charlotte was kissing him. And no longer tentatively. Their mouths were wide open, tongues entangled. Her hands were wandering over his T-shirt, his down her bare shoulders.

He hadn't meant to react like that to the sight of Charlotte in the bikini, but it was morning and she was gorgeous, and he had some control over his body but not that much. His insides were slowly igniting, like a flame licking at paper, then catching on something more substantial.

But why? What had changed? The beard, maybe, but that couldn't be it. Or had it been him? Had his obvious physical reaction to her red bikini given too much away? No, it wasn't just the beard standing between him and Charlotte and a long and wonderful life together. It was much more than that. Because Charlotte wasn't ready. Charlotte wasn't over Tim. Charlotte dumped every man she dated after a few dates.

Charlotte did not mean to be doing this.

Once Ben's brain was in gear, his mouth froze. Charlotte's lips quickly copied his reaction. Their mouths remained touching, locked but unmoving. As if that would change anything. Finally, she pulled back.

'Um…' Ben muttered, forgetting every word he'd ever known.

'Yes—um… I'm sorry,' she said.

'Don't be,' he replied quickly. 'That was nice.'

Nice! Are you describing a cup of coffee? It was amazing. Life-changing.

'Actually, it was more than nice,' he added.

Charlotte looked down shyly, but he could see the smile on her face. 'It was, wasn't it?'

He needed to stay calm. He needed to make sure that whatever he said next didn't panic her and send her running. Then he looked down at Charlotte in her red bikini and God help him. He'd always been careful about not letting his eyes linger too long on her low necklines, knowing that it was a line he shouldn't cross, but no, in his current state of arousal, it took every drop of his self-control to drag his eyes back up to hers. It was even harder to find the right words to say next.

He had to take this slowly, carefully. As if he were holding the finest glass. He had to make sure she wouldn't freak out.

He put his hands back between his legs, covering his lap. He was trembling, the sensation of Charlotte's mouth on his still vibrating through him. He also had to make sure *he* didn't freak out.

'Ben?'

'Yes.'

He looked up from his lap and back to her. Her eyes were wide with concern.

He opened his mouth to ask her what was wrong but before the words were out her lips were back on his. Warm and wet and asking the only question he wanted to hear.

Yes was his answer. A thousand times, yes.

Her lips were silken and tender and she tasted like Charlotte. Like the scent that surrounded her, like the way his apartment smelt when she left it. But best of all, the kiss was like continuing the conversation they had started the day they first met. Natural, sharing, mutual. He slipped his fingers into her hair and she pressed herself against him. The world dropped away. This was his entire existence.

Breathless, they both pulled away, panting. She leaned against him and he held her as they caught their breaths.

'I'm sorry, again. I don't know what's come over me.' She ran her hands over her hair, her cheeks were flushed and her lips pleasingly plump.

'Don't apologise,' he said gruffly.

If only, instead of deciding that he would never kiss Charlotte, he'd happened to imagine what might happen if he ever did, he'd have had a plan for this moment and wouldn't be floundering now for the right words.

Because he wanted her. He wanted to kiss her again.

More importantly of all, he didn't want her to run.

A first kiss—their first kiss—wasn't the finish line; it was the beginning of the race. He was now simply lined up at the starting line with all the other men she'd dated.

He was just like Don and the rest, waiting for his Dear John text message. Or worse, waiting for her to hop and skip out of here and onto the next flight out of Denpasar. No. He wasn't going to be like Don or the other men because he knew her.

And that meant also knowing that Charlotte wasn't over Tim. And knowing, as he knew the back of his own hand, that Charlotte was going to self-sabotage any new relationship because of it.

'You're my best friend. And I don't want that ever to change,' he said.

She looked down and nodded. 'Yes, that's right. Sensible.'

'Don't get me wrong, the kiss was great, but…'

'Yes, I know. Our friendship. I don't know what came over me.'

'So you're not going to freak out?' he asked, knowing that simply by saying that she might.

'I'm not freaking out.'

Not yet.

'I didn't mean... I know you're not.'

'And you shouldn't freak out either.'

'I'm completely calm.'

Charlotte laughed and picked up his hand. It was still shaking. 'No, you're not. If anyone's freaking out it's you.' She pressed his hand between both of hers.

Oh, God. Her hand was as steady as a surgeon's whereas he looked as if he had a tremor. He snatched it away and put it back in his lap to cover the other obvious giveaway about exactly what sort of physiological reactions were going on in his body.

There was a knock at the door and Ben jumped up to answer it. Whoever it was had impeccable timing and he would have to remember to thank them.

When he remembered his own name.

He smiled broadly at the man who was delivering them the breakfast of fresh fruits, bread and hot, steaming coffee, which Ben had ordered the night before.

Thank goodness he'd had the foresight to do that. Hopefully a large cup of caffeine would help him figure out what on earth to do and say next.

CHAPTER FOUR

CHARLOTTE'S KNEES TREMBLED as she stood and went to her room.

She noticed the plants, the white couch, the painting of the jungle on the wall. Everything seemed sharper. Brighter.

Ben. She'd kissed Ben.

She'd kissed her best friend. And it had been wonderful.

Until, that was, it had become weird and more than a little uncomfortable.

You're my best friend. And I don't want that ever to change.

That meant he didn't want it to happen again. The message was loud and clear. She'd kissed him, without warning and without thinking, and possibly jeopardised their entire relationship in the process. He'd taken it well—he'd even, she suspected, enjoyed the kiss—but that was as far as his feelings went.

She was such a fool.

In her room, Charlotte's hands shook as she took off her wet bikini. They still shook as she turned on the shower.

They couldn't even blame alcohol; they'd both been sober.

Jet lag, that must be it. Though was that even a thing? Did people do crazy things just because they were a bit tired? They might forget where they put their keys. They didn't forget that one wasn't supposed to kiss one's best friend.

Maybe she'd just wanted to kiss Ben. Maybe it was as simple and true as that, she thought as she let the warm water wash over her.

No, that couldn't have been it, there was nothing simple about what had just happened. They'd known one another for years, spent countless hours in one another's company and she'd never felt like this before. No, it was something else. And she had better figure out what it was before it happened again.

You're my best friend and I don't want that ever to change.

Ben was sensible. She didn't want to ruin their friendship either. Ben was...well, he was her closest friend. He made her laugh. News—good or bad—wasn't real until she told Ben.

She didn't want anything to change either. Especially not over something as insignificant as an impulsive kiss.

Even a really, really good kiss.

Charlotte dressed for exploring, in denim shorts and a T-shirt. The sun was fully above the horizon by the time she emerged, hesitantly, from her room.

Breakfast had been laid out on the deck, including fresh coffee, which she jumped on as though her life depended on it, and the most magnificent fruit platter she'd ever seen. Ben was nowhere to be seen, leaving her to look at the view alone. The fruit didn't taste quite as good without him. And certainly not with the worry about the kiss looming over her.

Surely one wasn't meant to feel like this about a kiss. Excited. Turned on. Joyful. Those were the emotions a kiss should elicit.

Not worry and a feeling of impending doom.

Exploring. That was what they were going to do today. As if everything were completely normal and nothing had changed. As if the kiss had been an early morning dream, gone with the sunlight. As if her heart weren't still racing.

But, she reasoned, they had to pretend that nothing had

happened. If they could just get through today, put her reckless actions behind them, then they would be okay. They had to be okay. For the sake of their friendship.

She waited what seemed like an age for Ben to come out of his room. She was about to knock when his door finally opened, revealing Ben, who waved and smiled and looked as though it were any other day.

'Shall we?' He pointed to the door.

She nodded. He was wearing a pair of shorts that came to above his knee and a slim-fitting blue T-shirt.

To match his eyes.

Oh, Charlotte, really? This is Ben, not some guy you met on the apps.

She had to stop ogling him.

She certainly had to stop thinking about the kiss. With that thought her finger flew to her tingling lips and touched them. Just as it did, Ben turned to look at her.

Caught.

He was going to think she was obsessed with him, and he wouldn't be too far wrong.

They left their villa and wandered down the coast. With every corner the view changed, from beautiful beaches to a village, to rugged limestone cliffs.

Nusa Lembongan was surprisingly hilly, and they made their way slowly up to one of the villages and explored a local food market and a Hindu temple, but, despite the new and interesting sights and the beautiful stone temple, their conversation was stilted and forced.

'It's magical.'

'Yes. Really pretty.'

Last week in London they had used words such as 'prepossessing', 'exquisite' and 'beguiling'. Now the best she could come up with was 'pretty'?

You can't push things, she told herself.

Something unusual had happened this morning, but things between them would get back to normal. They just needed to give it time.

They needed an activity, something to distract them both. As they emerged from the temple and put their shoes back on, they were approached by a young boy who handed her a pamphlet. Kayaking in the mangrove swamp. That was an activity! Something new they could try that would distract them both from the kiss.

Charlotte passed Ben the pamphlet.

'You want to go kayaking?' he asked.

'Maybe. I don't know. I never have.'

'Then let's learn.'

A driver took them the short drive to the north tip of the island and the mangroves, a dense forest of trees and a river that spread in a maze out to the sea.

They were shown to their two-person kayak, lying on the beach beside two paddles.

'Push it into the water and then climb in,' the guide said.

Charlotte slipped off her shoes and Ben pushed the kayak into the shallow water. It wasn't long before she realised the flaw in her magnificent plan to distract themselves—how was she meant to get into the damned thing? She lifted one leg very awkwardly over the side and tried to sit, but the kayak tipped.

She stumbled and Ben had to reach out for her to prevent her from ending up bottom-first in the water. He caught her with one strong arm and held her effortlessly. Her heart hit her throat. Instead of thinking about getting into the kayak she only wanted to slide her arms around him and pull him even closer. Strong, steady. Her Ben.

'Okay?' he asked, his hand still holding her and his blue eyes staring into hers.

She could only nod in reply.

'I'll go first,' he said.

Unlike her, Ben climbed in deftly, his muscular legs supporting his graceful movement into the kayak.

His shorts rode up and she could see the muscles defining Ben's strong legs. One more thing he'd been hiding under his heavily clothed London persona.

Ben held the kayak steady with an oar and Charlotte attempted her mount again.

She fell into the kayak with a thump, sending water sloshing over the sides, but thankfully without either of them ending up in the water. Her face burned. One more embarrassing thing to add to today's tally.

Ben manoeuvred the kayak in strong deft strokes, whereas Charlotte's oar hit the water awkwardly more often than not. She probably would have done a much better job if she hadn't been so distracted by the sight of the muscles in Ben's arms flexing and extending as he paddled. Her gaze travelled from the ripples under his T-shirt, past his firm biceps down to the veins in his forearm and hands.

Ben was different in the warm sun of the Java Sea. Half dressed, to be sure, but glowing in the sun. He was strong and capable; showcasing skills she'd never noticed in cold grey London behind a paintbrush or in an art gallery.

Physical.

The word made her mouth dry, even in close on one hundred per cent humidity.

If she wasn't looking at his arms, she was looking at his legs, his strong thighs.

Argh. She shook her head. She'd had way too much sun.

Charlotte tried to focus on what they were gliding past, the tangled roots, birds, and the occasional fish.

But the memory of the kiss floated just beneath the surface of their entire day together.

'It's cooler out here, don't you think?' Ben asked.

Is it? Charlotte wanted to reply. But she kept her mouth shut; the heat she was experiencing wasn't coming from the sky or the water, but the man in front of her in the kayak.

'Hey, are you just relaxing back there? Making me do all the work?'

Charlotte looked down at her hands. They were balancing a motionless oar.

She hadn't been paddling, she'd been concentrating so hard on not looking at Ben she'd forgotten even to row badly.

'Sorry, I was looking for the fish,' she lied.

Had he always had muscles? Did they always ripple when he moved? She was sure she would have noticed such a fine set of biceps before if he had.

To be fair, she didn't have many opportunities to see him do anything as physical as this in London. Sometimes he helped her move a large painting. Or held a door open for her, but hardly ever in a T-shirt. Never when his bare arms were exposed to the sun.

'Fish? Are there fish? Where?'

'Oh, I think I saw some before,' she lied again.

Normal. Everything was completely normal, Ben told himself as the guide dropped them back in the village after the kayaking trip.

They stopped for a late lunch before walking back to the villa. Charlotte had been jumpy earlier that morning but seemed calmer now they were sitting on a beach, eating spicy noodles they had bought from a street vendor.

Ben had grown up in Australia, had spent half his childhood at the beach, but the colour of the water here was like nothing he'd seen before. Fishing boats bobbed and the water sparkled.

A small group of people were standing on the beach pointing at something. When the crowd parted, they saw a pod of green turtles making their way slowly into the crystal-clear waters. A few younger, spritely turtles reached the water first, followed by a large, older lumbering one.

'Amazing,' she whispered.

Ben just nodded, captivated.

Even eating a meal together, something they had done countless times before, the conversation between them was limited. Whether it was due to the kiss or something else, he couldn't be sure, but he feared that the kiss had unsettled her completely.

Charlotte panicked at the first sign a relationship was going well.

And at the first sign it was going badly.

So he was stuck. The only thing he could do was to pretend that things were normal and hope that, with the passage of time, they soon would be.

He hadn't gone as far as telling her that they should forget about the kiss as that would insult the intelligence of both of them. Trying to forget was pointless, but agreeing to put it behind them and move on was sensible. At least they had both agreed that they didn't want their friendship to change.

He didn't have the first idea how he was going to navigate the next steps between them.

The first thing was that it shouldn't happen again.

Not because it wasn't good, but because it was *too* good. Kissing Charlotte was not something he trusted himself to give up easily, so he'd never kiss her again if that was the only way of keeping her in his life for ever. Losing her as a friend wasn't an option.

'What are you thinking?' she asked.

'I'm wondering what this colour blue is called.' It was a lie. The water was definitely cerulean but he had to say something that wasn't, 'I was thinking about that kiss we shared this morning, about your lips on mine and how they tasted of peaches and how, in all the years of knowing you, I've never let myself imagine what it would be like to kiss you because I was afraid it would be exactly like that.' There were so many things going through his head right now and almost none of them came under the heading of Things He Could Tell Charlotte.

'Always the artist.'

'The whole place is stunning.'

'Yes, it's so relaxing.'

He looked at her. She thought it was relaxing? It might have been relaxing were it not for the excruciating tension between them.

He'd been so grateful when she'd picked up the kayaking pamphlet, as it gave them something to do. As soon as he got back to the cabin, he'd look up more ways to fill their empty schedule with activities—surfing, cooking classes, trips to Ubud—anything—he didn't care—as long as it kept them busy. And kept their lips far apart.

'I'm glad I came.' She turned to him and smiled.

Her smile felt like a hug and he smiled back. 'I'm glad you did too.'

'I'm so glad to be away from London. I should have been doing this every year. It's so much better to be somewhere else on Tim's anniversary.'

The feeling of pleasure evaporated instantly. It felt as if an elephant had just sat on his chest. An elephant named Tim.

'Well, next year let's go somewhere else, even if my mother isn't getting married,' he said, his mouth dry.

She picked up his hand and squeezed it. 'Thank you for understanding, Ben.'

And just like that, they were friends again. Just friends. This was her way of telling him that the kiss didn't mean anything. That it was just some crazy early morning blip. That was better than her leaving, but he still felt disappointed.

'I know you miss him.' Her hand was still in his and he allowed his thumb to glide just once over the soft skin on the back of it. 'I know this time of year is hard for you, so I'm glad you came too.'

'Yes, but it's strange. It's been so long. I'm not sure if I miss him or the idea of him.'

It was a strange thing to say. 'Charlotte, I know you date. I know you see men. But I also know that you tend to end those relationships before they even get going.'

'I just haven't met the right person, that's all.'

'Have you ever considered that maybe you're not over Tim?'

'I don't think I'll ever be over Tim. But I promised him I'd find someone else.'

Her words flicked something in his chest and his next words came out without thought or planning. 'But how will that be fair to the guy you choose?'

'What do you mean?'

'He'll always be second best to Tim.'

Charlotte stood and brushed invisible crumbs from herself and gathered her things.

'Well, then it's a good thing I haven't committed to anyone else,' she said primly.

He was on dangerous ground, that was clear, but, like a fool, he stumbled forward into unknown and possibly hostile territory. 'I know that you promised him you'd find someone else, but you aren't going to be able to have a new relationship until you're over Tim.'

She shook her head. 'It isn't that. It's just that I haven't found someone who makes me feel the same way.'

Something collapsed inside him. It was as if she'd punched

him, but she was standing two metres away. Why would those words hurt him so much?

'I've never met anyone who gives me that same feeling. Of being swept away. Of violins, fireworks and grand gestures.'

Despite his best effort, Ben laughed. 'Real love's not like that. It's not violins and fireworks.'

Charlotte's face fell and Ben wished his words back.

'What do you know about love?' Charlotte crossed her arms. 'Well, what?'

She was right. What did he know about love? His relationship history was more barren than hers.

He pulled himself up and shrugged. It was the best he could do.

'Tell me,' she prompted again.

He shook his head. Despite being no more an expert in romantic love than Charlotte, he wasn't about to tell her what he thought true love was.

'Please don't lecture me on love when you can't even tell me the last time you were in love.'

'No, Charlotte. I wasn't—'

'Tell me what you think love is,' she insisted.

Standing there, with the sun bouncing off the water and straight into Charlotte's dark eyes, with the warm Bali air swirling around them, he looked at her, took a deep breath and gave it his best.

'Love is small, perfect moments. It's waiting. It's patience. It's being there, even when it hurts. It's forgiveness.'

He turned away and gulped. He had no idea where those words had come from. That that was even what he believed. What did he know about love? He had just picked a fight with his best friend over nothing. The person he cared about most in the world. He was in no position to lecture anyone about love after speaking to her like that. He turned back to apologise to Charlotte, just in time to see her brush a tear from her eye.

'Char, I'm so sorry.'

She waved his apology away.

'No, really, I am. I had no right to speak to you like that.'

'It's fine, really. What did you say about forgiveness?' She smiled weakly.

He was as surprised by his words as Charlotte was. Maybe more so. Patience. Small things. Being there even when it hurt.

She was no longer expecting an answer to her question, but he still tried to answer it himself. The last time he'd had a relationship that had lasted more than a few weeks had been when he lived in New York. He and Maya had had an amicable break-up when he'd decided to leave for London. They still emailed occasionally, and she'd even extended him an invitation to her recent wedding. He liked Maya, but their break-up hadn't left either of them heartbroken.

Who, then?

Instinctively, he looked across at Charlotte. Her mouth was tight, her footfalls a little too hard.

They both knew that was as far as things would ever go, so there was no point in feeling anything else. Less point in taking out the feeling that was causing a tightness in his chest and a heaviness in his gut and examining it in the tropical sunlight.

Yes, he loved Charlotte. Of course he did. But he wasn't in love with her. If things were different, then he might think about whether their relationship could develop further. Whether he would want to kiss her again. And again.

But things were not different, so it didn't matter what he wanted.

They walked the rest of the way back to the villa in silence. It couldn't have taken more than ten minutes, but it felt like hours.

As soon as Ben swiped the key card, Charlotte said, 'I'm feeling a little wobbly. The jet lag is catching up with me so I'm going to take a nap.'

'Good idea,' he muttered. 'I think I'll join you.'

Charlotte's jaw dropped and he realised what he'd unintentionally implied.

'I mean, I'll have a nap as well. In my own bed. Not in yours. That's not what I meant.'

Ben knew his face was burning. Despite their best efforts, the kiss hadn't just made things awkward between them.

It had made them excruciating.

Ben paced outside Charlotte's door. They were due to dinner in fifteen minutes, and she still hadn't come out of her room.

She's done a runner.

He calmed the pessimistic voice in his head. He knew she couldn't have gone anywhere as he'd been sitting in the living room all afternoon, waiting for her to wake up from her nap.

Far from spelling a new, wonderful phase in their relationship, the kiss had just made things between them strained. They needed to discuss it better than they had, but it would have been easier to walk a tightrope.

Discussing the kiss meant risking her saying that it was a mistake. It risked having her telling him something she hadn't earlier—that it must never happen again. All they had agreed was that they didn't want their friendship to change.

And what did that mean?

He knew they shouldn't take things further. One kiss, one mistake, could be forgotten. Could fade from memory. But as Charlotte napped and Ben brooded, other thoughts intruded.

Maybe they could kiss again? Things were already awkward between them, so maybe another kiss wouldn't make things worse. It might just let them know whether the one they had shared this morning was an outlier. A wonderful, miraculous exception. They could kiss again and find out if what they had this morning could be repeated without it hurting their friendship. Or was his head just addled with sunstroke?

Ben saw the doorknob turn and then looked away, so he could turn back towards her, pretending everything was normal and he hadn't been staring at her door willing it to open. 'Hey, it's nearly time for dinner,' he said as casually as he could manage.

She wore a pretty pink linen dress that skimmed her knees and her shoulders, revealing her long, bare arms. Smooth and lean. He resisted the urge to lift his fingertips to them and trace their silky length.

As they walked out of the door, Charlotte said, 'I'm looking forward to meeting the famous Will Watson.'

Ben clenched his jaw. His brother. Always the competition. And now he'd piqued Charlotte's interest. Great.

'What do you know about Summer?' Charlotte asked.

'Absolutely nothing.'

'You didn't meet her last year at the funeral?'

'I had no idea she existed until yesterday.'

'I thought they'd been together for years. Isn't that what your mother said?'

'He hasn't introduced her to the family before now. I've no idea why.'

'Hopefully we'll find out why tonight,' she said.

Or not, Ben thought.

Will's love life was his own business.

The sun had set and the moonlight reflected in the calm waters as they walked the short distance to the restaurant Diane and Gus had booked for dinner.

Charlotte seemed to be as touchy as ever after her nap. She knew he didn't like talking about Will, yet here she was probing Ben about his brother.

'Why don't you ask him?' she persisted.

'Ask him what?'

'About her? About Summer.'

'Why would I do that?'

'Because he's your brother.'

'We don't talk. Not like that.'

'Maybe you should.'

'Why?' Ben and Will had not been close for years. And there was no reason for them to start now.

'It might make you feel better,' she offered.

'I feel perfectly fine.' Ben's chest tightened.

She snorted.

'What was that about?'

'So you can dish out the amateur psychological advice but you can't take it?'

Ben stopped walking, closed his eyes and took a deep breath to stop himself from saying the first thing that came to his mind: Stay out of my family business.

'I am fine. And happy.'

'Are you?'

Ben opened his eyes to see Charlotte standing right in front of him, hands on her hips and staring him down as though she were trying to bore a hole into his brain.

'Are you happy? Content? Is everything in your life completely and utterly perfect? Is there *nothing* in the world you wish for?'

He swallowed hard, burying the true answer deep down inside.

'I am perfectly happy and content with my life.'

She turned to leave but he still saw her roll her eyes.

By the time they'd reached the restaurant he was wound tighter than a spring.

There was nothing wrong with him. He was happy. Well,

happy enough. He was content. His career was going well, he had good friends, including Charlotte. And no matter what the little voice at the back of his mind was saying, at least he and Charlotte were friends.

Thankfully, they soon reached the restaurant, and were shown through to a deck overlooking the water. The dinner was to welcome the wedding guests who had arrived that day, including Gus's parents, Diane's sisters and, of course, Will and Summer.

His mother was standing with Will and a woman he assumed to be Summer. When Diane saw him and Charlotte walk in, she waved and called, leaving him no choice but to go over and greet them.

Will looked the same as always—impassive, serious. He held out his hand and the brothers shook. Briefly.

Introductions were made and Charlotte gave Will a huge smile and a kiss on each cheek. Ben's gut twisted.

Summer Bright looked just like her name; she had flowing auburn hair, a long colourful dress, and sandals on her feet. She wore pretty bracelets on her wrists that jangled when she also greeted Ben and Charlotte with a kiss on the cheeks.

'They're so pretty. Where did you get them?' Charlotte asked, pointing to Summer's jangling bracelets.

'Back in Adelaide, but I'm hoping to go shopping for similar things here. I hear they have fantastic markets in Ubud.'

'Yes!' Charlotte exclaimed. 'Ben and I were planning on going tomorrow or the next day. You guys should come with us.'

'That'd be wonderful,' Summer replied.

The women were instant friends and Diane beamed as she observed Charlotte and Summer chatting. Will glowered and seemed to want to pull Summer away.

Ben shook his head. His brother would always be a mystery to him. A mystery he had no desire to explore.

Will's betrayal had been nearly as bad as his father's. Sure, it hadn't been Will who had treated Ben any differently, but Will had benefited from their father's favour. He'd never defended Ben. Will had stood by, accepting his father's time, attention and money, while Ben was made to feel like an intruder in his own home. Everything the family did revolved around the business and Ben's decision not to be involved was treated with scorn and derision.

While Charlotte and Summer chatted about Bali and their trips over, Will and Ben stood in silence, not making eye contact with one another. It surprised Ben that Will had chosen a woman so unlike him. Summer seemed genuinely warm and friendly. The opposite of Will.

At every dinner party, there was a good end of the table where there was loud laughter and another end that was calmer, even boring. Ben found himself at the latter. He was seated next to his mother's older sister, his aunt Sarah, and Gus's mother. The two women didn't appear to require him for their friendly conversation about bushwalking and grandchildren. Charlotte was, unfortunately, at the fun end, seated between Will and one of Gus's handsome friends.

Ben did his best to make conversation with Gus's parents and his aunt, while also straining to hear what Will and Charlotte were saying. And burning up inside.

He and Charlotte never bickered like this. Never picked at one another's wounds. He supposed he should have expected her response after he'd questioned her about Tim this afternoon. He hadn't planned it, but then nothing was going to plan today. Any plans he had had taken a U-turn when she'd sat next to him by the pool in the string bikini.

He knew why he'd leaned in to kiss Charlotte; it turned out the line between his platonic feelings for Charlotte and his desire for her was as thin as the straps on Charlotte's red bikini. But what had made her lean into him?

The look of desire she'd given him this morning hadn't been in his imagination. It had been real enough to hit him over the back of his head and push him towards her too. It had been real enough to make him forget that this was *Charlotte*, who still loved Tim, who fled from any connection that got the slightest bit intense.

It had been morning, just before sunrise, and they hadn't been the slightest bit intoxicated.

Maybe she just wanted to kiss you too?

The thought was so preposterous he almost laughed aloud.

He and Charlotte together would be a disaster, both of them running from any potential relationship the moment it looked like becoming serious. If their friendship was to survive, they had to keep their hands off one another.

CHAPTER FIVE

CHARLOTTE WAS RELIEVED to be seated at the opposite end of the table from Ben.

Bloody Ben! She'd spent the morning feeling funny in her belly each time she looked at him and barely able to keep her hands off him, but now, after their lunchtime discussion? Now she couldn't stand to look at him.

Fancy telling her she wasn't over Tim! Implying that she wasn't being fair to any of the men she dated because she knew, deep down, she didn't want a relationship. And then, to top it all off, he had the nerve to tell her what love was!

Ben, whose relationship track record was even patchier than hers. Ben, who couldn't even tell her the last time he'd been in love.

She knew she still missed Tim, but she was ready to fall in love. She had been for ages. She just hadn't met someone who made her feel like Tim did, and what was the problem with that? She wanted swelling violins and fireworks, and she would wait until she found them, no matter what her parents said. And especially no matter what Ben said.

Bloody Ben.

She was still steaming.

Ben's brother Will was lovely and she was very much enjoying his company. Despite their different appearances, she could tell they were brothers. He was about the same height as Ben, maybe a little broader, and his hair was much darker. Near black, it was cut into a style even shorter than Ben's new cut.

She doubted Will had ever grown a beard. No, she doubted he would allow his face to grow it. He struck her as the type of person who issued orders expecting them to be obeyed. The stubble on Ben's face was already pushing through defiantly.

It was hard not to compare them, even though that was what Ben had been afraid of, that she would start comparing him to Will and that she would find Ben coming up short.

But she'd never do that; Ben was the original, Will just a slightly similar copy. Will was charming and good company, but he wasn't the same. She didn't feel as relaxed around him as she did with Ben. And she certainly didn't feel any of the multitude of emotions Ben had inspired in her today.

She could reassure Ben he was her favourite brother and always would be.

With a stab of guilt, she realised she shouldn't have picked at Ben on the walk over, continuing their argument from lunchtime. She especially shouldn't have asked him if he was happy. It wasn't fair. She knew things with his family were tense and instead of helping him through tonight, she'd inflamed things.

She didn't know what had come over her today. Jet lag? Hormones? She had no idea. But something inside her was off kilter.

Despite Ben's protestations that all his father and brother cared about was money, she learned from Will that the family business had evolved over the years from plastic manufacturing into recycling soft plastics. Will's passion for it seemed to extend far beyond just making money; he had genuine concern for the environment and keeping the business profitable so it could stay operating and keep many materials out of the oceans and other ecosystems. He had built it into the major business of its kind in Australia. Charlotte doubted Ben knew about his brother's passion; if he did, he might understand his brother better.

She sighed. It wasn't her place to tell Ben to talk to his brother and try to mend things. That would likely make Ben even angrier.

After the first course Gus stood up and gave a short speech, thanking everyone for coming, and singling Ben and Charlotte out for travelling from London. After the speech there were hugs and people moved seats. Charlotte found herself sitting next to Diane.

Charlotte looked around at the restaurant, which had been decorated for the occasion with tropical flowers and tea lights. The ocean waves provided a calming backdrop.

'It's so beautiful here. Such a romantic location for a wedding.'

'I always wanted to get married on a beach.' Diane sighed.

'And Ben's father didn't want that?'

'God, no, David would have hated this.'

Charlotte's mouth dropped.

'It's okay, I was young when I married David and didn't have the courage to ask for what I wanted. We got married in a church because that's what our parents expected. That's what everyone expected. But now, it's my choice. And Gus's.'

Ben had told Charlotte about his overbearing parents; his father had been behind many of the decisions concerning Ben, but his mother had supported them. Charlotte wondered now how much Ben's mother agreed with everything her late husband had done, whether they had been the team Ben had always thought them to be, but she didn't say anything.

'I'm so glad he's here,' she told Charlotte. 'Thank you for persuading him to come.'

'Oh, I didn't,' Charlotte said reflexively. Then stopped. Ben had been prevaricating about whether he would come until Charlotte's offer. 'I gave him a nudge. But we're both glad we're here. Me especially. It's so nice to finally meet Ben's family.'

Diane picked up Charlotte's hand and it felt natural for her to squeeze it. 'You've been a good friend to him. I'm so grateful. I know he has other friends, but you're special.'

'Oh.' Charlotte felt her face grow red.

'It's hard living away from your family, even in another city, but on the other side of the world it can be especially lonely. We all need a person nearby. A person to call on in an emergency. It's such a comfort to me to know that he has you.'

'I have him too. Honestly, he's always there for me.' Charlotte spoke without thinking. The words were true. Ben was always there for her. No matter what she'd done or where she'd done it. Fixing things for her, coming to get her when she didn't feel safe on a date. Holding her hair off her face after that New Year's Eve party that got out of hand. Listening to her go on and on about her business and which artists she should be chasing and selling.

'He's my rock,' she said and suddenly felt tears welling in the back of her throat. She'd been callous to him on the way here this evening. More than that, by kissing him this morning she'd treated their relationship carelessly. She didn't want to do anything to ruin her friendship with him. She cared for him too much.

She didn't want to lose him from her life.

Diane didn't seem to notice the emotion that was welling up inside Charlotte as she continued. 'He never saw eye to eye with his father. They were always arguing about priorities. Never saw all the things they had in common. Their ambition, their drive. It broke my heart when Ben left.'

He left because he didn't have the support of his family, Charlotte wanted to say, but bit her tongue. He left because Will was given all sorts of support—financial and emotional—that was not given to Ben. Her desire to defend Ben was nearly overwhelming.

Her reaction surprised her. Parents should treat all of their children equally, not favour one over the other because of their career choice, she wanted to say. But for the sake of maintaining harmony, she kept the thought to herself.

'I knew he was immensely talented; I knew that he'd be able to support himself. And his father did too. But it hurt that he never visited.'

'Maybe he never felt as though he had your support,' Charlotte said, trying to keep her tone non-committal. She knew exactly how hurt Ben had been by his father's words and actions. Ben had not only been cut off financially, but his parents had not shown any interest in his work. Not in the same way they had followed and nurtured Will's career.

It was the differential treatment between the siblings that hurt him the most. But Ben had told her to keep out of his family business, so she stayed quiet.

It hurt her to know that they didn't think Ben was good enough. How must it make Ben feel?

Diane changed the subject deftly though and asked Charlotte about her gallery, and her parents. Charlotte began to relax as they talked about neutral topics, but then Diane said, 'I understand from Ben that you were engaged once.'

The nervousness returned to Charlotte's chest.

'Yes. We were young but we were planning on spending our lives together.'

'You never found anyone else?'

'I'm looking, but I just haven't found anyone who makes me feel like Tim did.'

Diane nodded. 'And Ben, he doesn't tell me much. Has he been seeing anyone?'

Charlotte felt unexpectedly sorry for Diane, who she now

thought seemed to genuinely regret the near estrangement from her younger son.

'No, at least not that he tells me. He's quite cagey about that sort of thing. I have to drag every detail out of him. It's strange, because he lets me prattle on about all my dates.'

Diane's brow furrowed and she gave Charlotte a look she couldn't interpret.

When the first guests began to leave, Ben caught Charlotte's eye across the deck and smiled. Her heart swelled.

They would be okay. No matter what had passed between them that day, they would get through it.

He raised his eyebrows. *Do you want to leave?* they asked.

She nodded. She was exhausted and unsteady. She could blame it on the jet lag, or the cocktails she'd drunk at dinner, but it was more than that. Confusion, being muddled. Despite coming to the other side of the world, Tim still wasn't far from her thoughts. But this year was different from the others. Because it wasn't just Tim in her thoughts, it was Ben as well. Confusing, overwhelming, twisting, all-consuming.

Their friendship was important, but it was more than that—*Ben* was important. And she wanted him to know that.

The kiss this morning and the conversation with Diane had made her wonder for the first time what it would be like to lose him from her life, and she didn't like the way that thought made her feel. Not one bit.

They didn't talk much on the short walk back to their villa. Ben swiped the card and the front door opened with a click. He held it open for Charlotte and as she walked within a breath of him to enter, she couldn't help but inhale.

Ben. Even his scent was different here. Sandalwood and jasmine. The soap provided by the villa. On Ben it was transformed. She made a mental note to pack some in her suitcase for the trip home and to leave it at his flat.

They stood in the foyer. She should probably go to bed, but there was still so much unresolved between them.

The conversation she'd had with Diane had been surprising and a little heartbreaking. She needed to talk about what had happened that day. Needed to know that they would be okay.

'What did you think of Summer?' she began.

'She seems lovely. Not at all what I expected.'

'How's that?'

'She's not the sort of woman I expected Will to find. You met him. He's buttoned up. Uptight in the extreme.'

'I think he's just shy.'

Ben snorted. 'You're thinking of Mr Darcy. Will is no Mr Darcy. He's ruthless and focused entirely on the bottom line.'

'I don't know,' Charlotte said and grinned at Ben. 'I saw him checking out Summer's bottom line.'

Ben smiled reluctantly.

What now?

'Call it a night?' he asked.

She was tired, but she still wasn't ready to end this crazy day.

'I had a nice talk with your mother.'

'Oh?'

'It was illuminating.'

'What does that mean?'

'It means I think I learned more about you tonight than I have in ages.'

'Really?' He scoffed.

'I didn't realise how estranged you were. And I didn't realise how much your mother regrets what happened.'

He shook his head. 'Charlotte, I asked you to not get involved.'

But she was involved. Ben was her best friend and she cared deeply for him. She hated to see him hurting. And she hated to think of him as feeling alone.

It's such a comfort to me to know that he has you.

She stepped over to him and slid her arms around his waist. It felt good to hold him like this. She pressed her head into his chest and squeezed him tight. She had no intention other than reassuring him that everything was okay, but as she felt him against her, the long muscular lines of his body against hers, something inside her shifted.

Charlotte lifted her head to look at him, but didn't pull away from the embrace. Ben's brow furrowed. He didn't say anything, but he didn't tell her to let him go. Or stop. Which was good, because holding him felt natural.

She lifted her hand and ran her fingers down his cheek, still bare, but now slightly rough. She liked doing that too. Touching him. Ben needed to be touched. And held.

And kissed.

She wanted to be the one to do that.

Ben still didn't talk, he was hardly moving, his frame still and hard against hers.

They'd kissed once without ruining things, hadn't they?

They could still be friends, but wouldn't this be better than being friends who didn't touch?

She wasn't sure any more about her fears from this morning. Friends could touch. Friends could hold. Friends could kiss. Couldn't they?

She lifted herself onto her tiptoes to find out. Her lips found his and thankfully his didn't pull away. He didn't immediately kiss her back either, but slowly, persuasively Charlotte moved her lips against his, teased them open and then all at once his grip tightened, his mouth opened, wide and luscious and dragging her in. She went willingly, gratefully. Their mouths danced and then tangled together. Wet and warm. Her heart swooped and her insides tightened with mounting lust.

Ben slid his hands into her hair and gently angled her face to fit her lips perfectly against his.

She felt her knees weaken and her inhibitions dissolve.

This morning hadn't been an aberration. Ben could kiss. *They* could kiss. They kissed so well together it would be a shame—practically a travesty—not to keep kissing.

Suddenly Ben pulled back. His blue eyes the colour of midnight. 'What's going on, Charlotte?' His voice was hoarse. Strangled.

'I don't know.' And that was the honest truth. If it had been any other man, she would have answered, 'Just fooling around.' But with Ben it was more complicated than that. Even though they were friends, couldn't they just see what happened and where it took them? 'Do we have to know?'

'No, we don't. We don't have to name it. But…' He rubbed his chin. She really liked beardless Ben, she really liked that she could see his lips properly. Liked that she could see his smile.

What she *didn't* like was Ben's hesitation. Didn't like the way he kept pulling away. He seemed to be into the kiss, he seemed to enjoy holding her. Wrapped tightly in his arms as she was, she could tell how much he was enjoying it, yet he kept pulling back.

'But?' Her voice was small.

'But I want you to be sure.'

She stepped back, untangling her arms from his.

I am sure, a voice inside her head said.

'I think we should both be sure,' Ben added.

That was it, Ben was not sure. Sensible Ben. He knew that every further caress was a risk. What would happen if they kept kissing and holding and touching and moved onto undressing…?

What then?

She was in no doubt sleeping with Ben would be quite

amazing. The question of what came after was too big, too scary, too unanswerable. Ben was right, their friendship was far too important to jeopardise. Already things had changed, their easy camaraderie replaced with awkwardness. The simplicity of trust had been replaced with uncertainty.

Charlotte nodded, but her heart was falling. Yes. They should both be sure. Her desire to be held by Ben wasn't worth risking their friendship for.

She stepped back. Despite every muscle in her body wanting to keep moving forward. This new need she felt for Ben was so surprising, both in its unlikeliness and its force. For years she'd looked at him as Just Ben, then the guy had had a shave and suddenly he was causing her insides to do gymnastics. What was going on with her? He was right, they did need to step back and wait until they were both in a steadier frame of mind.

Ben coughed. 'Ubud tomorrow?'

She nodded, and turned towards her room, still pondering the mystery of what was going on between her and Ben. Hormones? No, no change there. Grief? Maybe, given it was getting close to the anniversary of Tim's accident.

Warm weather and fewer clothes. Was she that frivolous?

'Sleep well, Charlotte.'

Commitment-phobe Ben was taking it slowly. Of course he was. It was what he did. Just as she dumped each guy after a few dates, Ben took relationships at the speed of a two-hundred-year-old turtle.

How was he so sensible? She was burning inside. A second later she would have pushed him onto the couch and straddled him.

He wants to take things slowly and carefully because he doesn't feel the same way.

He'd looked so devastated after their kiss, his brow creased with worry. He did regret it. He knew this had changed their relationship. If he'd enjoyed the kiss, he wouldn't have looked as though he'd just lost a pet.

Charlotte threw herself onto her bed. Now it was her turn to feel devastated.

Because despite what Ben felt, she wanted more.

Ubud was a ferry ride back to the main island of Bali and then a taxi ride up into the hills. They met Summer and Will at the ferry wharf and the two women greeted one another with a kiss. Ben waved to Will and Will grunted back.

Great. It was going to be a long day.

'I don't know why we have to go with them,' Ben grumbled softly to Charlotte when they were seated next to one another on the ferry.

'Because I like Summer. And because it's weird if we don't.'

Ben liked Summer too, but didn't think it was strange not to go on a day trip with them. Though he had to concede that, with all the kissing he and Charlotte now apparently did, they should be hanging out with other people to try and dilute the tension between them.

But they should have chosen another couple to hang out with; Will brought tension with him. It surrounded him like an aura.

'I don't know what she sees in him,' Ben grumbled and was rewarded with an elbow to the ribs. Which had the unfortunate effect of placing Ben's body on even higher alert.

'Shh, he's your brother.'

'But he's so uptight. And she's so not.'

Summer turned and looked at them from two seats in front and smiled.

'Shh. She heard.'

'She can't have heard over the boat engine.'

The elbow Charlotte bumped into him was yet another

reminder of the new physical nature of their relationship. They'd kissed again last night, and even though they had again told one another they didn't want to ruin their friendship, neither of them had come right out and said it mustn't happen again. He wasn't sure where that left them or how he felt about it. Terrified? Most definitely.

But also maybe a little excited.

He'd managed any attraction he might feel to Charlotte in the past by not getting physically close, but Bali seemed to be literally throwing them at one another. So far this morning they had brushed hands as they reached to pour the coffee, bumped into one another on their way out of the door and collided getting on the ferry. Each touch sent sparks through his body.

Now, on the ferry, they were sharing a seat that really was too small for two adults and their hips kept bumping, prompting warmth and feelings and making him sweat even more than the equatorial temperatures already were.

'It's so sticky here, isn't it? Do you think we'll ever get used to the humidity?' She fanned herself by pulling the neckline of her dress, showing him flashes of the cream of her chest and the swell of her breasts.

Despite the humidity she spoke of, his mouth was bone dry. 'I don't know.'

As much as he'd wanted to scoop Charlotte up and carry her to his room last night, as much as he'd wanted to lie with her all night, tasting and exploring one another's bodies, he knew it was possibly the worst thing he could do.

If they slept together, and it was anything other than anticlimactic, if she got the sense that he felt anything for her, she'd leave him for ever. And despite trying their entire relationship to hold his feelings back, he feared that sharing Charlotte's bed would bring those carefully suppressed emotions to the surface. He had no choice but to take things slowly. So slowly she would barely notice they were happening. Like grass growing. Or paint drying.

One day at a time.

One kiss at a time.

One claustrophobic ferry trip at a time.

Ubud was heaving with tourists and locals alike. He'd been looking forward to visiting what was called the cultural centre of Bali, but also missed the relative tranquillity of Nusa Lembongan.

The four of them found their way to the art market the guidebooks raved about. Ben tried not to think about what might or might not be going on between him and Charlotte while Summer and Will held hands and looked adoringly at one another. Something about Will and Summer's relationship worried him; he knew he and Will were no longer close to one another, but if Will had been dating Summer for years why hadn't he heard of her? Why hadn't she been at their father's funeral? Something wasn't quite right.

The market was crowded and more than once he lost sight of Charlotte's dark hair. When she drifted off in the opposite direction, pulled by the crowd, he reflexively reached out and grabbed her hand. She glanced at him briefly, then slid her fingers through his, entwining their hands. Their fingers stayed like that as they made their way across the market. There were amazing sights, sounds and smells, an absolute delight for the senses, but Ben couldn't tell you anything about that market in Ubud except how perfectly wonderful it felt to have Charlotte's hand in his.

He was nearly ready to succumb, and twirl her into his arms, but his resolve held.

He wasn't going to be another Charlotte statistic.

'This is the place I was telling you about,' Summer said

to Charlotte when they neared the other side of the market. As soon as Summer turned, Ben dropped Charlotte's hand.

The small shop was full of jewellery and clothes and Ben and Will stood outside while the women went in.

'Summer seems lovely,' Ben said.

Will nodded.

Making conversation with his brother was like pulling teeth. Will wasn't his favourite person in the world, but Will hadn't personally wronged Ben. That had been his father, Ben reminded himself.

'She's not the sort of woman I imagined you with.'

'What's that supposed to mean?'

Ben took a step back. 'Nothing, really. I guess I imagined you with someone more corporate. But it's good really.'

Will's shoulders noticeably relaxed.

'Sorry, mate. It's just… Do you want to leave the women to it and get a beer?' Will said and Ben nodded.

'Mum doesn't approve of Summer?' Ben guessed as the brothers took a seat on the deck of a small bar overlooking the bustling street.

'She's bemused, like you, but she doesn't disapprove. She seems happy I'm dating someone.'

'And Dad?'

The air stilled at the mention of their father. The brothers had not spent long together at the time of the funeral. Ben's visit had been short and he'd spent most of the visit with his mother making the funeral arrangements. Will had claimed to be frantic attending to the implications to the business. Just as it had always been with their father, business had come first. Even when your father had just died, nothing and no one was more important than the business, Ben thought bitterly.

'Dad never met her.'

'Really? I thought you guys had been together for a while.'

'Yeah, well, you don't need to be a member of this family to know that Dad would not have approved.'

It was as though Ben was suddenly seeing his brother for the first time. Sure, Will shared their father's workaholic tendencies, but what if Will didn't want to run the business but never had the same courage that Ben did to leave?

Poor Will, not even being able to introduce his girlfriend to their father because he'd feared his disapproval. Ben wanted to shake his brother and remind him he was a grown man and did not need the approval of a tyrant, and a dead one at that. Instead, he said, 'I think she might be a good fit for you. I think she might be just the type of woman you need.'

'Yeah, well.'

A wave of sadness washed over Ben; he and Will had been so close as kids, swimming at the beach together, playing cricket in the backyard, or computer games. If you'd asked Ben at any point up until high school who his best friend was, he would have answered, without hesitation, 'Will.'

But when they were teens, it had changed. Will had been enthralled with their father and Ben had drifted slowly but surely away from them both. Making money didn't interest him in the same way it seemed to interest them. And then his father had made Will his favourite and Will had stood by while he was given everything and Ben nothing.

'And what about you and Charlotte?' Will asked, but when he looked at Ben, it felt as though his interest was genuine.

'We're good friends, have been for ages.'

Will raised a single eyebrow and his lips quirked into a grin. For a moment Ben caught a glimpse of his brother of old.

'It's complicated,' Ben clarified.

Will lifted his glass and touched it lightly to Ben's. 'Yeah, mate, it always is, isn't it?'

* * *

The four of them had lunch and explored Ubud. In the afternoon, at the peak of the day's heat, they reboarded the ferry back to Nusa Lembongan. On the return trip, the two women shared a seat and Ben and Will did as well.

Once they had said their goodbyes, Charlotte grilled him on the walk back to their own villa. 'Did you talk to Will?'

'I didn't have any choice, did I, given that you monopolised Summer all day?'

'She's great. She's fun and such a free spirit. Did you know she's a cabaret singer?'

'A what?'

'And she sings in tribute bands. And she busks.'

'Seriously?' Ben couldn't have been more surprised if Summer had been a painter, like himself. The Adelaide Watsons were allergic to anything artistic or anything whose economic value could not be easily determined.

'I've told them they just have to come and visit us in London.'

'Us?'

The word hung between them like a grenade that had been activated but not yet detonated.

'Us. Yes, you and me.'

Were they now an Us? And when had that happened? He wanted to ask, but was terrified about what would happen if the grenade went off.

There wasn't a single part of Charlotte that was not burning up by the time they got back to Nusa Lembongan from Ubud. She was drenched in sweat, her face was red, but most of all her insides were tight and hot. She'd just spent a whole day being next to Ben, pretending that everything was normal and wondering what on earth was happening between them.

First, they had been seated together on the narrow bench

on the ferry, their arms bumping constantly. Next, they were squished together on the even narrower bus seat; their thighs pushed together, sticky with sweat. Then they were jostled along the street together. Finally, in the crowded market Ben had grabbed her hand so they didn't lose one another. The hand-holding was for practical purposes only but in those ten minutes she'd got to know what it would be like to always be holding Ben's hand. It felt strong, and protective, filing her with a sense of safety. She found herself wishing he'd keep doing it once they were back in London.

Which was silly because they both knew their way around London so there wouldn't be any need.

But still. It would be nice, she'd thought.

And not just hand-holding. But kissing too. She wanted to do more of that.

And more.

She wanted to see Ben, not just in his shorts, but without them. She wanted to get to know what was under his clothes as well as she knew the rest of him.

That thought made her hotter still.

What's the worst that could happen if we slept together? Charlotte had asked herself over and over on the day trip.

The sex might not be good, came the answer.

That was unlikely, given the kisses they had shared.

The sex might be great.

In which case that could be even worse. If the sex was great, she'd probably want to do it again and then what would that mean for their friendship?

And what if, amongst everything else, their friendship got lost?

Somehow, she didn't see that happening. A friendship with Ben would be strong enough to survive whatever happened.

If the sex is great and we wanted to keep doing it, would

that mean we were in a relationship? Does Ben want a relationship with me? Do I want one with Ben?

Those were the questions that she simply didn't have the answers to. That was probably why Ben was being so cautious—he wasn't sure if he wanted a relationship with her. And he clearly wasn't as physically shaken by their kisses. He seemed calm, reserved, whereas, inside, she was a mess.

Ben was always so cagey about his relationships, even though in almost every other aspect he was open with her. She knew some deeply personal things about him, like how his father had favoured his older brother, how he'd always wondered why his father's love had been conditional, how he felt happiest when he was painting. But, despite sharing all this with her, Ben still kept most details of his romantic relationships from her.

He had told Charlotte all about his teenage crush, she'd even once met Maya, the girlfriend he had left in New York, but he'd said next to nothing about his most recent dates, apart from details that she now realised were superficial—who the woman had been, where they'd eaten or drunk. But never how he *felt*.

And that was the one important thing that eluded her now.

As they left Will and Summer and approached their villa, undiluted awkwardness simmered between them.

'What next?' Ben asked, as they walked to the door.

It was a good question, but Charlotte was no closer to figuring out what was going on between her and Ben.

'I just don't know, Ben. I'm really confused.'

'I mean, do you want dinner? A drink?'

Charlotte's face burned even hotter than it was already.

'I mean, confused because I don't know if we should eat in the villa or find somewhere else,' she added, trying to cover her slip.

He nodded, but the sly grin that came over his lips made her wonder if she really had convinced him.

'I think the villa. I think we should get something in. We've been out the last two nights.'

As friends, they could talk about most things. Especially meal plans. But as potential lovers? She didn't know the rules to that.

Potential lovers? She was getting way ahead of herself. She wasn't even sure that Ben wanted to kiss her again. Let alone sleep with her.

A memory from their kiss the night before came back to her, a low, soft groan coming from Ben's throat as he pulled back from their kiss. Ben did enjoy their kisses, that was apparent from his heavy-lidded eyes, the flush of his cheeks.

Friends with benefits sounded crass to Charlotte's ears. But they were friends and they could also sleep together. Would that be such a strange thing?

She already knew she liked Ben, loved his company. And if they were lovers as well, wouldn't that be perfect?

If you were friends who cared for one another and slept together, what did that mean? Would it be really possible to keep things platonic? To keep the physical from the emotional?

All these years that was how she had managed her relationships because it was the emotion that was the problem, that was what led to heartbreak.

She'd managed with other men, but could she do the same with Ben? She already knew him and cared for him, so it wouldn't be like the others. Was that a good thing or a bad thing? She had no idea.

Exhausted, but wound tight, Charlotte flopped onto the couch.

'It's still so warm.'

'If only there were somewhere we could cool off,' he said with a laugh.

'You're right, we should have a swim.'

Yes, a swim would cool them both off. It would also do something about the butterflies that had been multiplying in her stomach all day, the sweat that clung to them both. She went to her room to get changed.

She'd brought a few swimming costumes, a black one-piece and the red bikini she'd worn the other morning. Charlotte's hand hovered over her suitcase for a long moment before she swallowed hard and chose the bikini.

Ben took his time changing. By the time he'd emerged from his room, Charlotte was already in the pool, floating on her back.

When Ben walked out and stood by the edge of the pool Charlotte's body stiffened, then began to slip under. She righted herself and stood.

Ben was wearing the briefest shorts she'd seen him in yet.

Best of all, he was shirtless.

In the four years of knowing Ben, she had never seen him without a shirt.

There was no reason why she should have, but she now felt slightly betrayed.

He'd been keeping something from her.

Sculpted and strong and perfectly proportioned pecs, just the perfect shade of caramel and with the slightest smattering of hair. Her gaze travelled lower to his stomach, flat and taut, and her fingers itched to slide over it.

Heaven help her.

Ben sat on the edge of the pool and lowered himself in before diving under the surface in one fluid movement and doing some lazy laps. The muscles in his back and arms rip-

pled under his skin with each movement. As he turned at one
end, he caught her eye.

He'd seen her watching! Though perving was more like it.

Charlotte dropped under the surface, her face burning.

To stop herself looking at Ben and his secret muscles she
copied him and started silently swimming laps of the pool,
determined not to stare. She glided through the water with
purposeful strokes. Yes. This was better. Exercise would help
take her mind off Ben's chest and the soft smattering of chest
hair she now knew he possessed.

The problem was that by not looking at him, she accidentally swam straight into him.

They bounced back from one another, then stood, facing
one another other, chest deep in the water. She curled her
hands behind her back to stop herself from involuntarily
reaching out. There was no end to her embarrassment. She
was trying to stay cool and calm, but her attraction must be
written across her face.

'Sorry,' she muttered.

'Charlotte, are you okay?' Ben tilted his head.

No. She wasn't. She was confused, but excited. Worried,
but there was an inevitability to what she was about to do.

She stepped right up to him. The water swirled around
their bodies and she reached for his bare shoulder. Golden
and strong. She rubbed it with the soft pad of her thumb.

Ben turned and climbed out of the pool in a hurry, as if
he were running away. But she wasn't going to have it. They
had to talk about this.

'What's the matter?' she asked, following him.

'Nothing.'

'Then why are you getting out?'

'Because I've cooled off.'

Charlotte scrambled out of the pool. They were going
to talk about this, because for starters she wasn't going to

be able to sleep tonight if they didn't and, for seconds, she thrummed with need. With want.

'Do you...not want to touch me?' she asked.

'Oh, Charlotte.'

He looked pained. As if she were offering him a root canal and not her body.

He doesn't want you. He knows this could all go very wrong.

Charlotte stepped back, at a loss of what to do.

Be honest. This is Ben. You can be honest.

'I'm sorry. I really am. I don't know what's come over me. Something's changed and I don't know what or why.'

If she couldn't be honest, then what was their friendship worth?

'I want you to hold me.'

Ben's face reddened.

'And sometimes I get the feeling that you might want to hold me too.'

Ben couldn't respond. He was torn between lying and disagreeing with her or pulling her into his arms and showing her how correct she was. So he stayed frozen to the spot. Slowly, hesitantly, Charlotte stepped towards him until she stood within a breath of him, and Ben was almost lost. He couldn't argue with her without lying: he wanted her with a ferocity that almost frightened him. But he had to stop; he had to be sure that she was sure and that this was not a spur-of-the-moment idea she would regret with a new day.

What if, despite everything he thought, she was sure? What if she truly was ready to put Tim behind her and move on? What if he, Ben Watson, could buck the trend that was Charlotte's love life? His resolve, his plan was unravelling as quickly as he suspected her skimpy bikini top could.

'I want you. I want this,' she said, and his heart almost

stopped. She took half a step forward and their wet skin met. Their hands remained at their sides but the exquisite swell of her breasts pushed gently against his. Her hip bone rested against his and he almost swayed with longing. He moved one bare foot between hers and their bodies were suddenly flush.

She wanted sex. He wanted sex. But sex wasn't as important as everything else.

'I can tell you want this too. At the very least I can tell you're interested.'

Charlotte shifted her leg between his. His lips might be able to lie, but his body couldn't, and it was apparent to anyone nearby that he was very, very interested in Charlotte and her wet, bikini-clad body that was currently wrapped around his almost naked one.

What was holding him back?

Charlotte asked him the same question. 'Don't you want to?'

'Of course I want to. Very much.'

'Then?'

Then...nothing? Before the doubt in his mind could speak one more word, Ben slid his arms around Charlotte's waist and pulled her tight. Their lips met before he could take a breath. Soft, wet, eager.

They continued the conversation with the kiss, their tongues saying everything that needed to be said.

I want this.

I want you.

Charlotte's bikini hid nothing. When he slid his hands down her back, he felt only glorious, soft skin. When her hands explored him, she felt only his bare chest, with his heart hammering like a drum under his ribs. And it was wonderful. Everything he'd never let himself dream.

But as her fingers began to explore the waistband of his shorts he realised they were approaching the point of no return. A friendship might survive a few kisses, but the next step would be different. He lifted his mouth from hers.

'Charlotte, you know that if you keep doing that, everything will change,' he murmured with his last breath of restraint.

'I thought you wanted it too.' She slid her palm down his back and into the waistband of his shorts.

'I do. Very much. I'm just checking in with you again.'

'Ben, if today is anything to go by, I'd say something in our friendship has already changed.' She moved her hand from the back of his shorts and to the front, her fingertips coming so close to him he could feel their warmth.

She was right; the kisses had already made things strained between them. But what they were going to do next would change it again. He knew that he couldn't make love to her and walk away. Once they crossed this line, any lies that he might have told himself about his feelings for her would be shown to be that: a convenient fabrication to protect his own heart.

'Promise me we'll keep talking?'

'Why wouldn't we?'

'I mean, keep talking with one another about how we're feeling. That way if things start to get weird, or strange or uncomfortable, we can deal with it.'

'Of course.'

'Promise me,' he insisted. 'As long as we let one another know how we're feeling, we'll be okay.'

'I promise.' Charlotte nodded.

He exhaled and Charlotte lifted a hand behind her back, untying the knot of her bikini with a single tug. She shed her bikini to clear the last remaining distance between them, shattering the last of Ben's remaining resolve.

This was it. It was happening.

He lifted his hand to her bare shoulder and rubbed her

tender skin with the pad of his thumb, mirroring her motion from moments earlier. Her eyelids lowered, and she exhaled. Exquisite. She was perfect. He lowered his mouth to her shoulder and kissed it. She tasted of sunshine and desire. His lips traced their way slowly across her collarbone and he felt her shoulders shiver. He was going to explore every inch, every curve, every corner of her.

Ben tilted his head and met Charlotte's gaze. Her eyes lowered to his lips and hers beckoned. Slowly, savouring each moment of anticipation, their mouths gradually came together again.

Tasting, exploring. Their tongues slid together in a beautiful dance. Charlotte leaned further into him and he felt her sighs vibrate through her.

He was aware of her hands moving slowly tentatively over his body, down his back, pushing down his shorts. Realising his knees might give way at any moment, he scooped her up and carried her to her room.

He laid her on her bed and she pulled him on top of her, her warmth exhilarating beneath him. She wrapped her legs around him, pulling him even tighter to her. Only his shorts and her skimpy bikini bottoms lay between them, but their thin fabric was a technicality only; his hand slipped under the wet fabric and over her gorgeous buttocks. They could both tell how aroused he was through his wet shorts. They had never been closer, or more intimate. He lowered his head and took one of Charlotte's perfect and perfectly erect nipples between his lips and even at that simple touch her back arched and she moaned. Her restraint was even thinner than his.

He lifted his mouth away.

'No, Ben, don't stop. Please.'

When she begged, he gave in. Who was he to deny her something that they both craved? Something that felt so perfect. He lowered his mouth again, pleasuring one breast and then the other, while Charlotte's fingers carefully relieved him of his shorts and stroked his length so perfectly he worried he would embarrass himself.

When he thought her touch might shatter him, he wriggled away…and trailed kisses down her belly, to the hem of her bikini bottoms. He eased them lower, breathing hard, shaking as he did so.

Charlotte… Charlotte… he repeated over and over in his head.

This was Charlotte. He'd never even let himself contemplate the next step.

He must have been too slow for Charlotte because she wriggled herself out of them, revealing the last of her beautiful body to him, confident, eager and without the slightest hesitation. He lowered his head, tasted her, heard her soft moans, and stroked her over and over again.

She nudged his head away and said, 'Stay right where you are.'

'Where are you going?'

'Two feet to the left to get a condom from my bag. Don't even think of moving.'

Her direction was firm. She was ordering him not to change his mind at the final hurdle. His head started to spin and he rolled onto his back. She was right to warn him. This was the point where either of them could stop and change their mind.

He sighed. No, he couldn't. He was too deep in. He'd felt Charlotte, tasted her.

The next step was already inevitable.

He insisted on sheathing himself, not trusting himself to hold himself together if Charlotte's fingers slid over him again at this point. He found her mouth again and kissed her, harder this time, as her legs wrapped around him, pulled him against her. Instinctively, they knew what the other wanted.

She was ready. He'd been ready for years and could only hope he didn't disappoint her.

He was hoping to hold himself together for as long as she was going to need, but didn't anticipate she would reach her climax so quickly, so forcefully. He fell mere seconds after her, as her body was still shaking. Pleasure tore through him like a blaze but he held her, kept her safe, kept her steady.

When his peak subsided, it took him a moment to realise over the waves of his own climax that Charlotte was still shaking, but his shoulder suddenly felt wet, and he realised she was crying.

CHAPTER SIX

CHARLOTTE'S BODY FLOODED with pleasure, it coursed through her, more powerful, deeper than she'd known in years. But one convulsion was slowly replaced with another, more un-stoppable, unexpected vibration.

Rising in her throat, pushing behind her eyes, filling the back of her nose.

The vibrations were no longer orgasm, but sobs. They rose up through her and shook her even as she was still lying tan-gled in Ben's arms.

He rubbed her back in soothing circles, realising what was happening even before she did.

She swallowed and gasped and tried to hold the tears in but they came from somewhere deep, hidden behind a wall she hadn't even known was there, and flooded her uncontrollably.

'It's okay, it's okay,' Ben whispered.

But it wasn't okay at all.

It was shocking. Mortifying.

She pulled herself up and turned away from him. It was a wrench, but it was necessary. She took deep breaths to steady her body and turn back the tears. She grabbed the sheet and wiped her face, vaguely aware of Ben lying on the bed be-hind her as she pulled herself together.

'Oh, God, Ben, I'm so sorry. I'm so embarrassed.'

'Don't be,' he said gruffly.

'No, I am, I don't know where that came from. I don't know what just happened.'

'It's all right, really.' Ben sat up behind her pressed a quick kiss on her bare shoulder before grabbing his shorts and leaving the room.

She caught a glimpse of his bare arse as he left and the feeling stirred inside her again. She was attracted to Ben, deeply, crazily attracted.

But it was attraction laced with more bitter emotions.

Embarrassment.

Shock.

Guilt.

She groaned and flopped back onto her bed.

She stared at the ceiling, the intricate patterns carved in the wood, and tried to figure out what on earth had just happened.

She had nothing to feel guilty about. Embarrassed, yes. But not guilty.

She was willing, Ben was willing.

Sex had not been like that for her in years. Not since Tim.

The tears rose back up again but Charlotte quickly got off her bed and went to the bathroom. She splashed her face with cold water and washed them away.

Maybe these tears, this pounding in her chest was about Tim after all? She'd run away from the London autumn but couldn't really escape the feelings that swamped her each year.

What if this new attraction to Ben was simply a symptom of her grief? A way of trying to forget about Tim.

If so, it had backfired spectacularly.

But sex with Ben was good.

No, sex with Ben was *great*.

Sex with Ben had opened up a place she'd forgotten was even there. The place where you were at one with each other, entirely attuned to the other person. Where the other person knew you so well, they knew exactly how to hold you, touch you, stimulate you.

Opening up that place had surprised her. She hadn't even realised what had come over her until it was too late.

She was such a fool. And poor Ben! She'd practically begged him to sleep with her, promised it wouldn't change their friendship and then this had happened.

Charlotte ran herself a bath and sat on the edge while she waited for it to fill.

Outside her room she heard a door bang. The front door. It was dark outside, but Ben must have gone out. She buried her face in her hands and groaned. She'd messed things up spectacularly. Pursued her best friend and then cried after the best sex she'd had in years.

As long as we let one another know how we're feeling, we'll be okay.

It was just as well he'd left, because she didn't know the first thing to say to him. She didn't even understand what was going on herself.

She slipped into the warm relaxing bath.

When Ben got back the first thing she needed to do was explain that the crying was not a review of his love-making ability. Quite the opposite. Ben's hands had known just the right pressure to apply, his fingers had known just where to stroke her. He'd been attentive, focused. Caring.

He'd known just where to touch her. And that had been the problem. No other man had been able to reach her there. Not since Tim.

The warm bath, the long day, the love-making, all conspired to make her drowsy. She pulled herself out of the bath, put on her pyjamas and opened her bedroom door so she would hear Ben's return. Once he was back, they would talk. She fell onto her bed, spent and exhausted, and she slept.

* * *

It was morning when Charlotte woke and saw the door to her room was closed. Ben must have closed it when he returned. She opened it slowly and padded out into the main room. Ben's side of the villa was quiet and his door was closed as well.

She wanted to walk across the foyer, open his door and slip into his bed, just to hold him and feel his warmth against her body.

But he didn't want that. He probably wanted space, which was why he'd left last night.

No wonder. What must he think? She hadn't just cried, she'd sobbed uncontrollably. She would explain, but he had to be ready to hear it, and clearly he wasn't. She had no idea how late he'd got back last night. She had no recollection of him returning to the villa. Where had he gone? For a walk? To a bar?

You pushed him away. You shouldn't be surprised if he took himself off for a drink or four.

She turned back to her room, slipped on a dress. She needed coffee. And food. She'd skipped dinner and with all of yesterday evening's excitement neither of them had placed a breakfast order. She'd go get coffee, bring one back for Ben and then they would talk.

Charlotte hadn't slept with too many people, but enough to know that last night she had made a terrible faux pas. It wasn't even as though the sex had been tear-worthy, just the opposite, but she didn't know how to explain that to Ben without sounding silly.

Making love to you was so good I had to sob my eyes out.

She needed to come up with something that made more sense than that.

Charlotte was surprised to see Summer at the nearest cafe, sitting on the deck, writing in a notepad.

'Hey there,' she said.

Summer looked up and her face lit up. 'Hi.'

'I'm just going to grab breakfast. Would you like to join me?' Charlotte looked around. 'Unless you're meeting Will?'

'No, I mean, yes, please stay. I just ordered a coffee.'

Charlotte pulled out a chair. 'Where's Will?'

'I'm honestly not sure.'

Charlotte nodded, but didn't say more, remembering Ben's concern that something was not quite right between Will and Summer.

The two women drank their coffee then ordered some breakfast. Charlotte ordered a sweet Indonesian porridge with coconut milk, ginger and sugar. It was delicious but she also salivated over Summer's order of *bubur ayam*, which was a type of rice, with chicken and sliced boiled egg on top.

With food and coffee in her, Charlotte's mood brightened, but she still felt unsteady. Her new attraction to Ben was confusing and threatening to destabilise their friendship. She could rule out alcohol. Her jet lag had passed. That left hormone fluctuations. But those had never made her react like this in the past.

'Is thirty too young for perimenopause?' Charlotte blurted out.

Summer snorted. 'I'm not an expert, but maybe. Why?'

'Because I feel strange. Like my hormones are off balance.'

'You're not pregnant, are you? That's more likely in someone your age than perimenopause.'

Pregnant? Charlotte almost choked on her coffee. Even if she was pregnant, it would be way too early to know. Besides, they had used protection. And she had an IUD.

But what if she were pregnant? With Ben's baby? Ben would make a wonderful father. She touched her stomach. The thought of having Ben's baby didn't make her distressed. Strangely, it made her calm. Would it have Ben's gorgeous curls? His bright blue eyes? His dimple?

Where was she?

Charlotte shook her head and returned to the conversation. 'No,' she answered.

Summer laughed. 'That looked like you aren't quite sure if you could be pregnant or not.'

'No, I'm not pregnant, it's not that.'

Summer grinned. 'Are you and Ben...? I thought you were just friends.'

Discussions about new relationships were usually the sort of conversations she had with Ben, but of course she couldn't have this conversation with Ben. Not when it was her feelings for him she was trying to figure out. But Summer already felt like a friend, and Charlotte desperately needed to speak with someone about what had happened.

'It's new.'

Summer's eyes widened.

'It's very, very new,' Charlotte added.

'That's exciting.' Summer leaned closer. 'Congratulations.'

'But it's confusing and...scary.'

'Scary? Why?'

'Because it's Ben. He's my best friend.'

'That's the best way to start something.'

'Is it? Because it feels terrifying.'

'Why?'

Charlotte took a deep breath. She might as well tell Summer everything. 'I had a boyfriend once, we were engaged. But he died.'

'Oh, no, I'm so sorry.'

Charlotte nodded. It was her standard response. She never really knew what to say, especially when someone who didn't even know Tim expressed sympathy. 'I don't want to hurt like that again. I want to find someone, have a partner. But I just don't think I can go through losing someone again. And because it's Ben, it's as though the stakes are higher than ever.'

Her best friend, the man whose company she felt most comfortable in, was also a wonderful lover. She should feel over-the-moon excited, but the overwhelming feeling she had right now was fear. Fear that she would lose Ben one way or another. Fear she would mess up this new part of their relationship.

Fear Ben might decide it had all been a mistake.

Or...

There were plenty of things that might happen to cause her to lose Ben for good. She didn't want to make a complete list.

'Is Ben pressuring you? Does he want more than you can give right now?'

'No, see, that's just it. I don't think he does. He's the one holding back. I'm the one with the crazy hormonal stuff going on.'

Summer laughed. 'My advice, for what it's worth, would be not to think too hard about these things. Feel more, think less. I think you're in safe hands with Ben.'

Safe hands. Lean, strong hands. Talented hands. The memory of them on her breasts the night before flashed into her mind and her muscles clenched.

'You don't have to know where you're going to end up, you don't have to know the future from the start. Because no one ever does.'

Charlotte nodded. Summer was right; even the best-laid plans could unravel in front of you, under the wheels of a lorry. She just had to see how things went with Ben. She had to give it a try.

She would go back to the villa, Ben would be awake and they would talk and make things right. They had to. Their friendship was too important. Charlotte downed the last of her coffee. She was going to go back and talk to Ben. Try to explain what had happened the night before. Tell him how she felt. What was the worst that could happen?

She stood and heard a voice. Diane.

'Just the two ladies I wanted to see,' she said. 'I hope you're both ready to party.'

* * *

I don't know what just happened.

Charlotte might have been surprised by her tears. She might not have understood.

But Ben did. He knew exactly what was wrong.

She wasn't ready.

By the time Charlotte had peeled her warm, shaking body away from his, he, too, was close to tears.

Making love with Charlotte had nearly ripped him apart as well, but for a different reason. Ever since he'd first met Charlotte he'd known, on some level, that he needed to keep her at a distance—emotionally and physically. He'd known that Charlotte had the capacity to break his heart irreparably. He'd understood that she was not ready to open her heart again, and maybe she never would be.

And now it was more important to remember that than ever: sex with Charlotte might have been good, it might have even been great, but that was all it was. A sexual need. A physical desire. Nothing more.

He left her room, tided himself up, slipped on shorts and a T-shirt. Then he stood outside her room and paced. Past the rumpled bed, probably still warm from their bodies, he could see the bathroom door was closed.

He heard the bath start to run, a massive tub, identical to the one in his room. It would take ages to fill.

Charlotte might be content in the bath, but the four walls of his room were closing in on him. He slipped on his shoes, grabbed the room key and left.

The road near the villa was different at night, and so different from London. It was much quieter, and very dark. He was a world and a tumultuous week away from where he was when he first learned of his mother's wedding.

If Charlotte hadn't decided to come with him, she'd be back in London and none of this would have happened, and things would be as they were between them. Safe. Steady. Stable.

Is that what you want? To go back in time a week? For this never to have happened?

Maybe.

As amazing as the last few hours had been, they had still been a mistake. As perfectly wonderful as it had been to hold one another, entirely bare themselves to each other, Charlotte hadn't been ready.

She wasn't over Tim.

Of course she's not over Tim, he scolded himself. *If she was, she wouldn't have wanted to escape the rainy British autumn to come to the other side of the world with you!*

As a rule, Ben avoided self-reflection when it came to his feelings for Charlotte, afraid of what he might find if he analysed his heart too closely. He tried not to now, but thought and worries kept resurfacing—despite his best efforts to push them away, they bobbed up like a buoy.

You love her. You're in love with Charlotte.

He shook his head.

He couldn't love her; they didn't have that kind of relationship.

He wouldn't love her, it would ruin everything.

His mind was just confused after making love with her. Scratch that, his mind was confused after having sex with her.

Energy coursed through him and he walked on and on. The night air was cooler before he knew it. He'd covered so much distance he'd reached a part of the island they hadn't been to before. Below him he could hear waves crashing into cliffs.

He had no idea how long he'd been walking, having left his phone and watch back at the villa. All he had on him was the villa key card.

Charlotte probably needed her space anyway. She needed

time to process what had happened as much as he had. Maybe more.

But what if Charlotte's way of processing involved up and leaving? It wasn't an inconceivable idea; Charlotte did have form for running away whenever a man got too close.

If she does leave while you're out, you know where to find her in London.

Far from reassuring him, the thought made him worry even further. Just because he knew where she lived and worked didn't mean she'd want to speak to him.

Ben resisted the urge to scream at the sea.

He knew she wasn't ready! Why did he let himself get pulled into that situation? Of course he wanted to kiss her, hold her, be with her—he always had—but he'd never let himself because he knew, deep down, this was exactly where he'd end up.

Not on this dark beach in Bali, exactly, but alone, with Charlotte panicking somewhere else. Ready to flee. Suddenly overcome with exhaustion, he let his knees buckle and he sat on a nearby bench.

Ben was always going to be second best. He saw that now.

Second best to Will.

Second best to Tim.

He'd never be the man Charlotte wanted and that was all there was. He had to accept that and get on with his life. He couldn't change his father's feelings and he'd never change Charlotte's.

All he could do was get on with things the best he could.

He moved his breath in time with the waves—in and out, in and out. He wasn't happy, not by any stretch, but he was calmer.

Ben made his way slowly back to the villa, rehearsing what he was going to say to her.

Charlotte, I'm sorry. Can we pretend this never happened?

That was laughable—pretending wasn't helpful when they needed to be honest.

Charlotte, I'm sorry, I know you still love Tim. I can move past this if you can.

But could he? Could he continue to be her friend, sit across from her at her gallery or in some London cafe and not think of the red bikini?

Charlotte, I'm sorry. If it isn't too strange for you, I'd really like us to remain friends. Please tell me what I can do to save our friendship.

That was it, that was what he had to say. She might never be his lover, but he couldn't lose her from his life for ever.

He unlocked the door and took a deep breath, his heart pounding so hard his ribs ached. But Charlotte wasn't in the living room. His heart picked up speed. *Please don't let her have left.*

The door to her room was wide open and Charlotte was fast asleep, sprawled out in short shorts and a tank top on top of the unmade bed. He could hear her deep, steady breathing from the doorway.

He watched her, wondering if she would wake, but she didn't. He covered her with a sheet and closed her door quietly behind him and went to his own.

Ben lay on his cold bed and at some stage his mind succumbed to the needs of his body, and he fell into a deep dreamless sleep.

He woke, disoriented, not knowing what time it was or even what hemisphere he was in.

Ben stretched, splashed water in his face and went to speak to her.

Please tell me what I can do to save our friendship.

A figure sat at the table by the pool, looking at the view. But it wasn't Charlotte.

It was his mother.

CHAPTER SEVEN

'LIKE A HEN NIGHT?' Ben asked.

'It's not really a hen night, it's more a women's afternoon, and Gus is having a gathering with just the men. He'd really like you to join them.'

It seemed unnecessarily traditional to Ben, but what really worried him was that it meant more time without seeing Charlotte. Where was she now? He looked past his mother to Charlotte's room. The door was open, but it was empty. He'd know if Charlotte was in the villa, he'd be able to sense her.

He was such a fool, sleeping so late. Letting her go.

'Do you know where Charlotte is?' He tried to keep his voice neutral.

'Don't you?' Diane asked.

'No, I just woke up.'

His mother gave him an unreadable look.

'She had breakfast with Summer, and now they're doing some things for me. Helping me with the party.'

The relief he felt was physical; Charlotte hadn't left the island. She was simply with Summer.

'Please go. I'd really like you and Will to have a chance to get to know Gus without me. And besides, I'd like to spend some time with Summer and Charlotte. They tell me more about my sons than my sons do themselves.'

Ben was going to open his mouth to remind his mother

that he and Charlotte were not dating like Summer and Will, but he held his tongue again.

What would he tell his mother anyway? How could he explain what was going on between them when he wasn't even sure himself? They weren't dating, but were they still friends? Could their friendship recover from earth-shaking sex that had ended in tears?

In the bright light of day his fears from last night had not disappeared. They seemed as rational as ever. Running away was what Charlotte did. She'd dumped other men for far less than tears after sex. Not liking the way he chewed. Living on the other side of the city...

'So you'll go? To Gus's shindig?'

Do I have a choice? he wanted to mumble, like a teenager. But he knew the answer. Charlotte would be busy with Summer and his mother. Even if she wanted to talk, which seemed unlikely, she couldn't.

At least this way, Charlotte was less likely to abscond.

Ben nodded. He and Charlotte would have to talk later.

'Will's going too,' Diane added.

That wasn't a positive.

'It'll be good for you to spend some time together.'

Ben wanted to contradict his mother but bit it back; he and Will were practically strangers, ever since Will had supported their father's decision to cut Ben off and Ben had left Australia.

He expected his mother to leave, now that he'd promised to spend the afternoon with Gus, but Diane stayed seated.

'Ben, darling, I'm so glad that you came for the wedding. I know it isn't easy for you. And I know that Gus and I are doing this quickly.'

'Yes,' Ben said. 'Why is that exactly?'

'Because we love one another.'

Yes, but that didn't mean you got married instantly. 'Sure, but why the rush?'

'Because you never know what's around the corner.'

Ben didn't feel like arguing with that. Something around a corner could jump out and upend your life in a few hours of reckless passion. His next question came out in a rush. 'Were you and Dad happy?'

Diane pulled a face. 'Why do you ask?'

'Because I'm curious, but you can tell me to mind my own business if you like.'

Diane considered his question.

'We were. But…'

She looked at the ocean, as though the answer were there. His mother's hesitation made him sad. And more than a little angry at his dead father.

Diane sighed. 'I wasn't unhappy, but things were not always easy between us. He was obsessed with his company and put it first. You know that.'

All too well. 'And?'

'I didn't always agree with all of your father's decisions.'

But you went along with them, Ben thought bitterly.

'Like deciding not to pay my tuition?'

'That was difficult. You know your father thought that since you didn't plan on working in the business, there was no reason for him to pay for your studies. It was a business decision, not a personal one.'

But it *was* still personal. Saying it was a 'business decision' was just his father's way of trying to manipulate Ben into giving up his dreams and passion and falling into line.

'I know that it looked as though your father was favouring Will.'

'It didn't just look like it, he was.'

Diane sighed. 'I think he really wanted to protect you.'

'How?'

'You chose a tough road, Ben. And I know you have done amazingly, but a decade ago, fresh out of school, I think your father though that the best chance you had to lead a stable and happy life was to choose the safe option.'

'Working for him.'

'Yes. I know he could have handled things better. *We* could have handled things better. But I think he truly just wanted you to come and work with him and Will.'

Ben thought it over.

No. It was his mother rewriting history. Trying to forget all the other things his father had done over the years. Withholding not just support, but also love.

'It wasn't just about the money. It was everything.' His father would ask Will about his studies, his life. Each time he'd see Ben he'd refer to him as a freeloader or lazy. Or ungrateful. 'He belittled me. Made fun of my dreams. But Will? There was nothing he wouldn't do for Will.'

Diane pursed her lips together.

'But it wasn't Will's doing. It wasn't his fault.'

No, it wasn't Will's fault. And it wasn't even their mother's; Diane had always showered Ben with affection and treated him exactly as she'd treated Will.

Ben still seethed. He'd had a privileged upbringing, but his father's love had been conditional. Maybe he was being petulant, still holding a grudge about something like his university tuition. Or the car. And the apartment he'd bought for Will. Maybe. But it still hurt. Being second best hurt. And now his father was gone the emotions were just as complex, still uncomfortable. No wonder he stayed away from his family. It was easier than dealing with them.

'But then why rush into marrying Gus?' Realising his question might have overstepped a line, Ben rushed on. 'I'm not disapproving, but I want to make sure you're okay.'

Diane picked up his hand and squeezed it.

'Your father and I were happy. I loved him very much. But it is possible to love more than one person in your life.'

Was it? Ben wanted to ask. That hadn't been his experience at all.

Ben showered and dressed for the afternoon with Gus and his friends.

A knock at the door sent his heart into his windpipe. Charlotte was back! He yanked open the door, but it wasn't Charlotte. It was his brother. Looking annoyed.

'Are you ready?'

'For Gus's thing?'

'Yeah, Mum said you were coming too.'

'I was waiting for Charlotte.'

'She's already at Mum's.'

Ben's throat closed over. Even Will knew where Charlotte was, when Ben didn't. She was avoiding him. It was clear.

Ben contemplated giving Will an excuse and begging off Gus's thing, but Will was giving him a look that was saying, 'Get yourself together.'

Despite being the same height, Will still somehow managed to stare at Ben as though he were looking down at him.

'Let's go. The sooner we get there, the sooner we can leave.'

His logic was sound. And then, Will added softly, 'She's with Summer. They're together, they'll be fine.'

Something inside Ben uncoiled. His brother was right.

Across the bay, the lights from another bar sparkled. Charlotte was there.

Now that the sun had set, the afternoon was definitely over. Will was talking to Gus's father, no doubt about something business-related that would put Ben to sleep. Ben figured he'd served his time. He'd waited long enough to see Charlotte and with each moment that passed he felt more and more on edge.

'You're not leaving already?' Gus said when Ben bade him goodnight.

Ben nodded. 'Congratulations.'

Gus, several beers in, unexpectedly pulled him into a hug. 'I'm really looking forward to getting to know you better. I know this is awkward, but I love your mother more than anything in the world. There's nothing I wouldn't do for her.'

'I know that,' Ben said. It wasn't a lie. Gus did seem like a great guy and his mother deserved to be happy.

'So stay?'

Ben shook his head. 'I have to talk to Charlotte.'

'Is everything okay? Sorry, you don't have to tell me. But you can. Unless that's weird?'

Gus's earnestness was endearing. He was nothing like Ben's father—they were polar opposites.

That's probably what my mother loves about him.

His mother hadn't found a replacement for his autocratic father, but a gentler, calmer man and Ben was relieved. For everyone's sake.

The only thing that made him sad was the past: his mother being married to a man who saw family decisions as business transactions. If you weren't in the business, you weren't in the family.

'I'm not sure if Diane told you, but we're planning on coming to London in a few months,' Gus said.

Ben shook his head. 'She didn't mention it.'

'Well, we are. She'd love to see you again; we both would. And Charlotte too. But I'd better let you get back to her now,' Gus said with a wink and Ben didn't mind the implication at all. He was going to find Charlotte and finally talk about what had happened last night.

Ben's heart hammered against his ribs. He felt his pulse in a hundred places throughout his body as he waited outside the restaurant for Charlotte. He'd sent her a message asking if she wanted to walk home with him, but she hadn't answered and he had no idea if she was still at the party. Even less idea whether she would want to speak to him, but a few beers with Gus and the boys had given him the extra nudge of courage he needed. They had to talk at some point, didn't they?

Then there she was. Wearing a short floral dress, her hair tied up loosely on her head, her face flushed.

She smiled at him and it felt as though he was breathing properly for the first time that day.

'Hey,' he said.

'Hey.'

'I thought you might like someone to walk home with.' The sunlight still lingered in the west, but it would be dark by the time they reached the villa.

'You're not kicking on with the boys?'

'No, it was remarkably restrained.'

Charlotte laughed. 'Unlike Diane's do.'

'Do you want to stay?'

'No! I was ready to leave. I'm exhausted.'

They walked along the dark path, occasional lights and half a moon guiding their way.

'I'm sorry,' they said simultaneously.

They laughed and before she could say anything he began the speech he'd been rehearsing all day.

'I'm so sorry, Charlotte. I know you're still upset about Tim.'

She kept walking and kicked the ground a few times with her feet. When she finally spoke she said, 'Ah, no, I don't think that's it. You see, I think my reaction last night was the opposite.'

'What do you mean?'

'I mean, I didn't cry because I was sad about Tim. I was

crying because I wasn't. Sad about him. I was crying because I finally wasn't holding back.'

Ben had failed exams that made more sense than what Charlotte was saying.

'I still don't understand. Holding what back?'

'You know…' Charlotte made a rolling motion with her right hand.

'No, I don't.'

She stopped walking. 'Ben, I've been on a lot of dates but it's never…never been like that. They never made me feel like you did. I never managed to…' Charlotte made the rolling motion with her hands again.

'Orgasm?' he asked, so there could be no doubt what she was saying.

'Yes.' Charlotte looked down, as though she was embarrassed.

She'd cried because she'd climaxed. And no other man she'd been with since Tim had done that? Except him. At that moment Ben felt a hundred feet tall and would have taken on any predator that approached them. Seven-foot body-builder? He'd take him on. Angry tiger? Let him at 'em.

'Oh, I see.' Ben tried to keep his voice even. 'You're not upset about it?'

'No, well, I'm embarrassed.'

'You don't need to be, really.'

'Ben, come on. Me bursting into tears must have seemed like a pretty brutal review of what we'd done, but that wasn't it at all.'

Feeling happier than he had since the previous evening, Ben almost didn't hear what Charlotte said next. 'So, I was wondering if…'

Ben stopped walking.

'I was wondering if you would give me another chance.'

'Another chance?'

'Yes, Ben, I'm sorry and… I thought maybe I won't mess it up next time.'

Was she suggesting what he hadn't even dared to hope?

'You want to…again?'

'I think I do. That is…only if you do?'

'Yes, I do.' And because those words were not enough to convey how he was really feeling, he added, 'Very much.'

Ben's hand was shaking when he lifted the key card to the lock. Charlotte lifted her hand to steady his and held his hand as he pressed the card to the lock and the door clicked open.

He reached for her, slid his hands around her waist, then down over her hips and up her body again. Charlotte wrapped her arms around his neck and he felt her fingertips slip into his hair.

He kissed the soft skin of her neck. The place he'd studied hundreds of times. He tasted it, breathed in her scent, inhaled until she completely filled his lungs.

All day she'd thought he was avoiding her. Waiting until she was asleep to return to the villa, waiting for her to leave before getting up. Or maybe she'd been avoiding him. She certainly hadn't been looking forward to the conversation they had to have, fearing he'd be upset. Or worse, that he would say they mustn't begin a physical relationship.

But there he was, waiting outside the bar for her. Hands in his pockets, looking nervous. Shy. And her heart exploded. Every worry, every concern, every fear she'd had evaporated at that moment. He wasn't upset; confused maybe, but he wanted to listen to what she had to say.

Last night had been a major turning point for her. Not just because Ben had brought her to climax, though that had been unexpected, but because she'd realised that the reason he'd been able to do that was because this was right between them.

He might be trying to be sensible by giving her space, by

taking things slowly, but that couldn't change the fact that whatever was going on between them was right. She was excited about this new thing between them and maybe she was being a little reckless, but her body throbbed with desire for him. His lips were on her neck and her insides were already molten as he kicked the door to the villa closed.

His kisses stayed restrained at first, but as she pushed deeper, he followed. His hands stayed in a chaste zone, but hers slid down his hips and to his bottom.

He mirrored her actions. Quickly followed her lead.

She slid her hands under his shirt to feel his hard, muscular back. She tried to ease his shirt up but Ben shifted position so she couldn't. Never mind, she'd head in the other direction. Her fingertips slid under the waistband of his shorts and began to manipulate the button.

His kisses stopped and her neck went cold.

He's holding back. He doesn't want this.

'Are you okay?' Her voice trembled. She wanted this. She wanted him.

'Yes.' He nodded. 'Are you?'

'Never better,' she murmured.

He paused and looked deep into her eyes.

Then he scooped her up and carried her to his bed. He pulled his shirt off in a movement so swift she was surprised not to hear ripping fabric. Then she gazed at his broad chest. Abs. Ben had abs. She lifted her finger and traced them.

'Did you always have these?'

'As far as I know.'

'You might have told me.'

'You never asked,' he murmured against her chest, his kisses exploring lower and lower.

He pulled her dress over her head and the air hit her skin for a moment only before he covered her with his warm body. They kissed and kissed, her body growing tighter, wetter, more impatient. Ben moved lower, ran his hands over her breasts then took them one at a time into his mouth. She stifled a moan.

She wanted him.

Needed him. Like air. As soon as possible.

Ben unbuttoned his shorts and slid them over his hips, but before he could kick them off, she reached greedily for him, rubbing her hand over him, feeling the length of his arousal, every muscle between her legs tightening. He was tender, yet firm. His kisses delicate, his body hard. Every muscle in her body reacted to him, from the ones in her toes to the ones in her heart.

He scrambled for his bag and a condom, even as she straddled him.

Ben's eyes widened in appreciation as she moved on top of him. She knew what was coming, knew, with a certainty that she hadn't felt in years that Ben could satisfy her, bring her to an earth-shaking climax. But even as he moved inside her, touched parts of her that no one had been able to reach, she knew she never wanted this to end. The orgasm would be the icing on the cake, being close to Ben, feeling him, tasting him, was the main event.

'Don't hold back,' she said. She wasn't talking about his body, but he didn't need to know that.

Don't hold back, let every part of yourself go. I want all of you.

She reached a climax before him, but rather than the reaction the evening before, she was revitalised, and pulled him even closer to her, rocking, marvelling at what it was like to make love with her best friend. Marvelling at the way he felt against her and the look on his face when he too broke apart.

Ben slept next to her, flat out on his stomach. She watched his beautiful back rise and fall with each gentle, contented breath.

Her heart tugged towards him. What on earth was going on with them? It was wonderful and terrifying all at once. Last night's love-making had not been a one-off. Ben had shown her, again and again this evening, that he could make her body feel things she hadn't felt in years.

And he was having the same effect on her heart as well.

Was it possible to fall in love so quickly?

Of course, it hadn't all been fast, they'd known one another for years, but three days was very fast to go from platonic friendship to love.

Love.

She pushed the word aside. It wasn't a helpful word to use. Of course she loved Ben. But love as a friend, or as a person, was very different from making love, falling in love.

This was lust and need and desire.

This was wanting to spend every moment with him, waking and sleeping. This was also touching her belly and thinking back to what Summer had asked her.

Are you pregnant?

She wasn't, they'd been careful again, but the idea of carrying Ben's baby didn't fill her with fear or dread, and now that the idea had been planted in her mind, she couldn't shake it.

Did *that* mean she was falling in love with him?

How was it possible to know someone for years and then suddenly fall in love? The idea felt strange and reckless. Unlikely, even impossible.

Risking waking him, she slid her hand over his warm back and rested it on his muscular shoulder.

Ben wasn't reckless. That was why he was being the sensible one and holding back, because he knew that three days was far too fast for their feelings to change like this.

Ben was cautious, he hadn't been swept up in whatever tropical fever had taken over her. Ben was her best friend and now she knew he was a great lover. She wanted to stay up all night watching him sleep, but she had to check herself, pull her feelings in.

Because what if Ben didn't fall at the same speed she found herself plummeting? Where would she be then? Awkwardly in love with her best friend while he just carried on unaffected.

Ben kept his feelings so close to his chest, she would have to tread carefully, but she needed to know how he felt and whether she had to protect her heart, or whether she could let herself fall, knowing that he would be there to catch her. She lay down and pressed her cheek to his shoulder. Safe, firm. She couldn't lose him.

Tomorrow she would make him open up.

CHAPTER EIGHT

THE FIRST RAYS of sunlight began streaming into Ben's room. Charlotte marvelled at how it hit his soft brown hair and brought out every highlight. She lay on her stomach next to him with her chin resting on his shoulder blade and drew circles across his back.

This man was gorgeous. Everything about this moment was gorgeous. The new day, the new relationship and sense of completeness in her chest. This was where she was meant to be.

Ben rolled over onto his back with a groan.

'Are you okay?' she asked.

'Never better,' he replied groggily.

'You don't sound like it.'

He met her gaze and smiled. 'We just didn't get much sleep last night.'

'It's almost like we're not even on Indonesian time,' Charlotte agreed. She kissed a sweet spot just behind his ear. 'I think we should just stay in bed all day.'

She loved this, the freedom to touch and feel any part of him she wanted. And it was all the more amazing because this wasn't some random stranger that she didn't know and didn't trust, this was Ben, who she could trust with her own life. And maybe even her heart.

But she still had to be careful. The new day hadn't brought

any more certainty to her about the new nature of their relationship.

Yes, they were friends. Yes, they were physically compatible, but did he have the same feeling of a swarm of butterflies in his stomach as she had? Did he feel the same racing in his heart each time he looked at her?

'We do have a wedding to go to the day after tomorrow though.' Ben pulled himself away slightly from her kisses and her heart dropped.

'You're not freaking out about this?' she asked carefully.

Ben laughed. 'Me? Freaking out? You're the one most likely to panic.'

Charlotte sat up and pulled the sheet to her chest. 'What do you mean? Why would I panic?'

Ben shook his head. 'Never mind. I'm sorry, that came out wrong.'

But she understood. He was being careful and making sure that she wasn't falling too fast. It was his way of saying, 'We need to take this one day at a time.'

He was right. Even though she was ready to give him all of her heart, she knew it was happening very quickly.

Charlotte traced a line from his eyes down his cheek to his chin and then around his lips. 'I'm not freaking out,' she whispered and planted a quick kiss on his lips before going to the bathroom.

When she emerged, Ben was dressed in shorts, but nothing else and sitting on the deck overlooking the pool and the ocean. If she had her way, this was how he would dress, always.

He passed her a fresh cup of coffee. 'What do you want to do today?'

'I want to stay here.'

And just look at you. I don't want to share you with anyone.

Ben grinned.

'We have to go to that thing tonight.' Gus and Diane were

really making the most of having all of their friends and family in the one place and had organised yet another gathering. This time all the wedding guests were invited.

'I know, but until then, we could stay here.'

'Are you sure?' he asked.

She felt a stab of guilt at the fact he might want to make the most of their short visit to Bali, so she said, 'But we can play tourist if you like.'

He gave her a knowing grin and shook his head. 'There's nowhere else in the world I'd rather be.'

They drank their coffee and ate some breakfast, but only for long enough to gather their energy before they returned to the bedroom. This time it was Charlotte who fell asleep afterwards, feeling safe and secure in Ben's arms.

But she was alone in her bed when she awoke many hours later and the sense of security she'd felt earlier had vanished, replaced again with the uncertainty that was slowly but surely gnawing at her. She told herself to take a breath, let things take their course, but it was hard to reach that stage of Zen. Even with the scene she found when she walked out onto the deck. Ben, with his feet up, head facing the sky, eyes closed. The sun dancing across the water of the pool and the azure ocean. If she didn't feel calm here, what chance did she have in the bustle of London, when they went back to their normal lives?

Charlotte sat on the day bed and stretched out, letting the sun warm her limbs as well. After a while, Ben stirred and noticed her beside him. The smile that broke across his face made her stomach swoop.

'How are you doing?'

His question was open and honest, and she was almost tempted to say, 'I'm confused and worried because I don't know what you're thinking or feeling and whether this is a big thing for you or whether it's casual and I'm wondering what happens when we get back to London and whether we're in a relationship. Is that what this is?'

But she bit those words back.

'Freaking out?' he prompted.

'No,' she said firmly. 'I'm...' Worried, concerned, apprehensive...so maybe, yes, maybe freaking out a little.

'Usually when I don't know about a relationship, I come and talk to you,' she began.

Ben nodded.

'But in this case, it's tricky.'

'Because you want to talk about me.'

She nodded.

'You can still talk to me.'

'But...' No, she couldn't. There was no way she could give voice to all the questions circling in her head.

'How about I start?' he said. 'So, Charlotte, did you get lucky last night?'

It was the first time Ben had asked that question and actually wanted to hear the answer. She looked at him through narrowed eyes, then her face brightened as she realised what he was getting at.

'I did, as it happens.'

'Lucky you.' He couldn't suppress his smile.

'Yes, and lucky him.'

Ben laughed.

'Can I take it from your answer that the sex was good?'

'The sex was great.'

'Just great?'

She swatted him. 'You're fishing for compliments now.'

'No, I'm just trying to understand. Tell me about him? What's he like?'

'He's very good with his hands. But I shouldn't be surprised by that, he's an artist.'

Ben sat where he was, forcing himself not to go straight to her and climb on top of her on the day bed. She wanted to talk and it was so important that they kept talking.

'An artist? You need to watch out for them.'

She laughed.

'So the sex was phenomenal.' He steeled himself for the next question. 'But how do you feel about him?'

He held his breath, fearing that he'd gone too far.

'He's one of my favourite people in the world. So, there's that.'

'That's a good start, isn't it?'

'It's a great start. The best. But…'

Oh, God, this was it. *But I don't think I want a relationship with him. Or anyone.*

'But I'm not sure how he feels.'

Ben allowed himself to exhale. 'Ahh…'

'And we talk a lot about how I feel but we don't talk as much about how he feels. I'm worried he's holding something back. Or that he's not as interested. He seems unsure.'

Unsure? Him? That was not what he was expecting her to say.

'Well, from what you told me and relying on my knowledge of being a man, I would guess, and it's just a guess…'

'Of course.' Her lips curled into a delicious grin.

'I would guess that he feels the same way you do.'

There. He couldn't possibly know if that was the truth, because he wasn't sure how she was feeling about him.

But it wasn't a lie, exactly, he told himself.

'Would he, you know, from what you know as a man, have thought the sex was good?'

Ben leaned towards her. 'I'm pretty sure he thought the sex was phenomenal. Probably the best he's had in his life.'

A lovely blush spread across Charlotte's cheeks.

'And how do you think he feels, theoretically, about what's going on?'

'I'm pretty sure he feels the same way as you,' he repeated.

'But could you be more specific?'

She looked down at him, eyes full of uncertainty and questions.

He thinks he might love you.

The words in his head made him pull back and Charlotte mirrored his actions, startled, eyes wide.

He loved her. But that was the last thing he could tell her. She'd fly out of the door without a backward glance if he confessed that. But he had to say something, because she was sitting across from him now looking crestfallen.

'I think he's excited about the new developments in your relationship.'

She tilted her head. That answer wasn't good enough for her. But it was all he could say without frightening her.

'He's very excited. And happy. But he's also a little nervous, because you are so very important to him, and he doesn't want to stuff anything up between the two of you.'

'But he's excited? Pleased?'

'Very. Because you are also one of his favourite people in the world. And the sex was phenomenal.'

She laughed.

'And I think he'd like to show you again how good it can be. Just to put that question beyond doubt.'

'Oh.' Charlotte considered this. 'I think that would be okay.'

Ben moved back to her and his lips dropped to kiss her beautiful shoulder as he let his fingers stroke her silken arms. He felt her relax under his touch. Her lids lowered. She might not love him yet, but he would do everything within his power to make sure she did eventually. And if that meant holding back his true feelings for a little longer, then that was what he had to do.

* * *

Charlotte looked at her wardrobe.

She wanted to wear something that would wow him. An outfit that would make more than just his jaw drop, an outfit that would make him fall in love with her.

She sighed. She only had what was in her suitcase. It would have to be the green. A long cotton sundress, but with a fitted bodice and low neckline. She showered and dressed and scolded herself for being so wound up about this. If Ben were any other man, she'd be relaxed. Nonchalant even.

But he wasn't just any man, he was her Ben. Their conversation earlier had been fun, and she supposed that she should be happy with everything he'd told her, but she couldn't shake the feeling that he was still holding something back. He'd agreed the sex had been phenomenal.

Probably the best he'd had in his life.

That should be enough for now, shouldn't it?

Part of her knew that she shouldn't push things, but the other part of her felt as if she were in limbo. Not knowing if they were moving forward or back or anything. Not knowing if he thought this would last when they got back to London.

Ben's relationship track record was as sparse as hers. He also never lasted beyond a few dates. Was that what he thought would happen between him and Charlotte?

She wanted him to like her. She wanted him to love her.

She walked out of her room and waited for Ben to turn around. Her palms were damp, whether from the humidity or nerves. She wiped them on her dress. At the rate she was going the dress would be soaked by the evening's end.

Ben turned and smiled. For a moment she forgot her mission and could only look at him. He was wearing a soft shirt, open at the neck, and loose trousers. His hair was washed and he'd shaved. She bit her lip and considered simply undressing him there and then, and forgetting about dinner.

He stepped up to her, eyes wide. 'Charlotte, you look amazing.' He brushed his lips against her cheek and she felt her knees weaken.

'Shall we?' he asked. 'The sooner we get there, the sooner we can get back.'

That sounded like very good logic to Charlotte.

They held hands as they walked, but he let go as soon as they approached the restaurant. It disappointed her, but she told herself it was okay, he wasn't ready to announce the changed nature of their relationship to the world. It was sensible even. But for once, she wished Ben was not so utterly sensible.

'Is everything okay?' he asked, as if he could read her thoughts.

'It's fine. No, great!' She forced a lightness into her tone.

'I'm sorry we have to do this.'

'No, don't be sorry. This is why we came. Why I came. It'll be a good night.'

Ben looked at her as if he didn't believe her and motioned for her to enter the restaurant first.

So much for wooing Ben and getting him to open up more. Tonight Charlotte was at the quiet end of the table. She was seated next to Ben's aunt and Gus's brother, who seemed considerably older than Gus and nowhere near as charming. Ben was at the other end of the table with a group of younger people, including a couple and their two young children. Ben's cousins. Charlotte was not great at guessing children's ages, but one of the children, with a mop of messy brown curls, was toddling around and chatting to people. The other was being passed between its parents' laps.

When the food arrived in front of them, Ben stood. Was he leaving? Giving a speech? What was he doing?

Ben reached down and said something to the child's

mother. She smiled and then passed the baby to Ben, who held it and rocked it while the child's parents ate their dinner.

He knew how to hold a baby. When on earth did he learn that?

Watching Ben hold the baby did very strange things to Charlotte's insides.

I just must be hungry, she thought, and loaded up her plate with more noodles.

Charlotte did not pay any attention to what the people around her were talking about, too busy watching the scene at the other end of the table. Once the baby was passed back to its mother, the toddler tugged Ben's sleeve and he lifted her onto his lap. Within moments Ben had the toddler laughing at something. Charlotte strained to hear what on earth he was saying. Not only was he comfortable holding the baby, but he also knew how to talk to them. She'd thought she knew Ben inside out, but now she felt as though she was getting to know him all over again. It was unsettling.

And wonderful.

Ben picked up her hand again once they were out of sight of the restaurant.

'Are you okay?' he asked.

'Yes, just tired.'

Back at the villa, she washed her face and brushed her teeth. Ben gave her a sheepish grin. 'So, I've run out of condoms. I thought I had more, but I clearly did not anticipate I'd be needing so many. Do you happen to have any more?'

Clearly sleeping with her had not been on Ben's radar at all. If she hadn't thrown herself at him then it wouldn't have crossed his mind.

What was she going to do with all these feelings that were getting stronger every day and pulling her towards Ben?

Charlotte held her stomach. It felt empty. Which was strange given she'd eaten half a Balinese feast at dinner.

She didn't want the condom. She didn't even want her IUD.

For the first time in her life the thought of getting pregnant didn't terrify her. The idea of a baby growing inside her, of *Ben's* baby growing inside her, didn't scare her—in fact she craved it. A baby that would grow up into a little child like the one he'd been talking to at dinner, with a mop of light brown curly hair on its head and his big blue eyes.

She clutched her stomach tighter. Now that the image was planted in her mind, she couldn't shake it. Kids were not on her agenda; they were on a five-year planner that hadn't even been printed yet.

She wanted Ben's babies.

And it was terrifying. She wanted to wake up to Ben's smiling face looking at her when she woke up every morning.

And Ben still thought they were friends. Ben who didn't want to hold her hand in front of his family.

'Actually, I want to go for a walk,' she said.

'A walk? The chemist will be shut.'

'No, yes, not for that. I just need a walk.'

'Okay, I'll get my shoes.'

'You don't need to come,' she snapped more forcefully than she'd intended.

Ben didn't blink. If anything, he became calmer. He was still as he said, 'I'm not letting you walk around in the dark alone.'

'Fine, come,' she said. It was the only way of not having to explain the excess energy rising inside her and her sudden need to get out of the villa where they had spent most of the day making love.

Being with Ben negated the whole purpose of the walk, which was to get away from him, to have some time to think and process what was going on in her head. And her stomach. And her heart.

There were no streetlights and, once they'd passed the cluster of hotels and villas near them, only the occasional house. She grudgingly admitted to herself that Ben was right, she didn't want to be walking alone. While the island felt safe, it was still an unfamiliar place.

'When did you get so good at kids?' she asked.

He laughed. 'I wouldn't say I'm an expert.'

'But with those kids at dinner?'

'My cousin May's kids? The toddler is Isabelle. The last time I saw her was at Dad's funeral last year. She was only just walking then. And the baby is Teddy.'

Isabelle and Teddy. Lovely names. What would they call their kids if they ever had them? She'd always liked Jacob. And Emilia.

'You were good with them. You knew what to do.'

'Hardly. I know that parents need to eat. And need every break they can get.'

'So, you don't want kids?' Charlotte froze. She couldn't believe she'd just asked that.

She couldn't believe she didn't know. They'd known one another for years, but never discussed this. If only she'd asked him this question three weeks ago when nothing was hanging on it.

'I…ah…' Ben stopped walking.

'You don't.'

'Char, I never… That is, I don't know.' A taxi truck drove past and its headlights crossed Ben's face. She could see the look of shock on it.

'I don't mean with me, I mean, just generally. In theory,' she clarified.

'I guess, one day, I suppose so,' he said.

He supposed so. As if he were doing her some sort of favour.

'Fine!' she barked, declaring that everything really was *not* fine.

'Charlotte, what's going on? What's the matter?'

She couldn't tell him. She couldn't tell him about everything that was whirling around inside her. New feelings, new desires. Some of the desires were so unexpected and so powerful she was overwhelmed by them.

Ben, I think I want to have your babies and it terrifies me.

She turned away and took some steadying breaths. Ben hadn't said he didn't want kids, he was giving her a perfectly rational and calm answer to her questions. They'd slept together for the first time less than forty-eight hours ago and she was now expecting him to say that they would have babies together?

She wasn't all right. She was confused. Shaken.

But he was so unruffled, as if this wasn't affecting him at all.

She tried to study his face in the almost dark. 'How are you not freaking out?'

'What do you mean?'

'I mean...' She waved her hands around hoping he would understand without her having to spell it out. 'I mean, about this. Us. You're so calm. Don't you care?'

Ben walked over to her, slowly. Still so bloody calm.

'I'm not calm.'

'You look calm. You seem positively bored.'

'Bored!'

'Yes, bored, as if you sleep with your best friend every day.'

In the darkness, his hands found hers. 'I am freaking out,' he said. 'I'm just internalising my freak-out.'

'But you are freaking out?'

'Totally. I'm panicking and excited and...and I'm trying to appear calm so you don't panic.'

Could that be it? Ben was more sensible than her, in some ways. He had the neat apartment, he was always on time. But she sometimes had to remind him how to get where they were going. Together, they always managed to figure things out.

And they would now. She squeezed his hand.

'Is that true? Are you really freaking out on the inside?'

He nodded. 'Like a duck in a pond. Calm on the surface, paddling like a mad thing below.'

'What are we going to do?' She needed to know how to handle these feelings, whether she should be holding something back or letting herself fall entirely and irretrievably.

'Take each day as it comes. Is there anything else?'

'It might help me if I can see you freaking out a bit more?'

'How would that possibly help?'

'I don't know, but I'd feel less crazy.'

He pulled her against him. He kissed behind her ears, down her neck. A warm feeling began to fill her belly.

'Paddling madly?' she asked.

'Madly. Frantically,' he murmured tenderly into her neck. 'So am I.'

CHAPTER NINE

BEN LAY ON his back in Charlotte's bed and she curled against him. She held his hand and was twirling her fingers through his. To an outsider it might have looked like a dreamy scene, but Charlotte was on edge. Oh, she might not have been on the brink of leaving the island and going back to London, but she was giving him sideways glances and screwing up her face with worry when she thought he wasn't looking. He had to remain steady for both their sakes.

They had shared their most honest conversation so far, but underlying it all he sensed she was worried about her feelings and about hurting his. She was worried about the future.

He wanted a future with Charlotte. He wanted to give himself to her body and soul for the rest of his life.

He didn't know where this new path would take them, but the last thing he wanted was Charlotte out of his life, so he had to take things slowly if things were going to have a chance of working out between them.

'What are we going to do today?' he asked.

'Stay here?' she answered.

It was so tempting. After all, they had everything they needed. A pool to lie beside, food to be delivered. Each other. They could, he rationalised, stay here for ever.

But this was Bali! On the other side of the world. A long

London winter lay ahead of them and there would be plenty of time to cuddle up in bed during the next few months.

He was getting ahead of himself. They had discussed the fact that they were both excited but nervous, but neither of them had broached the subject of what would happen back in London. Would they be able to keep their new relationship alive? Or would it die out slowly? Or worse, end quickly. Dramatically. Irretrievably.

Just because he wanted to spend all day in bed with her, that didn't mean that was what they should do. They were friends first and foremost and he was trying not to forget that important fact. They should do something that friends would do. They had to preserve that part of their relationship.

'That would be nice,' he replied.

'You left off the "but".'

'Don't you think we should make the most of our time here?'

'I thought we were?' The smile that broke over her face made him tingle all over. He was about to roll over and pull her to him, but he held firm.

'I think we should make the most of our last couple of days. The wedding is tomorrow and we leave the day after that. There's still a lot we haven't seen.'

If he didn't get out of bed, they would make love again and, yes, it would be wonderful, but every time they made love, he felt a little closer to her. Fell a little more.

She sighed. 'You're right. We should explore. Where would you like to go? Swimming? Surfing?'

'Gus said we should really visit Nusa Ceningan. It's the next island over and there's a famous yellow bridge between the two. Nusa Ceningan is meant to have beautiful beaches. Romantic.' As soon as the words slipped out, he wanted them back. So much for not spooking Charlotte.

But to his delight, her face lit up. 'Let's do it.'

* * *

Ben was holding back.

Oh, not in bed. In bed he was very much on board with what was happening. But he was still holding something back.

Just because you're friends and you have sex, that doesn't mean this is a relationship, she reminded herself.

Except that he'd suggested a romantic island visit. That was what he'd said, wasn't it?

Ben had pulled his phone out and was scrolling through his emails as though he hadn't just dropped the R word.

At what point did 'friends who had sex' become something more? At what point were they in a relationship? If only he'd give her a sign that this was more than just a two-friends-having-sex arrangement.

He'd told her that he was panicking too but, given the infuriatingly calm way in which he seemed to be approaching this, she assumed that was largely for her benefit. Besides, he'd also told her repeatedly that their friendship was the most important thing, the thing they had to protect above all else.

She knew—logically—that she had to give their relationship time to evolve. They were on the other side of the world, away from their real lives, and neither of them could predict what might happen when they returned to London.

In the meantime, they were going to a romantic beach.

She climbed out of bed, naked in the daylight. Ben looked at her appreciatively and she felt herself blush. It was a lot to get used to, seeing one another naked. Though, she was convinced, a thoroughly positive change in their relationship.

She ran a finger down his bare foot, sticking out over the edge of the bed, tickling him. 'Let's go see these beaches.'

After breakfast and dressing they walked out of the villa and to the concierge that operated the accommodation to find a means of getting to the island.

'Where are you off to?' the assistant asked.

'Nusa Ceningan.'

She shook her head. 'There are no cars allowed on Nusa Ceningan either. But you can rent scooters,' she said, pointing to a row of small motorcycles.

'We could walk,' Charlotte suggested.

'No, it's too far. And too hot. Take a scooter,' the woman insisted.

'Change of plan,' Ben said. 'We'll find a closer beach.'

But Nusa Ceningan was *romantic*. He wanted to go. And she did too.

Charlotte stared at the scooters. They weren't actual motorbikes. Not exactly like Tim had been riding. More like mopeds.

'We don't have to go,' Ben said softly.

'But you want to.'

'Not this much. Charlotte, it's okay.'

'Just give me a moment.'

It wasn't her preferred mode of transport, but they wouldn't travel fast.

Ben stood still and Charlotte went to the bike.

At university, she had ridden a bicycle everywhere. Tim had as well. One the paths, on the roads. In London owning a car was impractical, not to mention expensive, so Tim had decided a motorcycle was the mode of transport for him. Charlotte had thought him lazy, more than anything else, as she preferred walking and the Tube, and it hadn't occurred to her that a motorbike would be dangerous.

Tim was a good rider, and for nearly two years he rode the motorbike without incident. But even the best riders could face trouble in cold, icy rain. It was always the rain that had worried her most, slippery, blinding, and unpredictable.

She knew she didn't have to do this. She and Ben could turn around and walk to a nearby beach. Or go back to the villa and bed.

But she didn't want to be stuck any more. She was tired of being scared and Ben wanted to do this.

Romantic.

She walked up to the scooter and placed her hand on the seat, as if touching it would answer her question. The leather seat was warm from the sun. She nodded.

Ben didn't say anything but raised his brows to confirm.

'Yes, I'd like to do this.'

'You can share, you know?' said the woman.

Ben and Charlotte looked at one another. Cosying up on a bike behind Ben? Where could she sign up? She nodded.

'You trust me?' he asked.

'Of course I do.' *With my life.*

They did the paperwork and the woman offered to show them how to ride. It was a relatively simple matter of turning the key and accelerating or braking. Balancing was easier than on a bicycle, not that she'd ridden one of those in years either.

'Helmets?' Ben asked and the woman handed them two.

Once their helmets were on, they got on the scooter, Ben first and Charlotte behind.

'Just yell if I'm going too fast or if you want me to stop.'

'I will, but I'll be fine.'

Ben looked even more worried than she felt as he turned forward and started the scooter. He drove slowly onto the road.

The road was smooth at first, but as they made their way across the island the more potholes they came across and the rougher the road became. She didn't feel worried, but she did have to concentrate on holding onto Ben. Though it was hardly a problem. Holding onto Ben was her new obsession. After a while, Ben pulled over to the side of the road.

'Is everything okay?' she asked.

'Yes, I just wanted to check how you're doing.'

'I'm fine. It's actually fun.'

Ben smiled, but only with his mouth. She reached over

and rubbed his arm reassuringly. 'Really, it's fun. I'm glad we're doing this.'

'The yellow bridge isn't too much further.'

Charlotte got used to the rhythm of the scooter accelerating, braking, and taking the corners gently.

She let go, not just of fears and worry about her safety. Or Tim. But also, her fears and worry about her future with Ben. After a while she stopped concentrating on the bike and began to notice everything else around her—the rush of the green scenery running past, the feel of the sun on her hands, the air brushing her face. In the humidity it could hardly be called a breeze, but it wasn't unpleasant. Most of all, she focused on the way Ben's back felt against her cheek. The way the muscles in his arms and legs looked as he steered and manoeuvred the bike. The world looked different from the back of a scooter, but maybe she was just looking at the world differently.

The yellow bridge was a narrow suspension bridge spanning the waterway between the two islands of Nusa Lembongan and Nusa Ceningan. It was made of wood and slightly rickety, reminding her of one of the suspension bridges over deep canyons in movies, only the bridge was low and crossed a strait of clear blue water.

There was a queue to cross the bridge, with only a certain number of people and bikes allowed at a time and traffic from both sides taking turns to cross. The crossing was also slowed down by tourists stopping halfway for photos of the beautiful view, taking in the seaweed farms and colourful fishing boats. But no one seemed to mind, no one was in a hurry. Not when they were all in such a beautiful, tranquil place.

Charlotte took out her phone and started taking some shots as well.

'Smile!' She caught Ben's handsome face by surprise.

She had plenty of photos of Ben, but that was Bearded

Ben. Friend Ben. This Ben—her Ben—was different. This photo would be different.

'And a selfie.'

He stood dutifully next to her, wrapping his arms around her and standing close. She moved in even closer, their cheeks touching. Sparks shot down her arm, causing her hand to tremble slightly. Charlotte angled to get the bridge in behind them and just as she was lining up another shot, Ben glanced away from the camera and towards her. As Charlotte hit the button Ben was looking directly at her. And smiling.

He stepped away and when Charlotte regarded the photo her stomach swooped. Anyone looking at this photo would see two people who were more than a little comfortable with one another's bodies. Tanned faces, close cheeks, bright eyes, bodies wrapped around one another's. She even fancied, for the briefest of moments, that her camera had captured a look of desire crossing Ben's face.

She'd look at these later and they would either make her happy or crush her.

Depending on what happened next.

'Are you going to post those?' he asked with a guarded voice, as though he'd read her thoughts.

If you post these, people will speculate that we're more than friends.

She had last posted a picture of them supping champagne in the airport lounge and another from the craft shops in Ubud, but apart from that she hadn't posted any photos of the trip to social media.

The highlights of the trip had all been decidedly not for general viewing.

She shook her head.

If Ben wasn't ready to announce their new-found intimacy to the word, then neither was she.

While they waited to cross, Charlotte looked up the history of the bridge.

'Did you know it's also called the Bridge of Love?'

Annoyingly Ben had put on his sunglasses and she couldn't read his expression as he said, 'No, I didn't know that.'

The Bridge of Love. That was his opportunity to use that word.

Throw it out there. See how it felt, how it sounded on his lips.

Love.

But he didn't.

Of course he didn't. This was commitment-phobe Ben. Two-date Ben.

They were, as everyone said, firm members of CA: Commitment-phobes Anonymous.

If you're not going to use that word, why are you expecting Ben to?

Ben might not have used the L-word but he did keep looking from the scooter to her with concern, so she smiled broadly. 'I'm okay. I'm having a good time,' she insisted. As she spoke, she realised it was the truth. No exaggeration was necessary; she was having a great time. The scooter wasn't fast, there wasn't much other traffic and it had brought them here, to this beautiful spot and this charming bridge.

They crossed the bridge, stopping with everyone else in the centre for more photos before continuing on to the island and the beach Ben wanted to visit.

Like all the other beaches in the vicinity, it was picturesque, with clear turquoise water and small waves that lapped gently up the white sands. The beach, like a few across the islands, had a swing. Not a large rope swing for daredevils to launch themselves into a lake or river, but a swing like at a children's playground, where people could sit and swing, dipping their toes in the water. This one had a double swing and was shaded by a broad umbrella. One swing each.

Romantic.

They bought some cool drinks from a nearby cafe and returned to the beach.

He handed her one of the drinks and said, 'You want to try the swing, don't you?'

She nodded. 'Don't you?'

Luckily the swing was unoccupied and they both claimed their seats. It had been years since Charlotte had swung on a swing, and the sensation of swooping in her stomach from the lifting and falling was a lot like what her body had been through the past few days with Ben.

It really was romantic. Clear blue, clean, amazing water, swinging, feet dragging through the water.

She laughed.

Ben turned to her and spoke earnestly. 'Are you having a good time?'

'Of course. I'm having a great time.'

'Thank you for coming.'

She shook her head. 'No, thank you for bringing me.'

Not having come to Bali with Ben was inconceivable. This week had changed her life. She just wasn't sure yet how much.

They passed Will and Summer on their return to the village, Charlotte still filled with endorphins after her ride. She felt energised by the exercise, but something else as well. By overcoming her fear of riding she'd unblocked something that had been holding her back. Ben was beside her, beaming, and she felt on top of the world. She greeted them both warmly and Summer gave her a hug.

'We've just ridden to the yellow bridge. It was great,' Charlotte enthused.

'We're just about to go surfing. Do you want to come?'

Charlotte looked to Ben and his eyes were wide. Charlotte had hoped they would go straight back to the villa, but she knew Ben loved to surf. At least he had once. He'd told her several times that it was one of the things he missed most about Australia.

'Ben?'

Ben looked to his brother and back to Summer. Charlotte, not caring what the others might read into the gesture, rubbed Ben's arm. 'You want to, don't you?'

Ben nodded. 'But do you?'

'I don't have to surf. But I'd like to watch,' she said low and suggestive, so only Ben could hear.

He straightened his spine and nodded. 'Sounds great. Just let us get our things.'

The four of them headed off to the famous surf beach at the northern end of the island. Charlotte was relaxed, and finally felt Ben was too. He was chatting away happily with Will about what they all might do that evening. Diane and Gus were having a quiet night alone as it was the evening before the wedding, and Summer suggested the four of them have an early dinner, to which Ben quickly and surprisingly agreed.

Maybe his attitude to Will was thawing.

Charlotte wasn't sure why it bothered her that the brothers didn't get along, but it did. Having no siblings of her own, she had always envied those who had them. It seemed like too important a relationship to toss aside capriciously.

Will hurt him.

Maybe, though Charlotte wasn't exactly sure why, Ben blamed Will for the actions of their father. Charlotte doubted that Will told his father not to pay Ben's university tuition. Or to refuse to extend the same perks that Will received.

Still, she didn't know everything that had gone on in the Watson household and had promised Ben she would not meddle.

Charlotte had dressed in her swimsuit, but felt she had exhausted quite enough courage and adrenaline for the day. Besides, the view was far better from the beach. It was hard to suppress the smile from her face as she watched Ben carry his board into the surf, his muscles rippling under his bronzed skin as he paddled out. She pressed her lips together as she watched his lean, strong body balance on the board as he rode a short wave in.

This was, she was quite convinced, paradise.

Charlotte stretched out on the beach and let the sun soak into her skin. Two more sleeps till they went home. Two more nights sharing the villa with Ben. Her body still thrummed from the night before. Summer was right, it was better just to see what happened and take each day at a time and not think too far ahead. She had to keep reminding herself that planning your life out perfectly was often a waste of time as too many unpredictable things would always be thrown your way. Charlotte knew that better than most.

Ben was more relaxed today as well. After speaking last night, she'd realised that his hesitation wasn't due to a lack of desire or interest, only caution and a wish not to see the friendship unravel.

But right now, she pushed the future from her mind. She watched Ben, in the shallows with Will, both of them showing Summer how to surf. Charlotte couldn't help but smile. She liked seeing the brothers getting along cooperating, not competing.

She closed her eyes and let her body relax, remembering how it had felt when Ben's fingers had stroked her the night before. She felt so alive with him, yet so comfortable. A strange mix of excitement and security.

She must have been dozing when a sound to her side shook her from her daydreams. She sat up, rubbing her eyes.

'Sorry to wake you,' Will said, rummaging in his bag.

Charlotte stretched. 'You didn't wake me. I was just being lazy.'

Will picked up his phone and moved a few metres away. It looked like he was making some kind of work-related call.

Charlotte shook her head. She wondered how Summer coped with Will's workaholic tendencies. She and Ben at least had the same amount of drive and ambition. They could both get lost in their work and, particularly before a big exhibition, it could become all-consuming for both. But they also knew how to wind down and experience the other joys in life.

Ben and I are well matched.

She shook the thought away again. She was meant to be taking things one day at a time, not thinking too far into the future.

She looked out at the waves and spotted Ben and Summer moving into the water. Ben holding his board confidently and surely. Summer with a smaller board. Ben managed to climb on first and began to paddle.

Charlotte knew in theory that Ben had spent much of his childhood at the beach swimming and surfing, though she'd never quite imagined the scene before her now, watching him, with his broad shoulders and tanned chest, navigating the waves as if he'd done it all his life. Summer was less certain and, unlike the brothers, she'd avoided the more challenging waves. But she climbed onto her board now, lay on her stomach and followed Ben.

There were so many things about Ben that Charlotte was only just discovering. He was a revelation. Ben and Summer moved further out, both of them deftly navigating the waves.

She watched Ben climb onto the board, then his knees, and catch a superb wave. The look on his face was priceless. It was worth travelling halfway around the world to see him look so happy and fulfilled.

It was worth travelling around the world for many other reasons too, she reflected.

Charlotte's eyes didn't travel far from Ben so, like him, she didn't see the giant wave until it was already on top of him.

The wave crashed over the boards and Charlotte lost sight of them both.

CHAPTER TEN

CRAP.

That was Ben's overwhelming thought as the wave loomed over him and Summer. He saw her on her board a few metres to his left.

'Breathe!' he yelled to her with his last breath, the instant before the wave came down on them with the force of a collapsing brick wall.

The water pushed Ben under and he felt himself being washed around, water swirling and tossing him everywhere at once. He tried surfacing but was pushed down again. Just when he thought he was out of breath his face hit the air and it filled his lungs before he was sucked down and back into the churn again. He held onto his board for as long as he could, but his fingers were no match for the sea. It slipped from his fingers and the tug from the ankle rope pulled him further down. Or up. He could no longer tell.

Then, mercifully—or dangerously, he wasn't yet sure—he felt the rope go slack. He'd lost his board, but free from its drag he managed to get properly to the surface.

The first thing he did when he could see was look around for Summer, but she was nowhere. The high swell blocked his view in every direction. He couldn't even see the shore and, momentarily disoriented, didn't know which way to swim.

But his priority wasn't getting to the shore, it was finding

Summer and making sure she was all right. Summer was a fair swimmer, but not as strong as him and Ben knew he was lucky to come through the wave that had just hit them. Summer, he feared, was out of her depth. Literally.

He looked around, but still couldn't see her. Panic slowly rose in his chest as each second passed without sight of her. He spun and spun. Seconds felt as though they were dragging out to minutes.

And then there she was. A flash of black and red in the blue. He yelled to her, but she didn't answer. He paddled towards her, but her body dipped beneath the surface again.

It only took a few seconds to reach her, but they were some of the longest of his life. He pulled her to the surface, twisting her so her face was out of the water. God knew where their boards were; his ankle stung where the cord had pulled and pulled before snapping. Summer's eyes were closed and her body limp and heavy. He tried to feel around her head for signs of an injury, but his arms were near dead with exhaustion. He turned onto his back, holding her to his chest and keeping her face and air passages out of the water. He didn't know if he could tread water like this for long, let alone swim back to shore, but he had no idea if anyone had seen the wave, or noticed them get swamped. He didn't have a spare hand to wave, so he turned his back to the beach and attempted a slow kick back.

He had to get there as soon as possible to get her breathing. There was no way he could attempt resuscitation here; he was barely keeping her face out of the choppy water. He kicked and kicked and shook her gently. 'Breathe, breathe,' he pleaded.

It was a dinghy that found them, washing small waves over them at first and, finally, two big arms reached into the water and hauled Summer, still lifeless, out of the water.

'Is she okay?' Ben asked the man piloting the boat, but he only shrugged.

As they approached the beach Ben looked at Summer, still lifeless, and he swallowed back vomit.

On the beach, his legs were like jelly. He shook as though it were three degrees instead of thirty. Someone covered him with a towel, but he could barely feel it.

A paramedic came over to assist him, but Ben wouldn't answer until he was assured that Summer was, indeed, breathing. They assured him she was and Ben almost cried with relief. They asked him some questions about what had happened with Summer and how long she had been underwater for, how long she was unconscious. Ben wasn't sure, but gave him his best guess as somewhere between ten seconds and a minute.

He looked around for Charlotte but found Will standing next to him. Ben couldn't meet his eyes. He was meant to be watching Summer, teaching her. Not letting her get swamped by giant waves. Will must hate him more than ever.

'We're taking her to the medical centre. Do you need a lift there?' Will asked gruffly.

Ben shook his head. 'No, I'll just go back to the villa.'

'Are you sure? I think you should get yourself checked out.' *Do you?*

Ben held back his petulant response. The last thing he needed now was Will trying to play parent.

Will touched Ben's shoulder and turned him to face him. Ben was about to shake off his brother's hand and ask what he thought he was doing when he saw Will's eyes. They weren't angry. Or annoyed. They were brimming with tears. Before Ben knew what was going on Will had dragged him into a tight hug.

Ben could smell the sweat and worry on his brother.

'Thank you,' Will choked. 'Thank you for being there. Thank you for saving her.'

Ben was too stunned to respond before Will released him, turning back to Summer.

Charlotte held Summer's hand as the paramedics explained that Summer would be all right, but they wanted her to get looked over at the medical centre and determine whether she needed to go to the main island to be checked.

Summer spoke slowly but clearly, and told them she felt fine. Just shaken.

'We're not taking any chances,' Charlotte said.

Summer was helped to a sitting position and Charlotte looked around for Will, but she couldn't see either Watson brother.

Her heart still pounded, so she sucked in a deep breath and then another and several more in quick succession before she noticed that none of the air seem to be getting to her brain. Will suddenly appeared and took her shoulders, turning her to face him. 'Charlotte, are you okay?'

She nodded, but she was still gasping.

'Charlotte, Charlotte, look at me.'

She found Will's eyes but they were grey, a dull and substandard version of Ben's.

'Now, breathe when I say. Can you do that?'

She nodded, still gasping.

'In,' he said. 'Hold it, now slowly out. Wait. Wait. Now, in again, slowly. And hold.'

She did as she was told, slowly exhaling, holding her breath and the gasping stopped, but she didn't feel any better. She felt as though she might throw up.

'Everything's okay, they're both in and safe. They're going to be all right. Everything's okay,' he repeated.

Ben and Summer might be on shore safely, but everything was most definitely not okay.

Once he was satisfied that Charlotte was still breathing, Will's attention went elsewhere. He scooped up Summer's things and said, 'They're taking her to the medical centre as a precaution.'

Charlotte nodded. She should be the strong one now, not collapsing in a hyperventilating mess. She needed to be there for Summer and Will. And Ben.

But she was having a hard enough time holding herself together.

'Call us,' she said to Will as he went to Summer without a backward glance.

It was over, they would be okay. Summer was breathing, probably a little bruised, but she would be fine.

Her eyes finally landed on Ben, standing a few metres away from her on the beach. His beautiful face was crest-fallen. His perfect shoulders slumped. She rushed to him and threw her arms around him.

'She's okay, you're okay. Thank goodness.'

Ben was shaking. She hugged him tighter, but the shakes were almost violent and she couldn't still them.

She didn't think she could do this. She didn't know how to deal with Ben's shock when she was barely in control of her own.

The wave had swamped them. Knocked them both under and sideways and she hardly knew what. She'd lost sight of him for ages. She didn't know how long it was in actual seconds, but it was long enough for the fear to travel from her brain, down her spine and to take hold, hard and heavy. Long enough that she'd had time to worry about how on earth she would feel arriving back at Heathrow alone.

And that was long enough.

She should feel delighted that he and Summer were both

all right, but now that the fear had taken hold in her heart, she couldn't shift it.

'Do you want to go to the medical centre?' she asked Ben.

He shook his head. 'I just want to go to the villa. Then check on Summer.'

'She's conscious. She's going to be all right. Thanks to you.'

'I should have seen the wave.'

'Ben, no one saw the wave! No one could have got out of the way quickly enough.'

Ben frowned. 'I was teaching her. I should have been paying better attention.'

Charlotte reached out her hand to take his, but something about the way he was holding himself, made her take her hand back.

They walked slowly back to the villa, neither of them speaking, both studying the people and the scenery as they went past. So much had changed since this morning. And not in a good way.

They showered and, after, Charlotte considered her available outfits. She guessed, without being told, that dinner with Will and Summer was no longer on the evening's agenda and she was relieved. She wasn't in the mood to socialise. She wanted a light dinner. Maybe a glass of wine and then to find something mindless on the television to fall asleep to.

And she wanted to do those things alone.

She needed to.

Ben was in her head and her heart. He was in her chest. Running through her veins. And she couldn't think properly when he was near. He was messing with her navigation system, like a magnet on a compass. And now, especially, she needed to think straight.

She chose loose cotton trousers and a T-shirt and put those on, then went, with trepidation, to speak to Ben.

He was by the pool, hunched over his phone. Oblivious to the amazing sunset that was happening over the water right in front of him. To be honest, the sunset left Charlotte a little cool as well, compared to the forces running through her.

'I'm guessing dinner with Will and Summer is off?'

'Will just messaged. Summer's going to be fine, but they've told her to rest.'

Charlotte nodded.

'We could go out. Unless...' He looked her up and down. She was not dressed for a night on the town. Even in Bali.

'I'm exhausted too, I think I'd like to stay in.'

'Sounds perfect. We can order in.' He stood and moved towards her, taking her in his arms and pulling her to him, but as her cheek rested against his collarbone Charlotte stiffened. He was dressed now, dry, and no longer shaking, but the feeling of hugging him on the beach flashed back into her mind. Both of them shaking. Terrified.

When she froze, Ben did too. He pulled back slowly and she stepped away, looked at the floor.

'Char?' His voice was questioning, because he knew her so well. As well as she knew herself. Maybe even better because he knew exactly what she was about to say, even while she was still trying to find the words to say it.

She wasn't ready to lose someone else. She wasn't ready at all. She looked at her toes.

'Ben, I need a bit of time.'

'Time?'

'It's a lot.'

'What? Ordering dinner?'

'No. Everything. Us.'

She only looked at him once she'd said it. He nodded. As if he, annoyingly, understood. Maybe he could explain it to her, why she was suddenly feeling suffocated. Overwhelmed.

Needing to flee. So she said what she knew, the part she did understand.

'I don't want to lose you,' she explained.

'You're not going to lose me.'

Charlotte shook her head. 'You can't promise that.'

She was going to lose him somehow. Maybe not to a wave, more likely because he didn't feel the same way about her.

'I can try. That's all anyone can ever do. I know you're upset about Tim—'

'No, I'm not. It's not that.' She'd ridden the scooter. She'd orgasmed with Ben, many times now. She'd let herself fall, finally, fall with abandon, gloriously. And hard.

It wasn't about *Tim*.

It was about fear. Fear that she would lose Ben just as she had lost Tim and the knowledge of just how much that would hurt.

'Do you want to…break up?'

'I don't know.'

The sound of those words sucked all the air from the space and surprised even Charlotte. She didn't want to break up with Ben, but she didn't know how she could do *this*.

'I don't know,' she scrambled. 'I know I need space. I need time. And I need to be alone.'

Ben's Adam's apple bobbed with a hard swallow. He blinked, didn't look at her. 'I understand.'

His reasonableness didn't make things easier, but it did make them smoother.

'Do you want me to leave?' she asked.

'Leave? Now?'

'Well, yes.'

'Of course not.'

'Given the circumstances—'

'What circumstances? It's seven at night, the evening before my mother's wedding, neither of us are leaving.'

'But I need space. I need to think. I could find another hotel.'

'Charlotte, no. Unless you would feel more comfortable?'

'Wouldn't you?'

He shook his head. 'I'll feel most comfortable knowing you're safe.'

'Ben...'

'I'm not going to stop caring about you.'

He was right, it was too late to run. It was too late to put a cork in her feelings—and his. She had to face them somehow. At some point.

Just not now. Not when, even though she seemed still, she was still shaking from the sight of the wave. She was still reeling from all the thoughts that had raced—no, stampeded—through her mind as Ben lay beneath the waves.

The difference between life and death was an instant.

'Can you please do me a favour?' he asked.

'What?'

'Don't leave. Please stay for the wedding.'

'I... I'm not sure that would be right. Wouldn't that be strange?'

'I think it would be stranger to come all this way and not go. Please don't change your flight. Stay here, I'll go somewhere else. I'll stay with Will. Just don't fly home yet.'

'Why not?' They could talk in London. Right now this villa was too small. This island was too small.

Though he was right, as much as she wanted space, she was exhausted and in no state to pack, get on a ferry to the mainland, let alone deal with the airline.

'I'll see in the morning. Ben, I just need space.'

Ben held up his hands. 'Take all you need.'

'Thank you for understanding.' She turned to go to her room and heard, 'Can you promise me we'll still be friends?'

She stopped mid-stride.

She needed time to think, and he was still wanting promises. Promises she didn't know she would be capable of keeping.

'I don't know. I honestly don't know.'

'Do you want to?'

Of course she wanted them to stay friends! And more. But as he kept saying, that wasn't the point.

'Friendship! You keep going on about friendship, like it's the most important thing.'

'But it is,' he pleaded.

'So that's all I am to you—a friend?'

'No, that's not all you are.' His eyes clouded over.

'But you think our friendship is the most important thing. You're so fixated on keeping our friendship that you're not even thinking of anything else.'

'That's not true.'

'It's exactly what you keep saying. Like a mantra. Like a broken record.'

His face reddened at her last words. Maybe she'd been a little blunt, but it was true.

'I'm just telling you that I don't want our friendship to end.'

She wanted to scream, release the hurt somehow. Because she saw now with perfect clarity that their friendship wasn't the most important thing to her. Their *relationship* was.

She certainly didn't want their friendship to end, but how could it continue when she loved him, and he didn't feel the same for her?

How could they go to gallery openings together and talk honestly about what they saw, while all the time she would want to be holding his hand? How could she go to his place for a cosy dinner when all she'd be able to think about was how she wanted to curl up in his bed? Feel him. Smell him. Touch him.

It hurt too much. Watching the wave take him out was bad enough, the bigger hurt would come every time they saw one another, and she'd be reminded that he didn't feel the same way she did.

If she hadn't known love with Tim, if she hadn't already experienced the crushing, ongoing, relentless pain of losing someone, then perhaps she could have been more casual with her heart. Perhaps she could continue to see Ben, casually, platonically. But she knew now she couldn't.

Losing Ben—either to a freak wave or to another woman— would be too much.

He didn't love her. Oh, he loved her as a friend, but he didn't feel the same uncontrollable passion that she felt for him. She had made the right decision.

'I hope we may be able to be friends again some time.'

'I don't understand. Are you saying you don't even want to be friends?'

'I'm saying I can't promise anything right now. That's what I've been trying to tell you.'

He dragged his hands through his hair and paced up and down the room. For a hotel it was spacious, but, still, it didn't allow him to take too many of his long powerful strides before he had to turn. The energy emanating from him felt explosive.

'I'm sorry, I think we need a break for a bit. I need a break and...' She motioned to him. 'I think you do too. I think we were too rash.'

'Rash? Charlotte, we've known one another for four years.'

'So? This week was...a lot.'

Ben closed his eyes and covered his face with his hands. A closed door would have had less effect.

Charlotte turned and moved to her room before either of them said something else, something there would be no coming back from.

Her room was empty without him. *She* was empty without him. She turned out the lights, drew the curtains, climbed into bed, and cried.

* * *

The sensation of a monster wave crashing over him was nothing—absolutely nothing—compared to how Ben felt now. Then he'd been flattened, half drowned, wind knocked out of him, water knocked into him. Disorientated. Shaken.

This was a hundred times worse.

Like the wave, it had been a surprise he hadn't seen coming. That morning, she'd ridden a scooter and he'd been so convinced it was a sign that she was managing to forget Tim.

She'd taken the selfie of them both and looked on the verge of posting it online. A sure-fire way of announcing their relationship to the world.

She'd even used the L-word.

The Bridge of Love. The funny, quirky yellow bridge of love.

She couldn't tell him why it was called that, but he knew. Because it was where you came with the person you loved.

And he loved Charlotte.

For four long years he'd tucked it away, pushed it down. Ignored it. Because if he acknowledged the L-word he'd have to acknowledge how much he loved her, how deeply in love he was with Charlotte.

He'd refused to use the word when they first met.

Refused to think about it when they kissed.

He'd even refused to think about it when she'd pulled him into her the first wonderful time they had made love.

But now that word was suffocating him, drowning him, flattening him under its weight. Not to mention he no longer knew which way was up or down. He'd lost his only true compass—Charlotte—and he might never know the right way up again.

He loved her. He loved her with his entire heart.

Had they actually broken up? It was unclear, hence the sensation of still being tossed around in the powerful waves.

Well, he'd messed that up royally.

Done the thing he'd been trying not to do for the past four years—fall in love with Charlotte—and at the worst possible moment.

And to top it all off she'd denied their friendship was important.

No, she said it wasn't the most important thing.

Their friendship was everything. Solid, central.

No. You have another type of relationship. It's new. But it's there.

No, Charlotte didn't love him like that. She would have said. She wouldn't have asked for a break if she loved him.

It was that simple.

This moment felt inevitable. It was what he'd been worried about since Charlotte had first kissed him. It had been what he'd worried about since they'd first met! As soon as the relationship developed, Charlotte would run.

He took little comfort in the fact that she was still back at the villa and he was the one currently walking down the street looking for vacancy signs at the hotels.

She was probably booking her plane ticket.

He had to figure out what to tell his mother.

Charlotte won't be at the wedding after all... There was a family emergency.

They should get their story straight, but that would require communicating with one another and he wasn't sure that was allowed at the moment.

I need time. I need space.

Ben approached one of the open-air bars that were along the street. He should eat dinner, but the thought of food made his stomach tighten. But beer? He could do that.

He ordered and pulled out a stool with a view of the street, not wanting to look at the ocean after today's misadventure. The beer was cold and refreshing but he hardly tasted it.

CHAPTER ELEVEN

'HEY.'

Ben looked up and saw his brother. 'Hey.'

Will looked at Ben as though he could smell the stench of recent break-up. 'Where's Charlotte?'

'I'm not sure.' He wasn't. She might be on the ferry to Bali.

'You've lost her?'

'You could say that,' Ben mumbled.

Letting his brother's ambiguous comment slide, Will pulled up a stool. 'Can I join you?'

'Sure.'

The bartender approached and Will ordered a beer as well.

'I was just picking up some food for Summer,' he said. 'She loved the noodles we had here the other night and I thought I'd take them back to her. Mum's with her now.'

'That's nice of her. The night before the wedding.'

'She insisted on coming, needed to see for herself that Summer was all right.'

Will drank a third of the beer in one large gulp, visibly relaxing as the alcohol spread through him. 'I'm glad I ran into you. I wanted to say thank you again.'

'For what?'

'What? For saving Summer. I'm so glad you were there.'

'I'm sorry I didn't see the wave coming.'

'No one saw the wave coming.'

Ben shook his head. He'd messed up so many things today.

This was very un-Will-like behaviour, being grateful. Kind. But nothing could make Ben feel better at this point.

'So where is she? Really?' Will asked.

'I don't know. We had a…' Was it a fight? A disagreement? A break-up.

'Whatever it was, shouldn't you go to her?' Will said.

'It's complicated.'

'So you say, but relationships are complicated. If they're not, then you're just acquaintances. And you and Charlotte are far more than mere acquaintances.'

'She's not over her ex.'

'Ex? When did they break up?'

'They didn't. Tim died.'

'Oh, I didn't know. When?'

'Seven years ago. Before we met. Motorbike accident.'

Will exhaled loudly.

'And you love her?'

This was businesslike Will back again. Straight down to the bare facts. Emotion be damned.

But Ben nodded.

'Did you tell her that?'

'No.'

'But you slept together?'

Ben bristled, but nodded again.

'And she said she wants to break up because she's not over her ex?'

'No.'

Will looked confused. 'Then what did she say exactly?'

'That she needed space. And some time to think.'

'Ahh.'

'You know I'm right.'

'No, you're not. That doesn't mean she's not over her ex, it means she needs space.'

Ben scrunched up his fists under the bar. Will saw things

in black and white, like numbers, but Ben's world view was full of shades.

'I think she's over this guy. Seven years? I'd say so.'

'What would you know?' Ben regretted his tone, petulant and like the spoiled brat his father always accused him of being.

Will stared at him and for a moment Ben thought he was about to be on the receiving end of one of their father's lectures. Probably the one titled 'You need to work for your money'.

But Will's face broke and he laughed.

'The guy's been dead for years, she freaked out when she thought you had died. Give her a break—she's not upset because she's not over her ex, she's probably upset because she thought she was about to lose you, too.'

Ben shook his head. No. Charlotte would have told him that.

'If she felt anything like what I did this afternoon, she'd still be freaking out. I know you and Summer had a scary experience, but it was just as terrifying for those of us sitting on the beach.'

Ben regarded his brother, his face flushed, clearly relieved Summer was all right.

He almost believed what he was saying about Charlotte.

If she loved him, she wouldn't have let him leave.

Even if the wave did make her upset, it was only because it reminded her of Tim's accident.

Not because she loved Ben.

'You have two choices: you can spend the rest of your life being jealous of a dead guy. Or you can just go find her and tell her how you really feel.'

He couldn't do that. He'd always be second best. He'd always be runner-up to Tim.

'Don't you have to get back to Summer?' Ben said.

'Tim is gone,' Will said softly.

Tim hadn't gone. Tim was always around.

'I think she loves you. That's why she's freaked out. Do you think she'd behave like this or react like this if she didn't love you? She may not know that she loves you, but she definitely does.'

Will didn't know anything. Ben couldn't believe he'd even considered confiding in his brother.

Will finished the last gulp of his beer and stood. He then wrapped Ben into an unexpected bear hug. 'I've got to get back to Summer.'

Ben nodded, but as Will turned Ben said, 'Will, I've got a question. It's a bit out there. Please don't laugh.'

Will moved back to the stool but didn't sit.

'Did you buy my painting?'

Will looked sheepish and kicked the ground softly. 'It was a good investment.'

Ben knew his mouth was wide open but couldn't do anything to stop it. He was floored. Will was his mystery buyer.

'It wasn't then. Not ten years ago. Dad called it rubbish. I was an unknown artist. It was my first big sale.'

'I liked it. No, I love it. And I did then. It reminds me of when we were kids. At Middleton Beach.'

'Yes, that's it.' One of the beaches they'd swam and surfed at as kids.

'That sale paid for me to get to LA.'

'I'm not giving it back,' Will said.

'I don't...' Ben didn't want it back. Though it would be nice to see it again some time. 'That's not what I meant.'

He didn't know what he meant. Will had been the mystery buyer who had been prepared to drop ten grand on an unknown artist.

Will had had faith in him, before anyone else did.

'I'm proud of you,' Will said. 'It's a great painting. Everyone who comes into my office remarks on it.

Not only did he love Ben's painting, he displayed it in his office, where everyone could see it.

'You don't think I'm an irresponsible fool?'

'I'm not Dad. I'm in awe of your talent.'

Ben gave this a moment to sink in. Will wasn't his enemy. Will had simply been caught between Ben and their father.

'Why didn't you say anything?' It would have saved both of them a lot of pain.

'I wanted to tell you. I wanted you to know that I supported you. And that I thought you were brave and talented. And that I thought Dad was wrong.'

'You did?'

'Yes, Dad was brilliant in many ways, but when it came to you, he was...well, he wasn't always fair. He thought he was protecting you, but I could see you didn't want a bar of the business. It was always clear to anyone with an ounce of perspective that it wasn't you.' Will shifted from one foot to the other. 'I'd better get back to Summer with this food.'

Ben finished his beer then headed across the street to the hotel with the vacancy sign.

He had to give Charlotte space, if it was what she wanted. And spending the night in a different hotel was better than risking Charlotte getting on a plane. Maybe by the morning she'd be ready to talk, but for now he'd give her the space she needed. Even if his body was aching to be near her. He'd do anything for her, even this.

When Charlotte finally got through to someone at the airline it was only to be told that they could put her on a flight one day earlier, but it was going to cost her several thousand pounds. She thanked the person and ended the call. Was she really going to pay so much money to be a coward? No, she wasn't.

Her phone pinged with a message from Ben.

I've got a room at one of the hotels near the beach for the night so the villa is all yours.

Charlotte threw her phone down, fell back on the bed and screamed.

This was what she'd asked for, wasn't it? Space to think?

Or space not looking at Ben, feeling all these things for him and being terrified.

She took a bottle of white wine from the mini bar, went out to the patio, and poured a glass.

The view of the moonlight was spectacular, but, without Ben, the wine tasted of vinegar. She drank it anyway.

He's your best friend...are you really going to cut him from your life?

It was inevitable she would see Ben again. She couldn't avoid him altogether.

But if Ben didn't love her—body and soul—then she was lost. She couldn't continue their friendship without being honest with him about how she felt. And once she did that, she was certain to ruin their easy, uncomplicated camaraderie. He'd probably want to avoid her anyway...

Eventually, Charlotte fell into a restless sleep, waking regularly, remembering the day before and despairing again. Finally, in the early hours, exhaustion caught up with her and the next thing she knew she awoke to find the sun was high in the sky. She wandered out of her room. The villa was cool, despite the tropical weather—she could tell that Ben wasn't here and hadn't been here. She wandered out onto the patio.

The place didn't feel right without him.

She looked out of the window, across the bay to Bali. The

sky was bright and clear and glorious, belying the turmoil inside her.

It was Diane and Gus's wedding day—in fact, the wedding was in a few hours—and she tried to imagine how Diane must be feeling. Excited? Nervous, maybe? Happy and relaxed, hopefully. Charlotte and Tim had only just started planning their wedding and hadn't even set a date.

Tim.

She wondered what he'd make of this mess she'd found herself in.

He'd tell you to pull yourself together.

She smiled. In the last weeks of his life, even when she was still hopeful that he'd overcome the wounds and infections that had ravaged his body, he'd made her promise she'd fall in love again. She'd promised that she would, but hadn't wanted to believe it would be a promise she'd have to keep. She'd still had hope.

She never gave much credence to a promise she'd made to placate Tim as he'd lain in pain.

He wanted you to move on. He'd say that you owe it to Ben to go to the wedding.

It was the whole reason she'd come to Bali after all: to support her best friend at his mother's wedding.

She wondered where Ben was. And she wondered how Summer was feeling.

Charlotte picked up her phone and sent a message to Summer.

Hey, there, how are you feeling this morning?

Her phone pinged soon after.

I'm doing so much better than yesterday. Still a little shaky but I had a good sleep.

Is there anything I can do?

Since you ask, I promised Diane I'd pick up her flowers. Could you possibly do it for me?

Charlotte wanted to say no. After all, she hadn't even decided if she was going to the wedding, if it would be right.

He's still your friend. He's still your best friend.

If she didn't go, they would all ask why and that would be awful for him.

Besides, it was Diane and Gus's day. She could hold herself together for a day if it meant not ruining someone else's wedding.

Charlotte messaged back.

For sure. What are the details?

'Charlotte, honey, what are you doing here?' Diane opened the door to her villa wearing a dressing gown. Her hair and make-up had been done and, even half dressed, she looked beautiful. Radiant.

'I've come to give you these.' She handed Diane the flowers. 'Summer asked me if I could.'

'Thank you, but, I mean, I thought you went home. Back to London?'

'What? No.'

'Ben said there'd been a family emergency.'

By the time Charlotte realised Ben had told his mother a white lie, Diane had as well. 'Is everything okay, or did my son just lie to his mother?'

'Um…everything… Um… I think he was just trying to protect me.'

'I think he was just trying to protect himself. Did you have a fight?'

'Not exactly. I was thinking of returning but I decided to stay. And come to the wedding, if that's still all right?'

Charlotte had worn her wedding outfit, the long blue dress she'd bought for the occasion. Physically, sartorially, she was ready to attend this wedding. Emotionally? She wasn't quite sure.

Diane studied her through narrowed eyes. 'Of course it is. I am glad you've stayed.'

Diane pulled Charlotte into an unexpected hug. 'Apart from anything else, Summer was supposed to help me zip up my dress. So you will have to do that.'

Charlotte sat and waited while Diane did the rest of her preparations. She took her gown out of its dust bag and Charlotte helped her into it, zipping up the back.

Diane looked stunning in the silver floor-length, one-shouldered crepe gown.

'How are you feeling?' Charlotte asked.

'Excited. And I think you should pour us a glass of bubbles while we wait for Gus to get here.'

'Gus is meeting you here?'

'Yes, we're going together. It's a second marriage for both of us so we aren't following rules that were set hundreds of years ago.'

Charlotte went to the champagne in the ice bucket Diane had pointed to.

'Do you mind opening it?' Diane asked. 'I might be happy, but I'm still shaking a little.'

Charlotte smiled, strangely glad that Diane wasn't entirely composed after all. Charlotte popped the champagne and poured them both a glass.

'To second chances,' Diane said and touched Charlotte's glass lightly.

Charlotte took a sip of champagne.

'Do you mind if I ask you something?'

'Of course not,' Diane said.

'It's a rather personal question.'

'They're the best kind.' Diane smiled.

'How did you know you were ready to marry Gus? After Ben's father died, I mean?'

'Ah. I'm sure Tim loved you and, because he loved you, I'm sure he would want you to find love again.'

'He would. I know he would. We had time to talk before he… Anyway, I know he would want me to be happy. Find someone, have a family. Have the life we planned. That isn't it.'

'Then?'

'I don't want to be hurt again. I don't want to feel that again. I'm scared.'

Charlotte tasted salt in her mouth but swallowed the tears back down. She refused to burst into tears on someone's shoulder half an hour before they were due to walk down the aisle.

'I think Ben loves you and I promise you there is no man more loyal, more loving.'

Charlotte nodded. 'None of that's in doubt. I know he is.'

Diane looked at her. 'Is it about yesterday? At the beach?'

Charlotte wanted to say no but couldn't bring herself to lie.

'It must have been awful, watching it. I'm so glad I wasn't there and only had to hear about it once we knew everyone was all right.'

'I could hardly breathe. I thought I'd lost him,' Charlotte admitted.

'But you didn't.'

For a moment Charlotte's whole world had stopped. It was such an awful and familiar feeling.

There was a knock at the door and Gus said, 'Honey, may I come in?'

'Yes, yes. Charlotte and I were just having a nerve settler.'

Gus came in and Charlotte felt like an intruder, though it was clear neither Diane nor Gus cared as they only had eyes for one another.

'Do you need anything else?' Charlotte asked.

'No, you go on. But just one thing.' Diane took Charlotte's arm. 'Think of this. If you don't see Ben again you lose him anyway. Is that what you want? It seems to me that your heart is going to be broken anyway, so why not take a chance?'

Charlotte nodded and attempted her best smile.

That logic would make sense if Ben loved her, she thought as she made her way down to the beach where the ceremony was to take place.

But Ben just kept telling her that their friendship was the most important thing. More important than sex. And desire. And lust. Maybe.

More important than intimacy? Than staring at one another across the pillow in the semi-darkness? More important than holding one another's hands in public, or announcing their relationship on the socials?

Maybe all those things were important.

Before she knew it, and before she was even sure she was meant to be there, Charlotte was at the beach.

Ben didn't want to risk their friendship for all those other things.

Or maybe he just didn't want to lose it.

Did that mean he didn't love her, or did it just mean he was scared too?

CHAPTER TWELVE

CHARLOTTE HELD BACK from the beach and watched the wedding crowd from a distance. Chairs were set out, decorated with green leaves and bright orange and red tropical blooms. A circle of flowers lay before the chairs, where the celebrant stood, waiting. Brightly coloured umbrellas stood around, providing partial shade. Some of the guests also held pretty parasols, to keep the sun away.

Ben stood to the left of the celebrant, next to Will. Her stomach tightened. Maybe it wasn't too late to change her mind and leave.

Ben wore long trousers and a white shirt, open at the collar and with the sleeves rolled up. He looked edible. Her heart soared and broke at once to look at him.

How could it hurt so much to lose something she never really had?

How could four years of beautiful friendship be ruined in one crazy week?

She willed her legs to carry her forward. When she moved closer, Ben looked in her direction. Charlotte froze. He smiled gently and nodded, but didn't make a move towards her, for which she was grateful. Charlotte took one of the chairs furthest away from Ben. Once seated, she noticed Summer seated up closer, but she didn't move. This was a family occasion and Charlotte was just a friend.

Thankfully, Diane and Gus arrived arm in arm soon after.

The guests stood, and even though Charlotte had already seen Diane and Gus dressed for the wedding, she still felt tears welling up. By the time they were saying their vows her face was wet and by the time they kissed she'd wet a whole tissue. She looked around and gratefully noticed she wasn't the only one shedding a tear. Though she didn't dare look in Ben's direction. She might start howling.

If you couldn't cry at a wedding, then when could you cry?

She felt guilty that they weren't entirely happy tears. Some of the tears were because she was witnessing the triumph of hope over loss, seeing someone take this leap again and find great love for a second time. But most of Charlotte's tears were because she didn't think she could do that same thing, because after yesterday and last night the thought of committing her life to another person felt further away than ever.

It was Ben she wanted.

It was Ben she wanted to marry. Ben's babies she wanted to carry. Ben's arms she wanted to lie in every night.

But what if something terrible happened to him too?

That was even assuming he would one day share her feelings. She didn't think she was strong enough or brave enough to do what Diane and Gus were doing now and that was why the tears kept falling, steadily, but quietly. Thankfully, most eyes were facing forward to Diane and Gus. She turned her head away from the direction Ben was standing.

When the ceremony was over, the guests followed the bride and groom to a table where champagne was being poured. Charlotte watched Ben follow his mother and new stepfather over with their families. Photos were being taken, but Charlotte was certainly not going to be a part of that. She stayed out of the way and sat on a bench and looked out over the water while she waited.

It would also give her face a chance to recover. Her skin was still tight from the tears, and probably looked a mess.

She was thankful she'd nearly given up on make-up since being in Bali as the humidity made it slide right off anyway.

She felt someone behind her and knew it was Ben even before she turned. Of course she did. She now had a sixth sense as far as he was concerned. Was this what her life would be like from now on? Her being acutely aware of his presence, feeling him in her bones, needing him, wanting every moment, while his heart remained untouched, immune?

Yes. That was what it would be like.

There was no way she could keep seeing him casually, just be friends.

But it was that or lose him entirely.

Would friendship be enough? Would it even be *possible*?

'Thank you for staying.'

'I... I was being rash. I shouldn't have said I'd leave.'

'Charlotte, I'm sorry.' Ben bowed his head.

'What on earth for? I'm the one who should be sorry.' She'd come to Bali to support her best friend, instead she'd let her feelings run away from her.

'I'm sorry for making you come to a wedding.'

She laughed. 'What? Why? It was a beautiful wedding. I'm glad I came.'

'But you cried.'

She looked down. So he had seen.

'Yeah, well, I've been doing that a bit lately.'

He nodded, but he didn't look happy. 'I know it must remind you of Tim.'

'Tim? Why? Because it's a wedding?' Not this again. No matter how many times she tried to get him to understand, he didn't see that it wasn't about Tim, at least not directly.

'Because you two didn't make it down the aisle.'

Then, because she didn't think what the gesture might mean or do to her senses, she stood up, walked to Ben, and picked up his hand. She intended to reassure him that this wasn't the case but it quickly became more. Because as soon as her skin touched his, she wanted more. She wanted to slide her hand up his bare forearm and all around him. She wanted to press herself against him. And never, ever let go.

'I wasn't thinking of Tim when I cried.'

'You weren't?'

'No. I was thinking of you.'

'Me?'

Charlotte's hand was still in his, but it was her words that touched him most. 'Why?'

'Because...because I don't know what to do about us. Because I'm terrified. And confused.'

Charlotte hadn't been crying over Tim, but over him. Ben Watson.

Could his annoying big brother be right? Could he have missed all the signs because he was stupidly hung up on the idea that Charlotte wasn't over Tim, or that she wasn't ready to move on?

Yes, he could have. Believing he was second best. Believing he was Charlotte's fallback.

'You don't have to be scared,' he said, and she gave him a withering look. He knew that look, because he knew Charlotte and he could tell that she was biting back a sharp retort.

One he would deserve, because he hadn't given her anything to feel secure about. He'd been keeping his own feelings hidden and disguised. He'd been purposefully keeping the full extent of his emotions from her so as not to frighten her. And he realised he might have gone too far.

Ben might be able to guess what Charlotte was thinking by that look, but she couldn't read his mind. Especially not when he'd been trying so hard and for so long to keep his true feelings hidden. He was so practised in denying them even from himself.

'I love you, Charlotte.' Her eyes widened and he got the feeling she was actually going to argue with him. 'And no, not as your friend. Well, as your friend, but as your everything. Your lover, your partner. Your boyfriend. And your best friend.'

Charlotte's mouth opened and closed several times as she searched for the words.

He stepped in and kissed her lips instead. For a second, she paused but then answered him with an unambiguous kiss. She surged towards him, grabbed him and pulled him to her. It wasn't the way you kissed someone if you were ambivalent or wavering. His heart soared, desire kicked in and he pulled her closer, deeper.

She drew back just enough to take a breath. 'I love you too,' she whispered. Everything around him stopped and there was only Charlotte, standing before him. He let the words sink in. 'And not just as a friend. But as my everything.'

Her face was still a little flushed but her eyes were bright. And maybe a little glassy. She'd never been more beautiful. Now he struggled for the words.

'I love you,' he tried the words again. Unfamiliar on his tongue. 'As my everything.'

She hugged him.

He felt her shaking.

She was crying. Again?

He pulled her back to wipe away her tears and reassure her that everything would be all right, but she wasn't crying, she was laughing. He wanted to swat her.

'What's so funny?' he asked.

'This! Us! We're idiots.'

'Not idiots just...'

'Lovesick fools? I was scared. So scared,' she admitted.

He took her hand and led her back to the bench she'd been sitting on earlier. They sat, facing away from the curious eyes of the wedding guests.

'I was so scared, I'm still so scared. Not just about what if something happens to you, but what if you change your mind?' she said.

He cupped her cheeks in his hands.

'Why would I do that?'

'Because…because people do.'

'Are you worried *your* feelings will change?'

She shook her head adamantly. 'No.'

'Why not?'

'Because I know you, I've been getting to know you for four years now and I know you inside and out. But why are you so sure?'

'My feelings didn't change this week.' Even as the words came out, he still wasn't sure he was going to say them. 'I have *always* loved you.'

Charlotte let go of his hand.

'Define always,' she whispered. Since a month ago, a year ago…what was he saying?

'Always. Since the first day we met. Since our first conversation about Picasso when you almost spilt champagne over me.'

'But…' Suddenly her mouth was too dry to make sounds.

'I have loved you since you told me about Tim. I have loved you since, since…always. And that's why I have been by your side for the past four years, listened to you talk about all your dates, watched you… After all that, I still love you. So, you see, I really don't think that there is anything you can do that will stop me loving you. Even if I wanted to.'

He gave her a lopsided grin, but Charlotte untangled herself from his arms.

He'd thought she'd be pleased, but she was annoyed.

'Always? All this time?'

This wasn't fair.

'You asked me—no, you made me promise—to tell you how I was feeling, but you kept this from me.'

'I didn't know how to tell you without scaring you. I didn't know how to say it without scaring myself.'

'Why? Ben, for the past few days I've been dying inside, thinking that you didn't love me. I've been thinking this has meant nothing to you.'

'It hasn't meant nothing, it's meant everything.'

But Charlotte's feelings went from desperate to furious.

'I nearly got on a plane! I nearly didn't speak to you again; I thought you didn't care.'

'No, Charlotte, I care.'

'You kept this from me.'

'Because I had to. For the sake of—'

'I know! Our friendship! I get it.'

Charlotte stood. But she didn't run.

There was no point. There was no part of the world she could run to where she could escape Ben. Because that would mean escaping her own feelings. Escaping herself.

Always. He'd always loved her. And she'd treated him like a girlfriend. She'd told him about the men she'd been with as if he were an indifferent... Nausea rose inside her. She'd hurt him. It had been unknowing, but she'd hurt him. Day after day.

'I didn't know, I'm sorry.'

'Of course you didn't know and you have nothing to be sorry for. Charlotte, I even tried to hide it from myself.'

'Why didn't you say something earlier?'

'Because I knew you weren't ready.'

The realisation dawned on her. Ben had been right. She might have accepted that Tim was gone, but she hadn't been ready to move on. Not last week, not a few days ago and certainly not yesterday. Not until this very moment had she been brave enough to tell Ben her true feelings.

'He's always going to be here. He's always going to be in my past. Ben, you need to accept that just as much as I do.'

'I realise that now. I know that Tim will always be in your past, but I intend to be in your future.'

Charlotte smiled at him, bursting with happiness.

He pulled her to him and cupped her chin in his hand. She fell into his beautiful sea-blue gaze and she stroked his newly shaven cheek.

'Is it because I shaved my beard off?' he asked.

'Yes. I mean no.'

He laughed.

'I saw you differently. As if for the first time.'

'So you don't like the beard?'

'I didn't say that. I just saw you anew. Afresh.'

One side of his lips lifted into a grin. Also a new look. Her stomach swooped.

'If I grow it again, will you still love me?'

She dragged a fingertip down his smooth skin.

'It wasn't just the beard. That was just when I realised I was attracted to you.'

'And?' Ben tilted his head.

'The attraction was one thing. It's pretty intense, as you might be able to tell, but it's also far more than that. I realised I want you to be my everything.'

He nodded.

She felt someone approach them and looked around to see Diane holding two glasses of champagne.

'We are about to do some speeches... We won't interrupt you, but I suspect you both might have something to celebrate as well.' She handed them both a glass.

Charlotte stood and hugged Diane. 'Congratulations, I'm so pleased for you both.'

Diane hugged her back tightly, then Ben hugged his mother as well.

She smiled at them both.

Ben took Charlotte's hand and they followed Diane over to where a string quartet was playing, filling the air and their hearts with the sound of violins, the exact way Charlotte had always dreamed.

EPILOGUE

CHARLOTTE'S HEART WAS RACING.

They would all be here in less than ten minutes.

She looked at Ben. He needed a haircut, but he'd had a shave. And his sweater didn't have any holes or stains. He still took her breath away.

She was wearing a new, loose-fitting dress and was happy with her appearance. Best of all Ben had tidied their apartment—formerly Ben's apartment. They had hardly needed to discuss that she would move into Ben's, given that his apartment was bigger and brighter than hers.

'Relax, there's nothing to worry about.'

'How are you relaxed? In five minutes our parents will get here. All of them!'

'Yes, and I'm excited.'

'Excited? What if they don't get along? What if it's a disaster?'

He pulled her to him. 'Then we have something to laugh about later.'

She pressed her cheek to his soft sweater.

Diane and Gus had arrived at Heathrow that afternoon and were expected at Ben and Charlotte's apartment that evening for an early dinner.

A week ago, it had seemed like a great idea to invite Charlotte's parents as well. That way they would tell them their news all at once.

Now, it seemed like a silly idea. Diane and Gus would be tired, her parents...well, her parents would be delighted. That only made Charlotte more nervous—high expectations and all that.

'It's going to be fine. In fact, it will be more than fine. Do you honestly think your parents will be anything but delighted when we tell them? My mother's going to be beside herself. Gus too.'

'Gus will probably cry,' Charlotte conceded. 'If their wedding was anything to go by.'

'So, the only thing we really need is tissues.'

Dinner was ready and in the oven—prepared, of course, by Ben, with Charlotte his trainee sous chef. Champagne was in the fridge.

Ben picked up her hand. The ring, sapphire blue like the Balinese water, sparkled on her ring finger. She lifted herself up and kissed him. His lips were as soft and welcome as always, his arms as strong. She hugged him tight.

'Will they think we're rushing things?'

'First, I don't care, and second, we've known one another for years. I don't think we can be accused of rushing anything.'

'But we're not just engaged, we've set a date. In two weeks' time!' Charlotte giggled. 'I guess it's at least more notice than your mother gave you.'

The plan was for Will and Summer to arrive just before the wedding. They were the only others who already knew Ben and Charlotte's plan for a whirlwind register-office wedding with a small party afterwards. They'd had to tell them so they could make their travel plans.

'Do you think your parents will be upset? You're their only daughter, maybe they want a bigger thing.'

Charlotte laughed. 'Dad will be delighted that all he has to do is turn up and Mum... Mum won't mind at all when she knows the reason we want to get married so quickly.' She gave Ben a knowing look.

'They'll think you're pregnant already.'

'I could be.' She grinned and Ben's mouth dropped.

She laughed. 'Kidding! But I want to start trying, you know that.'

Ben nuzzled the sensitive spot beneath her ear. 'We could start now. We don't have to wait until the wedding.'

Charlotte pulled him even tighter. She loved this man with all of her heart and could not wait to start living the rest of her life with him.

* * * * *

COMING SOON!

We really hope you enjoyed reading this book.
If you're looking for more romance
be sure to head to the shops when
new books are available on

Thursday 11th April

To see which titles are coming soon, please visit

millsandboon.co.uk/nextmonth

MILLS & BOON

MILLS & BOON®

Coming next month

SECRETLY MARRIED TO A PRINCE
Ally Blake

She watched as a dozen thoughts tangled behind those pale hazel eyes, before he said, 'I am Prince Henri Gaultier Raphael-Rossetti.'

He pronounced his name *On-ree*.

A burr of pain settled behind her ribs. For while she'd known next to nothing about him, she'd thought at least he'd given her his true name.

Then her brain stuttered and she backtracked a smidge. 'I'm sorry, did you say *Prince*?'

He nodded. Thought it was more of a gentle bow. Elegant, practiced, princely.

Matilda blinked. 'Since *when*?'

'Since birth,' he said, a flicker at the edge of his mouth that might have been a smile. Or a grimace. 'Though I have been Sovereign Prince of Chaleur for the past two years.'

Matilda looked at the ancient sandstone structure, the burly bouncers hovering nearby, Henri's gorgeous car, and the beast parked in behind it. She remembered the crowd in the street, surrounding him, calling his name.

Then she looked back at *him*. The way he held himself, the way he dressed, the way he spoke. How educated and hungry for knowledge he had been back then. That *je ne sais quoi* that had drawn her in from the very first moment.

'Are you freaking kidding me?' she asked.

'I'm not. Freaking or otherwise.' Again with the flicker at the corner of his mouth. This time it came with a slight thawing in his gaze.

The requirement of anonymity, the money, the access, the way they had breezed through Europe with absolute entitlement. It all made sense now. It hadn't been a weird hazing thing, or bored rich kid thing. It had been about protecting Henri.

A *prince*.

A prince that she had fallen for. Had married. Which made her...

No. Nope. Nope-ty nooooo. There was no point getting ahead of herself. Not until she had legal paperwork before her own eyes. Legal enough to satisfy George Damn Harrington.

As to the rest? Part of her wanted to kick him, right in the shins, for keeping such a thing from her. Then again, she had vowed to love him for a lifetime, before bolting to the other side of the world.

Maybe they were even.

Continue reading
SECRETLY MARRIED TO A PRINCE
Ally Blake

Available next month
millsandboon.co.uk

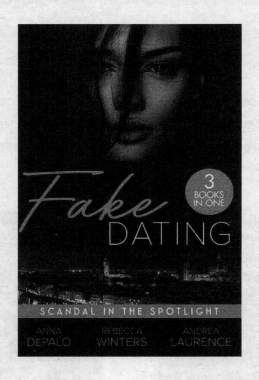

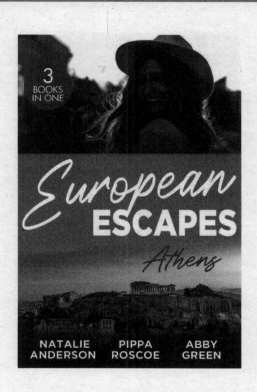

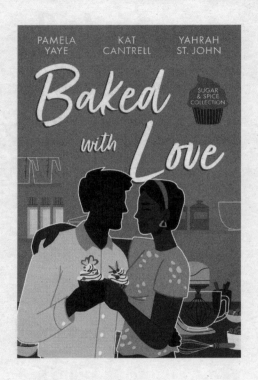

LET'S TALK

Romance

For exclusive extracts, competitions and special offers, find us online:

- **f** MillsandBoon
- **X** @MillsandBoon
- **⊡** @MillsandBoonUK
- **♪** @MillsandBoonUK

Get in touch on 01413 063 232

MILLS & BOON

THE HEART OF ROMANCE

A ROMANCE FOR EVERY READER

MODERN
Prepare to be swept off your feet by sophisticated, sexy and seductive heroes, in some of the world's most glamourous and romantic locations, where power and passion collide.

HISTORICAL
Escape with historical heroes from time gone by. Whether your passion is for wicked Regency Rakes, muscled Vikings or rugged Highlanders, awaken the romance of the past.

MEDICAL
Set your pulse racing with dedicated, delectable doctors in the high-pressure world of medicine, where emotions run high and passion, comfort and love are the best medicine.

True Love
Celebrate true love with tender stories of heartfelt romance, from the rush of falling in love to the joy a new baby can bring, and a focus on the emotional heart of a relationship.

HEROES
The excitement of a gripping thriller, with intense romance at its heart. Resourceful, true-to-life women and strong, fearless men face danger and desire - a killer combination!

 **afterglow BOOKS**
From showing up to glowing up, these characters are on the path to leading their best lives and finding romance along the way – with plenty of sizzling spice!

To see which titles are coming soon, please visit

millsandboon.co.uk/nextmonth